FOUR CROWS

A romantic thriller by Lily White

This is a work of fiction and any resemblance to any person, living or dead, any place, events or occurrences, is purely coincidental. The characters and story lines are created from the author's imagination or are used fictitiously.

Four Crows: Copyright © 2017 by Lily White

lily@lilywhitebooks.com
http://www.facebook.com/authorlilywhite
www.lilywhitebooks.com

If you are interested in reading additional books by Lily White or would like to know when new books are being released, Lily White can be found on:

Facebook and

Twitter

Join the Mailing List!!!

If you are interested in receiving email updates regarding additional books by Lily White or would like to know when new books are announced or being released, join the mailing list via this link.

http://eepurl.com/Onoeb

Join the Facebook Fan Group!!!

If you are interested in receiving exclusive previews for upcoming novels, or to participate in giveaways, join the fan group for Lily White Books.

FAN GROUP LINK

Author Note and Disclaimer:

This book is intended for entertainment purposes solely. This novel discusses sensitive subject matters. Readers who sensitive to triggers are advised to proceed with caution.

Other Books by Lily White

(Book title hyperlink directs to purchase page on Amazon)

Her Master's Courtesan
(Book 1 of the Masters Series)
(Available on Smashwords and Barnes & Noble)

Her Master's Teacher
(Book 2 of the Masters Series)

Target This

Hard Roads

Asylum

Wake to Dream

Table of Contents

PROLOGUE

Dear Katie:

Maybe this is a stupid way for me to start this letter. You're so much more than dear, but I can't wrap my brain around another way to begin. It may even be stupid for me to be writing you at all. There's no place for me to send this. If there were, I'd be standing with you in person taking you back from whatever evil has stolen my life away.

For the first time, I don't know what to say to you. We never had that problem before. From the moment we met as kids, we were each other's safety net. We laughed easily. We smiled brightly. We kept each other warm during the winter storms, and we played in the sun during the long summer afternoons.

I've done something wrong, baby. I've done many things wrong because I've lost the sounding board you've always been in my life. I've lost my confidence, my strength, and my common sense. You were all those things, and now that you're gone, I'm wandering lost.

Without you to guide me home, I fear I'll never be found.

My actions have hurt a girl. I've hurt her without remorse and in ways that would make you hate me if you could see what I've done. I don't want to think of myself as a monster – but maybe I am. I'm not done hurting her, and when I'm finished, I know she'll be destroyed.

1

She's so young, this poor creature that I'm dragging through my insanity, the one who's trapped and helpless to a man who lost his mind fourteen years before she met him. I held a gun to her head. I kicked dirt in her eyes. I threatened her life until she was cowering beneath me begging for me to forgive her for everything she'd done. But even her tears weren't enough to smother the rage that pulses inside me, they weren't enough for me to let her go, to give her a safe place to run to while I annihilate everything she's ever known.

You never knew her because she was just a child when you disappeared. If Michael hadn't been taken away from me when I was off at war, she would have been the same age as our son. Maybe they would have met in a sunlit field as kids like you and me. Maybe they would have grown up together, their bodies developing and changing as their hearts taught them what it was to truly love one another. I should feel protective of this girl, should feel a need to watch over her as I'd intended to watch over Michael, but the drive inside me to return the pain I've lived with has led me to use her in the worst possible ways.

Please don't hate me, Katie. I couldn't live with myself if you turned away. Seeing your smile disappear would shred my heart. Hearing the disappointment in your voice would force me to my knees. Not seeing the bright blue of your sparkling eyes because you lost your faith in who I am would absolutely destroy me.

But I can't lose those things, can I? I can't see your smile, I can't hear your voice, and I'll never see the light in your eyes again.

I'm a rabid dog off his leash, a hungry tiger uncaged, a feral wolf that's been injured and abused, only to be set free. Without you to hold the leash, I've become focused and intent on destroying everything in my path.

They took you from me. They stole you and they stole my son. They stole my heart, my soul, my happiness, and the perfect beat that pushes blood through my silent and broken heart.

I wasn't given the chance to save you from the shadows. They took you when I wasn't there to protect you.

Who does that? Who waits until a man is off at war to come in and steal away the only thing that gives him the ability to breathe?

2

They could have stolen my arms or legs, my heart or lungs, my teeth or any other part of me and it would have hurt less than taking you. The pain is unbearable. It's never ending. And over the years that I've endured the agony, it's developed into something far darker, far more deadly, than anything I knew could exist inside me.

If I could crawl to you just to hear your voice once more, if I could drop to my knees just to see one last glimpse of your face, if I could give up my life just to hear the love that was always in your voice, I would forgo my pride, my strength, my entire being just to have you in my arms for one second longer.

All that's left for me to do is confess the sins I've committed, to confess the sins I still have left to do.

I know you will disapprove of the man I'm becoming, but I don't know how else to ease the aching that consumes me every second of every hour of every day. Not even sleep relieves me of the agony. And not even death will allow me to forgive this world for the pain that remains when you're not there.

A man is dead because of me, and three more will die before I'm done.

A young girl is crying because of me, but my heart can no longer care about the tears I've caused.

I haven't hurt her in ways that make me pure evil, not like the men that stole you away. However, every day has me inching closer to the line that separates a good man from the monster I'm becoming.

Vengeance has blinded me to my actions. More blood will spill once Maggie leads me to the men that stole you from my life. All I can do now is ask you to understand me, and to beg you to forgive me for my crimes.

Forgive me for the heartache that consumes me.

Forgive me for not having the ability to let you go.

Forgive me for the pain I've caused Maggie, and for destroying a girl who's too young to know what it means to live.

The world has made you a woman shining among the stars, and left me behind as a broken and crippled man.

For that, I won't stop, Katie. I won't relent, not until all three of the Crows are dead and gone.

And you'll just have to forgive me, Darlin', for all the messed up and unforgiveable things I'm about to do.

CHAPTER ONE

MAGGIE

Do you remember what you were doing an hour ago?

How about a day ago? A week? Or even a year?

Or how about when you were four years old, on a warm summer day, hours after a rainstorm had washed away the languid heat just enough to cool the breeze that blew in from an open window?

I do.

But I wish I didn't.

On that day, and with small, fat fingers, I awkwardly gripped a red crayon in my hand. Situated on the dirty linoleum floor in the kitchenette, I stabbed at the white rectangle of construction paper in front of me, worrying my bottom lip between my teeth, a habit I had when I was trying to concentrate.

The paper crinkled each time my fist flew down. Another dot. Another splash. Another spray of liquid ruby that twinkled on the blades of grass in my front yard in bright and brilliant sunlight.

The wash of gemstones was the most beautiful thing I'd ever seen, but it was as scary as it was pretty, I just didn't understand why.

"Well, there she is, my little slice of pumpkin pie. Why don't you get up here and give your daddy a hug?"

A wooden chair creaked to accept my father's weight. I squealed a delighted sound, my small body pushing up from the floor to climb in the lap of the biggest person I knew. I'd seen other mommies and daddies in the parks as they hovered over their children, but none of them were as big and strong as mine.

With a smile on my lips, I clasped the drawing in my hand and laid my head against his chest to listen to the steady rhythm of his heart. It was always warm and safe when he held me.

"What did you draw, Maggie Pie? Let Daddy have a look."

His fingers brushed over the mess of black curls that framed my cherubic face, his heart beat slow and strong beneath his ribs. The paper rustled as he pulled it from my hand, a smile creasing his lips to look at the rubies I'd scattered across a field of green.

"Well, would you look at this?" A smile tilted his lips as I pulled my head away to look up into his proud face. Grinning down at me with a gleam behind his eye, he barked out a laugh before asking, "Do you know what this is, angel?"

Nodding so hard the curls bounced around my skull, I looked at my father with wide green eyes and said, "Red rain." My chubby finger pointed at those pinhead dots of color scattered across the grass. "Rubies."

"Rubies, huh?" His mouth pursed, a shrill, loud whistle cut from his lips before he looked at me again. "And why do you think they're rubies?"

"They sparkle," I answered.

Heavy steps rattled the floor beneath the chair where my father sat with me in his lap, my brother, Finn, answering my father's whistle. "What's going on?"

Finn was big like my daddy, leaving me to often wonder why my siblings weren't close to my age. I'd seen other brothers and sisters in the park where they played together and were the same size. But my two brothers were too big to play. With me, at least. They always played with their friends at night with no problem.

Holding up the drawing for Finn to see, my daddy laughed and said, "She says it's red rain. And rubies. Didn't I tell you to run that damn wood chipper at night when she's sleeping?"

Finn crumpled the drawing in his hand, his narrow eyed gaze slicing down across me. Palpable anger from someone much larger than myself caused me to shrink against the only person that made me feel safe.

"Daddy?"

Strong arms held me tight as bitter words that I didn't understand, much less care for, were exchanged between the two men. Eventually, Finn let out a bark of disgust before stomping his feet out of the room, disappearing into the dimly lit interior of the small home.

"Now, don't you worry about your brother, Maggie Pie. He's just mad because he got caught breaking the rules. It's not your fault he's a dumbass."

The vibrato of his baritone voice soothed me. Settling against him, I pressed my ear to his chest to feel the familiar rattle that happened when he spoke. His voice was so big his lungs and ribs could barely contain it. When he talked, the words came out of his mouth, but also vibrated along his entire body.

"I'm taking you to the park today, little one. Do you remember that new friend you've been talking to? Michael, I think, or Mitch?"

"Michael," I answered, the hint of a smile in my voice because I loved going to the park. I made new friends every time I went, and daddy made friends as well. Daddy was so lonely. I wished he'd make friends for longer than just a night.

"Yeah. Michael. I can drop you off, little one, but I won't be able to stay that long today. I have to get everything hitched together for the long drive we're taking tomorrow out to old man Maxwell's farm. You like that farm, don't you?"

"Yes," I answered.

I did like it. The horses were pretty and the goats were funny. But I hated the hogs. They had high-pitched, keening squeals that threatened to make my ears bleed. It scared me, the way they threw themselves at the gate of their pen desperate to eat whatever came their way.

Daddy and my brothers liked the hogs, but I didn't.

"Maybe we can take Michael to the farm. He'd like that, too. Don't you think?"

Nodding my head, I cuddled closer.

"When Michael's mommy comes to get him, you should ask her to give you a lift home. That way you don't have to find your way here in the dark all by yourself."

"Okay, Daddy."

It wouldn't be the first time I brought a friend home. And their mommies always had a good time.

🐖🐖🐖🐖

It was perfect weather to be at the park that day. Two peas in a pod, Michael and I played like we'd known each other our whole lives. We both liked bugs, liked to swing so high on the swing set that its feet would lift off the ground, Michael's mother reprimanding us every time the chains went slack and sent us into free fall.

I loved the thrill, and so did the friend that was so much like me.

Eventually, dusk settled around our shoulders and Michael's mother told him it was time to go home for dinner and bedtime. He was a good kid, didn't argue, and when he took her hand to walk to their car, he turned back to see me sitting alone in the sand, the only child left in a park that had been deserted to the brilliant color of the setting sun.

"Where's your daddy, Maggie? Is he coming to pick you up?"

She'd been so worried and I knew that despite the late hour, his mother would drive me home.

⋏⋏⋏⋏

"Why is she screaming like that?"

Shrugging my tiny shoulders, I scooped two fake sugar cubes into Michael's cup. Teal with pink rims and tiny sparkles, my tea set was one of my favorite things. Beside me sat Cuddle Bear, and next to Michael was his stuffed rabbit, Floppy Bunny.

"They're just having fun, I guess. Grown ups are so weird," I answered. "You don't have to be scared. As long as your mommy gets enough sleep tonight, she'll wake up in time to go to the farm with us tomorrow."

It's when the mommies didn't wake up on time that was really bad. My friends were always scared when that happened - too scared to smile when they saw the farm the next day.

"Does Floppy Bunny need more sugar in his tea?"

Staring at Michael with wide, expectant eyes, I ignored the loud music they always played when there was company. With loud guitars and pounding drums, the music was sometimes happy and a lot of times mad.

The mommies would make a lot of noise, but I knew it was just in fun because Daddy and my brothers would always laugh. Not the quiet kind of laughter either. They laughed like someone was tickling their sides until they couldn't breathe. I was glad they always had a good time, and often wondered if I'd get to see the party when I became a grown up.

There was one thing I hated about these kind of nights. Every time they made new friends, I knew it wouldn't last.

One night only, my Daddy always told me, *and then we move on to a new place for a while and make friends there.*

He'd always ruffle my hair.

We'll come back, Maggie Pie. This is our land and we'll always come back to it.

CHAPTER TWO

Fourteen Years Later...
MAGGIE

"Man, it's good to be home. I never thought I'd miss this place as much as I have over the past two years."

Nudging my shoulder with his own, my father smiled at me with exhaustion shadowing his eyes and the sweat of late summer heat tacky against his skin.

"What do you say, Maggie Pie? Did you miss it?"

Turning to him with equally tired green eyes, I gave him a thin smile. I hadn't seen our place in so long, I wondered if it would hold the same magical appeal it always had when I was a small girl growing up.

My eyes scanned the distance outside the windshield of our beat up red truck, and I could barely see the roof of the old barn and dilapidated house over the tall grass of the overgrown field.

"I missed it," I finally breathed out, lying to keep the old man happy. "I'm sure once we clean up, it'll feel like home again."

Although it'd only been a few years since I'd seen the place, it was a long two years. It was the time during which I became an adult, legally, at least. And it was the time I finally grasped onto the understanding of the life fate had decided I would live.

In many ways it wasn't a bad life. I had three men who loved me and looked after me, even if two of those men had grown distant over the last few years. Anything material I wanted in the world was at my fingertips. Never denied, I could talk my father into buying just about anything. But money wouldn't buy my freedom. Money couldn't buy friends, or love, or even a different life.

The tire of the truck dipped in a pothole on the dirt road, viscous mud splashing up onto the side of the truck from one of the large divots that speckled the land. Behind us drove another truck that towed machinery my father couldn't be without. And behind that was a ratty old camper - a fifty square foot aluminum nightmare that was my home away from home.

The shocks on the truck were all but gone, the land rocking us to and fro like two babies in the cradle of a solitary life. Daddy didn't talk much on the long drives across country, but his silence was better than the way my brothers would prattle on if I rode with one of them. I only accepted the passenger seat in one of their vehicles if I was sick of the thoughts that invaded those long empty periods of silence that came with riding with my father.

The bark of a phlegmy cough caught my attention, my head spinning left to see the bloody spittle that covered my father's palm. Clenching his hand quickly, he lowered his arm to wipe the evidence of a burgeoning disease along the side of dirty jeans.

"Don't think I didn't see that."

Despite the sheltered and guarded life the old man had forced on me, he was all I had, and I loved him. "You need to get that looked at, Daddy. What'll happen to me if you're not here, huh? You think Finn or Brody are going to look after me? They'll sell me off just as fast -"

"Don't you be talking about that, Magpie. Not one damn word. And don't ever accuse my sons of not looking after you, neither."

Side-eyeing me, the old man's shoulders rattled with another cough, this one small enough that he was better able to hide it.

His coughing fits were like earthquakes, small pre-shocks that rumbled in his lungs until the pressure became too much. Everything inside him rattled then and the filth trapped in his lungs came up. He'd suffer the small aftershocks for at least a half a day later.

As far as I was concerned, it was getting time the stubborn man see someone about it.

"Don't look at me like that. I'm still the parent around here, whether you think you're a grown up or not."

Rolling my eyes, I turned to catch my reflection in the side window. The moon had settled low on the horizon and it was that mysterious space between night and the first light of day. It was my favorite time because it was an in between space where anything could happen.

A round face framed by wild black hair stared back at me. Green eyes the color of a forest at dawn were slanted at the corners, just enough to give me an exotic look, but not enough for me to pass as foreign. Daddy always said I got my eyes from my Native American momma, but I wouldn't know. The woman lost her life while bringing me into the world.

Every time I was told the story of where I came from, the tale became more magical and surreal. Born inside an old, deserted church, Daddy swore the angels and God himself were looking down at me, blessing me with beauty and sweetness when I took my first breath. Unsure whether that was true, I swore they must have left immediately after. No child worth the love of angels was raised in a family of Crows.

My full mouth was drawn into a thin line as I stared into eyes that seemed vacant. Where had the little girl gone that was happiest in the rare moments she had alone with her father? Why did she have to grow up and *want* more?

It took years for me to realize that life wasn't made up of toys, pretty dresses, and friends for one night only. Once the

13

understanding hit me, though, I'd never been able to escape the longing for something beyond what I'd been given.

Leaning my head against the cool glass, I recalled the first time I truly understood what my family was doing. Not too old, perhaps eleven or twelve, I listened to the screaming that echoed out from behind the loud, raucous music they always played when company was over. The pleas from that woman's mouth never stopped haunting me from that night forward.

Please stop...

No!...

I have a family...

The words never stop repeating in my head, becoming an endless loop of sorrow and pain, of torment and new beginnings.

Daddy stopped letting me bring friends home after Old Man Maxwell died when I was nine, and I never understood why. Not until that night at least, the night a stranger's frightened screams painted a clear picture of the life my family was living.

Red rain. God, I'd been so stupid to believe anything so unnatural could exist.

"The field has really filled out since we burned it last." My father's hand touched my arm, dragging my attention back to the present. "Ain't that the way it works, little one? I'm telling you, Mother Nature sure knows what she's doing. Ashes to ashes and all that. Destruction by fire feeds the new life that grows."

A chill slithered along my spine, the buried knowledge of what lay in that field and now fed the grass that reached for the sky. A small plot of earth that sat to the left of the barn, a place where the rubies would shimmer beneath the bright sunlight. Those gemstones were always lost to the dirt my brothers tossed over them, before the gasoline they poured caught flame and the field became a raging fire, contained by trenches, that burned all the rubies away.

14

The night after I discovered the horrifying truth to the *parties* my family threw, I'd sat on my father's lap and asked him if we were all destined for the gates of Hell.

Laughing so deep, I thought he'd dump me from his lap, his arms held me tight when he explained, *"it's the nature of life, Maggie Pie. Kill or be killed. Us against them. A man's gotta have the ability to feed his family, and those women bring in good money."*

He'd squeezed my shoulder when I flashed him a grim expression. *"Now don't you worry, little one. The sins of the father don't lie on the shoulders of his daughter. It's the sons that bear that weight."*

Scooting me off his lap, he gently nudged me along. *"Go play with your dolls, Maggie. You let Daddy worry about the things that are too scary for you to know about."*

It was as if that conversation had torn the veil off their sinister deeds, as if it had freed the three men to openly play, because the baby had finally learned the truth. Nothing was the same after that conversation, and I quickly learned to stay silent.

On the nights they brought those women home, I'd gather my things and disappear into the fields of whatever place we were staying. Always far away from any city, always out where the stars were my friends, we only stayed in one place for a few months at a time.

We moved around so often I didn't know what it meant to have a permanent and stable home.

After the parties, the women would be gone by the time I returned in the morning. If they'd been smart, they were packed up and shipped out to wherever Daddy sold them. If they weren't, well, they became the sustenance for the fields that would eventually be burned to ash. Finn never did run that chipper during the day again, and I didn't miss the shine of rubies across the grass.

His voice a mellow hum across the surface of my thoughts, my dad broke through the storm of memory. "Don't you worry, Maggie Pie. We've got enough money to last us a while. We won't have to move out again for at least another year or so."

I hated the constant moving. He knew it. But his words were always the same, nothing more than a bunch of sounds with no true promise or meaning.

In a few months, their skin would itch for another party, and we'd be back on the road again.

CHAPTER THREE

ELLIOT

"It's been fourteen years, Elliot. At some point, you have to let all of that go."

The fear in my mother's voice didn't shake the need inside me to discover the truth of my wife and son's disappearance. It didn't settle the constant crush of anger and rage, the deep-seated sorrow that broke through the stillness of the night to stab my heart and tear my soul to pieces.

In the beginning, she'd played along. She'd listened to me cry through the cold, lonely nights when I swore that the heavens above had abandoned me. But as my mother's acceptance of their loss grew stronger from year to year – as well as her need for me to move on - my thoughts of revenge became more pronounced until it became my obsession.

My hand gripped the phone so tight, the blood rushed from the wrinkles in my callused skin.

"I'm not forgetting about them, Mom. I'm not just rolling over on this and accepting it. Something happened to Katelyn and Michael and I'm not letting it go until the bastards that took them pay for it."

"Let the cops handle the matter, Son -"

"The cops have done nothing but store the case file away and mark it as unsolved! I've tracked more potential suspects than they ever cared to find."

From the second I returned home from my last tour, I'd devoted every waking moment to finding my wife and child. The horrors of war, the slaughter of angry and proud men, it was nothing compared to the agony of not knowing. I was a specialist in the Marine Corps and had been on assignment at the time my family disappeared. It took the military a month to finally get the message to me because, to my country, the assignment had been more important than the soldier. Perhaps if they had told me sooner - if I'd returned home sooner - I could have saved my wife and child.

"You need to calm down, Elliot. Your anger won't bring them home. All it'll do is tear you up inside until you're as lost as them."

I was already lost, but I didn't pass that thought on to my mom. She was worried enough as it was.

"Listen, mom. I'm going to let you go. It's late and -"

"Get some sleep, Elliot. Take your pills and get some rest."

I never took the damn pills, but she didn't need to know it.

"Love you, mom."

My thumb hit the button to end the call, my hand clenching the phone so tight, I wouldn't have been surprised if it was crushed to dust in my hold.

Before I even knew what I was doing, the phone crashed against the opposite wall, the glow of blue light beaming from where it lay atop a layer of dust that gathered in the corners.

Those poor phones. The salesman at the cellular store thought I was just some unfortunate klutz, his smile far too bright every time he saw my shadow darken the large glass doors. How many phones had I gone through this year already? I wasn't sure, but I didn't really care either. All that mattered was hunting down the bastards that took my wife and son.

I should have been home protecting them, but instead I was somewhere in a foreign country fighting a battle that meant little to me besides the piss poor amount of money it sent home to my family. I'd left home to take care of them, and all my absence had done was leave them alone and exposed to the homegrown monsters that plagued this country.

Aggravated thoughts constantly spinning, my brain wouldn't stop asking the same questions over and over again.

What had Katelyn been thinking? She was always so careful. She knew that predators lurked in the shadows, ready and waiting for someone as beautiful as her to come along.

But damn if that woman didn't have a soft heart. It must have been some stupid stray that distracted her, some lost soul struggling to make it through the world that she took the time to help. That was the only thing I could believe would have left her open and vulnerable, the only thing that would have distracted her enough that she and Michael could be stolen.

Pulling a smoke from the crushed pack that sat on a pile of papers, I slipped the butt between my lips and fired up the zippo. The first tug was always like coming home to something familiar. Blowing it out, I watched the cherry transition from red to grey, the ash gathering at the tip like what remained of my life after my family had vanished.

While overseas, I swore I'd quit the nasty habit as soon as I was home and safe. With nothing but an empty house to return to, I saw no reason for quitting a habit that would put me in an early grave.

Drawing a deep drag of death into my lungs, I blew the smoke out to dance above my head, my eyes staring at the handwritten notes of the journals I'd been keeping for years. At first, every time I came across a new possibility, a new clue, I took it to the police, hoping like hell they'd follow it up and locate the two people who meant the world to me.

They may as well have taken my hope, stomped it beneath their state issued shoes, and spit on it for good measure.

For the first three years, they played along with my visits.

Yes, Mr. McLoughlin, we'll look into it.

Yes, sir, we can definitely check it out.

Thank you, sir, for your service to this country.

All bullshit. All lies. The slack jaws never bothered to look into even one of the leads I came across. After the third year, all I got from them was their pitiful stares and the barely spoken whispers that I needed a shrink.

I gave up going to the cops when those whispers started, and for the eleven years that followed, I investigated the leads on my own.

Nothing concrete had turned up in the years I'd been pouring over document after document about the people who lived in my rural town. As far as I could decipher, most of the people in the area were good folk, their noses clean of illegal activities.

However, one family always stuck out to me. A foursome of oddballs, three men and a girl. The Crows owned an old farm on the outskirts of town. They operated a landscaping company that mainly performed large lot clearing, storm cleanup and tree removal.

On its own, I wouldn't have considered their lifestyle strange, but the family had a pattern of taking off for a few years at a time - normally after a string of crimes occurred within the county surrounding the small town.

It took me too long to make the discovery, and it was just another mistake that buried my family deeper in the crevice of their mysterious fate.

By the time I was discharged from the military and returned home, the Crows had been long gone. It took another few years for them to return and draw my attention.

They were a strange lot, three grown men - one much older than the others - and a young girl that I discovered later was near the same age as my son. Asking around, I learned that the foursome were comprised of a father, two sons and a daughter that had been a surprise child for her aging parents. The mother didn't survive the birth of the girl according to what little information I could obtain on them through townsfolk.

The Crows - as they were called by the town - lived off their land mostly, rarely coming into town to purchase tools, sparse food, clothing and other odds and ends. Packages were often delivered to the mail center on the main boulevard of the town, and once a week when they were staying on their property, the eldest Crow, Jonah, would drive in to fetch the packages. Every so often, he'd bring one of his sons along to assist, but rarely the young girl.

After several years of watching the family's patterns - as much as I could without drawing attention to myself - I became concerned when a woman went missing twenty miles outside of the county at a strip mall in another rural city. Two days later, the Crow family packed up and was heading out.

It was by coincidence only that I'd seen them leave, but news of the woman's disappearance was playing on the truck radio at the same time I saw them hauling out. Perhaps God himself finally found it within his heart to lead me in the right direction.

From what I'd learned about Katelyn's disappearance, she'd been frequenting the park on a daily basis with Michael, each time staying for a few hours and leaving just before sundown. I couldn't find anybody who'd witnessed her at the park on the day she was taken, but that didn't mean she hadn't been there.

Sitting exhausted over the notebooks I kept, my eyes endlessly searched the words written over the pages, as if by reading them enough, some concrete answer would appear.

"Damn it, Katelyn," I quietly hissed, "what were you doing that day?"

Finding the bottle of whiskey I'd been nursing all night, I brought the rim to my lips, and settled into my chair to pour over the notes. It was a task I did every damn night, a task I'd never stop doing until the day I found my wife and son.

CHAPTER FOUR

MAGGIE

I've always loved animals. All creatures, big and small, it doesn't matter. There are certain ones that frighten me more than I care to admit, but despite my fear, I still respect the lives of those creatures.

However, that respect wasn't enough to prevent me from cowering in a corner when faced by one of those dreadful pests, the eight legged variety in particular.

"It's just a spider, Maggie. It's not going to reach out and get you. Just smash it."

Shaking my head, I fixed my eyes on the eight legged threat. "Please, just get it outside." Pleading with my father, tears welled in my eyes.

There was too much death in my life already. I had to wonder if I could call myself a good person if I, at least, stopped some of it.

Even if it was just a spider.

My father shook his head in disbelief before running a frustrated hand through his hair. "I'll never get you, Maggie. You've seen stuff a hell of lot worse than a spider getting squished. What is it with you and these animals?"

"Daddy, just scoop it up in a cup and take it outside where it belongs." My breath came out on a rattling huff. "Please?"

Shaking his head again, Daddy snatched a dirty glass from the table and chased the spider into a corner. He trapped it between the glass and his hand, standing up so fast his knees popped. "Open the damn door."

Running to pull open the door, I jumped back before my dad could get close to me with that nasty, little thing.

I watched the old man place the spider in a bed of weeds that bordered the overgrown field, and I hoped the small arachnid would be smart enough to leave that bed before my brothers mowed down the grass that afternoon.

Peeking my head around the frame of the door, I gripped the wood trim and stood in embarrassed silence as my father plodded back towards the house.

An angry finger waved in my face, but when I looked past it, all I saw was love and concern behind my father's blue-grey eyes. "I'll never get you girl. You care too much about things. And you know what caring gets you."

"Thank you, Daddy."

Putting as much saccharine sweetness as I could into those words, I watched the old man's heart melt right there in front of me. For as evil as Jonah was, he still cherished me, his only daughter.

All he had left in him was another disbelieving shake of his head. "Your brothers and I are going into town. We need food and supplies to fix this place up. You think you can manage to stay out of trouble for a few hours?"

"I'll stay inside," I promised.

"No answering the door, neither. You never know who's standing on the other side."

My lips pulled into a smirk. "Nobody ever comes here, Daddy. Hell, I'd be surprised if half the town even remembers we live here anymore."

"Clean up your language, baby girl. Sweet women don't say sour words."

His steps shook the floorboards as he crossed the kitchen to call my brothers, but I wasn't quite done with him yet.

"While you're in town, are you going to see a doctor about that cough?"

He didn't bother to look back at me. "Mind your own business, Maggie," was his barked response.

Taking a seat at the small, round table that stood on unbalanced legs on the linoleum, I picked up a pencil to idly sketch as the three men made their way out the house, their low murmured words indecipherable from where I sat.

Despite the way my father and brothers doted on me and kept me safe, I was never included in the bunch, always an outsider of their exclusive group. I didn't need to wonder why I'd never feel included. Theirs was a party to which I'd never receive an invitation, a fact that didn't cost me much sleep.

My hand brushed over the paper as I shaded the large butterfly, graphite lead dust a shimmering black smudge over the skin of my palm and fingers. Dropping the pencil so suddenly that it bounced over the table and onto the floor, I sat back in appraisal of the artwork I'd created.

That butterfly with its shaded wings of one color stared back at me accusingly, a symbol of life that was as sweet and serene as the soft wind I imagined held it in place.

At least you're not trapped, I thought. *You might have a short life, but at least you live it free.*

Struggling with that thought, I wondered if a brief life lived fully was worth more than a long one lived trapped beneath the thumb of cruel men. Not that they were cruel to me. It was quite the opposite, in fact. But I still felt the strain on my soul for the cruelty they imparted on others.

Dustmotes danced their erratic patterns through the glow of fractured sunlight in the room. The windows hadn't been cleaned in years and dirt now caked the glass. The result was a depressive ambiance, a shroud of filth and detriment that I was desperate to escape.

I'd promised my father I'd stay inside, but I knew he'd be gone for two hours, giving me one to explore around outside.

Stretching my lean body backwards when I stood from the chair, I winced at the pull of tight muscles along my spine. I was always cramped and crumpled after the long drives between my ever-shifting homes.

A walk would do me some good, and I knew it. No longer caring about my father's fears that some monster would snatch me the moment I was alone, I packed a bottle of water and some light snacks to take with me out into the fields.

A bark of laughter flew over my lips when I realized that the true monsters had just driven away in their beat down red truck, and they wouldn't be snatching me when they returned.

I had that, at least. Not having to fear the crazies because I was related to them was one less thing I had to worry about.

Hauling my weary body out the door, I ignored the way the screen slammed shut behind me and leaned askew as it broke away from its top hinge. The crappy house was falling apart at its seams. I knew just how that would feel.

Grass tickling the backs of my knees, I meandered my way through the field, settling down on the ground when I found the small stream that trickled its way across the property.

Lying on my back, I closed my eyes against the glare of the sun, a brief thought crossing my mind that if I opened my eyes and stared for long enough, the sun would burn away the faces of the children and women I knew would be lost forever.

Some still lay as dust and ash in the field that was growing high and strong just feet away from me, while the others were left to a fate that was concealed to me as soon as money changed hands.

I couldn't bring myself to cry for the grown women. But the kids? I'd shed far too many tears for them already.

Letting those memories trickle away with the slow moving current of the stream at my side, I turned my attention to fantasy.

Reality was a dark and dismal sequence of days that ticked by with no rhyme or reason. But fantasy was a place where I could live a normal life, where I had friends, a boyfriend, and a future that didn't include hiding in the shadows of society.

What would that be like? I thought. *Never having to hide?*

It was a question that would never be answered. Even when my daddy died, I'd be lucky if my brothers ever let me out of their sight. I shuddered at the thought, memories creeping in of all the times I'd caught Finn standing in my doorway at night while he thought I lay sleeping. Without my father alive to protect me, would Finn finally cross the threshold into my room?

Longing for just one glimpse of something beyond the life I knew, I imagined the feel of soft lips on my own. From movies I'd seen and books I'd read, I knew that when two people kissed, love would fill their hearts. I couldn't believe that love was as warm as the books described it, but I knew the lust had to be real because I felt it.

Images of the characters played through my mind. The description of the way hands felt on a woman's body brought my own palms scrubbing up my abdomen, tracing the line of my rib cage.

It would be so sweet, so right, so pure if I could ever find it. Fighting against the crushing reality of the life I'd lived, I dreamed of new beginnings with a man that made me feel something other than the sickening guilt and crushing fear that was hardwired into my young mind.

Slipping my fingers beneath the hem of my shirt, I pushed the material up higher, revealing my skin to the scorch of sunlight, the bottom of my breasts to the whisper of wind that brushed across my body.

One finger tracing the shape of my nipple, I opened my mouth to release a breath filled with the desires I kept trapped inside.

Another hand crept towards the waistband of my shorts in search of that sweet spot I'd read about, but had never been lucky enough to find. Pulling the button free, I opened the zipper, the thin cotton of my panties soft beneath my touch.

And just as I slipped my hand down farther, a stick snapped within feet of me, my body going still after the sudden sound made me jump.

CHAPTER FIVE

ELLIOT

"Not sure when they came back," Norm Granger mumbled, a thick wad of tobacco stuck between his lip and gums. He spit out a string of sludge before turning his narrowed eyes back to me. "I assume they rolled in last night, though."

Leaning forward against the counter, I lowered my voice so nobody else in the small general store could overhear my questions.

"Why do you assume that?"

Casting a sidelong glance towards the large picture window at the front of the store, I watched Jonah and his two sons enter the post office across the street. The old man's hair had gone full silver since the last time I laid eyes on him, his shoulders withered and strained as he coughed. He looked to be on his last leg, but his sons were still as strong as ever.

"They usually crawl in on the first day they get back. Not sure if you've driven past their property lately, but it's going to take a lot of work to make it livable again. I'm sure they need supplies." Another shot of dark sludge was spat into a bucket beneath the checkout counter. Ned eyed me with suspicion. "Why are you asking, anyhow? I didn't realize you were keeping tabs on the Crows."

I shrugged, my eyes still trained on the three men entering the post office. It took them less than a minute inside before they reemerged with a handful of packages.

"I'm not. I just haven't seen them around much."

Flicking a quick glance at Ned, I forced an innocent smile over my lips. "I haven't been out near their farm in a while, so I was just surprised to see them in town. I wonder why the daughter's not with them?"

Ned huffed out a breath. "Damned if I know. The entire family is a little off. They come in every couple of years, but when a big storm hits the news, they head in the direction of whatever unlucky town got pounded by it. Must be good money because I've heard about the shit they buy around here. It's not cheap."

While Ned prattled on, I watched Jonah and his sons drop off their packages into the truck before turning to walk into a local bar. Figuring they'd be inside for a while, I tapped my palm on the counter twice before casually nodding to Ned as goodbye.

Ned shook his head at my hurried exit and turned his attention away to watch the old war movie blasting from the television behind the counter.

A sheet of heat wrapped around me as soon as I stepped outside, thin beads of sweat dripping down my temples by the time I reached my car. Where was the girl? I wanted to know. Was she left at the house while her family tied one on?

Going out to the property wasn't the most brilliant of decisions, but if I were caught, I'd cross that bridge when I came to it. My curiosity was too much to let go.

The drive out didn't take more than a half hour. I was thankful for the quick trip, but also realized that if the men had left closely behind me, they'd be pulling up at any time. Climbing out of my car, I pulled the lever to pop the hood and walked to the front to give myself an excuse for sniffing around the property.

Lifting the hood, I pulled up the thin metal bar to hold it in place. I wiggled the connector loose from the battery and decided I'd play stranded and dumb if anybody showed up while I was sneaking around.

With my excuse in place, I trudged across the overgrown lawn to approach a house that was one strong wind away from being demolished. A screen door listed pathetically to the side, the top hinge broken away from the rotted wood. Slapping against the house with every small breeze that blew by, the door practically crumbled in my hands when I pulled it fully open.

Knocking twice on the interior door, I released the screen and stepped back. If the girl was home, I assumed she was inside. But if she weren't, I'd take that as freedom to explore the grounds. Nobody answered and I breathed out a sigh.

Turning to scan the overgrown field, I noticed a small, freshly crushed trail through the tall grass. My eyes darted out to the street. The men hadn't yet returned home. I followed the trail.

The path wasn't too stomped down, which meant whoever made it couldn't have weighed much. My thoughts went to the girl seconds before I saw her.

Lying in a small clearing by a stream, she had her face tipped up to the sky, her eyes closed tight against the sun. Black, wavy hair flared out over the ground at the sides of her head. Her long legs were bent at the knees. Held together, they swayed from side to side, a lazy rhythm in the mid-afternoon heat.

The girl couldn't have been older than Michael would have been if I'd been home to protect him and keep him safe. Noticing she was beautiful, a sickening thread of attraction surfaced as I watched her. Gritting my teeth, I remembered what family she belonged to, and the thread snapped apart entirely.

Taking another step forward, I plastered on a fake smile to call out to her, but she moved suddenly, her lips parting on a soft sigh as her hand traveled up her body. I froze before I lowered my foot down slowly.

I shouldn't have been watching her, shouldn't have been lingering silently while she lifted the hem of her shirt. But when the bottom swell of her small breasts came into view, I found myself captivated.

Never the type to watch women, I wasn't the type to approach them or talk to them either. That wasn't to say I hadn't taken a few to my bed since Katelyn died. But it took ten years before I broke down enough to touch another woman, only because I couldn't spend another lonely night in bed. The woman had stuck around long enough to warm the sheets after we'd had sex, but by the time I was through with her, the guilt of what I'd done surfaced and I'd kicked her out.

It was nothing against the woman. It was simply that she wasn't Katelyn.

My eyes still stuck on the girl touching herself in ways that had my body reacting, I thought about my wife and son, and it brought my thoughts back into focus.

I couldn't want this girl because I hated her for being a Crow. She would have been too young to take part in my family's disappearance, but that didn't excuse who she was. That girl represented a group of men who could be the answer to what happened to Katelyn and Michael.

Teeth gnashing over that thought, my jaw ticked with anger. And as the girl's hand slipped down to disappear beneath the waistband of her shorts, I stepped forward to purposefully crush a small branch in my path.

CHAPTER SIX

MAGGIE

"Who the hell are you?"

My eyes flew wide to see the strange man standing within feet of me. Younger than my father - but possibly older than my brothers - the man stood still watching.

I yanked my hand out from my pants and sat up. My lips parted to scream at him, but nothing came out.

Embarrassment flooded me for what I'd been caught doing, especially because the man who caught me was beautiful for someone much older.

With brown hair that framed his face in a disheveled mess, and with cheekbones that cut sharp angles across his face, the man stared at me with an intensity that made my stomach clench, every muscle in my body pulling taut as I stared at him.

His eyes were the stark color of gunmetal and he had a peppering of dark scruff across his cheeks and square jaw. Beyond his looks, there was nothing nice about that man. And I knew it the minute I saw him.

"You might want to leave before you do something stupid. My daddy and brothers are in the house. They'll kill you if you touch me."

"I'm not here to touch you," he answered, his eyes narrowed and his voice as rough as coarse sandpaper. Obviously struggling over something, he stood there balancing his weight between his feet.

My voice pitched higher. "You need to leave."

"My car broke down outside your house. I was seeing if anybody was home."

"Well, my *home* is about a thousand feet back the way you came." Pulling my shirt into place, I glared at him. He hadn't done anything wrong to me, but I couldn't shake the tremor of unease I felt just for him being in my space. "What's wrong with your car?"

His brow wrinkled in surprise, a smile spreading across his lips that looked forced. "I'm not sure. If I knew that, I wouldn't be standing here harassing a seventeen year old girl."

"I'm eighteen," I bit out.

"My apologies."

Huffing out a frustrated breath, I planted my palms on the ground behind me and leaned back on my arms. He really was a handsome man. It was too bad he looked about as safe as the ones who'd raised me.

"Listen," he said, "if your dad's home, do you think he can help me fix my car?"

I knew better than to admit I was there alone. "What's wrong with it? Maybe I can help you figure it out."

Curiosity arched his eyebrow. "You know something about cars?"

I found it odd that he didn't. There weren't many men in rural towns that didn't know a thing or two about engines. Maybe he was from out of town?

A single nod of my head was my simple answer. Constantly being on the road meant I'd had ample opportunities to help my father and brothers work on engines. I'd been turning wrenches since the moment my hands were big enough to grip the tools.

Whoever the man was, I wanted him gone before Daddy and my brothers arrived back. They wouldn't be happy to see him on the property and I'd hate it if there were a fight. "I'll take a look at it, but if we get it running, you'll need to be on your way."

Pushing up to my feet, I wasn't looking at him when he asked, "What if we don't get it running?"

"Then I hope your legs aren't too tired because you'll still need to be on your way."

Leaving my stuff behind, I approached the man. "What's your name?"

He stared at me like he hadn't heard my question, but eventually opened his mouth to answer, "Elliot. What's yours?"

"Maggie," I answered, my voice flustered. If I hadn't seen the man blink or heard him speak, I would have sworn he was a statue. No normal person could stand so perfectly still. It was as eerie as a snake staring at you, coiled and ready to strike.

Caution sparked over my skin as soon as I was within arm's reach of him. "Are you going or what?" Careful not to walk past him, I spurred him along to take the lead. I wouldn't chance having him at my back.

Waving his hand in the direction of the house, he said, "I was going to follow you."

My eyebrow arched, distrust a slithery thing along my spine. "I don't know where your car is. You need to show me the way."

Elliot paused, his eyes studying me with questionable intent. A few moments of tense silence passed before he said, "Fine."

It was obvious he didn't want to turn his back on me either. Turning, but placing distance between us so he could keep me in sight, he led me back up the path I'd traveled earlier. Crossing the yard quickly, I spotted the truck off the shoulder of the road.

A black 4x4 with silver trim and back passenger cabin, the truck looked brand new. It didn't make sense that he'd already be having problems.

"What's wrong with it?" I asked.

Elliot shrugged. "Don't know. It was driving normally but then just slowly died. The radio went out first and then it was just dead."

I prayed it would be an easy fix.

We reached the truck and I shifted around a bit until I had Elliot by my side and not at my back. The battery cables were the first things I reached for. As I'd suspected, one of them was loose.

"Here's your problem, right here. Your battery cable came loose."

"I thought I'd checked that."

A chill ran along my skin from the way Elliot stared at me instead of the engine. Inching away from him, I wiped my hands on my shorts.

"If you have a wrench, it's an easy fix."

Another tense moment of silence passed between us. Shaking his head like he was snapping himself out of something, Elliot flashed me a forced smile.

Unable to miss the straight white teeth and the dimples that dented his cheeks, the tightening in my stomach happened again, a shiver coursing through me that was surprising.

"Yeah," he finally said, "I have one in the truck. I'll take it from here."

I nodded and stepped away, but he called out to me.

"Hey, that was really impressive. Most girls your age don't know about cars. Where did you learn that?"

Dressed in a black, short sleeve shirt that hugged his broad shoulders, jeans gripping at his narrow waist, and a pair of black work boots covering his feet, Elliot was the picture of fit. I traced my eyes over the planes and valleys of his arms, chest and abdomen, my mind appreciative for what I could see beneath the tight cotton of his shirt.

Even though he put off an air of *something* that made me want to run and hide, I stepped towards him.

My thoughts raced and I struggled to convince myself that there wasn't something wrong with Elliot. Something was wrong with me.

How long had it been since I'd been alone with a stranger? As a child, I'd been left at the park to play with other children, but once I'd grown too old for those games, my father and brothers had kept me under lock and key. I was only allowed to spend time with their friends - people they knew they could trust - and never a man on his own.

Perhaps the caution I was feeling wasn't a result of anything Elliot had done, but more because I was alone for the first time with a man, one that I felt attracted to despite the marked age difference. How old could he be? Not old like my father, but just by the way he carried himself I knew he had to be older than my brothers.

"My dad and brothers taught me," I finally answered. "We travel a lot for their work, which means we're constantly working on the trucks and equipment while on the road."

He gave me an easy smile, less stern than the ones he'd flashed before. I liked the way his face looked when it softened. My body relaxed as I allowed myself to trust that he didn't intend to do me any harm.

"That must be hard. Being so young and moving around all the time."

Shrugging a delicate shoulder, I reached up to brush my hair away from my face. An odd desire to fix my hair into place overcame me, a desire to make myself attractive to this man. I'd never wanted to attract attention before. But then again, the people my family hung around weren't the type who's attention any person would want.

"It's all I know. Their business requires that they travel around. Storms hit all over the place and they need to be where the money is, you know?"

It wasn't anywhere near the truth of where my family got their money, but it was the lie I'd been forced to tell my entire life. I hadn't had many opportunities to tell it, but my father had shoved it down my throat so many times, he never had to worry that the truth would come up in its place.

Idly kicking at a stone on the ground, Elliot pulled his focus away from me for only a split second before those grey eyes locked to mine again. "So, I take it that means you haven't lived here that long?"

I shook my head. "No, we've lived here since I was a kid, we're just not here all the time."

It didn't occur to me until that moment that he was asking a lot of questions. He was a handsome man, probably the most handsome I'd seen in real life, and he'd told me he was impressed with me. That small bit of a compliment had been enough to make me want to preen where I stood. Nobody complimented me anymore. Nobody.

"You said you were eighteen, right?"

My eyes widened and a small, shy smile pulled at my lips. "Yes."

Elliot nodded. "Well, if you've been here since you were a kid, maybe you knew my son when you were younger?"

My body froze in place. I didn't want to answer any more questions, didn't want to continue a conversation that might get me in trouble if I said the wrong thing. But I didn't want to walk away from him either.

Then again, I wasn't sure I had much to worry about. If this man still had his son in his life, it was a good indication that I'd never known the child.

If I had, he wouldn't be talking about his son like he was still alive.

Glancing down the long, two lane road that led past my house, I couldn't see a car out in the distance, which meant I had more time before my daddy and brothers arrived.

"Probably not," I finally said. "I don't really know anybody around here."

Refusing to drop the subject, Elliot took a step towards me. "Well, maybe you knew him. His name was Michael. He had brown hair and blue eyes. He always carried around a stuffed rabbit he'd named Floppy Bunny. Does that ring any bells?"

It rang the alarm bell, and because of that fact, I wanted to run as fast as I could back to my house.

My eyes rounded with fear as I inched backwards. Yes, I remembered the boy, but only parts of him. Like the way he'd cried when his mommy was so tired she'd slept the entire way to the farm. Or the expression he had on his face when my family and I drove away from that farm and the boy realized he was being left behind.

"Listen, I didn't know him and your car is fixed, so you need to leave," I said, not giving Elliot time to respond or react before I sprinted across the field towards my house.

Slamming the door as I ran inside, I locked the place up tight and refused to even look out the windows until my father and brothers returned.

CHAPTER SEVEN

ELLIOT

My eyes tracked Maggie as she ran away, my hands clenching into fists when her sudden flight made it obvious she knew something. Fighting against the urge I had to chase her down, I remained in place and watched her until she'd disappeared into the ramshackle house.

Her reaction had been all the confirmation I'd needed to know that her family had something to do with Katelyn and Michael.

I didn't think my fight was with her. She'd have been too young at that time, innocent just like my son. However, her father and brothers hadn't been. And men like those three could have easily overtaken and controlled Katelyn. They could have easily made my family disappear.

After rounding my car to grab a wrench from the glove box, I ignored the sweat dripping down my brow as I tightened the battery cable back in place. Every muscle was tense along my bones, my teeth clenched together as I slammed the hood down and turned to stare at the small house where Maggie had run.

It took everything in me to resist marching up to that house, to force the door down, if need be, and pull the girl out by her hair. I needed to know what she was hiding, but I couldn't be stupid about it either. Tempering the rage that was festering inside me, I turned my attention to the length of highway I'd passed over in route to the Crow farm, and my eyes focused on the small cloud of dust being kicked up by the tires of a distant truck.

Jonah and Maggie's brothers were returning home, and I wasn't prepared at that particular moment to take on a fight that would be three against one.

Cursing under my breath, I walked around the truck to climb up into the driver's seat. Flinging the wrench into the glove box, I slammed the lid shut and turned the key to start the engine. The truck fired up with no problem, and by the time my hand gripped the gearshift to slam it into drive, Maggie's family pulled up in their beat down truck. Three sets of angry eyes locked on me as they pulled to a stop beside me.

Waving to them like I had no idea who they were, I grit my teeth when I rolled down the window.

"Is there a problem with your truck?" one of the brothers asked, his blue eyes studying me from where he sat, his elbow hanging out the open window.

I tipped my chin towards the hood and forced a smile. "The battery cable came loose. It was a quick fix and I'll be on my way now."

Old man Jonah leaned forward in his seat to get a good look at the stranger parked outside his property. After a quick appraisal, and a glare behind his narrowed eyes that made it clear he didn't trust me as far as he could throw me, Jonah inclined his head.

"Just be sure you are on your way, son," was his slurred warning.

Rage coursed through my body in tumultuous waves, but I kept a level head despite the way my fist gripped the steering wheel until the knuckles turned white. I wanted nothing more than to pull the gun I kept beneath my seat and level each and every one of them, but I wouldn't get answers from them if they were dead. A bullet was too kind a death for the price I wanted those bastards to pay.

Answers. I needed answers. And to get them, I needed those men alive.

Giving them a mock one-fingered salute, a byproduct of the time I'd spent in the military, I nodded my head once before driving away.

ᐱᐱᐱᐱ

Sitting in the old leather chair by my desk, I stared at a picture of my wife and son.

I'd carried that picture with me into the Middle East, and I'd cherished the note written on the back of it from my beautiful Katelyn. There was a scribble in blue crayon that ran through her note, the only remnant I had left of my son.

Leaning back against my chair, I sympathized with the way it groaned to take my weight. In many ways, I was that chair, still strong in structure, but ragged and torn apart on the inside and out. Years of unbearable anguish had drawn wrinkled lines across my skin, just like years of neglect had torn holes in the black leather of the armrests.

And much like that chair, I appeared older than I actually was.

Katelyn and I had been young parents, Michael a surprise addition that neither of us had been prepared to take on. It was the reason I went into the military immediately after I'd graduated high school. At the time I'd joined, the United States wasn't involved in many wars, but after an attack that occurred in New York, everything changed and I was deployed.

It was during my first tour that Katelyn and Michael went missing. As soon as I received word of their disappearance, I'd lost my mind. The military discharged me a few months later because I was a danger to myself and any soldier who fought beside me.

I'd come home to an empty house where I no longer heard my wife singing out of tune while she cooked or did dishes, a house that was so quiet because the laughter of our son was no longer there.

And through those years that I sat in agonizing silence, I'd aged faster than I should have, but I didn't really care.

At thirty-four years old, I could easily pass for forty.

Slamming my palm down on the desk, I ignored the flutter of paper from the breeze kicked up by the motion. Staring at the photograph, I considered what I would do with the new information I had.

Running to the police wouldn't do me an ounce of good. I'd attempted that when I first suspected the Crows. The cops laughed it off as the ruminations of a heartsick husband, as nothing more than the need to place blame by a shattered and broken father.

They were quick to clear the Crows, even went so far as to show me what little they could find on the timing of large storms and the dates the Crows left town. They used the date my wife disappeared, specifically, and then pointed to the reports of a hurricane that had just finished pounding the East Coast. To them, that coincidence was good enough.

Never once did they visit the property. Never once did they lift a finger to try.

No. Taking this to the police would only draw their attention to the fact the Crows had returned home, and I didn't want that. It was better to remain quiet - better to watch and wait - until the moment presented itself to strike.

With a bottle of whiskey tilted to my lips, my mind wandered to that young woman by the side of the stream. What had she been thinking about when her hand skittered up her stomach? What thoughts had been running through her head when her shirt slipped up so high I could see every curve of her young body? Were those bastards doing to her the same things I assumed they'd done to my wife?

The questions were killing me, so I gulped down the burning liquid in hopes it would smother the flame of rage inside me.

More than that, I hoped it incinerated the odd flare of interest I had in Maggie Crow.

There wasn't a thing about her that should have drawn my attention, not in the way a man should be interested in a woman. If anything, I should have felt protective of the girl. That, or hated her. Even if she wasn't part of a family that made my skin crawl just at the sight of them, she was too young for the thoughts that had whispered to me when I watched her.

She was off limits in every way, and for every possible reason.

Draining the bottle, I threw it in a small trashcan to the side of my desk. The glass clamored against the metal and shattered.

Hands running through my hair, I clenched my eyes shut and let my head fall back. She was just a girl, young and skittish. I couldn't fathom what the hell I'd been feeling.

It didn't matter. It *couldn't* matter. She was part of the family I wanted dead.

Cursing under my breath, I practically hissed out the words. I didn't know if I'd be able to easily pull the trigger and kill her.

Despite the skittish behavior that all but screamed *I know what happened to your kid*, Maggie had impressed me. She was confident about her knowledge of cars, and her eyes were much older than her years. It made me wonder what horrors those eyes had seen.

Promising myself that I'd give her a chance, I made the decision to help her if she was there against her will. But if she fought me, or if I found out she was somehow involved in the crimes her family had committed, her death would have to be a simple means to an end.

CHAPTER EIGHT

MAGGIE

"Did that man outside come to our door?" My brother, Finn, took a step towards me. We shared the same hair color, the same face shape, but where I had green eyes, Finn had blue. And where I was small, Finn was tall and broad.

Shrugging a delicate shoulder in response to his question, I turned to busy myself with pencil and paper. I sketched for an excuse to avert my eyes, because, in truth, I was a horrible liar. Although, with as boring and controlled as my life had been, there was never much for me to lie about. My family was with me practically all the time. But what few secrets I did have I wanted to keep, and now Elliot was one of those secrets.

My heart beat harder at the thought of Elliot. I wasn't sure if it was due to attraction or fear, but that small jump in pace was noticeable. It was probably for the best that he'd brought up a subject that made him dangerous. I wouldn't have walked away without it. Now that I knew he was connected to a family that could spell trouble for my father and brothers, it made him off limits in every way. I didn't need the temptation of a fantasy I couldn't have dangling right in front of my face.

"What man?" I asked, feigning ignorance with a voice that was timid and soft.

"The one whose truck broke down. You didn't see it? A black, shiny 4x4 with its hood up? You didn't notice that?"

Another shrug, my hand working the pencil over the paper. "Daddy said I couldn't go outside. So I didn't see anything."

Finn smirked. "Yeah, because you've always been one to listen to what daddy says."

"I'm a good girl," I mumbled. Too afraid to take Finn on directly, I made my argument, but with little strength behind it. "I don't do anything wrong."

His lips tilted at the corners, an expression that mocked me with every drop of cruelty Finn had in him. "Really? That's funny, because I could have sworn that's not exactly true."

Taking a seat at the table opposite me, he watched with a passive stillness that shot a chill along my spine. I loved my brothers, but I couldn't deny there was a rancid sickness that infected them both. Finn just happened to be the worst of the two. It was his laughter that was the loudest. No woman alive could scream as loud as my brother could laugh.

With a voice that was halfway between a whisper and an angry hiss, he taunted, "I seem to remember some books of yours that I found. The ones you had hidden beneath your bed. Do you happen to know what books I'm talking about?"

Giving me a slimy grin, he folded his hands together over the surface of the table.

I cringed because I knew exactly what books he'd found, and I didn't want my father to know anything about them. Regretting not throwing them away immediately after reading them, I prayed that Finn wouldn't say anything.

"Please don't tell Daddy. He'll kill me."

Finn's smile broadened. "I know."

"Why are you even bringing this up?"

Holding his hands up in feigned placation, Finn said, "Don't worry, Maggie. This can be our secret." He laughed a sharp bark of a sound that caused me to jump. "I mean, I get it. You're a growing girl. You've got *needs* just like the rest of us."

45

My nose scrunched. "Ew, Finn. I don't need to know about your needs."

Another bark of laughter, and Finn's expression became dead serious. "The reason I'm bringing this up," he said flatly, "is because I know you're not as good as you pretend to be. And I know there was some strange guy outside our house when we weren't home."

His inscrutable gaze locked to mine, anger wrinkling them slightly at the corners.

"I just want to make sure you know what would happen to any man we find that's been alone with you."

A lump formed in my throat. It didn't take a genius to figure out what my family would do.

"A man has many parts, Magpie."

Speaking slowly, there was a subtle threat weaved into his words. "Fingers, toes, arms, legs, other parts..." He canted his head to the side and grinned. "Well, hell, you've read the books. You know what parts I'm talking about."

Tired of his game, I tipped up my chin. "So? What's your point?"

His expression dripped with venom, his voice so eerily calm, I shivered just to hear it. "So, it would be a shame for a man to lose all those parts. Don't you think?"

Averting my eyes once again, I went back to sketching pencil over paper. There was an obvious tremor in my voice when I answered, "You don't have to worry about that today, because I didn't see any man."

"Sure you didn't, Magpie." A saccharine sweet response. "Sure, you didn't."

The legs of his chair scraped angrily over the linoleum floor. His heavy steps shook the table beneath my hands as he walked away. Releasing a shaky breath, I fought the urge to cry.

CHAPTER NINE

ELLIOT

Three days passed quickly after that brightly lit afternoon when I met Maggie. And in the seventy-two hours that followed, my mind had been focused on the family. The hours I spent holed up in my house were filled with research I hoped would paint a clearer picture of the Crows.

A man obsessed, I'd poured through records of abducted women and children throughout the country, tracking the disappearances alongside any major storms that had occurred. There wasn't a definite pattern I could follow, and that fact alone drove me to the bottle time and time again.

I'd missed three days of work and couldn't afford to miss more, but my boss was a good man who understood when I told him I was sick.

Sick drunk was more like it, but still sick just the same.

Scrubbing my palm over the stubble on my cheek, I stared at the countless images of missing women. My eyes memorized the details of their bright smiles and pretty faces. I wondered how many of those women were fortunate enough to meet a quick death, and how many had been tortured for hours, or possibly days? As far as I knew, there was a very real chance that some of those women were still alive out there, but the ruminations were just a momentary distraction from the true task at hand.

There was no clear pattern I could make out from the abundance of information I found online. In truth, it was a testament to my belief that we were already living in Hell.

Rape, murder, storms that raged...plagues, heartache, and illness. I couldn't possibly list every sad topic and event that made this world an unsafe place, couldn't possibly recite every evil that existed. The God-fearing men had it wrong the entire time. Hell wasn't a place below our feet and separate. Hell was what we lived through every day.

The lessons I'd learned in church had all but told me that fact when they mentioned that God had given the Devil dominion over this place.

I couldn't take on the Devil himself, but I sure as hell could take on three of his demons.

Nothing I found was concrete, nothing that could definitively tie three men to the countless loss suffered by the missing victims and their families. Judging by the property and the state of their lives, I wouldn't have considered the Crows brilliant, but it didn't take intelligence to stay out of sight, and by remaining in shadow they'd masked every trail I might have followed.

All I had left was gut instinct, and my gut was churning over the thought that the Crows had everything to do with my family's disappearance.

Lucky for me, I wasn't a court of law and I didn't need DNA or some other damning bit of evidence to convict them. Circumstantial evidence and Maggie's reaction had been enough for me to sentence those three fucks to the gallows.

Pushing out of my chair with such force I left it spinning in place behind me, I moved with weighted steps through my small house in route to the bedroom. Despite the alcohol sloshing around in my brain, I moved with a level step, only bumping my shoulder a few times against the wall as I went down the hallway.

A sharp turn right and my eyes focused on the seven foot gun safe I'd moved into the bedroom from the garage a year after returning home. The dark grey steel contrasted sharply against the soft, bright fabrics Katelyn had used to decorate the room. Except for the addition of the safe, I hadn't had it in me to change anything else in the space.

Within that safe sat three rifles, two shotguns and ten handguns, all sizes, high to low caliber. They weren't the weapons I planned to use to kill the Crow men because that would be too humane, but they were the weapons I'd use to get close to them and take control. Fighting the urge to open the safe and clean the guns, I reminded myself I'd just cleaned them the other day and hadn't used them since.

I knew I was unraveling, breaking apart slowly until all that was left of me was my basic, primal instincts. Eat, drink, sleep, shit, kill. And every once in a while...fuck. That's all there was. Everything else had died on the day my wife and kid disappeared.

Put in the simplest terms, I was damaged. I was broken. I had nothing left to lose, which made me the most dangerous type of man. I lacked fear. I lacked morality. I lacked every decent thing inside myself that made me care about consequences. Nothing mattered. And because of that, it made me the perfect predator too.

𝕴𝕴𝕴𝕴

I should have called out of work for a fourth day, but a sudden extended absence from the job I'd been loyal to for the past ten years would have drawn suspicion. That was the problem with rural towns. Everybody knew everybody's business.

As long as patterns and the usual crawl of life continued forward without interruption, people went about their day and kept their noses down. But as soon as something unusual happened, you might as well print it in the paper because every person would know.

That's why I was outside in the scorching heat, my body half buried in the engine of a large combine, wrench in hand as my feet dangled precariously off the frame. Harvesting season would be approaching soon and the farmers had been lining their machines up at the shop where I worked to get them prepped and ready for the grueling task of plowing fields and making what money could be made from the haul.

A tractor sat behind the combine, the green paint stripped from its sides from years of neglect and work, its tires in need of a change and its engine blowing out a billow of black smoke that had the owner worried the loss of the machine would be costly.

On any other day, I would have consoled the owner of the tractor and promised him it would be up and running in time, but I couldn't wrap my head around the job enough to care...not since the Crows returned.

I had another hour to burn before I could call it a day and drag my weary body away from the mechanic's yard and back home. But home wasn't where I'd be going that day. There were other matters far more important than drowning myself in a bottle.

Unsure how I'd venture onto the Crow property again without being noticed, I became lost in my thoughts. Their farm sat on the outskirts of town, far enough away from any other occupied property that I wouldn't have an easy excuse for driving by. The fact that I hadn't been questioned more thoroughly by the men the day they found me sitting in my truck outside their house was shocking. I had no reason to be out there, no reason to be driving by, unless it was their property specifically I was seeking.

Fortunately for me, the men hadn't asked, but they sure as hell saw my face, and if they were intelligent men, they would have dedicated my features to memory.

"Well," a deep voice drawled behind me, the sweet stench of a small black cigar alerting me to the identity of the person speaking, "you think you'll have her running by tomorrow? Tate is getting antsy. He's already called four times today asking for a time estimate."

Laughing to myself, I pushed my body away from the engine, sweat dripping from my brow into my eyes as my feet found and balanced my weight on the running board of the combine. I dragged a rag across my forehead to wipe away the stinging sweat, most likely replacing it with oil, dirt and whatever else had spotted parts of that red rag a putrid black.

My eyes met Henry Dodd, my boss and long time friend. "Tate hasn't stepped foot on this machine in ten years at least. I doubt that crotchety bastard could lift his foot up high enough to climb on, much less see where he's going enough to drive it. Why does he care?"

Henry laughed, puffs of smoke blowing out of his nose as he pulled the thin cigar from his lips. "He cares enough to force his grown boys up onto that machine. His body might be feeble, but his mind's not. Said he needs it up and running by tomorrow afternoon."

"Yeah," I barked out, my palm wiping the drops of sweat from the back of my neck. "Then go ahead and call him. You can let him know she's ready."

Surprise wrinkled Henry's forehead, his raised eyebrows disappearing beneath his hairline. With a grin twisting his lips, he said, "I knew there was a reason I hired you. Had to be something decent about your work to convince me to put up with your piss poor attitude every damn day."

I grinned. "I come here to work, not talk. It's not my fault you can't seem to stay away from me."

Not one to miss a beat, Henry smiled brightly. "Well, if you weren't so sweet out here looking all dirty and sweaty, I'd be able to control myself better."

Unable to hide the smirk that pulled at my lips, I stepped down from the combine, wiping my hands on the dirty rag as I approached my boss. "I'll tackle the tractor tomorrow. Although that black smoke is a bad sign. Not sure what's causing it. Could be some leaked oil burning itself out, or it could be a death rattle. Won't know until I open it up."

Casting a sidelong glance at the machine in question, Henry shrugged a tired shoulder. "It'll be Tobias' call once we know more. A patch job might get it through this season. Might not. But don't worry about it tonight. Go home and get some rest, Elliot. You look like shit."

Without responding, I shuffled past. I didn't make it five steps toward my truck before Henry's hand landed on my shoulder, preventing my retreat. Spinning on my heel, I squinted my eyes against the blinding sunlight that framed Henry's large frame.

"I know, to you, I'm just your employer, but I also like to think of you as a friend. And I can't allow a friend to get himself in trouble, if you know what I mean."

Henry's words sent a warning chill along my spine. Rolling my shoulders back, I kept my mouth shut while thoughts raced through my head about the type of trouble Henry knew I was getting myself into. Was my interest in the Crows so obvious that the entire town already knew my plans?

"You're hitting the bottle again pretty hard." Giving me a knowing look, Henry blew out a frustrated breath between stern lips. "Trust me, son, I know the difference between the flu and drowning in a bottle of whiskey."

Sympathy softened Henry's expression, his baritone voice a vibration on the wind. "I know you've been dealt a sad hand, but at some point you need to move past it. Stewing yourself in the tears of your past and the alcohol your swallowing to forget it won't help you survive."

He stared pointedly at me, concern burning behind his eyes. "Don't you want to move past this? Don't you think that's what Katelyn would have wanted you to do?"

I didn't respond because there was nothing for me to say. Henry had hit the nail squarely on the head, jamming it down so deep there wasn't an excuse I could give that would force the nail out. But despite how Henry looked at me with pity behind his eyes, I felt relief. If the only thing my boss was worried about was the bottle I nursed nightly to force myself into dreamless sleep, I'd take it. There were far more concerning thoughts running through my mind that I preferred remain hidden from view.

"The anniversary is coming up," I explained after a tense moment of silence. It wasn't a lie, in fact it was the date I planned on taking my time to exact revenge for the loss of two people who had been my entire world. The anniversary was in two weeks - giving me fourteen days to plan the end of the Crows. The end of what had once been my eternal nightmare. I wasn't sure I'd survive, and on some deep-seated level, I wasn't sure I wanted to.

"She wouldn't want this for you," Henry repeated. He'd never met Katelyn, but he'd known of her. That's how small towns worked. The adults were friends with the adults, their children carrying out their friendships and disputes as a tiny mirror image of the parents. If Bob Fargo didn't like Chad Green, you could bet money on the fact that Bob, Jr. was arguing with Chad, Jr. on the playground.

Henry couldn't speak for what Katelyn would have wanted because he didn't know her, not like I did. She was a strong woman, but still skittish. She had a love for stories and often kept her nose buried in books on every subject. That's how she knew that not even a small, tight knit community could save you from the monsters that lurked in shadow. If they wanted you, they'd find you.

Although, he hadn't known Katelyn as well as me, or any other child growing up in our generation for that matter, Henry had known her folks. The pain of her loss sent her mom and dad running for another town hours from where she'd been born, had grown, and eventually disappeared. I couldn't blame them. They wanted to move on and they needed to escape the shroud of pain that wrapped them in her absence. It made sense that Henry would believe that Katelyn was the same...that she would have run from the memories in order to move past them.

However, that wasn't Katelyn.

Katelyn would have fought tooth and nail to discover what happened to the people she loved. She would have gone just as crazy as me until she found the truth as to what happened to her son. Katelyn would have wanted revenge as much as me, and for that reason, I wouldn't let go until I had it.

Tipping my head in acknowledgement of what Henry said, I gave my boss a sad smile. "Maybe you're right."

There was nothing left to be said.

Henry waved goodbye as I turned to close the few feet of distance between my boss and my truck, climbing in to go home and shower before driving out in the direction of the Crow farm.

CHAPTER TEN

MAGGIE

There was nothing more familiar to me than the roar of engines coming from my father's machines. The smell of fresh cut grass filtered through my senses. The clean scent that belonged to the land spreading out around me promised eternity if I'd just take those few steps that would allow me to become lost within it.

Lowering myself down the three cement steps from the front door of the house, I looked out across the field watching the cloud of dirt that kicked up from the back of my father's mower. I paused and wondered how much of that was the leftovers of whatever evil thing my family had done. The wind shifted and kicked that cloud in my direction. Closing my eyes against the onslaught, I didn't dare breathe it in as I covered my nose and mouth to run across the expanse and find the small trail that led out to freedom.

I'd read once that whatever you smell, taste, or touch becomes part of you. There was no way I'd allow the death that littered this land to sneak its way into my body.

The woods were my playground, the stream a trickling beginning of the river that would carry me away from it all if I only knew how to build a boat. Every so often I'd send a stick down that slow current imagining myself riding aloft it and escaping the lonely existence my father and brothers had created for me.

Secrets were my friends and threats were my chains. My old man didn't mean anything by it, I knew that. On my head he'd fashioned a crown of the moon and stars, settling my body on a pedestal he'd created in memory of the mother I'd never known. I often wondered if he hadn't become a monster because the pain of losing his wife had been too much. There were times I'd wanted to ask if they'd killed when my mom was still alive, but I was too smart to start conversations I knew would only lead to trouble.

Despite the joy they found in hurting others, they never talked about it like it actually occurred. Like an insidious nightmare, my memories crept through my head at night, but there was no person who would acknowledge them out loud and admit they were real. I was always told it was someone else's burden to carry. But how heavy of a burden could it be? Not enough to stop them from committing another.

Tall grasses in the fields closer to the stream tickled the backs of my legs as I walked. My father never mowed out this far. It wasn't like the farm was intended for anything more than a residence. There was no need to keep the outlying areas clean, no reason to clear the fields so that they could grow more food than what we needed to survive.

A person would never hear me complain about the natural landscape. It gave me a place to hide, a place where I could imagine a life outside of the one I was living. No. Not really a life. What I lived was more like a cage, the lock of which had been welded together so that no hope existed for escape.

The small clearing by the stream came into view and I realized I considered it more home to me than the rundown shack that barely remained standing at the front of the property. Releasing one end of the blanket I was carrying, I allowed the wind to pull it out fully before settling the thick material over the dirt. I kicked off my flip-flops and shivered in response to a breeze that blew across the expanse. Cold weather would be coming soon. I smiled because I knew that meant there wouldn't be any hurricanes or other storms that would give my family the excuse to kill and head out again.

Even if it would only be a handful of months, I was pleased to know I'd stay settled in one place long enough to take a deep breath.

Lowering myself to the ground, I tilted my face up into the scant amount of sunlight that remained. The day had been hot, but late afternoon had dragged with it a touch of the cooler weather that was approaching.

My eyes hadn't been closed for more than a minute before I heard something walking around in the woods behind me. Pushing up to rest on my elbows, I squinted my eyes against the shadows, instinct chasing a warning along my spine as I scanned for even the smallest movement.

Dead leaves swirled in a gust of wind. A thick shadow moved from left to right. The hair on my nape stood on end.

Pushing up until I was crouched on the ground, I continued to peer out. My voice low, I warned, "I don't know what's out there, but I see you."

I didn't know if it was an animal or a man, and I hoped the fact that I'd spoken out loud would chase either option away. Nothing skittered off at the sound of my voice. The tension ratcheted higher.

Pushing up to my feet, I crept forward, my unblinking eyes taking in every detail I could distinguish from the swirl of decaying leaves and rattle of thin branches that hung low enough to slap the ground.

My body crossed the threshold of the woods, the sunlight fading at my back as I pushed forward, my hand finding and settling on something warm and hard. A gasp of breath flew over my lips when I looked up into the eyes that watched me.

A large hand wrapped over my mouth preventing the scream that would have torn from my lips, but remained trapped in my throat instead.

"Don't scream. It's just me."

I didn't recognize the hiss of the whispered words, but I knew the earthy scent that wafted past my nose. Alarm instantly tightened my shoulders. Had it been anybody else, I would have fought and struggled. But not him. Not my secret.

Lips grazed my ear as the man bent over my tiny frame to ask, "If I let you go, do you promise not to scream?"

Nodding my head, I thought of all the women I'd heard scream when they understood their fate. It was too late for those women, but not too late for me. However, I didn't fear this man like the women had feared my family...I just wasn't sure why. Perhaps my fantasies had led to stupidity, but I liked him more now that I'd had a chance to build a fantasy about him, even more than I had on the afternoon we first met.

His hand released my mouth and I backed up a step to look him in the eyes, disapproval pulling my lips into a thin line.

"What are you doing here? This is private property, Elliot. My family is home and if they knew you were out here..."

"I got lost," he explained, although I didn't understand how that was possible. The only adjoining property was another abandoned farm. He had just as much business there as he did on my land.

Fear drove a sharp line across my abdomen, my interest in this man cut through by the weight of the question he'd asked me before we parted ways the last time we met. Craning my neck to look behind me, I wondered if I shouldn't run as fast as my feet would carry me. Did he know that his son had been at this house all those years ago?

"I'm thinking of buying the farm next to yours. I decided to explore around, but I think I took a wrong turn."

Each word he spoke settled my shoulders a touch more. I wasn't sure if the relief I felt was in the explanation itself, or the hope I had that it was true.

Returning my gaze to his face, I felt a flutter in my belly. He was so beautiful. Even if he was dangerous.

Keeping my voice low so that it wouldn't travel on the winds that continued nipping at my cheeks, I blinked a time or two before answering, "I don't think you should explore if you don't know how to keep yourself from getting lost."

What was wrong with this man? First, he didn't know how to fix his truck, and now he couldn't find his way through the woods if someone had drawn him a map. From what he'd told me, he wasn't new to the area. I couldn't understand why he wasn't like every other person I knew around here. Not that I knew many, and that realization made me pause.

Perhaps I was comparing Elliot to the only men I really knew, and it wasn't a fair comparison. My father and brothers could live off the land. They could strip an engine and piece it back together faster than most people could watch their favorite movie. But those were the skills required by people who had good reason to live off the grid. Elliot must not have much to hide if he was so dependent on civilization to survive.

Relaxing even more at that thought, my stomach fluttered again. Elliot wasn't like the men that raised me, and my curiosity was piqued by that clear fact.

Questions continued flooding my head despite the attraction I felt for him. I wasn't dumb enough to instantly believe everything he said, even if I wanted to.

Narrowing my green eyes on him, I asked, "Why didn't you show yourself when I called out?"

A sheepish grin played over his lips, his hand reaching up to rub at the back of his neck. And damn if those dimples in his cheeks didn't make me want to smile right along with him. "You want the honest truth?"

My eyes widened. "Yeah. What else would I want?"

His shoulders shook with quiet laughter. "It was a rhetorical question."

"So then give me your rhetorical answer."

His brow furrowed at my words. "No, that's not -" Shaking his head, he didn't finish the comment, choosing instead to finally tell me what he was doing lurking around like a creep.

"I didn't want to scare you," he explained, a note of embarrassment on his voice. "And I didn't want to be rescued by a girl."

"Woman," I insisted. "I'm eighteen."

His eyes peered down at me, the corner of his lips twisting into a condescending grin that made me want to slap the expression off his handsome face. I was sick and tired of people viewing me as a child. I hadn't been a child since the day I learned how my family made their money.

"You'll have to forgive me, sweetheart, but it's hard for me to look at you and not see a child."

My face twisted in anger. "I'm not the one lost in the woods, now am I?"

He laughed, the sound warm and soft against my senses. I wanted to stay mad, but couldn't stop myself from drawing closer to a man that had dug himself into my thoughts little by little since the time we first met.

"I guess you have me there." Twisting his body around, he looked in the direction of the adjacent farm. "It's getting late. I should probably get back before the sun sets fully."

"How are you going to find your way?" I wouldn't admit it openly, but I liked the feeling of superiority. It wasn't often I knew more than the people around me.

My brothers had gone to school when my mom was alive, but I hadn't been given that option. We moved around too much and, most likely, my father was afraid I'd say the wrong thing around other kids and adults. He'd attempted to homeschool me, but that went as far as engines and survival skills. I knew how to read, I knew math, I knew enough to live off the land, but I wasn't book smart. Judging by the way I was still standing there with a man I knew to avoid, I wasn't the best student in common sense either.

But I had a leg up with Elliot at the moment. I knew how to get to the farm, and he was stuck unless I decided to help him. It made me proud enough to preen where I stood.

"I can walk you back."

His fingers worked over his neck again, the movement causing his bicep to flex beneath the short sleeve of his grey shirt. I admired the view, my eyes chasing the lines of quiet strength beneath his tan skin.

"No. I don't think so. The sun will be down by the time you can turn around and come back. I don't want you hiking around in these woods at night. There's no telling what can happen to you."

Canting my head to the side, I didn't know whether to feel special because he wanted to protect me, or angry because he thought I couldn't take care of myself. Giving it a moment's thought, I decided to meet the two in the middle.

"I appreciate the concern, but I've been hiking these woods during the day and night for as long as I can remember. And if you want to make it back to the other side before the sun sets, it's best we get moving now."

His eyebrows shot up to his tousled hairline, and I had to suppress a laugh.

With a sly smile pulling at his lips, his rugged accent was thick when he answered, "Well, in that case, show me the way."

Rolling my shoulders back with the pride I felt, I stared at Elliot and hoped I was right about him. He didn't seem like the type of men I lived with, but I still knew there was danger about him, both physical and otherwise. It might be the dumbest decision I'd made in my life, but I walked out in front of him to lead him through the woods.

Heavy steps sounded behind me for another ten minutes. I hated the silence between us, hated that I was missing an opportunity to learn about a person whose face invaded my dreams.

Unable to keep quiet any longer, I twisted my body to look back at him, damn near tripping over a tree root in the process.

"Is that why you were out here the other day? Because you were looking to buy the farm?"

He didn't answer immediately. Tossing him another sidelong glance, I wondered what was on his mind that kept him so silent.

"Yeah, actually," he finally said, his voice distant and cold. "I drove right past it the first time, which is why I ended up in front of your place."

Nodding my head, I stepped around a large rock, my skin crawling when I saw the large spider that skittered beneath it.

"Why did you run away from me the other day?"

My body flinched at the question, even more than it had at the spider.

Instinct kicked in, the lies that rolled so easily off my tongue filling my mind, just waiting to be spoken. Drilling me had been my brother's job, and Finn took the task seriously. I wouldn't slip, wouldn't accidentally allow the truth to leak out with the excuses I'd been trained to give.

"Your truck was fixed and my family was on their way home. I didn't want to be seen with you. They're protective."

His silence bothered me, the way he seemed to dissect every word in his quest to know what I knew. It was a result of my bad judgment, the simple fact that I couldn't run this time without confirming I had something to hide. How I'd ended up here with this man in this place: it was a consequence of my heart having become so lonely I would risk everything for just a moment to pretend I could have something real.

"I thought you said they were home. Now you're telling me they weren't?"

I wasn't a stupid girl, and I wasn't falling for his surprise at learning I'd been alone that day. My father and brothers had seen Elliot on the road. It was almost certain he'd seen them as well. He shouldn't be this shocked to discover I'd lied.

"I was home alone. Telling you that would have been stupid, don't you think? You could have done anything you wanted."

"I could do that now, couldn't I?"

Spinning to face him, I stopped short, my eyes locking to his with hesitation tracing my spine. It wasn't that I couldn't outrun him, especially here where every path looked like another. If nothing else, I could get him so scrambled and lost that I could sneak home without worry of him finding me again.

What had once been inviting was now set in a stern line. His mouth gave away his feelings more than his eyes. But at the moment I found the resolve to let this fantasy go to run back into the arms of a family that would kill to protect me, Elliot smiled.

"Not that I would do anything. I'm just saying that you've put yourself in a position where I *could* do something. It doesn't make sense. Why protect yourself then, only to leave yourself open and vulnerable now?"

Vulnerable. Yes, I had left myself open to a certain extent, but not in the way he thought. I believed I knew enough about Elliot to be certain that I could outmaneuver him in these woods. This wasn't the first time he'd come to me for help. But that didn't mean I was entirely safe.

Not entirely.

My heart was a different vulnerability altogether.

While my mind had been tripping over that thought, Elliot snuck closer, and by the time I realized my mistake, his warm, strong hands had wrapped around my shoulders to hold me in place. Tipping my head up to look at him, the breath was forced from my lungs.

Sharp, grey eyes stared down at me, his arrogant mouth crooked in such a way that his bottom lip pushed out until it was practically impossible not to want to know what it felt like against my own. The shadow of stubble defined the line of his strong jaw, and his hair was just messy enough to force my hands into fists to keep from reaching up to run my fingers through it. A jolt of need shot through me, the same jolt I felt in the moments I'd allowed myself to feel what the characters in the books I'd read had been feeling.

"You're a surprising person, Maggie. And it's not often that I find myself surprised. I've lived a long life. A hard one at that. And then you come along and make me wonder."

Wonder what? I thought. Worrying the back of my lip between my teeth, I focused on controlling the rate of my breath. There wasn't much I could do about my heart thumping painfully quick behind my ribs, and I hoped like hell he didn't notice how shaky I'd become in his presence. It was ridiculous to feel this way about a man I barely knew, but it was the first time I'd been this close to someone other than my family or their friends.

Releasing one of my shoulders, he gripped my chin between his finger and thumb, tipping my head up even more. Tension was a vice grip on my spine as his eyes bore down to search my face for every secret I had to hide.

With a voice as soft as the wind that played my hair across my back, he said, "We should get going." There was a grittiness to his words that made my legs weak beneath me.

Despite what he'd said, neither of us moved to take another step, both frozen in a moment where I wanted him to kiss me.

Knowing nothing about him didn't stop me from wanting him, and the danger that he wore only made me want him more. He was off limits, I reminded myself, but it wasn't enough to force me away, to break whatever hypnotic spell he'd wrapped around me with nothing more than the feel of his heat against my skin.

CHAPTER ELEVEN

ELLIOT

"You're shaking."

My voice came out softer than I'd wanted, and the reason behind that velvet touch to my words concerned me. Maggie wasn't a person I should show kindness. She held a secret behind those startled green eyes - a secret that had kept me imprisoned in my own shame, regret and pain for fourteen long years.

Dressed in nothing more than a thin, cotton sundress that showed off her shoulders and gave just a hint of what was hidden beneath the light blue colored fabric, Maggie stared up at me with fear and something else. Excitement, maybe? Or promise?

Many women had looked at me with that same promise in their eyes, but none of them, since Katelyn, had caused a shot of interest to tear through me as a result. Shaking off that inkling of desire, I pulled my hands from Maggie's skin, stepping back quickly to place distance between myself and a girl I had no business wanting.

She was nothing more than the key to my revenge, the weak link that would allow me access to the men I blamed for everything that had gone wrong in my life. My plan to use her hadn't formed until I pulled my truck up to the abandoned property next to the Crow farm. It had been the best option - at least until this moment when I was staring down at a girl that pulled at something inside me I thought had long been dead.

Maggie was impressive. I could tell she wasn't the brightest woman I'd run across, not in the typical estimation of intelligence. She wasn't Katelyn with her perfect grades in school and offers for college that she'd turned down regardless of my protests. But I had no doubt this girl could survive the worst of circumstances.

Despite her short stature, despite the way she trembled even more after I pointed out her reaction, she continued to glare up at me with no reservations. Most women take their peek and look away. They're too shy to openly want something. But not Maggie. This girl had strength in her spirit - strength and the damn misfortune of being a Crow.

"It's getting cold," she explained, as if there weren't so many holes in that excuse the wind could tear right through it.

I hated this. With every fiber of my being, I hated what I had to do. But that's the thing with revenge. A man was willing to do whatever it took - hurt whoever it took - just to see that particular deadly sin to its end.

Stepping closer, I dropped my head to the side, my eyes trailing along every curve of her body without guilt or remorse. "Well, I can't let you be cold, Darlin'. Not when it's my lost ass you ran out here to save. Tell me what I can do to help you."

For every step I took forward, Maggie took one back. The distance she kept between us didn't escape my notice, and my smile pulled wider as a result.

"I'm fine," she insisted, but the hitch in her voice told me she wasn't as fine as she'd like me to believe.

"You don't look fine." Throwing as much charm as I could manage into the words, I closed the distance until she was backed up against a tree. My chest barely brushed hers as I stared down at the trembling form of her body. Reaching out, I swept my finger beneath the thin strap of her dress, tugging it to slide off her shoulder as the tip of my finger traced her skin. "Let me help you."

Her mouth opened slightly, her chest rising and falling with shallow, rapid breath. "Slipping off my sleeve certainly isn't going to help."

"Well," I grinned, "Then allow me to slip off mine."

"What?"

The question had barely left her mouth before I tugged at my back collar and pulled the t-shirt from my body to hand to her. "Take this." Shoving the soft material into her hand, I smiled. "It should cover you better than what you're already wearing."

Her eyes widened and trailed slow paths over the lines of muscle that hugged my frame. I've always been a strong man. The military only served to strengthen my physique, the packs I carried and the miles I'd run sculpting my body until it was a finely tuned machine. Coming home from the war hadn't done anything to diminish my build, not when I was constantly working it turning wrenches for Henry, or running miles down the road just to escape the pain of losing my family.

Leaning towards Maggie, I laughed softly at the way she stood frozen clutching the shirt I'd given her tightly to her chest. "Do you see something you like? Is that the real reason you ran from me the other day? Are you scared?"

It was all too apparent that I affected her. The way she struggled to pull in a deep breath, the way her eyes never left my body as if she were memorizing every small detail. I regretted having to toy with a woman who was so obviously lost to the attraction she felt, and I had to wonder why. Perhaps she'd been sheltered by that damn family of hers too much, or perhaps the cause of her behavior was something far more sinister and disturbing.

Maggie surprised me when she reached out to push me away, my body stumbling back as she moved away from the tree and tipped her chin up with an expression of pure defiance.

Surprising me again, she held my eyes as she pulled the shirt over her body, the material eventually hanging down to her knees. I'd expected her to throw it down, or if polite, to refuse it graciously and hand it back, but I didn't believe she would actually accept my offer.

"Thank you," she said, her voice as weak as her knees had been moments before. "We really should keep moving."

My head fell back and true laughter blew over my lips. Not much took me by surprise anymore, but this woman - this person I should have hated as much as the family she belonged to - she continued to mystify me with every decision she made.

Shaking my head in disbelief, I stepped towards her and motioned out with my arm. "Ladies first."

A grin pulled at her full lips, a flash of something behind eyes that were the color of a forest at dawn.

As we moved through thicker brush, Maggie kept looking back at me, concern shadowing her expression. "You're going to get eaten alive by bugs now that you don't have a shirt covering your chest. Guess you didn't think about that when you decided to give it up to me."

It seemed the ice had been broken between us, and all the tension and indecision in Maggie had dissolved in the few moments I'd attempted to stir up longing inside her. Refusing to miss the opportunity to gain information, I innocently said, "I'm not worried about the bugs. My father taught me to respect women above all else, so I'm just glad to help keep you warm. But I'm sure you know what I mean."

Casting me a furtive glance, Maggie shrugged a shoulder. "I guess so. My daddy treats me like I'm the most precious thing in his world. My brothers on the other hand..."

Her voice trailed off and the tension returned to my shoulders. "I don't mean to pry, but what about your brothers?"

She was finally talking, and as long as I didn't push too hard, I hoped it meant I would gain all the information I needed with this one trip. Perhaps her father hadn't been involved after all. It was a possibility, but something told me there was more to Jonah Crow than simply a doting father.

"My brothers," she answered, her voice far off and hesitant, "they're, I don't know. They're just mean. Not all the time, and Brody is better than Finn, but I think they're jealous of how much my father loves me." Her thin shoulder shrugged when she admitted, "I guess they just hate the fact that they have to watch over me all the time. Not that there's much to watch. I don't go anywhere or do anything. I don't have any friends or..."

"A boyfriend?"

Her head spun to look at me. Her cheeks stained red with embarrassment, she smiled shyly and replied, "No. I could never have a boyfriend. They'd kill him if he laid a finger on me."

My eyes widened in response to her words and Maggie was quick to explain, "I mean, they wouldn't actually *kill* anybody. They'd just scare him until he ran off."

There was fear behind her gaze, fear that I knew had been placed there by the secrets her family wished to remain hidden. I didn't want to run her off with too many questions, even if those questions were screaming in my head and causing my hands to tighten into painful fists.

"Sounds like a typical older brother," I teased, somehow forcing humor into my voice when all I felt was rage. Not at Maggie. Never at her. But at those men who stole my life away.

Not responding to what I'd said, Maggie's expression fell. She turned to walk faster. "The farm should be up this way in another ten minutes or so."

Passing the rest of the trip in silence, I took a deep breath when the neighboring farm came in to view. If I was going to ingratiate myself to her, I had to do it soon. The more information I had about the Crows the better.

"I have a confession to make, Maggie. I hope you won't get mad."

She pivoted on her heel, her eyes meeting mine with true fear behind them. "I got you to the farm, so I should get going," she snapped, not angry, but there was the trace of terror behind her words. I couldn't understand the reaction, and I wasn't about to let her run away until I knew what scared her.

The woman was quick on her feet, I'd give her that, but I had reflexes that had been honed by my days as a Marine. As fast as she ran past, I reached out to wrap my hand around her bicep and drag her back against me. She fought my hold, but stilled suddenly once my mouth pressed against her ear.

"I haven't even told you what I wanted to say," I whispered. "Where are you going in such a hurry?"

"I have to go," she muttered, her heart beating a frantic pulse beneath her skin, her breath coming out in shallow spurts. She was terrified, the trembling of her body, a vibration against my own.

"In my shirt?" Still practically whispering, I laughed softly, hoping the friendly sound might shake her out of whatever terror flooded her.

Her body stilled at the question, becoming weak against mine as she stopped struggling in order to listen to what I had to say.

"You can't take off in my clothes, Maggie. Not if you don't want your family to know you were with me."

Nodding her head, she reached down to pull the t-shirt up, but I placed my hands on her stomach to prevent her from lifting it over her head. "Before you give it back, can I tell you what I wanted to say?"

Her back was pressed to my chest, her hair soft against my bare skin. A chill ran through me, tightening every muscle across my bones as the scent of her shampoo struck me. Roses. The beautiful girl that was so terrified she could barely remain standing smelled like the flower that reminded me so much of my wife.

Gritting my teeth against the onslaught of memory, against the grating pain that tore me apart inside as the whispers of happiness I'd once had echoed in my thoughts, I softened the sharp edge to my voice, my mind focused on the task at hand. I needed Maggie to trust me. I needed Maggie to want me enough that she'd risk everything just to be near me. Without her, I had no chance at getting close to the Crows.

Bringing my lips down to brush her ear again, I said, "All I wanted to tell you was that it wasn't an accident I ended up at your place today."

Every muscle in her body tensed mirroring my own, but I kept going hoping that she would understand what I was trying to say.

"I couldn't stop thinking about you after the day I broke down in front of your house. I couldn't get those gorgeous green eyes out of my mind. I want to know you, Maggie, and I think you want to know me."

Pressing closer, I ran my hands down her arms, watching as goosebumps broke out across her skin. "Tell me you want to know me. I'm begging you, beautiful, tell me I wasn't wrong when I thought there was a spark between us."

CHAPTER TWELVE

MAGGIE

"I have to go," I insisted, forcing every word past my lips despite the way they clung to my tongue desperate to remain silent.

Unsure whether I loved or hated the fact that he released me so quickly, we stepped away from each other as I turned to stare at the first man who'd shot electricity along my skin.

"Thank you," he said, a flash of light reflected in his silver-grey eyes from the last ribbons of the setting sun. "You know, for saving my ass and all. I didn't mean to scare you."

I watched silently as his mouth twisted into an embarrassed grin, his hand reaching up to rub at the back of his neck. I knew then that it was a nervous habit on his part, much like the way I chewed at the back of my lip when I concentrated or didn't know what to say.

Breathing out on a rush of breath, he admitted, "Fuck, that was a stupid thing for me to say." He laughed, the sound so genuine it made me smile in response.

"I'm so bad at this romance shit. I -" His voice trailed off, but I wished he'd keep talking. His accent gave him a boyish charm, and the grittiness of his voice tugged at something inside me that caused my thighs to tighten together.

Shaking my head, I took a step closer despite everything inside me that told me to tuck tail and run.

"It wasn't stupid," I offered, my tone uncertain about everything this man represented. I knew who he was - who his wife and son had been - but I finally allowed myself to believe he had no idea about my family. The thought sent a shot of excitement through my body, my skin blushing with the anticipation of what this could be.

"It's kind of creepy that you lied to me about being lost." I wasn't lying to say it. I was flattered that he wanted to see me so badly he'd acted like a fool just to get close.

The setting sun shone like fire against the darkening sky, colors banding out as the moon climbed up from the horizon. Elliot glanced up at the waning light before leveling his gaze back on me.

"You should get going, Maggie. Or at least let me drive you home. I worry about you in those woods all by yourself." Flashing me a charming smile, one that caused those dimples to indent into dark points on his cheeks, he apologized. "And I'm sorry for acting like a creep. I just didn't think there was any other way for me to get to know you besides sneaking around."

"Are you really buying this farm?"

One quick nod of his head was his response before he turned to look out over the fields of grass and weeds. A two story house stood in the distance. Dark and abandoned, it was still more inviting than the small house where I lived. I could imagine myself in a house like that - with a man like Elliot.

"Yeah. I'll probably be out here every day for the next few weeks inspecting around. I need to see what should be fixed before throwing down money."

I grinned, my weight shifting between my feet because I knew I should get back home. The only problem was that I didn't want to leave.

"I can keep a secret," I said. Giving him a smile I hoped would say all the words I was too afraid to speak, I ignored the frantic beat of my heart. "So, maybe I'll see you out here tomorrow, if you can keep a secret, too."

Some unspoken thought flashed behind his eyes, quickly covered by the way his mouth pulled into a lurid smile.

"Darlin', secrets are all I have. I'm always ready and willing to take on a few more."

My stomach fluttered, my body tightening as I forced myself to keep from drawing closer to him. Shirtless and with jeans that hung from his narrow waist, he was the most beautiful man I'd ever seen. His chest wasn't smooth, but had just enough dusting of hair that it made me wonder what it would feel like against my palms.

Trailing my eyes down further, I hiccupped over my breath at the muscles that rolled beneath his tan skin. His arms were three times the size of mine and I knew their strength could tear me to pieces if I allowed him to wrap himself around me. I needed to go, needed to place as much distance between Elliot and myself before I did something stupid.

"Secrets it is, then. I'll see you tomorrow, Elliot." Turning to run back home, I stopped short when he called out my name.

"I think you're leaving with something that belongs to me." His eyes roamed over my body and I remembered it was his shirt I wore.

Breathing in deeply, I savored the smell of him on the shirt, but gripped the hem, reluctant to strip it off and return it. I hadn't had a chance to lift it off my body before he spoke again.

"No, beautiful." His hand touched mine and I jumped to discover he'd closed the distance between us. "I wasn't talking about the shirt."

Flicking my eyes up to his, I admired him beneath the thick fall of my inky dark lashes. "What were you talking about?"

Strong hands gripped my hips, my body jerked forward until I was pressed against him. Bending over, his lips brushed the rim of my ear when he whispered, "I'll let you go home to think about that for a while. Maybe tomorrow you can come back and tell me what you came up with."

He released me as fast as he'd grabbed me and I stumbled back a few steps.

A wolfish grin spread over his lips, his eyelids heavy and hooded over the stormy grey. "Keep the shirt so that you stay warm on your trip back."

Swallowing down the nervousness that sat lodged in my throat, I nodded once before turning away to walk into the woods between the two farms.

"And Maggie?"

Glancing at him from over my shoulder, I waited in rapt attention.

"Be careful. I'd hate to see somebody so beautiful get lost in the woods at night."

Thud. Thud. Thud.

My heart couldn't handle the sweet torment of his words. Unable to speak, I nodded again, running away fast enough this time that he couldn't stop me.

⁂

"Where have you been? The sun set an hour ago and dad's been looking everywhere for you. We thought a damn bear had dragged you off."

With my gaze lowered so that I didn't have to see the scorn written across Brody's face, I let myself into the house wishing like hell he would move aside so I could run down the hall and disappear into my room.

His hand wrapped around my arm, my entire body shaking back and forth as he forced me to look up at him.

Brody was every bit as big as Finn and my father, but somewhere along the line his hair had turned a sandy blond. His green eyes were the only feature he shared with his baby sister.

"Answer me, Maggie. You know we don't like it when we don't know where you are."

"I was out by the stream where I always am, but then I decided to take a walk through the woods. What's wrong with that?"

Angry green eyes narrowed on me, the color glimmering with something nefarious and revolting. Having Brody this close made my skin crawl. Stepping away from him, I tried to jerk my arm free. His grip was too tight and I hurt my shoulder from the effort to pull away.

"Let me go."

Dragging me closer, he lowered his head until we were nose to nose. "I'm not letting you go and you're damn lucky I found you before Finn."

A shiver coursed along my spine and I screamed, "Daddy? Daddy, I'm home!"

Soft laughter drew my attention back to Brody.

"He's not here, Magpie. The old man's out looking for his precious daughter, probably killing himself off faster for being out in the cold." His voice dropped to a shrill whisper, the words hissing over his smiling lips. "What are you going to do when he dies? Who's going to protect you then?"

Tears welled in my eyes and I fought to keep my thoughts from going to Elliot. A man like him could protect me. He could take me so far away from this house I'd be able to forget it ever existed in the first place.

My voice was an angry drawl when I demanded, "Let me go, Brody. Daddy's not dying and you're just going to piss him off by thinking you have the right to put your hands on me."

Despite the strength I'd intended to put in those words, they still came out weak. Brody and Finn had many ways to torture me and still stay in good graces with our father. All they had to do was pretend they were looking out for me - that whatever mean spirited thing they'd done was because it was in my best interests.

My brothers were a large part of the reason I was so sheltered. Constantly whispering in my father's ear, they kept it so I was always within sight. It didn't make any sense, especially when they complained about having to take care of me.

His fingers uncurled from my arm and I could still feel the heat of them against my skin. More than likely I'd bruise, but Brody would just lie and say I was doing something stupid and needed to be grabbed.

My dad loved me, but when it came to who he believed, it was always my brothers.

"Keep telling yourself that. You go ahead and continue believing that Dad isn't one step away from the grave." He laughed. "Women are always easier when they're off guard anyway."

Rounding into saucers, my eyes locked to his, my skin crawling in response to the expression on his face. Brody didn't have the chance to say anything else before the kitchen door slammed open behind me, a familiar cough filling the small room.

Brody stalked off as my father approached.

"Where were you? I've been out there for over an hour."

Batting my eyes, I spoke with as much sweetness as I could. My father never could deny me when I acted innocent. "I took a walk, Daddy. Through the woods and it got late before I realized it. I turned around as fast as I could."

Finn stood behind my father, scowling and angry because he was pissed I could play my *daddy* so well. If it were up to Finn, I would be punished in one way or another.

My father's shoulders withered and he coughed so hard and loud that he had to settle himself into a chair just to keep from tipping over. "Don't do that to me again," he said breathlessly, his coughing fit shaking his entire body. "I mean it, girl. Don't run off without telling me."

Tears streamed down my face, first for fear of my brothers, and second for the love I had for my father. He wasn't a saint. In truth, he was closer to a demon. But he was all I had.

Spoken on a bare whisper, I relented, "I won't, Daddy. I promise."

CHAPTER THIRTEEN

ELLIOT

Seven days.

It had been an entire aggravating week that I found myself loitering around an abandoned farm waiting for a girl I wished I didn't know.

Sitting in an old metal chair that was rusted at the feet and listing slightly to the left, I laid my head back against the side of the house and squinted my eyes against the harsh afternoon sunlight.

My back hurt from bending over engines all day, but I savored the pain. The minor aches and muscle pulls were nothing compared to the emptiness I felt inside.

If anything, to feel pain at all was a blessing. It filled that hollow part inside me that had rotted away to dust in the months following my family's disappearance. In the years following, the helpless, panicked breath I'd forced myself to endure when reality came crashing down blew away all that dust until I was left with nothing.

In the fourteen years I've spent alone, the emptiness and misery were the only things left inside me. But now there was a spark of something else, a spark I wanted to extinguish before it built into something hot and fierce, something that threatened to burn me from the inside out.

I felt worry. I felt concern and a twinge of need. All for a girl I had no business knowing.

Where the hell had she been this past week? Had her family found out she'd been with me in the woods? Had they done something to her as a result?

Unable to handle the possibilities that buzzed in my head like a swarm of angry hornets, I pushed myself up to my feet and paced over the packed dirt and weeds that littered the land surrounding me. A noise sounded in the distance, branches cracking together causing the leaves to rustle in the wind.

Spinning on my heel, I fought against the feeling of relief that nagged at me. She'd finally shown. Maggie was safe and okay. The feeling was unwelcome because it wasn't Maggie I should be concerned about. The only thing I knew anymore was the need for revenge, that and the acceptance that I would die as well when I finally had it.

No. Not *die*. I was already dead. I would just finally stop breathing.

But still, that relief was a pinprick of emotion and light cutting into the darkness that filled me, so when I spun expecting to look at the small, brunette beauty I'd waited to see for the past week, my heart twisted into knots at the sight of a set of squirrels angrily chattering as they chased each other along the threshold of the woods.

Disappointment stepped in to take relief's place.

Scrubbing my hand along the stubble on my jaw that I hadn't trimmed in so long it was becoming a full beard, I cursed under my breath and kicked at an errant rock that sat in my path. "Fuck, Maggie! Where the hell are you?"

"Right here."

I spun again, the dust beneath my feet kicking up into a cloud around me, my eyes finding and settling on a small, young woman who stared back at me with worry behind the greenest eyes I'd ever seen.

"Maggie." Nine parts relief and one part concern, her name fell from my lips as I stepped towards her, my hands clenching into tight fists when she stepped away in response.

"Maggie?"

Her eyes were directed to the ground at her feet, her body covered by a thin yellow dress that hung midway down her thighs. With shoulders naked to the sun except for the tiny straps that held the dress on her body, she stood motionless before me, a discolored ring of skin on her left bicep drawing my attention and igniting my wrath.

"What happened?"

I'd growled out the question, instantly regretting allowing my anger to bleed out into my voice. I needed to attract Maggie closer, not push her away, but I couldn't help the rage I felt towards the men that raised her. Biting off another hissed curse, I shifted in place fighting the urge to storm over and shake her, to force her to look at me.

Seconds passed in a thick soup that churned between us, the heat scalding my skin red and the air trapped from entering my lungs because it was too thick to breathe.

"Nothing happened." A whisper. A plea. A blatant lie wrapped up in those two simple words.

I was finally able to take a breath. It wasn't a deep one, and it did nothing to settle my nerves, but it was a breath nonetheless.

"I don't know what to say here, Maggie. I've been waiting for you for a week. I've been worried. And I can tell just by looking at you that something happened because the glitter and hope I normally see behind those eyes of yours is missing."

Her gaze shot up to meet mine.

Taking that tiny bit of eye contact as an invitation to move closer, I stepped forward like I was approaching a timid rabbit ready to bounce away at any second. What would I do if

Maggie ran from me? How would I get to the Crows if I didn't have her to lead me?

The truth was I could go in with guns in hand and level them all before they knew what the hell had struck them. I was dead already, wasn't I? It didn't matter if I made a scene or left evidence all over their land and house. I didn't plan to walk away once I'd ended each and every one of them. What did it matter how I approached them?

A small voice inside reminded me it mattered because shooting them would be too damn easy. A quick death wouldn't return to them the pain and anguish they'd forced on so many others. It wouldn't cut them all so deep that their minds shattered before their bodies took that last gurgled breath. There wouldn't be time for the begging and screaming, the anger and torment I wanted them to suffer because they had already made me suffer in that way.

Her voice hitched when she admitted, "I can't come over here again. I shouldn't be here now, but I wondered -"

Holding her stare, I stood stock still not daring to move and lose what little chance I had at keeping her close. This poor girl was caught in the crossfire between three evil men and the newly born psychopath they'd created when they stole my family away.

"You wondered?" Prodding her gently, I forced the anger from my voice and replaced it with what I hoped was the same velvet texture I'd used to seduce Katelyn when I was young.

This poor girl. This poor, unfortunate pawn.

Shy desire filled her eyes, hope and longing a flicker against the green that sparkled within the heavy rays of the sun. She believed me when I was soft with her. She wanted me when I pretended to want her. She became lost to me, making it obvious how innocent and naive she was. I was taking full advantage and I wouldn't go easy on her simply because I knew what I was doing would destroy her.

The Crows had destroyed everything good and pure in me, and I'd promised the phantom memories of my wife and son that I'd return the favor.

"I wondered if you'd actually be waiting for me."

My lips pulled into a charming smile, my shoulders rolling back as I dared another step in her direction. "Of course, I am. You're worth waiting for."

Close enough to touch her, I pressed my fingertip beneath her chin to tilt her face up to mine. "Don't you know that about yourself?"

A slight shrug of her thin shoulder was followed by a heartbreaking confession. "Nobody's ever waited for me before. I'm always left out."

Knowing what those men did, I had to wonder if it wasn't a good thing she was left behind. There was a small chance she didn't know what her family did in the shadows. Her potential innocence is what made my using her to get close to them all the more vile.

But I couldn't let that be a problem. I couldn't let it become something that kept me from delivering every ounce of pain I'd promised.

"Hey, Maggie?"

Her eyes blinked, the black lashes that framed them fanning out across her skin before the green was returned to me. "Yeah?"

"Am I still a secret?"

Her full lips pulled into a hesitant grin, her voice a whisper on the wind when she answered, "Yes."

Not missing a beat, not taking the chance that I could lose the connection I had with her in that moment, I leaned in until our lips were inches apart. Her breath brushed across my face and I smelled the same rose scented shampoo in her hair when wisps of it were caught and danced in the breeze.

"How long do I have with you before you go home?"

Possessively curling my fingers over her hips, I pulled her closer until our lips barely touched. Her breath left her lungs in shallow huffs, her heartbeat so erratic and strong that I could feel it against my chest. Dropping my voice to a dangerous, low tone, I spoke against her mouth when I asked, "Will you stay with me for just a little while?"

I didn't kiss her, didn't want to move until I knew she wouldn't take off and leave me a distant memory staring at her back as she ran away.

"Will you?"

Maggie breathed out.

I breathed in.

"Yes," she answered.

Our bodies melted together.

CHAPTER FOURTEEN

MAGGIE

"Come with me, beautiful. Let's go somewhere we can't be seen from the road."

Twisting around, I narrowed my gaze to stare off into the distance. The road was nothing more than a faint, shimmering line from where we were standing. I turned back to him with confusion wrinkling my expression.

"I'm not sure anybody can see anything from all the way over there."

I felt his fingers grip mine before he tugged me along. Without bothering to look back at me, or respond to what I'd said, Elliot led me to the abandoned house, around a corner, and to an old decaying chair that was propped up against the wall.

The feet of the chair sank down into the sand when he dropped his weight into the seat. "Come here."

My heart threatened to tear through my chest. Inching backwards, I stared at Elliot, my breath coming out short and spastic. I'd never felt fear like this before. Not even when I heard those women screaming at my family's *parties* and understood what those screams meant. This was a new kind of fear, a kind that caused sweat to mist across my skin and make it sticky. The kind that made me lightheaded and dizzy.

Crooking his finger to dare me to approach, Elliot smiled like he knew how frightened I was. The heat behind his eyes gave away the fact that he didn't care, and the way his eyelids lowered until they hooded over the grey made it clear he'd chase all those fears away.

"Come here," he cooed, "we don't have all night."

Air rattled over my lips, my legs trembling beneath me. What the hell was I doing with this man and why hadn't I told him to leave me alone like I'd planned on the walk over?

The past week had been the worst. My father had gone about his business like nothing happened, but my brothers took it upon themselves to keep me within sight.

They were always cruel when it came to me, but their attention was amplified over the past few days, their minds filled with suspicion. I didn't know if it was boredom on their part or the fact they'd seen Elliot out on the side of the road the day he first showed up, but I hadn't been given an inch of wiggle room until they both took off to visit with friends.

They told my dad they'd be gone for the night and I took that to mean something awful was happening at another house in a neighboring town. Guilt flooded me for feeling relieved they were gone when I knew that some other person might be losing their freedom or life.

If my father wasn't involved, I might have turned them in years ago just so I would be able to escape. My conscience was too full of guilt, too full of pain to sit silently while the monsters my brothers had become preyed on the helpless and unwilling. But what choice did I have? I didn't want to hurt my father. He'd loved me with everything he had. He'd provided for me and protected me. He just never learned to let me grow up, spread my wings and fly.

Because of that, I worried for any person who tried to be my friend. Especially Elliot. If my brothers found out I was here with him now, I knew they'd try to kill him.

"I don't think this is a good idea, Elliot. It's probably best I go back."

He stood up, inching his way forward as I inched farther away. It killed me to move away from him, but touching him would destroy every bit of my resolve. I wanted this more than anything I'd ever wanted in life, but to protect him, I had to leave.

Holding his hands up in placation, Elliot looked concerned. "Where did you go just now, Darlin'? Just a minute ago you were right here with me and now -"

"Now, I think it's best I walk away," I answered, pain woven into every word I spoke. "I don't want to get you in trouble, Elliot-"

"You've already gotten me in trouble," he grinned, his perfect white teeth flashing in the sunlight, "just not in the way you might think."

God, he was so beautiful. And he was such a ... *man*.

Thanks to the wonder of dirty books, I knew a thing or two about the difference between men and boys. Men were strong and reliable; whereas boys were flaky and selfish. Men knew what they wanted and took it; whereas boys were fickle and mercurial.

A true man knew how to treat a woman so that she found herself lost to all the emotions he created in her; whereas boys might make a woman's heart sing, but they could never make her go weak in the knees.

My knees were so weak at that moment they were knocking together - which meant that Elliot was definitely a man.

"Plus," he argued, still inching his way closer with careful, measured steps, "you can't get me in any more trouble than you already have. I'm a secret, remember? There's nobody else that knows about me other than us."

Waving his finger back and forth between our bodies, he drew my attention to the motion of his hand as he snuck closer. By the time I looked up into his eyes, he was near enough to reach out and pull me into his arms.

After stumbling over my own feet in an attempt to pull away, I finally stopped the struggle. He wasn't going to let me go and I didn't want him to. There was no point fighting it.

Elliot smiled when he realized I'd given up trying to run away.

It seemed like I'd spent my entire life doing the wrong thing, and now that I was trying to do something right for a change, this beautiful man wouldn't let me.

His feet moved to pull me forward, his arms like steel bands wrapped securely around my body. "You and I are going to sit in this chair for a while and talk. That's all. You have nothing to be scared of."

Laughter escaped me before I had the chance to stifle it. "There's only one chair. I'm not sure that both of us will fit."

He grinned wider, a glimmer in his eye that made my heart pound harder. "Oh, I'm sure if we get creative, we'll figure out something."

My heart skipped a beat entirely at the thought.

Elliot never took his eyes off me as he lowered himself into the seat, leaving me standing with my legs between his knees.

His fingertips brushed up the outside of my thighs. I shivered at the touch, fear rekindled in my heart, not because I was genuinely scared of Elliot, but more because I'd never been touched like that before.

On long nights alone, I'd imagined what it would feel like: the first touch, the first kiss. But deep down I'd known those moments would never happen for me - not while my father and brothers were still alive.

For the first time in my life, I felt surprised by the curveball life tossed in my direction.

"I don't think it's going to work like this so well," Elliot teased, a hint of tension in his voice and a roughness that made wild thoughts clamor around in my mind.

Gripping my thighs, he pushed me back until my legs were no longer between his. Closing his own, he pulled my thighs apart, the strength of his hands easily overpowering what little effort I made to keep my knees together. Tugged forward again, my knees bent as Elliot pulled me down to straddle his lap.

"Much better."

His lips twisted up into a dirty smirk and I felt that smirk all the way down to my toes.

"Much, much better."

My body shook nervously above his, but my eyes remained locked to the shadows that lined his face. Traveling up and down my body, his gaze took forever to finally lock with mine.

"Is this too much?"

I shook my head, desperate to pull in enough air that I didn't pass out right there on top of him. He was too close. I was too close. But I couldn't find it within myself to push him farther away. When he wasn't there staring at me, I could convince myself that I'd be able to live without a man like him. But now that we were together again, every decision I'd made to let him go flew out the window to become lost to a turbulent breeze.

"I think I'm okay," I finally answered.

His hands gripped my hips, his eyes never letting mine go. "Have you ever been kissed before?"

My heart jumped into my throat at the question, my tongue peeking out to lick along my lips. I noticed his eyes tracking the path of my tongue and it stole the breath from my lungs.

"No," I answered, my voice quaking over the one syllable.

Cocking his head to the side, he smiled at me until I found my gaze trapped to the smooth surface of his lips. They were red and inviting beneath the dark color of his mustache and beard. All I could do was grip my hands over his strong shoulders trying my best to play it cool.

How foolish had it been to admit I'd never been kissed before? Everything inside of me wanted Elliot to look at me as a woman instead of a girl, and yet, there I was, admitting so easily that I'd never experienced anything sexual in my life.

His hands released my hips to grip my knees and slowly creep up my thighs, his fingers pulling the material of my dress along with them.

Damn if that didn't make me shiver where I sat.

"Would you like me to kiss you?"

Nodding my head, I ignored the lump in my throat that kept me from answering him aloud. It concerned me that he would hear the fear and embarrassment, that he would change his mind if I said the wrong thing.

Letting go of one of my thighs, Elliot brought his hand up to curl a finger beneath one shoulder strap of my dress, using the small bit of cloth to pull me forward until our mouths were close together.

I closed my eyes, unable to handle the intensity of the moment. I hoped he couldn't hear the frantic beat of my heart, hoped I was making it seem like he didn't affect me as much as he did.

"Have you ever been touched?" he whispered, a finger sliding beneath the bottom hem of my skirt to press up against my panties. Stars burst behind my eyes, my knees attempting to lock together but stopped by his legs between them.

"Is this okay with you, Maggie?"

With my forehead pressed to his, I breathed out heavily and nodded again. His hand pulled me forward and his lips met mine.

Gentle at first, his mouth moved against mine, his tongue peeking out to run along my lips, but not pushing itself inside. He tasted of cigarettes and mint, and for some odd reason I liked the combination. Unable to move, I sat frozen in his lap as his mouth became more demanding, his lips parting to open mine as well. When his tongue slipped inside my mouth, I forgot how to breathe.

Dizzy and lustful, my head swam with possibility. I still couldn't find it within myself to move or touch him back, but I savored the feel and taste of him, jumping in place when the finger he'd moved beneath my skirt pressed harder against my panties and brushed back and forth.

Unsure of whether it was nervousness or pleasure that raged like wildfire inside my belly, my eyes shot open to find that his had been watching me the entire time. He smiled against my lips, the finger wrapped into the strap of my dress pulling it down off my shoulder until the top swell of my breast was exposed to the hot afternoon sun.

"Am I moving too fast?"

His voice was the sexiest thing I'd ever heard, even if it was a breathless whisper.

"No," I managed to say. "I don't think so."

"You don't think?" He smiled and pulled my dress down more, my entire breast now exposed between us.

His eyes never left mine, not even as he released the material of my dress to cup the weight of my breast in his palm. Enjoying the rough feel of his skin against mine, I pressed myself into his touch, craving more. When his thumb flicked over my nipple, I gasped against his mouth.

"I want to make you feel good, Maggie. But I don't want to scare you away. It seems like every time I get close, you run as fast as you can."

If only he knew I was running to protect him. Without the fear of my brothers and father, I would never let him out of my sight.

"You don't scare me," I whispered back.

"That's good," he replied, humor in his voice. "You want to feel good, right?"

I nodded.

That beautiful grin of his widened, his eyes flashing with heat like I'd never imagined possible.

"Well, then hold on, beautiful, because I'm about to make you feel every bit like the woman that you are."

CHAPTER FIFTEEN

ELLIOT

Maggie shook like a leaf above me, her mouth saying yes to feeling good, but her body so tight and tense that I feared I would break her with one wrong move.

I never planned to take it this far. A kiss maybe, a soft brush of my hand on her hip. But this...it was much farther than I'd intended to go. I needed her to talk, and that wouldn't be possible with my tongue shoved down her throat.

But I couldn't help myself.

She tasted like sunshine following a heavy rainstorm, all innocent, fresh and wild. It would have been better if she'd refused me - that's what I'd hoped would happen - but she was giving in to my every move, not bothering to consider the fact that she was straddling the lap of a practical stranger.

If she had been my daughter, I would have strangled her for being so trusting, but in this case, it worked to my benefit. I needed her loose. I needed her trusting. I needed her to become so addicted to the way I could make her feel that all the secrets she kept bottled up inside came pouring out into the open.

Slowly working my finger over panties that were becoming wet, I trapped her stare with mine, refusing to release the contact for even a second.

"How does it feel when I touch you? Does it make your body hum?"

Maggie's forehead was pressed to mine. She was fighting to keep from closing her eyes and becoming lost to the sensation of my hands on her body. Every emotion she felt was obvious behind her gaze, every question and concern buried beneath the feeling of being touched for the first time.

A virgin.

Damn, I wished that wasn't the case and I promised myself she would remain that way regardless of whether she begged for sex or not. My cock pressed painfully against my pants, but I ignored my body's needs.

Pushing my legs apart, I spread her legs wide, giving my large hand more access to her sweet spot. Her eyes closed and I clicked my tongue, a tone of disappointment on my voice when I begged, "Don't leave me, beautiful. Open those pretty eyes and stay right here with me."

She forced her eyes open. I dragged in a breath at the haze I saw covering them. Her body shuddered over mine and I continued stroking over her panties with one hand while cupping her breast with the other. Slow and steady, I wouldn't force her to go farther than either of us was willing to go. I needed her coming back for more. Satisfying her curiosity the first time wouldn't get me what I wanted.

"Answer me, Maggie. What do I make you feel?"

As much as my body burned to bend this girl over and take everything I knew she'd be willing to give, I wanted to laugh. She could barely stay focused, much less answer any question I asked. That just made asking the questions more fun.

Speaking low so that my voice was a bare whisper between us, I talked to her, leading her through everything she was feeling in hopes that hearing it would make it all the more real in her mind.

"Your body is getting wet for me. Do you realize that?"

Her eyes closed and I smiled at the way her cheeks flamed with need and embarrassment.

"Ah, beautiful, you don't have to be shy about what we're doing. It feels good and that's what it's supposed to feel like. It means you want this...that you want me." Pressing my lips to hers, I spoke against her mouth, "You do want me, don't you?"

When she didn't answer, I shook my head softly. Slowly, I pulled my hand away and her eyes shot open. "No."

"No?" A wolfish grin was painful against my cheeks. "You don't?"

She shook her head and swallowed. "No...I mean yes, I want you."

"Then why aren't you talking to me? You keep closing your eyes and leaving me all alone."

My hand found its way back between her trembling legs, my finger reaching out to push softly against a spot I knew would send her sky high.

Wrong. All of this was wrong. I was using this poor woman when her first time should have been something special.

Unfortunately for Maggie, my need for vengeance was stronger than the duty I felt to protect her heart.

I would use her. I would betray her. I would split her apart when I destroyed everything she'd ever known. And when I was done, I'd walk away from her, attaching the memory of overwhelming loss to the memory of the first time a man showed her love.

It was enough to cast a heavy shroud of distrust and pain over the rest of her life, but that couldn't matter. All that mattered was justice for the people I'd lost.

"It feels good," she breathed out, averting her eyes while her cheeks glowed pink for having to openly acknowledge what she was doing. Women learned to be vocal about their needs eventually, but their first time? That first time is when they need someone else to take the reins and guide them.

It was too bad Maggie had to be guided through her first time by a man who felt nothing for her.

No, that wasn't true. I felt one thing for her. I felt pity.

"Does it feel as good as when you touch yourself?"

Her eyes clenched shut and I laughed.

"Don't try telling me you don't touch yourself, Maggie. I know you remember what you were doing when we first met. Your fingers were all over this sweet pussy. Who were you thinking about that day? Who do you imagine when you touch yourself?"

I kept the motion of my hand slow and steady as I guided her to the moment where her body would find the heavens and praise God before shattering apart against me.

Her lips trembling against my own, she tried to respond, but her breath was becoming more labored and heavy as my hand massaged her breast. "I - I - oh..."

My shoulders shook with silent laughter. After pressing another soft kiss to her lips, I asked, "Hey, Maggie?"

"Yeah?" she breathed out, no longer able to open her eyes to stare into mine.

"Would you like me to shut up and make you come?"

Clenching her eyes tighter, she nodded her head so hard the curls in her hair bounced around her head.

I laughed softly again.

Taking her mouth with mine, I tasted her tongue as my fingers pulled aside her soaked panties to run through the slickened skin. Maggie's body jumped at the contact, but her mouth continued moving against mine, her timid tongue flicking out to explore my kiss.

Loving the way her knees tightened against my thighs, I silently called myself a bastard when I pushed a fingertip inside her. She jumped at the sensation, but eventually settled down when she realized I wasn't going deeper than just the tip. Not wanting to hurt her, I circled my finger around the tight muscle, my cock painful against my jeans in response to her wet heat.

"Does it hurt?" I whispered. I already planned to break her heart. I didn't need to break her body along with it.

Shaking her head, Maggie surprised me by forcing her body down so that my finger pressed deeper inside. Her hips moved over me and I bit the inside of my cheek to keep from taking every part of her.

"More," she begged, her voice barely recognizable.

I would make her come. She was so fucking sweet, she deserved that, at least.

Kissing her with a passion I hadn't known since Katelyn died, I released Maggie's breast to wrap an arm around her body and hold her in place. With my middle finger seated inside her, I used my thumb to rub against her clit. She lost control of her body when I began pumping my hand, her head falling back and her mouth dropping open. Small moans sounded from the back of her throat and I grit my teeth to keep from lowering her down to the ground and fucking her like she would disappear if I didn't.

Taking the time to watch her body bounce over my hand, I admired the dark, pink nipple that was the perfect size for her breast. I dropped my gaze down further to watch the muscles work in her thighs. Her hips rolled over my hand and she used me to get herself off as much as I was using her to get revenge.

Maybe this girl wasn't as innocent as I believed...

As her moans grew louder, I knew she was getting close. I didn't need her making so much noise that it carried on the wind. Releasing her back to grip my fist into her hair, I pulled her towards me to lock my mouth over hers and swallow those moans.

I kissed her as the moans turned into louder mewls. I kissed her as those mewls turned into tiny screams and begs. I kissed her until she couldn't kiss anymore, her body reaching its peak and every muscle tightening as she quaked over my lap. Pulling my head back, I admired the flush of ecstasy across her skin, smiling to myself when her body relaxed and melted against mine.

With her head resting on my shoulder and her chest beating against mine from her heavy breath, I brushed my hand down Maggie's long hair and said, "I've got you, beautiful girl. I've got you."

In more ways than one...

Damn.

I was a bastard.

CHAPTER SIXTEEN

MAGGIE

Singing softly to myself, I tracked my way through the woods, taking a few shortcuts I knew and watching out for the places that were so thick with brush there was no telling what nasty critters were waiting for me to come along.

My brothers had been gone for three days. I'd been able to sneak away and see Elliot every one of those days and my heart was beaming because of it. He was every bit the man I'd dreamed of one day knowing. Each time we met, he made me want him more.

Practically skipping with happiness, I tilted my head up to see the last desperate rays of the sun paint colorful ribbons across the sky. Elliot always made me leave when there was just enough light to make it home, but it was getting harder to do that with each passing day. Telling me he was worried about me and that's why he made me leave caused my heart to swell in my chest, my smile pulling apart so wide it burned the skin of my cheeks.

I liked Elliot far more than any sane person should and it bothered me to admit that fact to myself.

Knowing better than to trust anyone, I let my mind drift to those awful memories that tear me apart during silent and sleepless nights. Those women - those lost souls that were stripped from the world and secreted away to death or someplace much worse - every one of their faces were seared into my memories; every one of their voices adding to the symphony of agony and pain in my ears.

Through the years, I'd promised myself to never become one of those faces or disembodied voices, but having seen what one person could do to another so easily and so often, I wondered if I wasn't tempting fate each day I snuck away to spend time with Elliot.

Was I being smart to wonder…or was I being paranoid? I hated the constant questions in my head.

I would have liked nothing more than to get away from the house before the parties started just so that I didn't have to know of the women that disappeared. But I never could sneak away fast enough, not until all the men were so drunk they forget I was there.

Having lived with it for so long, I knew better than to trust a man so easily. I'd seen the way those women had been convinced to go to a place where my family could get her alone. I knew how easy it was to be drugged and dragged away.

But, there was something different about Elliot. Something good. He was the perfect gentleman whenever I went to see him. A playful, dirty minded one, maybe, but I liked that about him. Hell, he was a little too much of a gentleman at times. He still hadn't had sex with me despite the offers I'd made.

Elliot hadn't even let me touch him below his belt. No matter how hard I tried, or the pouty looks I gave him, he always turned me down.

The stupid man wanted to wait, wanted it to be about me, or at least that's what he told me. The truth was I wanted to wait as well. I worried that it would hurt, but still couldn't help feeling anxious and impatient about having sex with him for the first time.

Coming to the trees that lined my father's property, I smiled. For as much as Elliot frustrated me, he made me feel special too.

I'd never felt that way before.

Light on my feet, I wound my way up the path, a song on my voice and a smile that wouldn't stop no matter how I tried to hide it.

"Magpie," my father's voice called out, the deep baritone rolling over the green grass that waved beneath a darkening sky. "I've been looking for you."

Scanning my eyes over the side yard and up to the house, I finally found him at the top of the stairs standing in the doorway.

"Hey, Daddy," I called back, not having to fake the happiness in my voice for once. "I came back before the sun's completely down."

Waving away the concern in my voice, my father called out, "That's not what this is about. Hurry up and get inside."

Tension and fear tightened my shoulders at the sound of his words. Breaking into a jog, I raced up the stairs and into the house, my eyes falling on my father and brothers.

Forcing my voice to be strong and steady, I asked, "What's happening?"

Please don't let it be Elliot. Please, God, don't let them know.

They couldn't know, I tried to convince myself. If they did, Elliot would already be dead. My brothers would have killed him right in front of my eyes.

"Pack your stuff, Maggie. A storm's coming in. We're leaving in two days."

"What?" There was numbness at first and then panic - pure, unadulterated, soul crushing panic that tore through every cell of my body.

"What do you mean there's a storm? You said we could stay in one place for a while."

My father's eyes, a silver-blue that were bloodshot and stained red around the edges, narrowed on me. "I don't care what I said. Something's come up. Your brothers' friend will be coming in tomorrow night, there'll be a party the night after that, and we'll be leaving the following morning."

"Dad-"

"I don't want to hear any arguments from you." Cutting me off, he screamed so loud the walls of the kitchen shook around us.

At the moment the walls stopped shaking, Finn's voice slithered through the room. "That's what I'm talking about, right there. I told you she was breaking rules."

My gaze shot to my brothers where they sat glib at the table watching the results of whatever lies they'd whispered into the old man's ear since they'd returned. Daddy had been fine with me up until that afternoon, and I didn't have to guess why he was suddenly angry with me now.

"Maybe we should take a stick to her again, Dad. It's been too long, don't you think? The girl's going to run off and get herself in trouble if she keeps scampering around the way she has been." Finn's eyes locked to mine, a slimy satisfied grin pulling at his lips. "Where have you been going every day, Mags? It's not like you to disappear."

Fear crept along my spine, icy fingers scraping at the muscles and freezing the bones in place.

Finn was on the warpath and I knew he'd stop at nothing to wrestle me under control. I never could understand why. We had our fair share of sibling fights as I'd grown, and Finn had always gained the upper hand.

Ignoring the way he smiled at me, I turned to my father, desperation dripping from every word I spoke. "Daddy, please."

He wasn't hearing it. Whatever lies my brothers had told him - the possibilities they'd whispered into his ear until they became truth - that's what stuck in my father's head and wrinkled his expression. I saw the decision behind his eyes to punish me, the sorrow that turned his mouth down into a heavy frown.

"You've been lying to me, girl."

"Daddy, no -"

"And don't you keep lying to me now!"

Effectively cutting off my argument, Daddy gripped the kitchen counter to hold himself steady on his feet. With his body becoming frailer with each passing day, it was obvious how he struggled to remain standing. For fear it would only weaken him more, I wondered whether I should continue arguing or just sit back and accept whatever punishment he gave.

I loved him. More than anything I'd known in life, I loved my father. He wasn't the nicest man to most of the people who'd known him. He wasn't the best example of what a father should be. But he had been my world for so long, I was afraid to find out what life would be without him.

When all you have is the worst of the lot, the worst becomes your *normal* because it's all you've ever known.

Settling himself, he coughed a few times, wiping the spittle and blood from his palm onto his dirty jeans before leveling his stare on me. "Where have you been going, Maggie?"

"Daddy -"

Holding up his hand, he growled out a frustrated sound. "You know what? It doesn't matter. Not anymore anyway." All the anger had dissolved from his voice, resignation moving in to take its place. "I'm old, Magpie, and I'm dying."

Opening my mouth to argue, I snapped it shut when he gave me a look that promised punishment for every word I had to say. My father was done listening and I would be made to walk whatever line my brothers had convinced him to draw in the sand.

"I'm dying, Maggie. You know it and I know it. I don't need to throw money at a doctor to know it." Barely able to keep his eyes fully open, my father swayed where he stood. I saw the half empty bottle of liquor on the counter and understood that some of his weakness wasn't a result of being sick.

"Evil is coming for you, baby girl. It's been coming for you since the moment you were born, the moment the only thing good in your life - your mother - was taken away from you."

His expression fell until he looked tired enough to sleep for several days straight.

"I thought I could protect you from it. Thought that maybe if I was strong enough, that if we kept moving around, it wouldn't find you."

Biting off a hissed curse, he widened his eyes. "But now you're running off like a stupid female, probably directly into the arms of whatever evil chases after you. I won't allow it."

"I won't run off anymore," I promised, my heart shattering at the thought of never seeing Elliot again. They were too close to the truth and I wouldn't risk leading them directly to the secret I was desperate to hide. I'd protect Elliot simply by staying put.

"I'll stay right here if it means we can live in one place for a while."

Shaking his head, Daddy leaned heavily against the counter. "No, girl. I'm afraid it's already found you. I didn't want to believe it, but even your brothers agree. We need to get you settled."

"Settled?"

Breathing out a resigned sigh, his eyes flicked to Brody and Finn before returning to me. "Your brothers have worked out an arrangement for you, Maggie. For after I die. It's not right for them to have to take care of you when I'm gone, and you deserve more from life than what you've been given."

Another gust of heavy breath fell over his lips. "The man who's coming tomorrow night has agreed to marry you. He's going to take care of you when I'm gone, and you're going to honor him like a wife should...regardless of what he does to earn money to provide for you. Do you hear me?"

Shaking my head, I stared at my father with disbelief widening my eyes. "No. Please, Daddy. You're being ridiculous. I don't need a husband, especially not somebody Brody and Finn picked out -"

"Why's that, Magpie?"

Spinning to stare at Finn's condescending expression, I fought back the tears that welled in my eyes.

"Why wouldn't you want our friend? Jack's a decent man. He understands the lifestyle you live and can protect you. Plus, he'll treat you right because he knows he'll be dealing with us if he doesn't."

Finn's lips rounded, almost cartoonish in how precise the expression of feigned understanding twisted his face. "Oh..."

His words were soft over his mouth as he angled his head to the side. "Unless there's someone else." A smile stretched his lips apart. "Is there something you're not telling us, Maggie Pie?"

Elliot... I'm falling in love with a good man named Elliot...

"No."

"You're marrying Jack." My father's voice drew my attention back to him. "If it's the last thing I do in life, I'm going to make sure you're safe. You're not going to be able to survive on your own, baby girl. You don't have an education. You can't hold down a job -"

"You don't know that! You never let me try!"

"I'm sorry, Maggie. But I've made this decision for you and you're going to respect it."

No. No. No. This wasn't happening.

My entire world was imploding around me and I was losing my grip on every small ounce of freedom and happiness I'd just found. Why did my life always have to work out like this? Why couldn't I have just five minutes to feel happy and breathe?

"I don't even know this guy, Daddy!" A twig snapped by the weight of the world, my resolve burst apart, my voice shaking with anger and pain. "I don't -"

"That's what I mean, right there," Finn's voice rose over mine, the deep baritone smothering every plea that left my mouth. "She needs to be brought back under control."

Brody sat silently as usual. He never dared cross our older brother. Even if he had spoken, I knew it would only be to prod Finn along.

"Yeah, son," our father drawled. "I think you're right." Disappointment and defeat softened his shoulders. "I can't do it. I just can't. You two take her out back and get her back in line."

Finn stood from his chair, the metal feet scraping loudly across the linoleum. He'd crossed the room and grabbed me before I had the sense to move away. Knowing better than to struggle, I lost my battle against the tears in my eyes that demanded to fall.

Soon, Brody joined Finn to lead me out of the house. Turning before they'd shoved me through the door, I begged one final time.

"Please, Daddy. I'll be good. I'll do what you ask. Please don't let them do this." Hot tears streamed down my cheeks, every ounce of hope, possibility and goodness stripped away until I was left with only terror and despair.

Clenching his eyes shut, my father shook his head. "I'm sorry, Maggie, but your brothers are right. Something wild has gotten inside you and we need to keep you safe from yourself. You'll understand someday. I promise you, you'll understand."

Shoved out into the silent stillness of the deepening night, we paused long enough for Brody to ask, "How many, Dad?"

I heard my father sigh.

"Twenty should do it, son. Twenty should set her straight again."

CHAPTER SEVENTEEN

ELLIOT

Throwing a wrench into the large toolbox that stood to the side of the garage, I wiped the sweat from my brow with a dirty rag, instantly regretting the decision as soon as I saw the oil all over my hands. I had soap that would help remove the stains from my skin, but I'd have to scrub to ensure it all washed away before I went to see Maggie.

It would be hard to explain the telltale signs of a mechanic when Maggie still believed I hadn't been able to fix my truck on the day we first met.

Straightening my tired body, I turned my head to peer out of the bay, narrowing my eyes against the blinding light of an unsympathetic sun. I was seventy-two hours away from the anniversary of Katelyn's disappearance, and I'd begun the process of making preparations for the vengeance I sought.

My bags and truck were already packed with the tools I'd need to finish the job. I hadn't bothered packing any clothes or other possessions because I didn't plan to walk away from the property after the Crows were no longer breathing. I'd penned a letter to my parents to explain my decisions and to apologize for failing them as a son.

Mom had begged me to move on...but not in the way I'd chosen to do so.

Knowing my parents would sort out whatever personal effects I left behind, the only thing left to do was say goodbye to the man who had kept me together long enough for this day to come. It would take some finesse to get out what I wanted to say without drawing Henry's suspicion, but I couldn't move on to whatever Hell awaited me without letting my boss know what his concern and patience had meant.

Telling him now would be better timing than waiting for the seventy-two hours to be up. Henry would wonder. I knew that. But saying it now would give me two more days to come in to work, to pretend like everything was normal so that any suspicion Henry had over the word of thanks would diminish at seeing me return to life as usual.

"Hey, Boss. I'm taking off for the day."

Henry slid out from beneath the '65 Charger he'd been working to restore for over a year. He had the girl running pretty good. However, he still believed there were a few kinks that he might never be able to work out - despite the amount of times I'd told Henry he was full of shit.

The car ran like a dream, but Henry was a perfectionist and wouldn't accept anything less than the best.

Arching his eyebrow in question, Henry stilled when he saw my expression. "Everything okay?"

It was hard to look at my boss' face, to see the concern behind his eyes and the accusation written into the line of his weathered brow. "Yeah, everything's fine. I just wanted to say thank you, brother. For the job and all."

Reaching up, I scrubbed my palm over the back of my neck, wincing when I squeezed my fingers over a sore muscle. "I don't know. Just for being a good guy. You believed in me when other people didn't."

Scooting out from beneath the car completely, Henry sat up. "What the hell is going on, Elliot?"

"I'm not sure what you mean. I'm just saying thank you."

"No. That's not *just* what you're saying. You're not the feel good, emotional type."

Laughter blew over my lips. "It's just a thank you, Henry. Just grumble out a response and we'll both get back to our usual tasks."

His eyes pinned me where I stood. "And what tasks are those?"

"You cussing up a storm beneath a car that doesn't need any more work, and me heading home to drown myself in a bottle."

After another scrutinizing look, Henry nodded his head. "Just be sure you're drunk as piss when I get to your house tonight to check on you."

Somehow, I knew that would be Henry's response. Glad to have done this now instead of on the last day I intended to show for work, I smiled and said, "I'll see you tonight, Brother. If I happen to be sleeping when you get there, just be sure to spoon me nice and tight. You know how much I like it."

Henry laughed so hard the sliding board beneath him shook back and forth. "No problem, Elliot. Maybe if you're good, I'll even read you a bedtime story."

Smiling at the easy friendship we had, sadness settled over me. I'd miss joking around with Henry. After all was said and done, I hoped Henry wouldn't be upset for too long.

ㅗㅗㅗㅗ

Pulling up to the abandoned farm, I took my time crawling out of the truck. The past several days had been the same. Arrive, wait an hour or two, watch as Maggie emerged from the woods and then paint on a pretend smile as I worked her into such a frenzy she forgot to keep her secrets to herself.

The first day the smile I'd forced pained me. I hated to realize that each day it became a little easier to smile when I saw her stepping out of the shadow of trees into the brilliance of late afternoon light. Each day, that smile became less of a disguise and more of a truth I was irritated to acknowledge.

I liked Maggie. I couldn't deny that fact. But I could, and did, regret it.

109

Maybe I could help set her up with another life. Possibly pull all the money I had saved and place it in an envelope where only she would find it. I wouldn't be alive to help her rebuild from the loss of everything she'd known, but if the money would carry her until she planted her feet in a new life, at least it would help her recover.

There was another possibility for Maggie as well and I made a mental note to write one more letter. I'd ask Henry to give her a job at the shop, to give her a chance to show him how good she was at turning wrenches. She'd have a place to live. She'd have a job. And she'd have enough money to keep her going until she found the strength to let go and live again.

The thought was still bouncing around in my head as my feet hit the ground, but I hadn't yet shut the door to my truck before motion caught my eye at the perimeter of the woods surrounding the property.

Stumbling out from the tree line before pushing herself back to her feet and taking off across the field, Maggie moved like she was being chased.

My heart was in my throat as I took off at a dead run towards her. "Maggie!"

She waved her hands at me, saying something that I couldn't hear over the pounding of my heart and the heavy fall of my boots against the ground. The expression on her face when she was finally close enough for me to see it only made me run that much faster.

"Maggie!"

I couldn't be sure, but it sounded like the frantic girl was screaming for me to shut up.

Snapping my trap shut, I ran faster, dust kicking up around me in a cloud. I'd barely reached her and wrapped my hands over her shoulders before she was begging me to leave.

"You have to go," she said breathlessly. "You have to leave now and never come back, Elliot." Tears streamed down her face as she pled, "Please, get in your truck and leave. Just pretend like you never knew me."

"Whoa, whoa, whoa," I said, hating how she averted her eyes because I knew it meant she was hiding something. Gripping her chin between my fingers, I forced her wild and frightened gaze back to mine. "What the hell is going on?"

Unable to keep her eyes locked to my face, Maggie scanned the distance behind me. She twisted to look behind herself before grabbing my hand. "Dammit, Elliot. You need to leave."

Tugging on my arm, she attempted to drag me back in the direction of my truck, but I wouldn't budge. Like a stubborn dog, I dug my feet into the dirt and leaned my weight back in an effort to keep from falling forward with how desperately she tugged.

"I'm not going anywhere until you tell me what's wrong. You look like hell."

More tears fell from her eyes, her panic ratcheting so high she could barely stand on her shaking legs. "Fine, you dumb shit, but at least come inside the house with me. We can't be seen out here and I don't know if I was followed."

Wrapping my head around the fact she just called me a dumb shit, I watched Maggie spin towards the house, her skirt flying up in the wind to reveal an angry purple line across the back of her thighs. She hadn't made it a single step forward before I grabbed the hem of her skirt and pulled it up farther.

"What THE FUCK happened to you, Maggie?"

It wasn't just one ugly and angry line glaring back at me...it was absolute destruction of what should have been pale and smooth skin. Line after line ran up her thighs, over what I could see of her swollen ass, and ending at her lower back. Some were just raised welts in a vivid red color, others were deep and bluish purple, so new they hadn't had time to begin fading to a putrid black and green.

The ones that set my hair on end and caused my fingers to clench into painful fists were the lacerations. Thin, but long, those cuts were fresh with small wisps of blood seeping down her skin, most likely because they'd been reopened from running.

Her hand smacked down the material of her skirt, her eyes locking to mine with as much defiance as there was shame.

"The house, Elliot. If you're going to be a stubborn dick about this, then at least go somewhere we can't be seen."

It wasn't until I was walking behind her that I noticed her strange gait. She could barely stand, much less walk straight. I wondered how much pain she'd endured to make her way through the woods to meet me.

We made it inside the house without speaking again, but that rotting wooden door hadn't fully been shut and locked before I glared down at Maggie.

"I'm giving you one fucking chance to tell me the truth about what happened to you. You're a horrible liar, little girl, and if I get the feeling you're lying to me, I'll -"

"You'll what?" she asked, the anger behind her voice so sharp it sliced through every ounce of sweetness that had once been in her. If the marks hadn't alerted me to the fact that something was wrong, her voice would have. "Take off? Like I want you to do? Like an intelligent person would do? Dammit, Elliot, why do you have to be so -"

My hand gripped over her mouth, the tips of my fingers digging into her cheeks. Bending down so that the tip of my nose touched hers, I spoke slowly and succinctly.

"I don't know what you were about to call me, and I don't want to know. But if you don't tell me who the fuck gave you those marks, when I remove my hand, I'm giving you a few more."

Maggie's eyes rounded with a mixture of fear and anger.

I grinned.

112

"And don't call me dumb again. You're the one who is beat all to hell, yet standing here trying to tell me to leave so I can't find out who did this to you and return those marks right back to them. I'm not wrong when I say that makes *you* the dumb one between us."

Seconds passed as we stared at each other in tense silence. Feeling Maggie's body relax from defeat, I straightened my body and pulled my hand from her mouth. "Fess the fuck up."

"Elliot -"

"No, Darlin', I can tell you it wasn't a guy named Elliot, unless you've been sneaking around with another man by that name. So you can stop right there. The next time you open that pretty mouth of yours, I want to hear the name of the son of a bitch that hit you."

She flinched at the rage in my voice. It took her several times of opening and closing her mouth again for resignation to finally shadow her eyes, tears to slip down her cheeks, and the whispered words "my brothers" to fall from her lips.

My blood boiled at her confession, but I still managed to bark out, "Thank you."

When my hand slammed on the knob of the front door, Maggie lunged forward to grab me. "Where are you going?"

"To kill your brothers."

It felt good not having to lie for once. I'd planned on killing them anyway. All Maggie had done was give me more of a reason.

"You can't!"

"No, sweetheart, I'm pretty damn sure I can. Painfully and slowly, if you really want to know." Mad humor dripped from my words, a man on the verge of losing his mind.

"You can't, Elliot. My father told them to do it."

Every muscle in my body tensed, my molars gnashing together so hard my jaw felt like it would snap.

Forcing a few deep breaths through my lungs, I fought to control my temper. "Well, then I guess your father has to die, too."

What kind of sick-minded, hillbilly, woman-beating family did this girl have? I shouldn't have been surprised, not with what I knew about them already. But the way Maggie had always spoken about them, they protected her, at least.

"Please," her body shook as she sobbed, her eyes clenching tight enough to turn the skin around them red.

Releasing her fingers from my arm, she slid down giving me barely enough time to catch her. Settling her softly on the floor, I didn't miss the way she winced when her body touched the ground.

CHAPTER EIGHTEEN

MAGGIE

There comes a time in every person's life when they feel like they'll break apart completely under the pressure of some insurmountable problem. It didn't matter who you were, how much money you had, or how good of a person you've been, that problem was going to find you one day when you least expected it and rip you apart piece by piece, leaving you deflated, dejected, and detached.

For me, that moment had come and gone so many times, I didn't have enough fingers and toes to count how often, but never in my life had I felt it as thoroughly and painfully as this.

Losing the battle against the agony and grief inside me, I broke apart on the dirty floor where I sat. Elliot kneeled in front of me, his large, rough palm brushing down my cheek with a gentleness that was in stark contrast to the murderous look behind his eyes.

Unable to speak at first, I sat and cried, embarrassment coming in to fill the emptiness left behind by every tear I shed. Falling to pieces in front of a man who'd lost his family while he was off at war felt like a slap in the face.

Whereas he'd been so strong to continue living after everything he'd endured, I was contemplating what it would take for my life to finally end.

Instantly hating the gentleness of Elliot's touch because of the weakness and shame it made me feel, I pulled away. Pain shot along my legs, bottom and back from the effort, causing me to cry out in response.

"I'm sorry you're feeling this way, Maggie. No woman deserves what they've done to you." An edge of barely controlled anger tainted his caring words. "How often does this happen? What haven't you told me about your family?"

Too close, his questions were getting way too close for comfort. I didn't know if I hated them because he couldn't know the answers...or if it was because I wanted nothing more than to sing like a damn canary and finally release the secrets I'd held for so damn long.

He was too tempting, and here in his presence I could allow myself to believe that there was something he could do to make it all end, even if I knew deep down that he couldn't.

"I have to go, Elliot. They might have followed me and if they find me here with you -"

A finger softly pressed against my lips to silence my words, my eyes trailing up to lock with his. I broke apart all over again when the desire I had for him came flooding back like water through a broken dam. But those desires were quickly cut through by the harsh memories of what my brothers had done.

The sting of the stick they used to beat me was still fresh on my skin. Laughter filled the night sky, laughter and the words that taunted me left ringing through my body as much as the pain. "You thought Daddy would always be here to protect you. Stupid fucking girl. It was only a matter of time..."

"They don't scare me, Maggie. Stop telling me to run away."

Another strike, my scream cutting through the dark sky. More laughter. Always laughter. "Your Daddy thinks Jack will keep you safe. He thinks he'll keep you from the evil. Daddy doesn't know that Jack's only holding on to you until we both get our fill. Stealing a woman is one thing, Magpie. Raising her and destroying her when she's pretty enough to fuck is something else entirely. It's like raising a hog just to fatten it up for the slaughter."

A shiver coursed down my spine as the memories assaulted me. Elliot's observant eyes locked to every expression that crossed my face. "Talk to me, Maggie. Tell me what I can do to help you."

"You need to leave here and never come back," I whispered, my voice paralyzed by the fear and memories.

"Where have you been sneaking off to?" Another strike, this one cutting my skin from the force. "You better not have let some stupid fuck take what was rightfully mine." A finger violating my body broke me apart so thoroughly I lost the ability to breathe. "Do you know what I'll do to your boyfriend when I find him? Do you know that when I kill him, I'll force you to watch? What will he see when he's lying there dying, Maggie? He'll see your face as I'm fucking you from behind."

Swallowing down the lump of shame and regret, I cast my eyes at the ground, somehow finding the strength to speak again. "I need to go home. My brothers left for a few hours, but I don't know if they're out looking around for you right this moment. This farm is the first place they'd check."

"I'm not scared of them, Maggie. Tell me what they did to you."

Finn got so close to fucking me where I was bent over an old sawhorse in the backyard that Brody had to step in and pull him off. "Not now, Finn. The old man might look out here and see this is more than a spanking. Stand back, it's my turn with the stick." I glanced up when Finn circled to stand in front of me. His smile stretched from ear to ear. Unbuttoning his jeans, he pulled his dick into his hands, stroking himself with his eyes locked on me. "Be sure to hit her hard, Brody. It turns me on to hear her scream."

Fighting to keep from retching at the memory, I shook my head. I couldn't tell Elliot what they'd done to me. I was too ashamed.

Elliot's finger caught me beneath the chin and tilted my face up to look at him. "I can take you away, Maggie. I can save you from all of them."

Finn stroked himself long and hard, the motion of his hand speeding up with every strike of the stick against my ass. I opened my mouth on another scream and felt something warm and sticky hit my cheek. Unable to fight back, my body submitted when I heard my brothers laugh.

"Do you really want to stay with them, Maggie? Or would you rather be with me instead?"

"We'll have to clean you up before taking you back in. It might finally kill the old man to see how much of a whore you're becoming." Using an old rag, Finn wiped the filth away, his eyes catching mine before he threatened, "And don't even think about saying anything to him. He won't believe you."

"I can marry you, Maggie. I can give you a brand new life."

My eyes shot up to stare at Elliot from behind the blur of tears. "You would do that?"

"Did you really think we share the same mommy and daddy, Maggie? Did you really think we were all just one big happy family?"

A kiss pressed to my forehead, I gave in and let Elliot take me into his arms, the memories assaulting me and tearing me apart on the inside.

"I've got you, beautiful. And if you'll allow me to help you, I'll never let you go."

"Your mother wasn't someone the old man loved. She was just another useless whore pregnant with another man's baby."

They weren't my brothers. At least that's what they'd claimed. I preferred to believe them even if I didn't know whether they'd told the truth. Was the man I'd loved my entire life really my dad? Even if he wasn't my biological father, he was still the man that raised me. My love for him was true regardless. I wasn't sure I could leave him alone to die.

With each passing day, I was running out of options. I didn't know what to believe. All my life had been lies, hiding spots and secrets. What's to say that my entire existence hadn't been more of the same?

Dragging in a shaky breath, I settled on what portions of truth I would give Elliot. He didn't have to know the entire story. Carefully selected bits and pieces would suffice to make him understand without implicating my part in the sordid history of my family. He couldn't know the full story. If he knew, he would hate me for what I'd done.

My voice barely a whisper, I explained, "I told you my father and brothers raised me. And I've told you that they've protected me from the world. None of that was a lie."

"This doesn't look like protection," Elliot argued. "What this looks like is sadistic abuse."

Nodding my head, I couldn't disagree.

I'd winced while looking in the mirror that morning, covering my body with as loose a dress as possible to keep the material from aggravating the painful and angry marks.

"My father wants me to get married to some man I don't even know. A friend of my brothers. He's supposed to come to the house tonight and I told my father that I didn't want to marry a stranger. For arguing, I got whipped with a switch. I'm not supposed to talk back or complain."

Violence coursed through Elliot's silent stare. Cold and ominous, the reaction was a vibration rolling off of him in vicious waves that crashed against me. Shivering in response, I lowered my eyes, turning my attention to anything besides the man that sat in judgment of my train wreck of a family.

"What happens if you refuse to marry him?" His voice was rough, but somehow gentle, grittiness giving it an edge I could feel down to my bones.

"They'll make me marry him anyway," I answered on a trembling breath. "It's like Daddy said: I don't have a real education. I've never had a job. And my brothers certainly won't support me."

Shivering at the thought of my brothers, I remembered I was spending too much time with Elliot. Every second that passed was only putting his life in more danger. Moving as if to get up, I was forced back down onto Elliot's lap when his strong hand gripped my arm.

"You do realize that we live in the United States, right? And that the year is 2017?"

Narrowing my eyes at the odd question, I finally locked my gaze to his. "Yes. I might not have gone to school, but I'm far from stupid."

His lips pulled into a smirk. "Well, if you know that, then why do you think anybody has the right to tell you who you will and will not marry? That's your decision," he tapped the tip of his finger on my nose, "and yours alone."

"I don't know what to do."

"Marry me."

It was the second time he'd said the words. My heart stuttered over the hope I knew better than to feel. Wishing it wasn't that way, I hated that every time I let a little bit of light into my dark existence, the pain would come to take it all away.

Shaking my head, a tear rolled down my cheek. "You don't mean it. You don't even really know me -"

"I don't need to," Elliot answered. "Run away with me, Maggie. Let me take you from the life you've been forced to live and show you what it means to be happy with the life you *choose* to live. Right now, Maggie. Just walk away with me and don't look back. You have the strength to make that choice."

Choice. It was such a simple, one syllable word that rolled off the tongues of most people without true consideration of how fleeting the concept could be, at least that's the way I saw it.

"Choice isn't something I'm used to having. My family took that away from me from the minute I was born."

Arching a brow at the statement, Elliot settled himself on the floor beneath me, no longer holding me in place because I'd given up running. "Nobody can take away your choice. Your family told you what to do. You made the choice to listen to them."

Our eyes locked, my teeth worrying the back of my cheek. Lost in thought, and finally finding the answer I was seeking, I breathed out before saying, "What if the consequences of disobeying are torture or death?"

"You're still choosing. Even if the choice is to die, it's still yours to make."

Silence fell between us, pregnant and weighted with the unanswered question that still hung precariously in the air.

"What's your choice, Maggie?"

"What are you going to do when the old man dies, Maggie?" Finn's soft laughter sent chills along my spine, my entire body limp and shaking from the punishment I'd endured. Lifted from the sawhorse by Brody, I was dragged away. Barely able to open my eyes, I saw Finn smile one more time before Brody was able to get me inside the house.

Elliot's hands gripped my shoulders to shake me from the memory. "Maggie? You need to make a choice for once in your life. What is it going to be?"

It didn't matter what Finn and Brody said, my father was still a person I loved dearly. Tears streamed down my cheeks, my heart racing hard as fear crept through me and stole my ability to breathe.

"Maggie?"

Locking my eyes with Elliot's, I blinked away the tears that clung stubbornly to my lashes.

"I have to go home, Elliot. I have to say goodbye."

When Elliot opened his mouth to protest, I shook my head, placing my hand softly over his lips.

"I can get away tomorrow night when they have their party. I can run, Elliot, and I can marry you."

CHAPTER NINTEEN

ELLIOT

Henry showed up at my house late in the evening, which didn't surprise me in the slightest. After assuring my boss that I was doing just fine, I requested the following day off to handle some personal matters. Henry didn't ask questions, but simply told me to take as much time as I needed.

Thankful for that small favor, I made my final preparations through the night, including writing a letter to Henry about Maggie's possible skills as a mechanic. As soon as word got out that the Crows and I had died, I knew it would only be a matter of time before my parents came by my place to tear it apart in search of answers. They'd find the letter, and being the respectable people they were, they'd deliver it to Henry.

Only able to sleep for a few hours, I got up the next morning before the sun took its place in the sky. After giving myself a quiet moment to enjoy a cup of black, bitter coffee, I made my way to the bank and pulled out what was left of my meager savings. It wasn't much, but it would have to be enough for Maggie to get by.

Back at home, I set three envelopes - the letter to my parents, the letter to Henry, and the money intended for Maggie - on my desk. I had to believe my parents would do the right thing with the money by finding the girl I regretted having lied to and giving her the envelope.

Technically, I still had forty-eight hours left until the anniversary of Katelyn and Michael's disappearance, but from what Maggie had admitted to me, the Crows would have flown off to their next destination if I waited that amount of time.

Only a fool would wait and pass up the opportunity to make things right.

I didn't regret that tonight would be the end of my life. The people I loved and who loved me in return would just have to understand. Without Katelyn or Michael, I hadn't truly lived a single day for the past fourteen years. Sure, my heart had beat its vengeful rhythm, and I'd drawn fetid breath into my lungs. My brain had fired and my body had moved through the usual motions, but none of that had been life.

My life had vanished into thin air with my family - their bodies, their laughter, their spirits lost to me so long ago. Finishing myself off once my vengeance had been sated would only be a small courtesy I paid for having endured so long to discover the truth of their fate.

Maggie still hadn't admitted her family's involvement. She'd been careful to never cross that line. But she had given me enough information about the men that raised her to give me a damn good excuse to go in and demand that information from the male Crows myself.

Thankfully, I now knew I could do what needed to be done with minimal concern about Maggie becoming collateral damage.

She'd believed the lie that I wouldn't be able to reach the adjacent farm until after nightfall. She'd easily agreed to wait until late in the evening to meet me at the two story house that sat abandoned in the large field. But I would never meet her as I'd promised. Instead, she'd wait until her heart had shattered beneath the understanding that I never intended to run away with her, and she'd return to her home to discover the reason why.

It pleased me to know I wouldn't have to worry about Maggie's safety while taking my revenge, but it drove a sharp spike of pain through my soul to know that I would destroy her heart in the process.

Would she be able to survive on her own? That was the question that plagued me, the question that ran through my thoughts so forcefully that it tore me from sleep each night since I'd decided to end the Crows.

The question couldn't matter in the end. Maggie wasn't my concern. She wasn't one of the two people I'd sworn to protect on the day I married Katelyn and on the day I first kissed the cheek of my newborn son. I'd failed to protect those people, and I would fail to protect Maggie from the aftermath of what I had planned for her family.

I had to believe she was strong enough to survive, not that I would change my mind even if I knew she wouldn't. Nothing could stop me now that I'd set the final steps in motion.

Packing the final tools I'd need to carry out my plan, I fought to keep my mind from returning back to Maggie. I didn't want to consider her as part of the grand plan. I didn't want to acknowledge the harrowing truth that she would become collateral damage no matter what I did to prevent it.

She was as innocent as they came. Obviously sheltered her entire life, the girl knew nothing about the real world. From what she'd told me during the hours we'd spent together, her understanding of the world, beyond her family and home, came from the romance novels she'd been able to sneak under her father's watchful gaze.

I wasn't sure what to think of the old man. By Maggie's account, he watched over her, protected her, loved her. But there was more to the story about Jonah Crow. I didn't miss the way Maggie's eyes shadowed over when I asked about their family business. I didn't fail to notice the shiver of fear that crawled across her skin when she remembered back to events she was always quick to hide. She was skilled at changing subjects so quickly a normal person would only assume something more exciting had crossed her mind.

But not me.

I knew her mind was like an old steamer trunk, one that held far too many secrets and remained closed by a heavy iron lock to which only Maggie held the key. There were many times I wanted to wrestle those truths out of her, but I couldn't bring myself to damage a girl that had been hurt and abused by the very things I needed to hear from her.

Her father abused her by failing to protect her.

Her brothers abused her in ways I wasn't sure I wanted to know.

And the secrets she carried abused her by whispering in her ear the dark truth of what was hidden by the shadows of the world around her.

The lurid details weren't necessary to know how bad those secrets were, I just needed to put an end to the men who'd created them. I needed to stop them before the secrets became so numerous that they destroyed the beautiful girl who struggled daily to contain them.

Destroying Maggie in the process would be unavoidable, but hopefully, she'd have enough to put the pieces of her life back together. Hopefully, she'd finally learn that there was more to the world around her than the scant traces of humanity those books she read allowed her to see.

She deserved first kisses and broken hearts. She deserved furtive glances and shy smiles. She deserved the first time a man that truly loved her laid her down and made her body sing. But most of all, she deserved to know what it felt like to have her heart swell with love and the knowledge that, with the right person beside you, the shadows of her gloomy existence would practically disappear.

Above all, Maggie deserved to know what it was to love and to be loved in return.

I couldn't give her those moments, but I could clear the path for the person - for the lucky man - who could.

Glancing at the clock, I saw that it was time to go. My plan was to wait until I saw Maggie enter the woods, to give her enough time to reach the abandoned farm and two-story house where she wouldn't find me as expected. And while the hours ticked by breaking her heart into shards and filling her mind with the truth that I never intended to take her away, I would be ending the Crows, one by one, leaving a blood bath in my wake until the moment came where I ended myself.

Five steps had me outside where I turned to lock my door for the final time. Cool air washed against the skin of my face as I lugged the last heavy duffel bag I'd packed to throw it in the bed of my truck. And as I climbed up to sink my weight against the soft leather bench seat and wrap my fingers over the wheel, I convinced myself that Maggie would overcome this.

She had to.

There was no other choice.

CHAPTER TWENTY

MAGGIE

Red rain. It was a memory that relentlessly stalked me through my short life, the terrifying, yet beautiful sparkle of rubies wetting the grass in my mind each time I allowed myself to think back.

I couldn't remember what the rubies looked like once they dried in the hot sun. Couldn't remember much except for when they disappeared fully beneath a blanket of dirt my brothers threw over them.

Maybe if I'd been allowed to watch, I would have realized that those rubies changed from a bright red to a dull maroon, and finally disguised themselves within a festering black that mimicked the rough hue of uncut onyx.

If only I'd been given the chance to see what happens when that red is left to dry. Maybe it would have prepared me for the spot I stared at now.

"Just clean the shit up before your dad comes looking for you. I'll go grab some clean sheets to replace that mess."

Life hadn't prepared me at all. Not for the mess, not for the heartache, and not for the nightmare I'd walked into the second I'd returned home.

Especially not for the *husband* that stood waiting for me when I'd returned.

Refusing to think of myself as stupid, I tried to ignore the scathing words echoing in my thoughts. On my way home, Elliot's voice had been a soft caress in my head - his pleas for me to run away with him, his desperation to keep me from returning home one last time to say goodbye. I should have listened to him. But the simple fact that I didn't allowed the scathing words to intrude and drown out the rough grit of Elliot's voice in my head.

You stupid girl...
...idiotic...dumb...naive...
You can only blame yourself...

My fingers gripped into the wrinkled, white cotton sheets, my eyes fixed to the stain of red, a puddle this time rather than the sprinkle of rain.

Tears welled in my eyes, my vision blurred, and I fought to blink away the sting of memory that shook me. I was succeeding in not sobbing, at least until Jack's sudden intrusion broke me apart.

"You still haven't pulled the damn sheets off?"

The tears slipped slowly down my cheeks as soon as I heard his voice.

"Here," throwing a clean set of sheets at me, Jack paused and smirked. "Would you look at those tears," he taunted, the tone of his voice slithery and sadistic. "I remember those from last night. And here I thought you'd run out."

His smirk widened. "Guess not."

Jack took a step closer, his lewd stare touching every part of my body. He had electric fingers that hurt instead of tickling, claws that were rough and solid, with talons that could rip your soul right from your body. But all of that was disguised behind a crooked smile and dimples that were charming. Jack had a mess of blond hair, and brown eyes with flecks of gold. However, behind those eyes was the same sickness I had seen in my father and brothers over the years, the same sickness that invaded my dreams until I woke up drenched in the sweat of terror.

I heard the women scream when I looked into Jack's eyes, and now my scream was just one voice within the symphony.

Flinching at the small sensation of his fingertip trailing after one of my tears, I ground my teeth until my jaw ached. I knew better than to move away. Eventually, his finger moved down my cheek and along my jawline.

"There ain't nothing sweeter than a virgin's body. It's a shame I only get to have it one time with you." He chuckled, the sound causing bile to fight its way up my throat. "Thankfully," he added, "there's more women like you for me to ride. When the mood strikes."

His mouth dropped open in feigned surprise, but it was only seconds before it closed again and his lips pulled up into a lascivious grin. "Oh, but don't you worry, Maggie. It'll be months before I move on to something better. It'll take me that long, at least, to wear you out so much that you're not fun anymore. By the time shoving my dick in you feels like tossing a hot dog down a hallway, I'll have found better uses for you. Maybe your brothers can help come up with something."

Finding my breast, Jack's fingers wrapped around the weight, the tips digging into the bruises that were there from his attack the night before. With the sun beginning its slow rise over the horizon, shadows crossed over my bedroom, and my mind flashed back. Slumping forward, my shoulders could barely hold the weight of the memories that slammed down on me.

Hurrying home after seeing Elliot had been difficult. Taking those last few steps up the front steps and into the house had been nearly impossible. My father had called out to me as soon as he heard the door creak open and I'd marched through the kitchen, only to turn a corner into the living room and find a nightmare waiting for me from which there would never be the relief of waking.

My father sat in his favorite chair. Finn, Brody and a man I didn't know waited for me with anticipation blazing behind eyes already dazed with the alcohol I could smell permeating the air. Each man had a bottle in his hand and all four sets of eyes were glued to me as soon as I made my appearance.

"Meet your new husband, Maggie Pie. And don't give me no argument about it."

There was no proposal. No ring. No ceremony and no preacher. The cake was absent as were the flowers. There wasn't a bridesmaid wishing she could be a bride or a first dance. There was simply a sentence and a threat delivered by the mouth of a dying man. A demand that I had no choice to refuse.

I cried as my family joked and carried on. An hour passed before my father's eyes slowly closed as he slipped off into a drunken sleep. Not a minute passed after he began softly snoring before my brothers turned up the music blasting from a small radio and Jack dragged me back to my room.

The details of my first sexual experience are as harrowing as they are hazy. The pain was my first memory, the humiliation closely following. Not even my desperation to imagine Elliot's face over Jack's was enough to ease me through the degradation of my first *responsibility* as a new wife.

For once the music that hid the screams of the women my family abused was used to hide my screams, and for as loud as I became, for as desperately as I wanted my father to hear me and stop Jack from everything he was doing, the music only became louder.

Snapping me back to the present, Jack's voice filled the room, amusement set into the tone of his words that forced more tears from my eyes. "I knew that was too much blood for a damn virgin. Filthy bitch. You could have mentioned you were on your fucking period before I fucked you."

His fist hit the wall near my head. "Clean it the fuck up."

Leaving me alone in the room, Jack stumbled his way down the hallway toward the living room where my brothers and father still slept off the liquor they consumed the night before.

Unable to stop staring at the blood that covered the sheets, I crumpled down to the floor, pain lancing through my body when the memento Jack had given me to remember my first night with him touched the filthy carpet.

"Stop crying, bitch. They're just my initials. I want every man who touches you after me to know that I was the first person here."

It was just a small pocketknife that he'd used, something so small that a person wouldn't feel threatened by the blade. From the pain, I would have sworn he'd carved so deep that he was etching bone, however I knew that he'd barely sliced the skin where he'd cut me.

Sobs escaped me as my body shook violently, my teeth biting into my lip to keep the sound as soft as possible. I didn't need Finn or Brody hearing me cry. They would only punish me for not feeling appreciative of the *gift* they'd given me in Jack.

Gift. Yeah, right. They'd called him that as he'd dragged me away, but I knew better. But even knowing that I was being led off to have my choice stripped away from me, I never realized how bad losing that choice would feel.

I'd been handed off to become somebody else's problem, and in the process I'd been stripped from the only man that didn't see me as the burden I'd somehow become to the men who'd raised me.

However, even after I'd been used, abused and left to cry, I still found the strength to keep moving. It took me a few minutes to gather myself enough to push to my feet, and it took another few minutes for me to go through the motions of stripping the bed of the dirty sheets and replacing it with the new ones. What took longer was walking into the bathroom and staring at myself in the mirror – staring, but not really seeing, the girl who now stood before me.

She had the same green eyes, the same black hair and the same round face as I remembered. But the light was missing from her eyes, the hair was a mess of curls that had lost their bounce and luster, and the face no longer held the smile that Elliot had worked so hard to put there.

From one night to the next I'd changed in ways that made me a stranger even to myself. Reality was a crushing weight on my shoulders and the future I'd always wondered about and wanted was now nothing more than a curse.

Showering was as pleasant as it was painful. I washed away the heavy scent of cheap cologne that Jack had left on my skin. I hissed when the water washed down my body to erase the red stain of blood. Daring to look, I twisted around just enough to see that the initials carved into my bottom weren't so deep that they'd leave more than just a faint white scar when they finally healed. Thankfully the marks were in a place where I wouldn't see them on a daily basis, and if the opportunity ever came for me to get away from the man who put them there, those scars were something I could ignore.

Not wanting to give up the only time I had to myself, I stood in the shower until the water became too cold for my skin. Gone were the tears, the blood, and the smell of a man I detested – but the bruises still lingered, the pain held tight, and the shame clogged my throat as I climbed out of the shower and got dressed.

My reprieve ended all too soon when the door shook to my right. Someone's fist pounded against the other side, but they didn't speak to announce themself.

Pound. Pound. Pound. Each beat made my stomach turn as it vibrated through my battered body.

Swallowing down the scream of frustration that worked its way up my throat, I shuffled across the dirty floor to flip the lock.

"It's about damn time. There's something in there that we need."

Brody stared down at me, his large body blocking the single bulb light in the hallway. "Are you going to move out of my way or what?"

Stepping back, I let him enter the bathroom, the steam escaping out the door as if it, too, had no desire to be in the same space as my brother. Without speaking, I watched Brody pull open the medicine cabinet door and fight through the numerous bottles of out of date painkillers and expired antacids. His hand locked over a small black bag, but his lack of coordination caused him to drop it into the sink as he pulled it from the cabinet.

It wasn't like I'd never seen the contents of that bag before. Several hypodermic needles and a vial of clear liquid rattled at the bottom of the sink before Brody quickly picked them up and shoved them back into the black bag that contained them.

Turning to me, he grinned. "We're heading out to hunt. Dad's staying behind to watch you and make sure you don't run off before we get back. There's some groceries in the fridge and we expect dinner to be ready when we return."

All I could do was nod my head in response. Arguing, crying, screaming…none of those things would do me a lick of good. They would only ensure that the next beating I endured would be harder.

CHAPTER TWENTY-ONE

ELLI⊕T

The sun sank past the horizon at half past seven. Sending up a few brilliant rays in protest, it painted the sky a breathtaking rainbow of reds, oranges and pinks that caught my eye and reminded me that beyond this life there was something far more magical, far more fair and beautiful than what I'd ever had the chance to experience.

Peace existed in the afterlife, peace and the serenity of knowing I might see Katelyn again, knowing that I might have the chance to kiss my son one more time before I'm dragged down to whatever punishment God had in store for me. Sure, I hadn't committed the sins that would damn me just yet, but I would commit them before the sun rose again.

I would maim. I would torture. I would kill. And for that, I would fry. But I wanted to believe that I'd be granted at least one brief moment with the two people who were stolen from me, and that moment would be enough. To see them smile, to know they were okay and together: it would be enough to satisfy me so that I could release my spirit into whatever pit of fire awaited me, and I could smile while I burned.

On one side of me were the shadows of a thick forest. On the other were the wide opened fields of the Crow property, the landscape dotted with nothing but tall weeds, sparse trees and the dilapidated house that stood bastion against the ever darkening sky. The windows were lit by the inside, and every so often a shadow would pass by. I was too far away to see if it was Maggie that paced the room that faced my direction, but I hoped the girl was biding her time, packing her things and preparing to leave the property.

I'd asked her to meet me at eight, and I'd reminded her to wait as long as it took for me to arrive.

Although the sun hadn't fully disappeared and the moon hadn't yet taken reign of the night sky, a bonfire shot up in wicked, dancing flames in front of the old house. With clawed fingers, the flames scraped at what remained of a beautiful sunlit day and cast out bits of embers that twinkled upwards into the sky like fireflies released from a netted trap. I'd lost count of how many bits of ash I'd watched burst into the night air and become lost to the gentle breeze that flowed past me in a chilled whisper of sound.

Around the bonfire sat several chairs; dirty, white plastic that was as broken and weathered as the house from which they'd been pulled. Several times, I'd watched Maggie's brothers come out of the house to drag out a radio, some food and two oversized coolers that I assumed held the alcohol for the night. Classic rock was a gentle hum in my ear, the radio not loud enough for me to enjoy the music that was playing, but just loud enough for me to recognize a lyric or two before the voice of the singer became lost among the crackle of the bonfire and the rustling of the branches that moved above my head.

Crouched down, I was in the perfect position to monitor the house and as soon as I saw Maggie make her way into the woods, I would carry out the plan I'd been waiting years to finish.

It took everything in me to remain still as Jonah and his boys came meandering out of the house. Obviously inebriated, despite the young hour, they stumbled over the packed dirt and weeds, their low voices carrying across the expanse. I wasn't able to make out their grumbled words, but I didn't need to hear what they were saying. Just seeing them lit a fire under my ass that had me fighting myself to keep from ending this all in a quick round of bullets that would slice the night air open and spill Crow blood.

A high-pitched scream tore away from the house drawing my gaze from the Crows. Eyelids narrowed, I peered into the distance to watch a fourth man come ambling around the corner, a woman dragged beside him, her tangled black hair caught viciously in his hand. The woman struggled against his unrelenting hold, her hands grasping at his fist, her feet stumbling beneath her as she fought to free herself.

Maggie…

From one heartbeat to the next, I vacillated between running straight for them and biding my time per the plan.

Despite the woman's fight, the man dragging her inched forward, my blood boiling by the time he neared the fire. The light cast across her face helped me take a strained breath. It wasn't Maggie as far as I could tell, and when she screamed again, her panicked voice confirmed it. Every muscle in my body relaxed just enough so that I wasn't lunging forward anymore, but it still took all the practiced self-control I had not to run and help what I assumed was the Crows' next victim.

Jonah and his boys settled themselves into the chairs while the man I didn't recognize continued dragging the screaming woman around the fire, finally settling her in the dirt in front of the audience of Crows and kicking her in the side for good measure. A barked command flew from his lips, which silenced her scream, but started the puddle of tears I assumed was quickly developing beneath her. Even from a distance, I could see the way her body shook with her sobs, and my teeth gnashed together at the chorus of male laughter that followed. How any man could take pleasure by the smell of a woman's fear was beyond me. Women were meant to be respected. They were meant to be treated with care and protected against the injustices of the world, but I guessed that meant nothing to the thieves in the night – the monsters that fed on the fragilities and vulnerabilities of those who they considered weaker than themselves.

I'd attempted to crawl into the minds of those sick fucks every night when I searched for the identity of my family's killers. But, no matter how hard I struggled to release every shred of humanity I had in me, I could never truly understand what it was that made men like the ones I was watching tick. I couldn't lower myself that far, couldn't make sense of the need for violence or the taste for stripping the freedom from a woman or child.

Bile was a sickening flavor on my tongue as I attempted in vain to keep from seeing Katelyn kneeling in the dirt in front of the men. The thunder of rushing blood pulsed feverishly in my head as I imagined her crying and begging for her freedom.

Rage became a torrent of lightning in my veins. I fought to control myself when Finn kicked dirt into the woman's eyes, and my hands clenched into painful fists while she was shoved to the ground by the fourth man, whose face I couldn't make out.

It didn't take a genius to figure out what horror show I was about to witness, but it did take a soldier to determine what I'd do about it. Struggling to ignore the abuse the blond man committed against the woman, I forced my eyes to the house, my gaze locking on a solitary shadow that stood at the window in witness of the bonfire that burned outside the walls of the home.

Don't look, Maggie. Just grab your things, head for the woods, and forget you witnessed their crimes.

A silent mantra in my head, I begged Maggie to walk away, to avoid seeing the atrocities her family committed without guilt or fear of repercussions. She didn't need another scar on her psyche, didn't need another helpless face etched into her memory, a weight she would bear each and every day as she attempted to rebuild her life.

She'd never talked to me about the truth of her family, but I heard it between the lines. I saw the terror that flooded her green eyes and I could sense the tension that sat just below her skin, the secrets that threatened to burst forth if she ever found the strength to finally speak them and make them real.

The shadow inched away from the window and I whispered a prayer of thanks that she didn't see what came next. My gaze retrained on the bonfire and the men that surrounded it, I watched as the blond man stripped the woman of her clothes. Raucous laughter rose up into the darkening sky without remorse or hesitation. The music became louder and the lilting guitar solo rang out across the expanse, the crooned country lyrics heavily at odds with the scene that played out before me.

I wasn't in a position to help that woman as quickly as she needed it, but I memorized each atrocity committed against her and promised I'd return each act against the man who tortured her for the amusement of the audience that sat before him.

Within minutes that woman was stripped of every bit of clothing she had, the shirt, pants and underthings tossed into the fire to catch flame. Naked and desperate, she attempted to crawl away from the man. Amusing himself, he'd allow her a few feet of distance before he stepped forward to drag her back in place, his hand reaching out to pull at her hair or slide possessively over her body.

The metallic note of blood flooded my mouth, my teeth grinding so hard that I caught the inside of my cheek between them and released the pressure that coursed through my veins. I savored the flavor, sucking on my cheek to induce more of the taste of death and destruction - of life and rejuvenation - in order to saturate my senses and set me on edge for everything I knew I had to do.

Killing a man wasn't easy. Not unless you were so devoid of humanity that you'd become a basic animal or something else entirely alien and strange. While at war, I'd regretted the times I'd fired my weapon and I'd prayed for the families of the men my bullets had mowed down.

However, war was a constant theme since the beginning of recorded history. Nations fought as much as their citizens. The drive for territory, resources and power were as forceful as the need for protection and revenge. There was a time in my life when I wondered why humanity hadn't yet risen above the need to spill blood. However, that question was silenced on the day I learned that my family was missing.

I'll admit that in the first several years after I'd returned I continued to hope that I'd see Katelyn and Michael alive again. But as that hope slowly dwindled, the need for violence came in to replace it.

With her face pressed into the dirt, the woman was forced into a position where her ass was high in the air. Legs spread apart and her body exposed, she was held in place by the blond man as one of Maggie's brothers pushed up from his chair to approach her.

My eyes flicked to the house searching for any indication that Maggie was making her way to the woods. Caught between the need to help the woman and waiting in place, I begged Maggie to hurry up and make her escape. It was nearly impossible for me to remain still, to watch as that poor woman had unspeakable acts committed against her.

Inching forward on my knees, I crept past the duffle bags I'd hidden in the bushes attempting to glean a better view of the house. It took effort to keep from watching what was being done to that poor woman by the fire, but I had plenty of practice focusing on one particular place while hell broke out around me. What was being done to that woman was atrocious, but I'd seen worse. I'd seen death and destruction on a scale that no man should ever have the opportunity to witness. Women, men, children…babies. None were safe during war. None were spared the indignity of slaughter, rape, torture or death. Fast or slow, it didn't matter. The pain lingered for all who were involved.

Several minutes passed before the side door to the house popped open. Slowly crawling its way from the frame, the door was so unsteady, I worried it would break away from the remaining hinge to crash down and alert the Crow men to Maggie's escape. A head of black curls peeked out, but she was too far away for me to see the expression written across her innocent face. Perhaps that was for the best. I didn't want to know the reaction she had to the terror that took place on the grounds of her property. There was no possible way she didn't hear the woman cry. But it would be better if she didn't have to face the cruelty being committed by the men who'd raised her.

Her head turned to peer across at the bonfire, and once she saw that the men were otherwise occupied – their attention glued to the woman as one of the brothers took what wasn't his – Maggie ran.

A single bag was slung over her shoulder. It appeared light for a person who was running away to a new life, a small, sad collection of personal possessions that easily fit inside a knapsack. Although I was curious why this girl who'd told me she'd been given everything had so little that mattered enough to take it with her into the woods, I pushed that curiosity aside to focus on the task at hand.

Quickly covering the distance to the shadows of the forest that lined her property, Maggie disappeared into the trees and I breathed out a sigh of relief to know that she was safe where she was going.

It was finally time to end the torment I'd endured for the past fourteen years.

I was calm.

I was focused.

And I was prepared to rain down Hell's fire on the men who were still within my sight.

CHAPTER TWENTY-TWO

MAGGIE

The woods at night have never scared me. The shadows that move, the branches that rattle, the leaves that rustle above my head in chorus with the symphony being sang by the creatures of the night.

Owls warned of my approach, scavengers scurried at my feet, eyes caught the sparse light of the moon to become reflective orbs letting me know that life was always close by. Whereas most people would feel lost in the wonderland of ever shifting darkness and soft light, I felt at home, especially on a night such as this.

I never remained home for my family's parties. I couldn't stand the sound of the music, not when I knew it only grew louder to disguise a woman's screams. Normally, I would run as far as I could as fast as my body would take me, but tonight I was making a slow crawl. The bruises my brothers left on my body from the lashing were so deep in the muscles that pain lanced me with every wrong step. Adding to that pain was the sore area on my bottom where Jack had carved his initials. Although not deep, those cuts were irritated by the elastic of my panties, the material riding up beneath my skirt to rub over the raw and aggravated skin.

Determined to reach the other farm, I swallowed down the fear that threatened to paralyze me.

The day had been quiet while Jack and my brothers were out hunting, a sick apprehension thickening with each hour they were gone. Having anticipated the worst for their arrival,

I wasn't surprised by the woman they dragged in. Heavily sedated by the medication they'd injected into her body, she wasn't able to focus on my father or me as she was dumped unceremoniously to the floor in the spare bedroom. While she attempted pathetically to crawl away from the men that stood lording over her, she cried what small amount of tears she could muster before giving up entirely and releasing herself into dreamless, medicated sleep.

While locking the door to the room, Brody and Finn leered in my direction, their mouths pulled into smirks, no doubt from having heard what Jack had done to me the night before. They didn't vocalize their taunts, didn't dare incur my father's wrath for fear he would end the *marriage* and ruin whatever plans they had for me.

Throughout the day, I'd gone back and forth on whether I should show my father what Jack had done. There was no doubt in my mind that he would have killed Jack for daring to mark my body, but I had another concern that kept me from lifting my skirt to show him the truth.

After Jack left, my thoughts had gone to Elliot and the promise he'd made to take me away from the only life I'd known. His face was a picture of paradise in my thoughts, his voice a welcoming song that lulled me into the belief that there was something out there better than what I'd always had.

Telling my father what Jack had done would be a quick solution to the problems that faced me. I knew he would ensure Jack never touched me again…at least not while he was alive to prevent it. But that was the problem as well. My father's health was declining with each passing day. His will, his strength, his control over the family becoming less and less as he approached the death we all saw coming. I wasn't sure whether he had a few hours left, or a few days, but I knew it wouldn't be a month, much less a year, that he would remain alive to protect me.

Elliot was a different story. Still young, still strong, and still able to defend the people that mattered to him, he was capable of taking me someplace safe, of ensuring that neither Jack nor my brothers could ever harm me again. Knowing his history in the military, it was readily apparent that he had the drive, the training and the skills to keep me safe. And I believed him when he told me he'd kill my brothers. It was written in the expression on his face, in his narrowed eyes, his lips held in a thin line, in the skin that was pulled taut over the sharp angles of his masculine face.

An avenging angel with black wings so large they blocked the sun wouldn't have been more terrifying than the look I saw on Elliot's face the second he saw the bruises that lined my legs.

It was for that reason I chose to make this journey. Promising myself that I would make it, I packed what I could without the family noticing that I was up to something. Deciding what to take and what to leave behind had been difficult. But after careful thought, I chose only what was absolutely necessary, keeping my bag light in case I needed to run.

If not for the injuries I'd suffered in the past several days, I would have moved much faster through the woods on my way to meet Elliot.

My breath plumed out in front of my face as the cold night air came in to settle against the ground. A chill caused bumps to break out over my exposed skin, but I ignored the discomfort and pushed myself to move faster. The cold wouldn't bother me long. Elliot's arms were large enough and warm enough to prevent even the weather from harming me. In my mind, he was the savior I'd dreamed of for so many lonely nights.

Nestled in with the anticipation of seeing him, and the relief I felt to know I was being taken away, was a pervasive guilt that rode me since the moment I promised him I'd be his wife. I'd been a part of the worst tragedy of Elliot's life. I'd been complicit in the destruction of his family. And I'd hidden that information from him with the intent of never being honest for as long as I knew him.

It shouldn't have gone this far with Elliot and me. From day one, I knew better than to talk to him, to care about him, to have anything to do with him. Yet, here I was, crawling through the woods on a moonless night with the hopes of becoming his wife.

Sure, I'd been young when his wife and son were stolen away. I didn't understand the part I'd played until years later when I was old enough to make sense of the way my family had used me. But that didn't make me innocent of the crime – not entirely. I still knew what happened to his family. I still had a picture of them in my mind every time I looked at Elliot's face. Despite the pain that was so obvious behind his eyes – the not knowing, the torment, the passionate rage – I still remained silent rather than offering him the same relief he was offering me.

What did that say about me as a person? The fact that I would so easily accept the help he was offering without giving him the one thing he needed since his family disappeared only made me more of a monster. I couldn't return to him the love of his wife, or the safety of his young son, but I could end the pain of not knowing, I could close the book on that small amount of suffering that came with the lack of closure he carried.

Fear made me keep my mouth closed, fear and the guilt that rode me with every step I took in his direction.

There was nothing I could ever say to him to make what I was doing okay.

As each thought crossed my mind on that front, my steps slowed a little more.

What was I doing?

Stopping in place, I turned my face up into a soft beam of light that broke through the dark canopy of trees above me. Trembling in response to the breeze that crept across my skin, a tear slipped down my cheek as realization slammed into me with the force of a hundred running horses.

I was a bad person for what I was doing to Elliot. I was evil. I was secretive. And I was cruel.

Stopped in my tracks by the harsh truth now filtering through my thoughts, I buckled over myself, sinking to the ground beneath the weight of the secrets I was keeping from the only man who'd ever offered to help me escape.

He was too good for me. Too trusting and too giving. When all I've done in life is take from him both unknowingly and then willingly, he continues to try to help me.

I've lied to him and he's done nothing but be honest.

I've hidden myself from him while he remained genuine and true.

I've taken advantage of him in more ways than he could ever truly understand, and if I continued marching forward to meet him as I promised, I'll only be taking advantage of him again.

A line was being drawn at that moment. A line that, if crossed, would make me no better than the family from whom I was running.

No, my hand hadn't been the one to slaughter his family. It hadn't been the one to steal them away. But even if I hadn't been responsible for the loss of everything he loved and cared about, I was responsible for keeping Elliot in pain, keeping him in the dark, and keeping him from finding closure because I refused to tell him the truth.

I didn't deserve a man as good as the one who was waiting for me.

The sad fact was I'd be hurting Elliot more to be with him, and I'd be accepting the love of a man who was a far better person than me.

The guilt became unbearable as that realization hit me, and rather than pushing up to take another step forward towards the life I could have had, I turned back to return to the one that I now knew I deserved.

I was a liar and a thief, and I believed the universe had put me exactly where I belonged when it made me a Crow. By remaining silent, by harboring the truth, I'd proven myself no better than the men who'd raised me. My hand didn't have the same blood on it as theirs, but by my willingness to hide their crimes, I was just as much responsible for the deaths of those women.

My silence had allowed them to continue killing.

Wishing I were strong enough to turn around once again to tell Elliot everything I knew, I regretted my cowardice as I continued marching back in the direction of my home. My weakness tasted sour on my tongue, but I would welcome the life I knew I was crawling back to because the punishment I'd endure would be justified.

Approaching the tree line, I paused to hear the music blaring across the fields. The tempo was hard and angry, the guitars and drums a fetid beat that welcomed the violence I knew was occurring and being hidden by the rhythm of whatever song it was they were playing. Over the years, I'd grown to hate the sound of music because, to me, the only thing music was intended for was to hide the pain.

Breathing out a trembling sigh, I glanced over my shoulder one last time at the path that would lead me to the adjacent farm where Elliot was waiting. I wondered how long he would sit in the abandoned house until he realized I wasn't going to show. Would he worry that my family had somehow kept me from leaving? Would he show up at my property to help me escape?

A new layer of heartbreak and concern crept over me and I became stuck in place once again, unable to move forward or back.

Glued to that small spot amongst the trees, I was battling myself over what to do. How had everything become so complicated so quickly? How had I messed everything up so easily?

Complicated was too simple a word for the position in which I found myself. Dangerous was more like it...or disastrous.

Spinning in place like a damn merry go round, I didn't know what to do. If I continued forward back to my family, I ran the risk of Elliot showing up to see if they'd kept me from going to him. But if I took off back in the direction of where I knew he'd be waiting, I ran the risk that he wouldn't let me go.

I was damned by every possible decision I could make, and I was the only person responsible for the problem.

Back and forth, my feet paced beneath me, my body moving in circles as I pondered the right thing to do.

And just as I made a decision I thought would resolve the dilemma I was facing, a loud voice rang out through the cold night, a terrible sound that caused my entire body to stand frozen in place.

I ran towards the tree line and peered out across the expanse to discover that I'd taken too long making my decision.

There were five men around the bonfire. My brother, Brody, was laid out on the ground, his eyes closed and something dark puddled beneath his head. In a chair beside him was my brother, Finn, his hair a disheveled mess and pure rage drawn across his expression. From where I was standing, it appeared that rope was pulled taut against his body; the plastic chair where he sat bent at the sides from how tight the rope was tied. Jack was lying on the ground as well, his pants pulled to his ankles and his lifeless body draped across a naked woman. Neither was moving, and I wasn't sure if they were alive or dead.

My father's raised voice was barely audible over the music that continued blasting from a small radio that sat atop a red, plastic cooler. The pressure in my chest at the sight in front of me was unbearable, the need to run, to fight, to scream…to hide.

Held by the throat, my father was struggling to fight a man I didn't recognize. Dressed in head to toe black, the man looked like a mercenary, a blood-thirsty killer, a soldier…

Elliot…

My heart pounded out a frenetic beat and my body swayed over knees that were barely holding my weight. Standing in horror, I watched my father drop to his knees, Elliot's hand still wrapped around his throat as the two men screamed in each other's faces. Panic shot through me until every muscle in my body was painful against my bones.

Here again, I was trapped in indecision. I didn't want my father to die and I didn't want Elliot to die either. What happened in the hour that I'd been away and what was I going to do to stop it?

I had limited choices, and very little power to step in between two men that mattered to me. Helping one would only hurt the other. If I freed Finn so that he could help me save my dad, he would kill Elliot in the process. If I jumped in to break the two men up myself, I knew one of them would die. There was no right answer, no clear and direct path I could take that would stop the nightmare that was playing out in front of me.

From one second to the next, my father was losing his battle against Elliot. Finally forced to his knees, he was dragged to a chair next to Finn, tied up in much the same fashion, his head twisting violently to the side when Elliot struck him with a closed fist. Blood shot from his lips and I bit my lip to swallow the scream that rose instantly to my throat.

This couldn't be happening. Not like this. Not between these two people.

What does a person do when they're caught between two people they love most in the world? My mind raced with possibilities, but nothing seemed actually possible. Just when I thought Elliot would kill my father right there in front of me, he stepped back, his gaze sliding down to where Jack lay prone over the body of the women he'd dragged into the house just hours before.

Picking his limp body up, Elliot slammed it down into another chair before reaching into a black duffel bag to extract more rope.

For a brief moment, there was a lull in the violence playing out in front of me, and a thought came to mind, a thought that incessantly whispered in my head until I found the strength to take action.

CHAPTER TWENTY-THREE

ELLIOT

They made it easy for me.

I wouldn't have believed one man against four could go so smoothly, but that's what happens when two of those men have their pants pulled down to their ankles and the other two have at least a half bottle of liquor sloshing around in their stomachs.

Sneaking up had required no skill at all. There was no doubt in my mind that I could have walked up slowly carrying streamers and tossing confetti and these slack jaws wouldn't have noticed. I'm not complaining about the ease of catching them off guard, I was just a tad bit disappointed that the simple task hadn't helped to alleviate the rabid anger that was still boiling in my veins.

Fortunately for me, once Maggie had made her departure and I'd waited a decent amount of time to ensure she was far enough away, Jonah and one of Maggie's brother were called upon by nature, their bladders working overtime to expel the alcohol they were ingesting as fast as their throats could work it down their bodies.

The blond man and Maggie's other brother were taking turns on the woman they held captive. I continued logging each disgusting act they committed against her just so I knew the exact score I needed to settle once I had them in my grasp.

That poor woman had lost the ability to scream after a half hour of their torment and I imagined her vocal chords

150

were as shredded as my soul had been when I'd returned home from war to an empty and quiet house.

Using the tall grasses around the property as cover while I made my way closer to the house, I kept my eye on Jonah Crow. He was the weakest link as far as I could tell and the distance he placed between his son and himself made it easy for me to sneak up behind him. The idiot still had his dick in his hands when the butt of my gun came down at the back of his head and he didn't have time to shout out a warning to his son taking a piss around the corner. I would have felt bad for the bastard landing in a puddle of his own piss, but I'd lost the ability to give a shit about him on the day my family disappeared.

One down – three to go.

Rounding the corner, I peered out to find that Maggie's brother had his back to me, a steady stream of urine mucking up the dirt beneath his feet. The man was so drunk, he didn't have enough sense to shoot the stream farther out so that his boots weren't covered in mud. Thanking God for how fortunate I'd become in my quest, I crept up in a slow crawl, my steps light as I approached. Finally having drained his bladder, his body jerked a bit as he zipped up his fly, turning just in time to catch sight of me before I struck.

Bloody spittle sprayed from his mouth the instant my fist made contact, but he wasn't going down as easily as his father. Reaching out, he caught me in the shoulder, dragging me down with him as his foot slipped in the puddle he'd left behind.

It wasn't the best of circumstances when you had no choice but to wrestle a man in urine and dirt, but I clenched my teeth and endured. I'd been in worse situations and I wouldn't be shaken by the filth that now covered my clothes.

The man was one hell of a challenge. Even three sheets to the wind, he gave as much as he received, but a few well placed blows to the back of his head finally settled him down. Opening his mouth to scream had been an unfortunate decision when I took the opportunity to shove his face down into the muck and forced him to swallow the mess he'd dragged our bodies down into.

Reaching back, I pulled a gun from my waistband. It took another three successive blows against the back of his head for his body to crumple beneath me. Had it been any other man, I would have left him to drown in the puddle of piss, but I had other plans for him that included a slow crawl to his maker.

After turning him over to prolong his life, I grabbed a few zip ties from a pocket in the cargo pants I was wearing and bound his hands and feet. He wouldn't remain unconscious and silent for long, so I made quick work of rounding the building once again to check on Jonah. He was still out like a light, and I had little worry of him waking up at an inconvenient time.

Saving the bindings I'd brought in my pockets for the younger men still having their way with the woman, I rounded the house one more time to duck behind a bush and monitor the activity at the bonfire.

Cursing under my breath, I had to dial back my rage to keep from drawing my gun and ending them right there. Maggie's brother was taking his fill of the woman's mouth, while the blond man violated her body from the other side. Her arms dropped beneath her body, listless and swaying. I could see she'd lost the ability – or the desire – to fight back any longer.

Thankfully, she was still alive and I had a chance to make things right. Nothing I did at this point would take away the horror of the violence being done to her, but at least she still had a chance to leave this place and return home to the people who loved her.

Katelyn and Michael never had that chance, and on that thought, I crept forward to take control of the situation. I needed to see these men writhe in agony just about as much as I needed air to breathe.

Neither man was aware of his surroundings, their eyes too busy looking down on the victim they held between them. Choosing to take a longer path, I crept over the ground holding close to the shadows of the house before rounding the bonfire to come up behind the blond man.

Drawing a knife from my pocket, I slid the blade open and just as Maggie's brother's eyes caught sight of me, I reached out to slice through the blond man's Achilles tendon. He fell like I knew he would, blood spraying out from his ankle as a feral scream erupted from his lungs. Having lost the ability to walk, he was no longer a problem and I was left facing a one on one fight with the last man standing.

Pushing up from my crouched position, I smiled at the poor bastard, my eyes narrowing the moment a scream left his lips. My gaze lowered to find a pool of blood forming in his hands and I couldn't help the burst of laughter that left my lips. It appeared that at the moment the blond man went down, he'd dropped the woman along with him. Her teeth snapped shut from her impact with the ground. Unfortunately for Maggie's brother, his dick was still inside her mouth at the time.

My head fell back and my eyes were wide open as I gazed at the stars and mouthed a quick 'thank you' to whatever dumb luck was helping me along. Within seconds, Maggie's brother lunged forward, his bloody dick still hanging from his pants, his feet stumbling over the jeans that were wrapped around his ankles. He didn't have much time to set himself straight, but he fought regardless. I had to commend him for not going down as easily as I thought he would.

His boots trampled across the woman and the blond man who was now lying on top of her, his hands grasping my shirt as he pulled me towards him. Caught off guard, due to my hesitance to trample the woman and cause any more injuries than she'd already endured, I stumbled forward, losing my footing just long enough for the brother to drag me to the ground.

Fighting on the ground wasn't my preference, especially not with two moving bodies beneath me – one crying and the other attempting to grab my ankles to hold me in place. While Maggie's brother attempted to gain control of my arms and torso, the blond man did his best to grab onto my legs, resulting in his face meeting the bottom of my boot several times. Four quick kicks left him moaning on the ground and he quickly gave up the struggle, leaving me free to continue wrestling down the brother.

He was a worthy opponent, evenly matched in strength and determination, but completely lacking in focus and skill. Perhaps abducting and raping women hadn't prepared him for the struggle that would take place while fighting another person of the same size. I wanted to laugh at that thought, but it was too depressing at the same time.

Gaining the upper hand, I rolled above the brother, my arm snaking around his neck as I crawled my way higher. It didn't take long before I had him in a chokehold that he couldn't break. I looked down into his face as he struggled against my grip, the lines of his skin becoming deeper while a crimson shade turned to a darker purple. His mouth opened in desperation for air and within a few minutes, his angry glare disappeared as his eyes closed. It wasn't until his body had gone limp that I released the tension in my arm and dropped his body into the dirt.

The blond man was still fully conscious, but he was too focused on the damage to his ankle to notice that my eyes had locked on him. Brushing the dirt and grime off my shirt, I pushed up to my feet and leered down at the idiot who sat crying over his injuries. The woman beneath him wasn't moving and I worried that she'd not survived the violence committed against her.

Reaching down, I held my finger to her neck, not finding a pulse and grinding my teeth at the realization that, if she wasn't dead, she was damn near close.

A new level of rage roared through me, my hands reaching for the first thing I could find. I pulled a log from the fire, ash sparkling in a stream of rain as I brought it down over the asshole's head.

One good hit was all it took to sink him to the ground until he, too, was left a pile of useless meat. He wasn't dead. I hadn't hit him hard enough for that, but he would be before the night was over.

Pulling more zip ties from my pockets, I quickly bound the two men where they lay on the ground and went back out in search of the two I'd left by the house. I had many things to say to all of these assholes, and questions I needed answered. By the time I was through with them, they'd be my unwilling audience until the moment came that I executed each and every one of them.

I'd barely had time to retrieve the man I'd left lying in his own piss, drag him around the house and tie him to a chair before a voice rang out behind me.

"Who the fuck do you think you are coming on my land and attacking my family?"

It appeared Jonah Crow had woken up to rejoin me and I spun around to face down a man who looked too sick and beaten to be standing.

"The name's Elliot," I offered, my voice a bit rough from exhaustion. By the expression on his face, he didn't appreciate my entrance, the beatings, or the nonchalant response I'd given him.

A smirk pulled at my lips when I asked, "What's wrong? Were you expecting me to give you a different answer?"

"You're a dead man," he growled out before spitting blood onto the dirt at his feet.

I glanced around at the bodies of his bound sons and the blond man – whoever the hell he was – and laughed. "Oh yeah? How, exactly, are you planning on accomplishing that?"

All joking was tossed aside as soon as he lunged in my direction. My hands reached out the minute his fist came into contact with my body. My fingers gripped around his throat as he struggled to cause me even the slightest amount of harm. Although still strong for the condition he was in, he wasn't much of a match.

He continued pounding on my chest and shoulders with everything he had, but I took each blow and savored the pain while my hand tightened over his throat.

Once the fight he had in him slowly simmered down, I leaned in until our noses were barely touching. His face was turning a nice shade of purple from the lack of oxygen being drawn into his lungs.

Our eyes locked for several seconds before I smiled in the old man's face.

"Like I was saying, you pathetic piece of shit: The name's Elliot, and I'd like to have a conversation with you about a few things. Thank you kindly for the invitation to your house."

"I didn't invite you nowhere," he managed to answer despite my hand wrapped tightly around his throat.

Laughing at the comment, I stared him in the eye, my voice calm as I answered, "That's where you're wrong, Crow. You invited me here fourteen years ago. You just didn't know it at the time."

He dropped to his knees on the ground in front of me without another word and I made quick work of binding his hands and feet.

CHAPTER TWENTY-FOUR

MAGGIE

I was a damned fool for thinking I could come between my father and Elliot, but I was determined to try. I couldn't overpower either of the men. I knew that as well as any person would. I didn't have other options.

Lucky that both men had been distracted by the time I made it back to the property, I kept low to the ground as I ran back towards the house. I grimaced to pull the door open and hoped like hell nobody heard the telltale squeak of the hinges.

Once inside, I ran to the window facing the bonfire. Peeking out from around the curtain, I saw that Elliot had overpowered my father and was in the process of tying his wrists and ankles with little plastic bands. I breathed out a sigh of relief to see that neither man had killed each other in the few minutes it had taken me to get inside, but that didn't mean death wasn't coming.

Quickly glancing around, I noticed that Finn was still strapped to a chair, while Brody and Jack lay lifeless on the ground by the bonfire. Blood puddled beneath Jack's leg and I wondered if he was dead or alive. The answer didn't matter much, and I wasn't certain I cared what happened to my brothers. The only thing that mattered was keeping Elliot as far away from my father as possible.

I took the time to continue watching and when Elliot picked up my father to plant him in the seat next to Finn, I assumed he wasn't planning on killing him immediately. It was a small reprieve, but one I hoped gave me time to do something about the situation.

Releasing the curtain, I ran through the living room in route to the bathroom. Several prayers left my lips as I swung open the door of the medicine cabinet and reached inside in search of the only thing I knew I could use to stop Elliot without outright killing him.

Thanking God and the baby Jesus for big favors, I pulled the black leather pouch out of the cabinet and opened it to find a small vial of clear liquid, together with three unused syringes. I had no clue how I would get close enough to Elliot to inject him with the drug, or how much I was supposed to use, but it was the only plan I had.

While running back to the window, I attempted to talk myself down from the ledge of panic where I was currently perched. Perhaps there was a way to convince Elliot to leave well enough alone. I didn't know why he was here or what he planned to do with my family.

Glancing at the clock on the wall, I discovered it was only an hour past nine. That wasn't much later than when I'd agreed to meet Elliot at the farm, so it didn't make sense that he'd come here looking for me when I hadn't showed.

But maybe he had?

Or maybe he was here for an entirely different reason.

Swallowing down the lump of questions in my throat, I continued watching the scene playing out by the bonfire. With my dad safely constrained in his seat, Elliot made quick work of tying Brody and Jack to their individual chairs, each man glaring at Elliot as he turned his attention to the woman on the ground.

Crouching down, he gently turned her onto her back before lifting her body up into a sitting position. Her head fell back, her long dark hair hanging limply over his arm in a mess of dirt, twigs and tangles. Holding my breath, I watched as he checked her pulse and lightly tapped her cheek to see if she would respond. She coughed when he brought her back to consciousness and I released the breath I'd been holding. Relieved that they hadn't killed her, I continued watching as he stripped off his shirt and pulled it over her body. The dance of shadow and light from the bonfire played over his chest and arms, and I lost the ability to breathe all over again.

He stole my breath by how beautiful he was, inside and out.

He also stole my heart by how gentle he'd been with the woman my family had stolen just so they could use her before tossing her away like garbage.

Lowering her back down to the ground, Elliot reached out to brush the hair away from her face, his lips moving as he asked her a question I couldn't hear from where I was standing. She nodded her head in response to whatever he'd asked and his eyes tipped up to narrow on Jack. Afraid he'd look in the direction of the house, I stepped back into the room to hide behind the curtain.

There was no doubt about it...I was in one hell of a sticky situation. I didn't know how much time I had. I didn't know why Elliot was even here. And I sure as hell didn't know if I'd be able to convince him to leave. Maybe if he hadn't seen what they were doing to that woman he might have agreed to leave if I promised to leave with him. But now? I highly doubted there was any possible way he'd willingly step foot off this property.

Damn it! I didn't know what to do.

Taking a few steadying breaths, I attempted to calm the shaking of my body. My heart threatened to tear through my chest. My mouth was as dry as the Sahara. And my thoughts were racing so fast that I felt dizzy from the effort of standing.

Reaching up, I rubbed at my temples to relieve the headache that was quickly adding to the seriously fucked up time I was having.

"Okay," I muttered to myself. "There has to be a way to deal with this. There has to be a way to make this right. Elliot's a reasonable man. He loves me. He wants to marry me. That has to be enough to convince him to leave."

I was lying to myself, and I knew it. Saying the words out loud didn't make them any more believable. The only thing that was a definite in my mind at the moment was the fact that I was running out of time.

Pulling out one of the syringes and the vial from the black pouch, I wasn't exactly sure I knew what the hell I was doing. I'd seen plenty of television shows and movies that included scenes in hospitals, and I attempted to mimic what I could remember.

I knew air bubbles were bad, and I knew to stick the needle in the top and pull down on the plunger to create suction. But how far should the liquid go down? There were numbers on the sides of the syringe, but that was about as useful to me as a foreign language. I checked the vial, but again, I was met with gibberish.

Not wanting to run the risk of killing him, I only drew enough liquid into the syringe to hit the large, black number one on the side. I hoped it would be enough, but then wondered where I was supposed to stick it. Brody or Finn would know, but they weren't in position at the moment to be giving me any advice.

The only thing I could do was wing it, so I decided that if push came to shove, I'd jab him in the neck and hope for the best.

Carefully, depressing the plunger, I forced all the air out of the tube until a small squirt of liquid shot out from the needle. I tapped my finger on the syringe for good measure, and only because I'd seen them do it on television. Once that was accomplished, I shoved the black pouch with the other two syringes into my pocket.

Now that my preparations were made, I took another round of steadying breaths – which didn't help in the slightest – and on shaky legs, I walked towards the door that led outside. It was now or never as I forced myself out into the

160

night, my lungs dragging in the smoke from the bonfire that was thick in the breeze that blew by.

Creeping around the house, I pushed my body flat to the wall and peered around the corner to look at the scene around the bonfire. Elliot was nowhere to be seen, but my entire family was still tied to their chairs, anger obvious in the expressions on their faces. They stared out into the distant field and I followed the direction of their eyes to see a large figure making his way back to the house with two large duffel bags in his hands.

When he neared the bonfire, he glared at my family before turning around once again to walk back out across the field. From the easy pace he took, you wouldn't assume he was a man in a hurry – and definitely not one who'd just beat the shit out of four men and left them strapped to plastic chairs around a fire.

Guessing this might be the only opportunity I had to help my dad, I darted around the side of the house and ran out to the bonfire. Finn saw me first and shouted my name. Glaring over at him, I stuck my finger to my lips to remind the idiot to shut his damn mouth. I didn't know how far Elliot had gone and I didn't need him running back to prevent me from freeing my dad.

Notice I only mentioned saving my father. It didn't occur to me that Finn, Brody or Jack were worth saving. On some deep-seated level, I had no problem leaving them there to suffer whatever carnage Elliot decided they deserved. But I knew better than to think my father would leave them to die once he was free of his binds. It was a damn shame, too. The world would have been a better place if the three of them were no longer walking around in it.

"Daddy," I whispered loud enough for him to hear, but soft enough that it wouldn't carry across the fields, "Are you okay?"

"Untie me right fucking now, Maggie, and then get your ass back inside the house."

Unlike me, he didn't seem to care whether Elliot could hear or not, his words were spoken with enough volume to alert everybody in a two mile radius.

Inching forward, I glanced down at the half naked woman on the ground and cringed to see the developing bruises on her skin. Her eyes were closed, but her chest was moving up and down with breath. I sincerely hoped she wouldn't die, but I wasn't sure what would happen to my family if she didn't. Come to think of it, there wasn't much we could do at this moment without Daddy and my brothers going to jail. Elliot had seen what they'd done to that poor woman and the realization made me pause.

My eyes dragged from the woman back to my father. "What are we going to do, Daddy? Ell –" I stopped mid sentence. If I mentioned Elliot's name, my entire family would know I'd been sneaking off to meet him. There was no other way I could know who he was. "That *man* saw what you all were doing to her. How are we going to get away?"

Unfortunately, I knew exactly what my father would do, and that made this situation even more dire.

"Maggie. Untie me now, or I'll –"

The roar of an engine was louder than my father's words, dust flying up following the screech of tires that blended with the bonfire smoke in the air.

I turned around to see Elliot's black truck parked only a few feet away from where we were all gathered and the image was something straight out of a dystopian novel. The dirt, smoke and debris in the air masked everything in the distance, turning the house and trees into shapeless shadows cast red by the flames that roared up into the sky.

"Maggie! Untie me now, God damn it!"

The driver side door of the truck flew open and Elliott jumped down. His chest was still bare from having given the woman his shirt. The contrast of his skin against the black cargo pants he wore only made him look more feral and dangerous.

162

"Maggie…"

I couldn't hear my name fall from his lips but I knew just by the shape his mouth had taken, the wide set of his eyes, and the way his gaze was locked tight to me, it was, in fact, my name he'd spoken.

"Maggie…"

My father's voice roared behind me, but I was frozen in place, unable to make a move towards the man who raised me or the one who now had me locked in his stare.

Elliot's mouth moved again, the words lost on the smoke-filled breeze that tore across the field. Twisting to grab something out of his truck, he moved slowly to pull on another shirt before making his way towards me. My father continued yelling at me to untie him, Finn's voice now joining in. But nothing they said mattered at that point, nothing could break through the spell in which I'd been caught.

I was a woman torn between the loyalty for family and the reckless love I held for a man I never should have known.

Finally reaching me, Elliot wrapped his hand around my bicep, pulling me close to him. Angling his head down, his mouth brushed my ear, his voice far angrier and alien than I'd ever heard it before.

"What the fuck are you doing here? You're supposed to be at the other farm waiting for me."

For a moment, his voice scared me. I doubted myself right along with feeling that fear, doubted I truly knew Elliot as well as I'd allowed myself to believe. And right behind that doubt crept in the barest hint of rebellion.

Tilting my chin up into the night, I waited for his eyes to meet mine. My feet were planted beneath me with my refusal to give him an inch of space.

"Shouldn't I be asking you the same question?" I dared to ask, a fierce tone to my voice that surprised me.

We were locked together, neither one of us willing to bend when it came to the situation in which we'd found ourselves.

"What are you doing here, Elliot? Why have you come to my home and hurt my family? What right do you have –"

His hand wrapped over my mouth, his grey eyes staring down at me with malicious intent, the retinas so large they'd become mirrors reflecting my image back at me. I didn't want to admit there was fear in my expression – even while it was staring me so unapologetically in the face.

CHAPTER TWENTY-FIVE

ELLIOT

This wasn't right.

In fact, this was all incredibly wrong.

With my hand over Maggie's mouth, I looked down into a face that stared back at me with a mix of fear, anger and confusion behind eyes of jade green. She fought against my hold when I didn't immediately speak, but I held onto her, refusing to give her any leeway while I was desperate to decide what I would do.

The last thing I wanted was for Maggie to witness her family die. She didn't need that memory following her through life like a thousand pound weight slung over her shoulders. I didn't want her waking up screaming in the middle of the night, or being stalked by the guilt of being unable to save them while she tried to pick the pieces up and put them back together for her own life.

The road to Hell truly is paved with good intentions, it seemed.

"You shouldn't be here, Maggie. I told you to stay at that farm until I came to you. I told you to wait for me where you'd be safe."

Pain shot along my hand, Maggie's teeth firmly planted in the skin of my palm. Ripping my hand free, I glared down at her, anger swelling inside me and the first trace of concern. In this moment, she was making a choice, and what side she chose would decide whether she lived or died. I never wanted to hurt her, but I remembered my promise to myself that I would if she tried to get in my way.

"Tell me why, Elliot? I went to the damn farm like you asked, but..."

"But?"

When she stopped talking, I knew there was more to the story she was telling me. Behind her, Jonah and his boys were shouting her name, however she didn't blink an eye in response. Her focus was entirely on me, her eyes asking a million questions that she hadn't yet voiced.

"Come with me, Elliot. Let's get in your truck and leave right now. I'll marry you. I'll run away with you and never look back. Just let my family go and –"

"And what? Allow them to kill the woman they were busy raping when I ran up here? Have you not seen her yet?"

My fist wrapped into her hair, and I twisted her head down to look at the poor woman who lay unconscious in the dirt. I'd reacted before realizing that the force I used on Maggie would hurt her, but I'd lost all sense of control the minute I'd crossed the fields to play out the vengeance I'd sought against the Crows.

I was a man possessed. Possessed with rage, with indignity, with hatred and pain. There was nothing that could stand in my way tonight, not even the beautiful girl who hadn't asked to be abused her entire life. I couldn't feel sorry for her, not now that she'd threatened to prevent everything I'd waited to do to the bastards who'd stolen my heart away from me fourteen long years before this moment.

Screaming in pain from the way her hair was being ripped from her head, Maggie cried out at the sight of the woman on the ground. Her knees gave out beneath her and she sagged, her body barely able to crouch because the hair I still held was holding up all her weight. Releasing her, I watched as she fell over, her arms bracing her body from falling completely over. Wide eyes were locked to the woman her family had tortured, those same eyes searching that poor

166

woman's body to see what indignities had left their permanent mark.

Kneeling down, I continued ignoring her family screaming at her to do something. They had to know she was powerless to fight against me. Yet, in their desperation to be free, they were willing to walk Maggie into danger, to beg her to give up her life on the off chance she would be successful in saving theirs. It was another mark against them that I ticked off on the score sheet I had yet to settle.

"Why?" she cried, her tears mixing with the dust and soot that was a thin blanket across her cheeks. Tiny rivulets ran down in streams as she stared at the teeth marks on the woman's skin, as she reached out towards the hair that had been ripped from the woman's head during her family's attack. Blood caked the woman's scalp where that hair had been torn away, but I doubted Maggie had seen it until she took an up close and personal look.

"I can't tell you why they did the things they did to that woman, Maggie. But what I can tell you is that it's the reason I can't just walk away with you now. I need you to leave on your own. I'm begging you to walk away while you still have the chance. Take my keys, take my truck, take this woman and drive as fast as you can without looking back. It's the only way you'll survive."

My voice was soft despite the rage that still boiled beneath my skin. I wanted her to go...she HAD to go. Forcing myself to remain still while she made her decision, I held my breath, my teeth grinding together each time her father or brother screamed out her name. Time wasn't ticking by fast enough and each second was adding oxygen to the flames of hatred that burned inside me. I was a ticking bomb, the pressure becoming so intense that there were only a few minutes left before I exploded and took out every living thing that existed around me.

Reality was melting into something unrecognizable, as if the flames of the bonfire were hot enough to fragment and distort truth and consequence, compassion and hope, until there was nothing left but primal instincts and pain.

What small amount of compassion I had left was balanced on a thin precipice, and one wrong move on Maggie's part would be enough to push me over the edge.

Her tears wouldn't stop flowing down her dirty cheeks, her lips held in a tight line that betrayed nothing of what she was thinking. Pushing herself up from the ground, she brushed her hands down the skirt of the dress she wore, her hand disappearing into the folds as her eyes held tight to the woman who remained motionless beneath us.

Twisting her head to the left, she looked at her family where they were tied to the plastic chairs that weren't heavy enough to hold them in place. Twisting back to the right, she stared up at me, the flames of the bonfire reflecting in her eyes, the haze of fire coloring her skin in shades of orange and crimson.

For a single second, I believed she'd make the right choice. But she fooled me in that one second, and unleashed the killer inside me in the next.

Her hand swung out towards me; her speed and strength unable to match the keen reflexes I'd hidden from her in all the time that I'd known her. Before her hand could make contact with my body, I'd wrapped my fingers around her wrist, the strong grip causing her to cry out as the fragile bones beneath her skin threatened to shatter.

Why she believed she'd stood a chance against me, I'd never know. And my heart broke apart in my chest to realize she'd drawn her line, she'd made her decision, and that she chosen her family over me.

Staring into her face for several seconds more, I matched her expression of fury with my own.

My gaze flicked down to the hand I held, to the syringe that sat lodged in her fist, the needle aimed directly at my body.

"I'm sorry, Elliot," she cried. "But I can't let you do this. Not to my father." Her voice shook as much as her body. "Not to him."

Shock tore through my system, shock and the faintest sense of betrayal. I hadn't done much for this young woman in the time that I'd known her. I hadn't saved her from the nightmare in which she lived. I hadn't rescued her from the depraved darkness in which her family had raised her. But I liked to think I'd given her three things her family never could: I'd given her freedom. I'd given her a choice. And I'd given her hope.

None of those things must have mattered as much as the loyalty she felt to the man who'd raised her, the loyalty that would now get her killed.

All emotion left me in that moment. Every bit of compassion, of warmth, of affinity I felt for Maggie dissolving as I stared at the needle she'd intended to use against me. I wasn't sure what liquid was housed within the plastic tube. I didn't know if it would kill me or simply knock me on my ass. But I was damn determined not to find out.

"No, Maggie. Don't apologize to me. I'm the one who should be saying sorry."

Her lips trembled as tears rolled across her cheeks to drip along the line of her jaw. Her eyes wide as saucers, she stared up into my face, panic lighting her gaze even brighter than the flames that roared behind me.

"For what?" she asked, her voice so soft I barely made out what she'd said.

Staring at the girl with what was left of my heart breaking apart in my chest, I released a breath filled with everything inside that made me a decent person. Pity was no longer a part of me. Hope had been driven away as soon as that needle left her pocket. And my concern for her was lost to the errant wind that drove past us as I realized there was nothing more I could do.

I hadn't been able to save my wife. I hadn't been able to save my son. And I feared I wouldn't be able to save Maggie.

There was nothing left. No concern. No interest. No empathy or understanding. All that remained flowing through my veins was the pervasive need to kill.

"For not convincing you to go that farm and stay put. For not saving you the heartache of watching your family die."

Her eyes rounded when she understood my intent, the bones of her wrist snapping when I forced the syringe from her hand. Opening her mouth on an ear-piercing scream, tears burst from her eyes once more. I smiled to hear her father's scream rise up to meet her own.

"Take your fucking hands off my daughter! Let my baby go! I'll kill you myself if you fucking hurt her.'"

Refusing to release the grip I had on Maggie, my gaze slowly crawled from her face over to where her father sat bound in a white plastic chair. It wouldn't have held him if not for the zip ties that prevented him from doing anything more than sitting as a helpless witness to the carnage I had every intention of bringing to the table.

My lips pulled into a feral grin, my eyes locked to a man I wanted nothing more than to slaughter like the fat pig he was.

"Here again, I have to ask how, exactly, do you plan on killing me, Crow?"

Rage was a purple mask on his face, the wrinkles and sagging skin only adding to the deep hue that now marred him. At a distance, I could still see the bloodshot red that streaked his eyes, the yellow of a decaying liver casting a sickening film over his glare.

I wasn't sure if I'd broken Maggie's wrist. It was impossible to judge my strength now that everything inside me had turned dark. She cried where she was kneeling beneath me, her wrist still caught in my hand and her body having lost every bit of fight it once had. Pulling her up, I ignored the cry of pain that tore from her lips, and I continued ignoring it as I dragged her over to stand in front of her father.

"You hurt my girl one more time, you son of a whoring bitch, and I'll -"

"You'll what? Scream at me some more? Wiggle around in the chair until it turns over and your face is buried in the dirt beneath your feet? There's not much you can do while you're bound, now is there? How does it feel, Crow? How does it fucking feel to be helpless to me? I'd like to know, because I've been wondering how my wife and son felt on the day you made them helpless to you."

As soon as the words left my mouth, I felt Maggie's entire body flinch against mine. Turning, I looked into eyes that held secrets too large and too horrible to share. I saw guilt mixed in with the horror, shame and the truth that she'd known all along exactly who I was, and exactly who my family had been.

It pissed me off to discover she'd known. And I'll even admit it took me by surprise.

"You knew?" I asked softly. "You knew this entire time?"

She didn't have to answer for me to know just how well she'd known the truth about what her family had done to mine.

And for as angry as that made me, it hurt, too.

Laughter rattled my chest, the laughter of a man who'd lost every ounce of sanity he had in him. Gone was the concern for a girl I'd never wanted to hurt. And gone was the promise I'd made to do everything in my power to help her live through this night. She was one of them, through and through. A Crow by birth - and now, a Crow by choice. Her silence had made her complicit, and for that I would carry no guilt if she died.

"She's just a child. This fight is between you and me."

Jonah's voice dragged my focus back to him, our eyes locking to each other, both narrowed with the rage we felt.

171

"That's good to know. Why don't you begin this conversation by telling me where I can find my wife and son?"

"Let go of my daughter, and I'll be happy to tell you whatever you want to know."

I wouldn't exactly have called his tone of voice *happy*. It was far from happy, in fact. But just having him talking was enough to calm the need inside me to rip his head from his withered shoulders. At least until I had the answers I wanted.

His angry glare softened when his eyes caught sight of Maggie crying, and for a brief moment I wondered if he didn't care about her more than I assumed. However, that moment was lost as soon as I remembered the marks I'd seen across her bottom, the angry lines that scored her skin from the bottom of her thighs up to her lower back.

"We seem to have a problem, Crow. I offered Maggie the opportunity to leave, but she declined. And as you are probably aware, her refusal is as good as telling me she's one of you. I can't let her go now. Not when I know she'd just run off to call the police."

"She wouldn't do that." Tipping his chin in the direction of his daughter, he said, "The girl knows better than to bring the law into family matters. Just let her go and we can keep this between us. There's no point hurting an innocent girl."

"Really?" I laughed, the sound becoming darker and more malevolent as the minutes ticked by. "Why don't you tell that to the woman your boys almost killed tonight? Wasn't she innocent? Did she deserve to get hurt?"

This conversation was lasting far too long, but I hadn't planned for this to be a quick execution. The night was still young, and I had all the time in the world to carry out the revenge I'd been planning for so long.

"Or, better yet, why don't you tell that to your boys when it comes to their own sister?"

Jonah's eyes narrowed, his mouth pulling into a thin line as his nostrils flared open.

My lips formed an 'O' of surprise, a smile tilting my lips right after because it appeared my suspicions were true. "What's wrong, Jonah? Didn't you bother to check and see what your sons had done to your precious little girl when you gave them the go ahead to beat her?"

"I don't know what the hell you're talking about."

A panicked cry cut through the night as I spun Maggie in place. Lifting her skirt in front of her father's eyes, I didn't give a shit if I was embarrassing her. At that moment, the only thing I cared about was showing the piece of shit in front of me exactly what he'd allowed two grown men to do to his daughter.

"Well, then allow me to show you."

With my voice booming over the other sounds that accompanied the night – the roar of the fire, the crackling of the wood as it broke apart into ash, the cry of the cicada that was a symphony of sound piercing the sky – I watched Jonah's face, searching it for the exact moment when he realized what his sons had done.

The intensity of his stare was locked on me, anger for having lifted his daughter's skirt quickly dissolving when he looked down to see the bruises and cuts her brothers had left on her body. I saw every emotion in his eyes that betrayed his thoughts, the exact moment of discovery seared into my brain as I absorbed the anguish and pain the realization had caused him.

"You see what I'm talking about, Crow? Did you tell them to do this to her? Did you ask them to leave scars?"

Screaming with the vehemence that consumed me, I held Maggie in place despite the fight she was giving me. Her tears continued falling until they become a puddle of mud beneath her feet, but I couldn't give a damn about the pain I was causing her. Nothing was more important than delivering to this man every ounce of fucking pain he'd delivered to me.

"Is that what you allow to be done to a child you love? Is it?"

Jonah's eyes continued glaring at the marks on Maggie's behind, his eyes narrowing into focus on one particular mark as rage turned his skin purple once again. Glancing down, I wanted to know exactly which mark it was that made him so angry, wanted to memorize every minute detail so that I could carry the feeling of retribution to my grave.

But rather than finding a simple bruised line, or one of the thin slices I'd seen when Maggie had met me at the farm the prior night, I found something that turned my own skin a brutal purple, a mark that stole the breath from my lungs and shot pain through my jaw from how hard I gnashed my teeth. Without thinking, I reached down to drag her underwear up the cheek of her bottom to get a better look at whatever had caused that large splotch of blood. What I found went beyond a simple lash mark or bruise. What I found was mutilation.

"What the fuck is that?"

Dropping Maggie's skirt, I turned her towards me, my fingers gripping her chin as I tilted her face up to mine. "Who the fuck carved their initials into you, Maggie?"

Her eyes bugged out of their sockets, tears still dripping down from the bloodshot orbs. Shaking her head, she attempted to refuse to answer, but my grip on her chin only became tighter, my face lowering down until we were nose to nose.

"Tell me which one of these motherfuckers did that to you."

While I questioned Maggie, I heard her father in the background threatening to end a man's life. After listening to what he had to say, I knew exactly who'd carved those initials into her skin, but I wanted to hear it from her mouth as well.

"Who was it?"

Her eyes flicked to the right, betraying her knowledge of the man who'd carved her skin. Following the path of her gaze, my eyes landed on the blond man whose ankle I'd sliced open with my knife earlier that night – the man who wouldn't live to hurt another woman again.

"Who is he?" My voice was deceptively soft, concern dripping from the words and a gentleness to my tone that dragged her attention back to me. She searched my eyes for several seconds before swallowing down whatever panic and heartache still pulsed in her veins.

Closing her eyes, she spoke around trembling lips to admit, "That man is my husband, Elliot. He wanted people to know I was his."

Shock tore through me, shock and a wave of rage so violent that my body became stuck in place. Most people reacted to anger with instantaneous action, decisions made without thought, and voices so loud that everybody within a mile radius knew what had pissed those people off.

But not me.

When my rage reached this level, I became cold. I became focused. I became as lethal as the rounds of a high caliber assault rifle, the edge of an expertly honed blade, or the blast of a nuclear missile that struck its target with ferocious grace.

"Was he your choice?"

Her eyes blinked up at me, her head shaking to the left and right so quickly I wasn't sure I'd actually seen the response.

"Then it's decided, isn't it?"

Tears slipped over her lips. "What's decided?"

Grinning down at her with a smile I knew scared her more than made her feel safe, I spoke slowly when I answered, "It's decided that this night isn't just about my family any longer. This night is about you as well."

It was wrong of me to put what was about to happen on her shoulders. If she survived the night, she'd have to carry the weight of her guilt for the rest of her life. But she needed to know that there were men out there who weren't as evil as her father or brothers – who weren't as evil as the jackass strapped to a white plastic chair who was about to learn what pain and mutilation truly felt like.

I hoped Maggie would find another man in her life who was willing to protect her. A man who would defend her honor and would love her no matter what the world threw at her. I couldn't be that man, but I sure as hell could show her what it looked like.

Breathing out a shaky breath, I closed my eyes and tilted my head up towards the night sky. It was time to end the nightmare that had held me prisoner for too damn long.

Angling my head back down to her, I opened my eyes and told her I was sorry, but I didn't give her a chance to ask why before I began my lethal dance with the men seated around the fire.

"It's good thing you like whoring out your daughter, Jonah. I'll be sure to enjoy her when your body is burned to ash. Maybe I can make her scream for me like the husband you married her off to."

Glancing over Maggie's head, I locked my stare to the yellow and bloodshot eyes of her father. A wicked grin pulled at my lips to see the anger pull his mouth into a tight line.

"Would you like to know what I plan to do to her?"

If looks could kill, Jonah would have just sliced my body open from belly to throat. His entire body went perfectly still. "You leave my daughter out of this. I don't know who the fuck you are, but I recognize you now. You're the man who was sitting outside my house a few weeks ago. I should have killed you then."

A bark of laughter shook my shoulders. "Yeah, you should have. But you didn't and now you get to see your daughter go through the same thing you did to my wife."

"We didn't touch your fucking wife."

My head snapped to look into the face of Maggie's brother, the one I'd previously left laying in his own piss while I worked on taking down the blond man and the other brother. Gripping Maggie's hair, I forced her head in the same direction. "Which one is that?"

An audible gulp sounded from her throat, her voice barely a whisper when she answered, "Finn. That one is Finn. The one on the other side of my dad is Brody."

My smile stretched wider. I'd been itching to dance with Finn ever since Maggie admitted the way he abused her.

"I suggest you shut the fuck up, Finn. You and I will get our turn later on this evening. I promise you that. Be a good boy and show some patience."

"I'm not –"

"What part of that statement sounded like you have a choice?"

His voice buried by mine, he snapped his mouth shut, his expression matching his father's, making the family resemblance impossible to ignore.

"Don't worry, you sick son of a bitch. I have plans for each and every one of you, so just sit tight and wait to see what I have planned."

My fingers locked around Maggie's wrist and she cried out in pain from the hold. I still wasn't sure whether I'd broken the bones when I'd forced the syringe from her hand, but I couldn't allow her pain to slow me down. I had a point to make to every one of the assholes who sat watching us.

Dragging her over the dirt by her arm, I ignored the way she begged and pleaded to be let go. As soon as we approached my truck, I threw her body up against the side and flipped her skirt up from behind.

"No! Please, Elliot! Stop!"

She fought against me, but the little girl had no strength left in her. Careful not to touch the areas of her skin that were still bleeding from what her *husband* had done to her the night before, I ripped her panties from her body, enjoying the way her father screamed behind us. In truth, I had no intentions of hurting her the same way her husband had, but I had no intention of letting her father know it.

Leaning forward so that I could whisper in her ear, I gave her one simple command. "Keep screaming, Maggie. Keep screaming and don't stop, no matter what."

Her mouth opened and the sound that tore across the night sky was so full of pain that it tore my heart in two. Fear, terror, panic and agony were threaded into that sound, enough heartache to poison the land and trees with the evil that she believed was being committed against her.

Grinding my hips against her, I led her family to believe she was being raped right there in front of them. The men screamed right along with her, the sound of pure rage reaching out to intermingle with the screams that tore from her throat.

This scene didn't need to last long for me to get the point across, and when I was done shredding the heart of the asshole who'd raised her in such a vile life, I wrapped my arm around her neck, squeezing hard until her body went limp against the truck, until her mind was delivered to the darkness of a deep, dreamless sleep.

I hadn't killed her. But her daddy didn't know that.

Jonah and his sons continued roaring out their empty threats as I lifted her small body up into my arms. Opening the truck door, I laid her on the bench seat before closing the door to lock her inside. I didn't want her interfering if she woke before my plans were carried out, so I pulled two screwdrivers from the toolbox in the bed of the truck and jammed it between the door and frame on both sides to ensure she wouldn't be able to let herself out.

"You didn't kill her," Jonah called out. "Tell me you didn't kill her! If you had, you wouldn't be locking her inside like that."

For the first time that night, I heard the hint of panic on his voice. Maggie hadn't been wrong after all. Her father truly did love her; he was just too stupid to understand what loving somebody meant.

The uncertainty in his voice had a calming effect on me. No longer feeling like I needed to rush to the finish line, I turned to stare out across the field, to lock eyes with each and every man seated in those crappy white chairs. A grin tilted my lips as my body leaned back against the truck.

It felt good to relax for just a moment, to take the time to allow the scene to sink in. I had the bastards right where I wanted them. It would have been foolish on my part not to enjoy just a few minutes of what I'd already done.

"Don't know, Crow. I didn't care much to check," I answered back, my grin pulling wider to watch fear wrinkle his face. "However, on the off chance she did survive, I just wanted to make sure she sits tight until I decide what else I want to do to her."

A stream of colorful expletives burst from his mouth. I laughed as I pushed up from the truck to walk around the bed. Lowering the tailgate, I took my time pulling one of the duffle bags in my direction, unzipping it and choosing which tool I wanted to use for the first order of business.

The image of JLK kept flashing in my mind. Rough and bloody, the letters had been carved just deep enough to leave a faint scar on Maggie's skin for the rest of her life, but not deep enough to require stitches and alert her old man to the fact that her husband had mutilated her on their wedding night.

Curiosity flowed in to mingle with my anger, so I called out to the assholes who sat patiently waiting for me to make my first move.

"So, tell me: Was there a ceremony for the wedding you dumb fucks held last night?"

I glanced up as my hand wrapped over the wooden handle of a sledgehammer.

Lifting the heavy tool and resting it on my shoulder, I turned toward the men and slowly made my way over. When I was within ten feet of them, I stopped.

"Were there flowers or a cake? How about a preacher, or…I don't know…a choice for her about who she would marry? Did you give her any of that, Jonah? Or did you just sell her off to the highest bidder?"

"I didn't sell my daughter off. If you let me go, I'll kill the bastard myself for what he did to her."

Shaking my head, I laughed again. "Sorry, but I won't be letting anybody go this evening. I have too many questions to ask and I won't rest until every single one of them has been answered to my satisfaction."

Jonah coughed, his head spinning to the left as blood burst over his lips. Once he was done, he turned back to look at me. "What do you plan on doing with that sledgehammer, son?"

I grinned. "I plan on making your daughter a widow."

He simply nodded his head. My brows shot up in surprise. If I didn't know he was a rapist and a murderer, I would have respected him for the lack of complaint.

Turning my back on the Crow family, I locked my gaze to the blond man. "J.L.K. What does it stand for?"

The fucker actually spit in my direction in response.

Pulling the sledgehammer from my shoulder, I balanced it between my hands, the weight of the head a balm to the violence that ran through me. "It doesn't matter much," I offered, "I have ways of getting the answer out of you."

Three steps forward, my boot walked through the spit that he'd shot to the ground, and I was in perfect range for the first swing.

The sledgehammer swung sideways connecting with outside of the bastard's right knee. The sound of bone snapping was barely audible when accompanied by the unholy scream that tore from the man's throat. His knee was destroyed with that one hit, the bones sticking out grotesquely where the skin had been split and the cloth of his pants ripped open. Blood dripped down the legs of his trousers to mingle with the crimson puddle that had already formed beneath his ankle.

"Looks like you won't be using that leg ever again. Any chance you want to tell me what those initials stand for now?"

He could barely look up at me, his face twisted in so much agony that his eyes were glued shut and his mouth was open on a soundless scream.

"Ah, come on now. That wasn't so bad. I've seen worse injuries on the battlefield. But I guess it takes a soldier to grin and bear it. Not a weak little fuck that likes to take his anger and hatred out on women."

Finally cracking his eyes open, he glared at me. "Jack. Luther. King. That's what they stand for."

I couldn't help the smile that pulled at my lips. "That's good to know, Jack. I like to know the names of the arrogant assholes I kill."

Before he could react, the sledgehammer swung again, his left knee blown out just as wickedly as the right. Another scream tore through the night air and once it ended, I listened to find that all the creatures that normally sang had dispersed, most likely scared off by the threat of carnage and violence.

The night was so still and so quiet that only the crackling of the logs could be heard. Well, the crackling of the logs and the soft whimpers of a man crying over two busted legs.

"That had to hurt," I commented without the slightest hint of sympathy in my voice. "But I bet it didn't hurt worse than what Maggie felt when you raped her and carved your name into her skin. Probably didn't hurt as bad as what you just did to this poor woman passed out in the dirt by the fire. At least your dignity is still intact, the pride you feel for being a virile man."

His eyes shot up to mine.

"Allow me to take care of that for you."

He was a smart man to close his eyes and brace for what was coming. As the sledgehammer rose up into the sky, his fingers wrapped over the weak armrests of the plastic chair, his jaw pulsing with how hard he clenched his teeth. I could have told him there was nothing he could do to prepare for what was coming, but I figured it would be better for him to learn that lesson on his own.

Jack wouldn't be raping women anymore.

He wouldn't be walking, and he wouldn't be carving his initials into anything else.

What he would be doing is fertilizing the fields, his ashes mixing with the dirt to be returned to the Earth.

But first…he would be singing soprano for another few minutes before I removed the gift of agony to replace it with the blank void of a quick and final death.

Coming down with the force of the hammer's weight, the sledgehammer slammed between the bastard's legs. The scream that cut the air was so high I would have sworn he'd inhaled helium prior to having his manhood torn from his body. The chair wasn't strong enough to support his weight any longer, not with the hole I'd knocked into the seat right in place of where his dick had once been.

A pile of broken plastic, broken bones, torn skin and a lifetime of regrets lay on the dirt in front of me. It would take one more swing to put him out of his misery, but I wasn't a kind man. My kindness had leached completely out of me fourteen years prior.

Savoring the way he continued to cry, I dropped the head of the sledgehammer into the dirt, and balanced my weight with one hand on the handle. Spinning around, I searched the expressions of the Crow men. It was easy to figure out what each and every one of them was thinking.

"Now that I got our buddy, Jack, out of the way, I think it's time we all have a friendly chat."

CHAPTER TWENTY-SIX

MAGGIE

I didn't hear anything when I first pried open my eyes to find myself face down on the leather bench seat of a truck. At first, I wasn't quite sure how I'd ended up splayed over supple leather, the carvings on my ass on fire against the cold air that was pervasive in the interior of the vehicle despite the shut doors and sealed windows.

It took me a few minutes to gather my senses together enough to realize that between one minute and the next, I'd been up against the side of Elliot's truck putting on a decent show of screaming and then waking up to a sickening silence hidden behind windows steamed up by my breathing.

How long had I been in here, and how had I passed out?

I remembered Elliot's arm wrapping around my neck. I remembered the fear I felt when I couldn't breathe and it felt like all the blood in my body was trapped in my face, the skin so tight I swore that the blood would burst through taking my eyes with it.

But I was still alive and in one piece, so I could only assume he'd choked me out just long enough to gain complete control of me.

Pushing up from the seat, I hissed when the skin of my behind met the cold leather. I wasn't sure where my panties were, but I wasn't too concerned with their absence. Tucking the skirt of my dress beneath me, I stared out the windshield to see a quiet, dark night in the distance.

From the corner of my left eye, I noticed the dance of shadow and light from the bonfire that still blazed in the middle of the field by the house. Instinct had me reaching for the door handle, tugging on it with as much strength I could manage only to find that the door was jammed tight.

I should have left the cloudy mist that concealed the view out into the exterior. I should have left well enough alone and sat in my place waiting to see when Elliot returned to cart me off to my next destination.

However, regardless of what I should have done, my hand reached up to wipe away the fog from the glass, my eyes opening wide when I watched the scene that was playing out in front of me.

Muted within the interior of the vehicle, a scream rattled the truck and the trees around me. Fear crept into my heart to think it was my Daddy crying out with the pain of a man split in two, but when I peered out to identify the pile on the ground at Elliot's feet, I saw that it was Jack laying in the dirt, broken and useless. His legs were unmoving and bent out of shape, blood a black puddle beneath him that looked like oil bubbling up out of the ground. His hands were held tight between his legs and that same crimson mess covered the skin of his fingers.

Elliot stood tall over a man that was most likely wishing for death. It had to be better than the agony he was feeling.

In Elliot's hand was a sledgehammer he'd used to tear apart the man who called me his wife for only one night.

Dropping the head of the sledgehammer to the ground, Elliot grinned like a tomcat in the middle of a group of felines in heat. His face was proud, his body relaxed, and his feet set apart like a man preparing himself for battle. With one hand balanced on the handle of the sledgehammer, he turned to face my family where they were still strapped to their chairs.

I couldn't hear what any of the men were saying, but judging by the looks on their faces, it wasn't a friendly conversation that were having.

Like a hammer against my skull, a headache pounded mercilessly behind my eyes. But the pain was nothing compared to the panic I felt the minute I saw Elliot take a step towards my father.

Their mouths were moving, but I couldn't make out a damn word they were saying. I tried to read their lips, but for all I knew they were exchanging recipes. It didn't help when Finn chimed in with whatever dumbshit remark he decided would be a good idea. Elliot's fist connected with his face in response.

I'd be a liar to claim I didn't smile to see Finn spit out a tooth along with the blood that was filling his mouth.

That small reprieve was lost when my father blurted out his opinions once again and Elliot's focus returned to a man who was way too sick to take a hit.

I had to do something.

Reaching down, I felt a lump in the skirt of my dress and thanked the heavens once again for small favors. I wasn't sure how I would knock Elliot out with the drugs I still had on me, but without time to formulate a decent plan, I had to go with my gut instinct.

Pulling out one of the two syringes I still had on me, I inserted the needle in the top of the vial and pulled the plunger down until the syringe was filled to the number two. Elliot prevented me from pricking him before, but if I had another syringe ready, I might have still had the chance to stick him with it while he was focused on the other. Plan made, I filled the second syringe with the same amount of the drug and sent up another silent prayer that it would work.

The only thing I could do now was attempt to get him over to the car and away from my father.

Turning towards the driver's side door, I banged my fists against the window and shouted as loud as I could. My throat was already torn to shreds from all the other times I'd screamed that night, but desperation and adrenaline were fueling me.

Within seconds, I realized that screaming my head off hadn't done a lick of good because the shouting men couldn't hear me over their own voices.

Still desperate to break up the fight that was occurring at the bonfire, I darted a glance around the interior of the truck searching for anything that I could use to bust myself out. There was nothing lying around that would help me break a window, so I pulled open the glove box hopeful there would be something inside.

After pulling it open, I realized that Elliot was nothing like the men who raised me. Instead of a gun, errant tools, or some other heavy instrument hidden beneath old receipts, food wrappers and whatever else my family typically shoved into the crevices of a car, there was only a leather bound case with neatly arranged papers inside. I knew damn well that Elliot's registration and insurance information wasn't going to do me any good and I tossed the book back in with a huff of frustration blowing over my lips.

Angry at the circumstances that prevented me from saving my family and Elliot, I banged my hands on the steering wheel, a small beep sounding from the hood.

The horn!

At a later time, I'd chide myself for having been so stupid, but there wasn't time now to wonder why I hadn't tried the horn in the first place.

Fists banging down, I blared the horn, my head turning to the left to see that it finally caught their attention. As soon as Elliot's eyes were focused on the truck, I banged on his window again and started screaming. His eyes darted between my family and me, indecision obvious in his expression. Dialing it up a notch, I laid on my back and began kicking the window.

It only took him a minute to approach the truck, his face peering in the window with a red haze of anger coloring his cheeks.

I sat up as his hand fidgeted with the door. Pulling it open, he allowed a draft of cold air to filter in before he opened his mouth to scream at me.

"What the hell do you think you're doing, Maggie? If your foot had gone through that window –"

My hand flew out to plunge the first needle into his neck. He caught it like I knew he would. A burst of pain shot through the bones of my wrist and up my arm, but I ignored it to swing out with my other hand, jam the needle in his neck and depress the plunger before he realized what I was doing.

He stumbled back as he reached up to pull the needle from his neck, the look of betrayal on his face causing my heart to shatter in my chest. I never wanted to hurt him. Never wanted to be the cause of any pain in his life. But he'd left me with no other option.

Praying that I hadn't used too much of the drug, I crept forward as his gaze grew hazy and he sank to his knees fighting whatever effects the drug had on him. When I thought he'd fall asleep and slump to the ground, he surprised me by shooting back to his feet instead. Charging towards the truck, he attempted to grab me, but I slipped back along the bench seat kicking out at his head, his shoulders and his chest. My feet didn't deter him.

Within seconds, Elliot had climbed inside, his eyes narrowed in anger, and for a brief moment I thought he would kill me for what I'd done.

I guess the universe and God himself were smiling down on me that night, because just as Elliot wrapped his large hand over my neck and began to squeeze, his eyelids grew heavy and the weight of his body sank down on top of mine.

Shaking him just to see if he'd wake up, I became scared when he didn't react. My hands roamed over his body until sneaking up to the pulse point in his neck. The frantic beat of my heart slowed down to find that I hadn't killed him with the drugs I'd forced in his body.

From outside the car, my father yelled my name, his voice strong despite the grittiness. I hated that he'd been screaming all night beside the smoke of a raging fire, but I didn't have time to worry about his lungs when Elliot was a far more immediate danger.

Not knowing how long Elliot would remain knocked out, I had to work to free myself of his large body. Eventually settling him on the bench seat, I crawled over the top of him and jumped out of the truck.

"Maggie! Get over here, girl, and untie us. You did good, baby girl! Real good. Now just free us so we can take over!"

His words stopped me in my tracks, the grim realization that they would kill Elliot if I freed them from their bonds. I didn't want anybody to die tonight – except for Jack – so I stared out across the field trying to determine what I should do next.

If only there were a way to free my father but prevent him from getting to Elliot. And then it hit me, the perfect plan for what I would do.

Spinning in place, my eyes searched the ground beneath the truck. I dropped to my hands and knees to see better in the dark, cursing under my breath when I couldn't find what I was looking for. Crouching down even lower, I was practically lying on my belly as my arms reached beneath the truck. Just when I thought I wouldn't find the unused syringe, it brushed against my fingers, just out of reach. Crawling forward, I stuck my head beneath the truck giving me just enough room to wrap my hand over the syringe.

After crawling back out, I stood up on shaky legs and took a second to wipe the dirt and dust from my clothing. I was a hell of a mess already and there was no point trying to knock the dirt away, but habits were hard to kill even in moments where time was running out.

Turning back towards my family, I made quick work of the distance between us, and I fell to my knees when I reached my father's chair. My hand shot up to cup his face, my eyes scanning his body to make sure I hadn't been too late. He didn't look injured as far as I could tell and a relieved breath rattled out of me.

"Daddy? Did he do anything to you?"

He didn't respond to the question I asked, his lips pulled into a tight line as he demanded I untie him. Brody and Finn were screaming to be released as well, but I didn't pay them any attention. I wasn't concerned about their lives in the slightest, and on some level I wished they'd met the same fate as Jack.

"I'm going to release you, Daddy. But I don't want you hurting Elliot. I can't have you two killing each other, okay? You'll just have to understand that I can't let this go further tonight. I can't."

"Untie me, Maggie, and then go inside the house. I won't let you get in the way of this."

Tears slipped from my eyes. I wasn't used to defying my father, not openly at least. A small bit of fear ran through me that I needed to tap down in order to finish what I'd planned.

Pushing up so that our faces were nose to nose, I whispered my apology before plunging the needle in his neck. His eyes widened in disbelief, and I waited as long as it took for him to finally pass out from the effects of the drug I'd given him.

"Why the hell did you do that, you stupid bitch? Are you trying to get us all killed?"

My head spun to the left at the sound of Finn's voice and I smiled. "I wouldn't give two shits if you got killed. But I'm still saving your ass one way or another. If I were you, I'd shut up and let me do what I need to do to save the entire family."

He continued screaming obscenities at my back as I pushed up on my feet and ran towards the house. As soon as I got inside, I ripped open one of the drawers and grabbed a kitchen knife before running back outside. Elliot and my father were still passed out as far as I could tell and I moved quickly

189

to free my father. After cutting away the plastic ties that bound his hands and feet, I dropped the knife in the dirt beneath me and turned to run back to the truck.

"Hey! What about me, Maggie? Untie me!"

"Screw you, Finn. For all I care, you can stay tied up in that position until the day you die."

It felt good to fight back against him for once. In fact, it felt so good that the worry I'd felt about everything I'd just done melted away leaving me proud of myself for having handled it. My father was free, but would be asleep for the next hour or so, hopefully. It gave me time to drive away with Elliot in the truck, time to escape this crappy situation and come up with another idea about how to keep this from happening all over again.

In truth, an hour wasn't all that much time to run away, but if I drove fast enough and took back roads, there was a chance I could get far enough that my family wouldn't find me. Beyond hiding from my family, I had to get the truck to a place where Elliot wouldn't immediately recognize where we were when he finally woke up. I hoped that meant I'd have time to talk him out of whatever plan he had for my family – that I could convince him to let it all go, run away with me, and start a new life.

⋏⋏⋏⋏

They say time flies when you're having fun. What they didn't mention is that it also flies when you're running for your life with an unconscious man lying next to you and your foot pressed so hard on the gas that the trees and other objects littering the side of the road became nothing but unidentifiable shadows as you blast past them.

Without knowing where the hell I was running to, I continued flooring the gas pedal without worrying of wrecking the truck on back roads typically only used by the locals. I'd worried that we'd run past a car or two on the way to wherever I was going, but fortunately I hadn't seen a soul as we weaved through the darkness that blanketed the lonely rural roads.

An hour passed before I realized it was gone. We were now approaching the three hour mark without Elliot having stirred beside me. Anxiety was my only companion as I dared to look over at him and wonder if I should stop just to ensure he was still breathing. What concerned me even more was the thought that I'd shot my Daddy up with the same amount of the drug when his body wasn't near as strong as Elliot's.

Visions of my father dying while my brothers were powerless to help him starting clogging up my mind, and I damn near broke down crying. If by trying to help I'd killed him in the end, I'd never get over the guilt.

Banishing those thoughts since they weren't doing me any good, I focused on the road ahead hoping that Elliot would eventually wake up enough to let me know he was okay.

Another hour passed by as I flew down the deserted roads. Eventually hitting a highway, I had no idea where I'd ended up, so I made the quick decision to take a right and see where the road would take me. I didn't recognize any landmarks along the way and the signs indicating exits weren't much help either. On one hand, it scared me to think that I was getting myself so lost I'd never find my way back home, but on the other I realized this was exactly what I'd intended to do. If I couldn't find my way back, than neither could Elliot. It would buy me the time I needed to convince him to let all of this go.

I hated being left alone with only my thoughts because it allowed the reality of the situation to sneak in.

Elliot knew my family had something to do with the deaths of his wife and son. Worse than that, he knew that I knew it, too, and had said nothing. I wasn't sure if he could forgive me for my silence. The thought crossed my mind that he'd kill me for keeping that information from him during the weeks that we'd gotten to know each other.

Reaching out, I turned on the radio hoping the music would help me relax or, at least, keep the frightening thoughts at bay. Old Southern Rock blasted from the speakers, my stomach in knots the minute I heard it. Turning the dial, I eventually found modern rock, the tempo so fast and the drumbeats so loud that it scrambled my mind just like I needed. Normally I wasn't a fan of this type of music, but it was perfect for distracting me from all the questions running around inside me.

By the fourth hour we'd been on the road, I settled back in the seat just to feel that something warm, wet and sticky was beneath me. It took me a few minutes to realize that nature had called when I hadn't been listening.

And, as usual, it called at the worst possible time.

Being a girl isn't easy. Once every month you have to constantly be prepared for whatever it is your insides decide to do with you. Some months weren't so bad and my period only lasted two to three days without any cramps or headaches to speak of. However, there were other months were it felt like my uterus was attempting to claw its way out of my body, the heaviness of my period causing me to run to the bathroom every hour just to keep from ruining my clothes. This was starting to be an in-between month, but in all fairness, I didn't really have a way of gauging it. I'd had sex for the first time the night before - which hadn't been pleasant in the slightest - and then I was run through hell tonight because of stubborn men.

Regardless of the reasons, I needed to pull over and get myself cleaned up. I also needed to buy some female supplies, but wasn't quite sure how I would do it. I didn't think to grab the bag I packed before hopping in Elliot's truck. I didn't have a change of clothes, food, money, tampons or anything else. I'd be kicking myself right now if I didn't also remember that I was dealing with unusual circumstances. Normally I'm the type to be prepared, but I hadn't been given much notice I'd be kidnapping a man for the sole purpose of keeping him from killing my family.

Blasting through another twenty miles had me well and good lost and the gas indicator flashing that the truck was running out of fuel. Glancing over at Elliot, I wondered if he had a credit card in his wallet that I could sneak to fill up the tank and purchase some hygiene products.

There was no other way to find out than to stop and search, so I pulled into the first gas station I could find at the exit.

The place was as deserted as the roads had been, but I didn't let the lack of activity bother me. As far as the attendant knew, I was just another normal girl, driving a normal truck, with her boyfriend passed out in the passenger seat. Deciding that I'd claim we were on a road trip if he asked any questions, I pulled up to the gas tanks and turned off the truck. Glancing over at Elliot, I realized he'd been snoring softly, but I hadn't been able to hear him over the radio. It was a relief to listen to him breathe - to know that I didn't killed him with the drugs I'd pumped in his system.

Slipping my hand into the back pocket of his cargo pants, I bit my lip not to whoop when I found a wallet. Slowly opening it, I wasn't prepared for the photo that stared up at me.

A younger version of Elliot sat smiling with a beautiful woman by his side. But, whereas his eyes were on the person taking the picture, the woman's eyes were cast down at the baby in her arms, a warm smile full of pure love pulling at her lips. There was hope in Elliot's gaze, something I'd never seen in him since the moment we met.

How had I been so stupid not to notice he never divulged much about himself? Granted, we hadn't known each other long enough to truly *know* anything about the other, but thinking back made it perfectly clear that in all the hours we'd spent talking at the abandoned farm, he'd been pulling information from me without offering much about himself.

I didn't know the Elliot I saw in the photograph, and glancing over at his sleeping body, I realized I didn't know the Elliot sleeping beside me either.

That wasn't entirely true, I guess. I did know some things about him. I knew that he'd been young when his son was born. I knew he had a wife and I knew that my family had stolen his family away from him. I also knew what happened to his family – not the specific details, but enough that I could have told him there was no hope in finding them alive and well.

Shame was a weight on my shoulders, and as I carried the burden of all the things I knew and didn't know, I slipped his credit card from his wallet and added yet another reason onto the long list of why I felt ashamed.

Carefully creeping out of the car, I shut the door as softly as possible and made my way across the parking lot towards the store. Anxiety followed behind me like a creepy stalker. It took a step when I took one, and it stopped to stand in my shadow when I paused to look behind me back at the truck. There was no sign that Elliot had woken up since I shut the driver's side door, but knowing that didn't help me shake my apprehension.

If you've seen one rural gas station, you've seen them all, and this one was no different. It was a small run down building with large windows that didn't appear to have been washed in quite some time. The parking lot was littered with debris, the concrete was uneven and the few parking spaces in front no longer had lines delineating one from the other. To the right of me was a two bay auto garage, the large steel doors slid down and locked in place for the night. The building could have used a coat of paint or ten, but it must have been good enough as it was to keep whoever owned it with a roof over his head and food in his belly.

Opening the glass door of the small shop, I heard the faint ding that rang through the store alerting the attendant to my presence. Nobody was standing behind the counter, but within seconds I saw an older man step out from a back room, his brown hair greying at the temples and his baggy clothes wrinkled across his body.

"Bit late for a shopping trip, isn't it?" He sounded like he'd just been woken by the bell and didn't appreciate the disturbance.

Smiling as brightly as I could manage, I edged towards the center aisles. "Just on a road trip with my boyfriend. He's sleeping out in the car, but I needed to pick up some female products."

As soon as I mentioned what I'd come in search of, his face wrinkled with embarrassment. It worked that way with most men, at least from what I could tell with the men in my family. They knew women had periods, and they understood the mechanics of how a woman's time of the month worked, but the mere mention of the subject had them itching to run from the room or ignore the issue as much as was humanly possible.

"Aisle two," he called out before ducking beneath a ledge and popping back up again behind the counter.

I didn't mind that he ended the conversation as soon as I mentioned what I was purchasing, it just meant there were less lies I had to tell.

Finding a travel size box of an off-brand feminine hygiene product, I dusted off the top and chuckled to myself wondering how long it had sat there untouched. Beggars couldn't be choosers at that moment, so I took the only product they had available and made my way to the counter.

"So," the man asked, his eyes darting to the box in my hand before a touch of red colored his cheeks. "Where are you and your boyfriend headed? Must be a long trip if you're still driving this late at night instead of tucked into a warm bed somewhere."

I hadn't thought that far in the lie I was telling. Given that I was a horrible liar as it was, I didn't have a quick response to offer him.

"Um, just driving, really," I said, looking everywhere but at the man who was now staring at me like I was an idiot. "Which reminds me: I need gas as well."

His fingers pressed some buttons on the cash register, electronic beeps filling the silent space between us. "Okay. How much do you need?"

Glancing over at the truck, I shrugged my shoulders. "I need to fill it up, I assume."

"How much does the truck take?"

In all honesty, I had no clue. Elliot's truck was a newer vehicle and I was well aware that gas tanks had grown smaller over the years to make room for whatever fancy options the automakers were offering. "I think fifteen gallons should do it."

His lips pulling into a thin line, the man peered out the window at the truck. "You sure? A truck that size should take more. If you want I could walk out there with you to help."

"No!" My voice was an octave higher on that panicked answer. The last thing I needed was the attendant to get anywhere near the truck where Elliot was passed out. Sure, I'd already told him that my boyfriend was sleeping, but what if Elliot woke up? I didn't want the attendant to be a witness to the heated conversation I was sure would occur. "I filled it up before and that's how much it took. If I need more I can always stop again later on."

Thankfully, the man dropped the conversation and rang up both the tampons and the gas. I handed him Elliot's card, but he returned it to me and motioned for me to use the card scanner facing my direction.

"If it's got a chip, you'll need to insert it. Otherwise, just slide it like normal. We just got the chip reader in the other day. It takes a minute for it to work."

Slipping the card into the slot, I selected debit, but then quickly realized I didn't have Elliot's PIN number. Cancelling the transaction, I inserted the card again and selected credit. Luckily it took, and I scribbled out an illegible signature as fast as I could.

The transaction was approved and I breathed out a sigh of relief. Handing me the receipt, the attendant nodded his head in my direction before mumbling, "Have a good night, Miss."

"You, too," I called out, my feet carrying me quickly towards the door before I realized I wasn't quite finished with the tasks I needed to accomplish. My hand hit the door before I turned back to the attendant to ask, "By chance, can I use your bathroom?"

He indicated to the back of the building with his hand. "Bathroom's around back. I'll apologize now for the condition of it. People aren't the cleanest when it's not their job to tidy up the mess."

I nodded my head in response and ducked out the door, hurrying as fast as I could to the restroom to use the toilet and clean up the mess I'd made of myself.

The attendant hadn't been kidding about the condition of the bathroom. Fighting the urge to cut and run when I flicked the light switch to see the brown linoleum floor that should have been white, the toilet that hadn't been flushed since the last person used it and the sink that had rust stains around the edges and some green goo covering the bottom, I held my breath as I went about my business.

As soon as I stepped outside again, I released that breath and stood still for a moment to pull clean air into my lungs and dispel the dizziness I felt after refusing to breathe the entire time I'd been inside. I hadn't been able to clean up as much as I'd wanted, but I did the best I could with the small amount of water that dripped from the sink and the lack of paper towels.

Crossing over the parking lot, I was in a rush to gas up the truck and get back on the road. A sneaking sense of something was brushing up against my thoughts, but I ignored it as I opened the gas tank and inserted the nozzle. The gas trickled in as slow as a snail. Eventually the fifteen gallons were in the tank and I set everything back to right before rounding the truck to climb back in to the driver's seat.

It had been my mistake not to check on Elliot before pumping the gas. And I'd been a damn fool for not searching my surroundings for any danger that might lurk in the dark.

A large, strong hand wrapped over my mouth just as I reached for the handle to the door, and a seriously pissed off voice hissed in my ear as my body was shoved against the side of the truck.

"Let me tell you now how this is going to go. You're going to get in the truck. You're going to scoot over to the passenger side. You're not going to make a fucking sound while following the first two instructions. And then you're going to tell me where the fuck we are before giving me the directions to get back to your fucking house."

CHAPTER TWENTY-SEVEN

JONAH CROW

The burning in my lungs was like nothing I'd ever felt before. My eyes were shut tight, my head lolled to the side of my body and my back ached with a vengeance for having fallen asleep in a damn chair. The smell of a dying fire was clogging my nostrils and my throat was as dry as a damn desert.

As my mind focused on clearing the fog that had it trapped, I fought against the hold my sleep kept on me. Anger was a pulsing beat in my veins, but at the moment I woke I couldn't remember why.

Hatred blazed. Betrayal a whisper on the night air. Muted sounds dragged me farther from the void of dark silence where I'd been dumped at the moment my eyes had closed.

Despite the pain in my body, despite the confusion that saddled me, I fought against sleep's hold, those muted sounds becoming words that made no sense when I listened to them closely.

Dad...

...the fuck up...

Maggie...

...kill the fucker who she ran off with...

At the sound of my daughter's name, I struggled harder, dizziness knocking me sideways while recognition came in to steady me long enough to understand it was the sound of my sons' voices I was hearing.

...untie...

Lifting my hands to my face, I pried my eyelids apart and the voices became louder and more demanding.

Nobody demanded anything from me. I'd taught everybody that lesson. What made these fucks think they had the right now?

Yeah, I was old. And I may have been dying. But that didn't mean I'd put up with anybody's shit. I was a Crow male. I gave orders. I didn't follow them.

"Dad! Wake the fuck up!"

I guess Finn had finally walked out of whatever tunnel he'd been in. His voice was closer now. It didn't echo in my head, didn't sound like he spoke around rocks that had been shoved in his mouth to muffle him.

"He's got Maggie. Wake up!"

Hearing her name for the second time caused my heart to beat harder beneath my ribs, it woke something in my brain. It caused panic to come in and rip me away from whatever warm blanket had kept me under.

Amber waves danced in front of me, the night sky coming into focus where flames had once been. Shaking away the exhaustion, I craned my head to look at my son.

"Fucking finally. Maggie drugged you, dad. She freed you afterward, but we're still tied up. You need to do something. We need to go after her."

No. Not my little girl. She wouldn't have betrayed me like that. Not Maggie.

"I'm going to kill that little bitch when I get my hands on her."

"No, you won't," I growled out.

Finn's eyes widened, his body jerking wildly in his chair with anger bunching his muscles beneath his skin. "She left us here. She left us for that son of a bitch who thought he could come here and –"

"I don't care what she did," my voice boomed. The boy had enough sense to shut his trap as soon as the anger rolled out of me in waves. "I'm still the father in this family. And I'll decide what happens to my children, including you. Do you understand me, son?"

Damn, if my lungs didn't protest just then, my words broken apart by the blood and mucus that forced its way up my throat. Coughing only caused more pain in my back, but I was used to it. These damn fits were going to kill me eventually, but not before I made sure my daughter was safe.

"Where'd she go?" I managed to croak out the question after spitting blood onto the dirt beneath me. "Did she say where she was going?"

"No," Brody answered. "She shot you up, cut your ties and left us here to die. Jack still ain't dead yet, and we've got a half naked bitch still lying by the fire. If the cops had shown up –"

"Well, if you two fucks are still sitting here tied to plastic chairs, I assume they didn't."

Wrenching my head to the side, I glared at my youngest son. He was a piss poor example of a man despite the many times I'd tried to beat some sense into him.

"How long have I been out?"

"Couple hours. Hell if I know. The damn sun ain't up yet, if that's what you're asking."

Shaking away the fog that still held me, I blinked my eyes to bring the scene around me into focus. On the far left, the fucker I'd allowed to marry my daughter lay passed out. Didn't know if it was from blood loss or extreme pain, but he lay motionless except for the shallow movement of his chest. The sledgehammer that had been used on his legs and crotch sat just where our attacker had left it, and I thought hard to remember what caused him to walk away and abandon his weapon.

"Maggie," I groaned. "Where is she?"

My gaze slid along the ground to find the woman we'd stolen for our entertainment passed out beside the dying fire. I couldn't tell whether she was alive or dead, and I didn't much care.

"After drugging you, she climbed in that bastard's truck and drove off with him. She said she was saving the family. It's a crock of shit if you ask me. I think she's been fucking that guy behind our backs for a while. Jack told me the bitch was loose as fuck on their wedding night."

My fingers gripped the armrests of the chair, my teeth gnashing together to hear Jack's name spoken aloud. "He still alive?"

Finn looked over at me, his expression twisted into something revolted and unsure. "Can't tell from where I'm still tied up, dad. You think you might want to do something about it now that you're done getting your beauty sleep?"

I was confused as all hell, but with each passing minute I regained my ability to think clearly. Fighting against the sluggishness of my body, it took three attempts to push up and out of my chair, the useless plastic tipping over in the dirt behind me as I stumbled forward, past Finn, past the sleeping bitch in the dirt, and rested my hand on the handle of the sledgehammer.

"Dad? What are you doing?"

It took another minute or two for the world to stop spinning around me. Using the handle of the sledgehammer, I stood in place, balancing myself until I felt strength return to my arms and legs - until I felt anger sweep in on a wave of adrenaline that chased away the pain.

"Dad?"

All I wanted was to finish what that jackass who'd stolen my daughter had started. I needed to get even with the bastard lying beneath me, needed to show him what happened when you dared leave a mark on my little girl.

His eyes cracked open as my shadow loomed over him. But despite the fact he was awake enough to look up at me, I didn't think he was conscious enough to understand the danger that was staring him in the face.

I spit in his eye before my hand wrapped around the handle of the hammer.

"You think to lie to me in my own house? You think you had any right to harm what was mine?"

"Dad! What are you doing?"

The sack of shit didn't even have enough sense to attempt to roll away or shield himself from what was coming. With the last bit of strength I had left in me, I lifted the hammer into the air, and brought it down on his head. Brain matter, blood and bone burst over the ground. His eyes bulged from their sockets and his arms and legs twitched as his body lay there dying.

Dropping the hammer to the ground, I turned around to look at my good for nothing sons. "And you two. What gave you any right to leave those marks on your sister?"

Finn's expression wrinkled the skin of his face, anger a purple cast across his cheeks and beneath his narrowed eyes. The moment his nostrils flared open, I chased the anger right out of him with my fist. Blood sprayed from his mouth and his head twisted awkwardly to the side.

"Consider that repayment for what you did to her."

Turning my glare on Brody, I was satisfied to discover that he had no complaints or arguments to give regarding what just happened to his brother.

"We'll settle this later," I warned him, my legs shaking beneath my body from the amount of time I'd slept in that damn chair. "But for now, we need to go find your sister."

A flash of silver caught my eye – a kitchen knife stuck in the dirt close to where my chair had been. Picking it up, I freed Brody first, disgust settling in my stomach over the way he complained that he couldn't feel his fingers. I thought I'd raised them to be stronger than that, yet both of them had been caught off guard by the prick that stole my daughter. They were two healthy, strong, grown men, and not one of them had enough sense to realize they were being ambushed.

After releasing Finn, I took a few steps towards the house, but turned again to bark out instructions. "Set that fire ablaze again. I want what's left of your friend tossed inside, along with the woman. We don't need bodies lying around to alert anybody to what happened here."

I didn't wait for them to answer before closing the distance between the field and the house with a few determined strides.

There was no man in this world that would take my daughter away from me without permission. There was no man that would sneak around with her and steal her purity from her without getting my approval first. Yet that dumb fuck had done all of those things while I hadn't been aware. He'd snuck under my nose, confused my girl with whatever empty promises he'd said to her, and he'd used her to get to my family in order to take her away for good.

My thoughts raced back to the bullshit he'd said to me. Some irrational crap about how I'd taken his wife and son from him over a decade ago. While he rattled off questions, I'd smiled to inform him that there was a damn good chance I'd fucked his wife and sold her off to die. I didn't give a shit about it neither. But if he wanted me to remember one woman among dozens…well…I didn't have any interest in sorting out their useless faces.

Those women were nothing but money. And their kids? They weren't worth much to me either, except for the money that sick in the head pig farmer paid me to drop them off to him. Every dollar bill looks the same once it's resting in the palm of my hand, and I'd told him that just as soon as he started demanding answers to his questions.

Dumb shit wasn't even man enough to finish killing off Jack for what he'd done to Maggie. I wasn't surprised. I knew

204

my daughter meant nothing to him. He'd made her a pawn in his stupid game, and I'd make him pay for that mistake when I saw him again.

Throwing open a cabinet door, I grabbed a bottle of whiskey from the shelf and practically ripped the wrapping and cap off the top. Bringing the bottle to my lips, I swigged down several swallows, my eyes closing as the burn chased down my throat to settle in my empty stomach. Numbness raced through my veins and rushed to all the painful places in my body.

When a good third of the bottle was gone, I slammed it on the counter and took a deep breath. Damn if that didn't start another coughing fit – this one worse than the last.

I didn't know how many days I had left, and only God knew my final hour. But I wouldn't let that stop me from freeing my girl from the clutches of a madman.

Out the window I saw the bonfire roar to life once more, the smell of burning flesh seeping in through the crevices of the house as they tossed their buddy in the fire. The bitch followed shortly after, her screams piercing the night until it fell silent once again.

A few minutes later, the door behind me slammed open, the walls of the kitchen shaking from how violently it struck against the frame. Heavy footsteps clamored over the floor as my pathetic sons stumbled in. I turned to tell them exactly what I thought about the mistakes they'd made tonight.

The pain didn't register in my gut immediately, but the smirk pulling at Finn's lips sure did. Reaching down, I felt blood seeping out from around the knife he'd stabbed into my body. My eyes remained locked on his insolent expression, on the look of betrayal and triumph that lingered behind his eyes.

"Sorry, old man," he said. "But you ain't worth shit to us anymore."

CHAPTER TWENTY-EIGHT

ELLIOT

"Where the hell are we, Maggie? What roads did you take to get us out in the middle of nowhere?"

A beautiful girl sat shivering in her seat beside me. She hadn't looked at me since I'd shoved her in the truck, and she'd barely said a damn word since I'd peeled away from the gas station parking lot in search of a single landmark that might tell me where the hell we were.

Several times now, I'd threatened to pull over and ask directions, but each time she swore she'd run screaming from the truck claiming it was *me* that kidnapped *her*. I had to admit she was smart about that threat. When I'd first laughed at the suggestion, she reminded me about the bruises on her body coupled with the carvings in her ass that proved she'd been abused.

The damn girl was a Crow, through and through, and my disgust with her was battling everything inside that reminded me I'd cared for her not even twenty-four hours before.

"Maggie," I growled. "I know what you're doing. I know you're trying to keep me away from your father and brothers, but I will find them sooner or later. You're only stalling the inevitable with this game, and you're seriously pissing me off in the meantime."

Why couldn't I have been an abusive man? One good slap might knock some sense into her, but no matter how many times my hand clenched into a fist, I couldn't bring myself to hit her.

Regardless of the arguments I made, she wouldn't respond, and I was stuck driving around in the pitch black of night trying to make heads or tails of the vast amounts of forest on either side of us.

The silence was like sandpaper against sunburned skin, every second of it that passed leaching me of the ability to give much of a fuck about anything. I'd had those bastards in the palm of my hand, but made the mistake of worrying about the woman seated next to me. I should have let her shove her foot through the window. I shouldn't have cared about the amount of damage she would done to her body in the process.

Had I not cared, I would have had my answers about my family. I could have slaughtered each and every one of those bastards and saved the woman they'd attacked.

I could have been dead by now and had one last moment of seeing my wife and son before God himself tossed me in the pits of Hell.

Tick, tick, tick – the silence kept building its pressure inside the truck until I thought I'd explode.

"That's it..."

Maggie let out a shocked scream when I veered wildly off the road, the back tires fishtailing behind us as dust was kicked up into a large cloud. I almost lost control of the vehicle as it dipped down into the dirt, the back end rising up from the sudden stop. Thankfully, I didn't hit any trees on my way into a clearing that had been hidden from the road for the most part. I'd seen it for just a second before making the split decision to ram my vehicle through whatever small saplings were in the way. Maggie was going to talk one way or the other, and I couldn't make that happen while we were on the road.

With thick dust still polluting the air in an impermeable cloud, I threw my door open and stepped out of the driver's seat. Four long legged strides had me rounding the front before my hand ripped the passenger door open. She tried to crawl away from me, but I was faster than she could ever hope to be.

When I'd first woken up in the truck while she'd been inside the gas station, I'd searched the inside of the vehicle for any surprises she might have stashed. I didn't find anything of any concern, and I'd hidden behind the bushes that lined the street in wait of the little traitor to come walking along. She'd been easy enough to take control of when she walked by unprepared, and after shoving her inside, I'd searched her entire body to make sure she didn't have another needle on her that she could use to knock me out again. She'd complained when my hands touched her breasts and between her legs, but I wasn't feeling like much a gentleman at that moment.

Unfortunately for Maggie, I wasn't feeling much like a gentleman at this moment either.

Another frightened cry left her lips when I pulled her out of the vehicle, dragged her around to where the headlights still beamed brightly and dumped her on the ground in a crying heap. The dirt in the air mixed with the tears streaming down her cheeks creating little muddy streams trickling down her skin.

On her hands and knees, she attempted to crawl away from me, but I grabbed her by the hair to drag her back into place. Crouching down, I made sure to lock my eyes to her before opening my mouth to scream out my demands.

"Tell me where the fuck we are! I'm not fucking playing with you, Maggie. If I have to kill you now and leave your body to rot in this fucking forest, I'll do it. I will find my way back to your place and I will kill every member of your family as slowly as fucking possible until I get the answers I want. Do you hear me?"

"I hear you just fine," she cried. "You're screaming loud enough to wake the dead, Elliot. You're scaring me."

"Do you think I give a shit that I'm scaring you? You can't possibly think that, Maggie. I know you're smarter than that.

208

Quite frankly, you should be pissing yourself with the fear that I might not let you live past tonight."

"Why?" She cried, her voice straining to formulate words through her sobbing. "Because of my family? I'm not one of them, Elliot. I didn't –"

"You can stop right fucking there, you lying bitch. Don't even try telling me you're not one of them. You made it readily apparent that, not only are you one of them, you're willing to do whatever it takes to cover up their crimes and save them from suffering the same fate as their victims. Don't you have a moral bone in your body? How can you not know it's wrong to stay silent while they're raping and killing women and children?"

"They didn't rape the children!" she screamed, her eyes rounding into impossibly large orbs as she glared up at me from the dirt where she was kneeling.

Laughter bubbled from my chest – the insane kind that only served the purpose of expending a small enough amount of pressure inside me so that I didn't reach out to choke the life right out of her.

"They didn't? They didn't rape them? Tell me what they did to them, Maggie. Specifically, what did they do to a four year old boy who had nothing to defend himself besides a stuffed rabbit?"

Spittle was flying from my lips, my voice so loud it boomed across the clearing and frightened away whatever creatures were out foraging for their meal. I was face to face with the woman who had lied to me the entire time she'd known me, the one who'd looked me in the face – who'd kissed me – while knowing what happened to my family.

"Elliot, please stop," she pled, but her begging was falling on deaf ears. I didn't give a damn how scared she was. I didn't care one bit if I was the monster in her life now. Nothing would stop me from discovering the truth of what happened to Katelyn and Michael and if I had to torture her to get it, I would.

"Tell me," I demanded.

"They – " she choked over her own words, barely able to speak past the sobs and shaking of her body. "I don't know what happened in the end, but I know my family didn't rape or kill your son."

Taking a deep breath to calm down the violence that was threatening to burst from my skin, I counted to ten while I brought myself under control. Deceptively soft, my voice was a bare whisper when I reached out to grip her chin, force her eyes to mine, and ask, "And how could you know that?"

Her eyes closed, her lips trembled, her entire body shook over the soil where she knelt. Opening her mouth to answer me, she was unable to speak out loud, not after one attempt, two attempts, or three.

"Tell me what you know, or so help me God, I'll –"

"I know they didn't touch your son because I was having a tea party with him the night he was brought to my house. My family didn't hurt him. He wasn't touched. He sat with me the entire night, but I can't remember anything more than that. I was only four. It's all a jumble of memory in my head."

"I suggest you think harder, Maggie. In fact, I suggest you think so hard right now to answer my questions that I don't kill you right here before finding my way back to someone who might remember a little better."

"I was only four! It wasn't my fault. I didn't know any better. You have to believe me. Please!"

"Please isn't good enough."

The anger took hold of me. Like a demon, it found it's way into my body and possessed me until I was powerless to fight it. I wasn't Elliot any longer. I wasn't the man who'd fallen in love at the age of thirteen, had a child at fifteen, and enlisted in the military at eighteen just to support the family I had when I was too young to take care of it. That man no longer existed.

What existed now was a man hell-bent on retribution. A man that would hurt whoever it took just to find the truth that had been denied to him since the moment he stepped foot back on U.S. soil. Guilt couldn't touch me any longer. And regret was so far off that I didn't worry about the burden of it, regardless of what horrible things I did to achieve what I was seeking.

Standing up, I shoved my hand against the back of Maggie's head, knocking her down to the ground so hard that she had to spit dirt out from between her teeth. I paced away from her in an attempt to quell the rage that was a fire in my veins, but then circled back again to kick at the dirt, to force more of it up into Maggie's face and into her eyes.

My hands clenched into fists and I imagined myself beating her down into the ground without remorse or hesitation. I imagined doing everything to her that her family had done to my wife and then bragging about it when I returned to kill those three bastards I left tied up around a bonfire. I imagined throwing her lifeless body into the bed of the truck and delivering her to them as revenge for what they had done to me.

But I didn't.

I couldn't.

I wasn't that man.

In a moment where I should have lost everything inside me that made me who I was as a person, a voice whispered up that reminded me there were two other spirits who'd shaped me. I could never lose them because I refused to let them go. Their memory held on to parts of me that kept me from becoming lost in the storm of pure rage that consumed me.

Gentle and soothing, that voice started so softly that I'd barely been able to hear it. As it grew louder, I recognized it was female. A little louder and I remembered the woman to whom it belonged.

My wife. The girl I met when I was just a boy. The heart and soul I'd fallen head over heels in love with once I knew what it was to love another. Her laughter was the wind across the clearing where I stood. Her heartbeat was the pulse that thundered in my head. The sunshine that always followed her warmed the places inside me that had grown cold since I'd lost her, and the happiness that was her entire being wrapped around me until I'd lost the ability to breathe.

That's the thing with the people you love. They start off as strangers who are separate and distinct. Through their beauty and kindness, they work their way inside you until you have no choice but to hold them close. Once your heart opens and accepts them inside, they become a part of you that is so indelible they are an essence of your soul that remains even after they die.

Katelyn was a part of me, and so was our son, Michael.

The parts of them that had become me wouldn't hurt Maggie for something that happened when she was four. And it was those parts that kept me from hurting her now.

But that didn't mean I wouldn't scare her.

Rounding the truck, I dropped the tailgate of the bed and pulled one of the duffel bags to me. Maggie continued wailing where she laid in the dirt, the pain of her sobbing reaching into me and ripping what little bit of my heart I had left out of my chest. She was just a child when my family disappeared and no matter what the circumstances had been, she couldn't be held accountable for their deaths.

She would be held accountable for lying to me – not that I'd done much better. I'd been lying the entire time I'd known her. Using her to get close to the men who had done my family harm.

Pulling a handgun from the bag, I zipped it closed and shook off the impulse to be a decent man. I needed answers and I was willing to walk the line between decent and monstrous in order to get what I was after.

Dirt kicked up beneath my feet and I took a few long legged strides to stand in front of the bawling girl on the ground. Cursing myself for adding to the torment I knew she'd suffered over the past few days, I pressed the muzzle of the gun to her forehead.

During my time in the military, I'd seen countless scenes of violence. I'd seen torture and pain. I'd seen destruction and pure hatred. I'd seen suicide and murder, rape and humiliation. I'd seen every horrible act one human could commit against another and I'd seen men break and surrender themselves to the pressure of carrying those images in their head.

However, never in the time that I spent serving had I ever seen anything as heartbreaking as watching Maggie surrender her will, surrender her fight, surrender her young life if that's what it took to save her family.

For as heartbroken as I was, I still had a duty to seek the truth. And I still had an unrelenting need for vengeance.

"We're sitting at a crossroads, Maggie. One where nobody lives in the end, except for maybe you."

Blinking away the tears in her eyes, she stared up at me without the light behind her eyes I was so used to seeing. "Take me instead, Elliot." A few more sobs rattled her chest, but she rolled her shoulders back regardless. This beautiful girl was going to walk into the afterlife with her head held high as she fought for the only thing she knew: her love of the father who'd raised her.

"I'm the one who made friends with your son. And I'm the reason your wife drove us home that night. I can't give you all the details, but I can give you that small bit. And if my family has to die because of what they've done, then I need to die right beside them. Because the death of your wife and son was my fault, too."

My hand holding the gun to her head trembled, the blood rushing from the tip of my finger where it was pressed to the side so I wouldn't accidentally pull the trigger. None of this was her fault. None of it. But she was willing to lay down her life to appease me.

Pulling the gun from her head, I dropped to my knees in front of her. Surprise flashed behind her eyes as the tears continued falling. And tears welled in mine to join hers. We stared at each other for several minutes before finally succumbing to the grief that trapped us both in it's cold, cruel hold.

Creeping forward, I tucked my finger beneath her chin and tipped her head up until her eyes met mine. My body trembled as much as hers. My heart pounded behind my ribs as my need for violence died.

Changing tactics, I calmed my booming voice.

"I'm not going to kill you, Maggie. What happened wasn't your fault. But I have to stop your family from killing again. And I need your help to do so."

"He's my father," she whispered.

"I know, Darlin'. I know. But that's neither here nor there when it comes to doing what's right."

A few tense seconds flew past until she swallowed down the grief that consumed her and nodded her head in agreement.

"Fine, Elliot. I'll lead you back home. I'm not sure where we are because I took different roads than my family normally drives when we're leaving town, but I'm sure we can stop and ask for directions. I don't mind you stopping Finn and Brody from killing again. I don't care if the two of them die. But I need you to promise me one thing – just one – and I'll help you finish what you came to my house to accomplish."

The tears in my eyes burned until I had no choice but to blink them away and drop into the dirt beneath me. "What do you need, Maggie? What will make you help me finish this?"

A shiver ran across her body. Drawing a deep breath into her lungs, she held it for a second before releasing it. And after rolling her shoulders back once more, she stared into my eyes.

"I want to be the one who kills my father."

CHAPTER TWENTY-NINE

MAGGIE

Desperation is a terrible entity. Unlike the emotions that creep in gradually and seduce you to love, to cry, to laugh or to tremble, desperation is a bully that charges you head on. Selfish and intractable, desperation consumes every part of you when it takes control. It bites down and shakes the life out of you, paralyzing you in its unrelenting hold until you're nothing but a puppet bowing and dancing according to the strings it has tied to its malevolent, skeletal fingers.

It wasn't simply despair or fear that I felt as I knelt before a crazed man holding a gun to my head, it was pure and undiluted desperation, the kind that left me without will, without choice, without anything but the instinct to submit to the dominant, immoveable force that stood above me.

I was desperate to survive. Desperate to save my father. Desperate to repair all the agony and chaos my family had created in the man who now held my life in his hands.

Only two nights had passed since Elliot told me there were always choices in life. The choice to live. The choice to die. The choice to fight against insurmountable odds, even if that meant you chose to give up breathing rather than succumb to the torture of being enslaved.

Elliot never mentioned you had to be strong to make that choice. And if he had, I wouldn't have believed him when he'd told me that choice had been my right.

The desperation had excised my strength. It had left me a shell devoid of hope, optimism or courage. A dog that had found its bone, desperation had gnawed me down to fragments of what I'd once believed I could have been. It left me covered in dirt, my eyes burning and my body trembling beneath an impossibly dark and moonless night.

Only when Elliot had removed the hard surface of the gun from my head had I been able to take a breath, but it wasn't enough to clear my head of the panic, to pull me from the arms of the desperation that crippled me while laughing at how easy I'd been made its victim.

Forcing myself to continue breathing, I listened to the words Elliot spoke, I reached out with that part inside myself that could feel the emotions of others, only to be burned by the desperation I recognized in him as well.

We were both slaves to the outcomes we wanted. Elliot wanted to destroy it all; and I wanted to discover a way to keep death from devastating my soul.

"Why would you want to kill your father, Maggie?"

Despite the way my eyes still burned from the dirt that continued to clog them, I stared unblinking at a man too beautiful to be real. It wasn't simply the sharp angles of his face or his square, strong jaw. It wasn't just the golden glow of his skin, or the hard muscles that were perfectly developed into defined planes that moved with a feline grace. It was the loyalty that consumed him. The love that destroyed him. The focus in his eyes that was so acute, it stole the breath from my lungs. His spirit was larger than life and I regretted not having known him when happiness infected his being, for not having known him before agony replaced the warmth and light inside him with turmoil and bitter cold.

"I don't want you becoming a killer," he whispered, his voice cradled softly by the cool night air. "You don't need that stain on your soul."

I couldn't tell him that desperation was the reason behind my sudden request. Explaining that I was buying time would only enrage him more. Despite the futility of the dividing line that had been drawn, I forced myself to believe that there was a possibility we could come together and see eye to eye.

Buying time had never been more important. Buying time was the only way I could ensure my father would survive.

Even though lying had never been my strong suit, it was the only option I had at that particularly difficult moment.

"Because you're right," I explained, hoping and praying that his own turmoil would keep him from seeing my own. "It's wrong what they've done. The kidnapping and killing. The parties they hold before we run away from the pain they've caused."

At first I'd been merely repeating back all the words he'd just said to me, but as I continued prattling on, a sickening realization hit me: The words he'd said hadn't been wrong.

I didn't approve of what my family had done, and if it had just been Finn and Brody's crimes, I would have turned my back on them a long time ago. My father was the challenging factor. It had been wrong of him to take part in the acts that had destroyed so many. And if he'd been any other man, I would have condemned him as fervently as any person standing on the outside of our family. I would have hated him for the victims he'd created. And I would have wanted to destroy him as thoroughly as Elliot planned to do.

To me, my father was a different man. He was the knight who'd chased away the dragons, the man who'd protected me against all the monsters that went bump in the night. He'd been the balm that chased away my childhood tears and the playmate that sat with me for tea parties, who'd danced with me and brought a smile to my youthful face. He'd given me everything I'd ever wanted or needed, and he'd used a soft hand in disciplining me when I'd gone astray.

Whereas other people looked at my father and saw him for the evil he'd committed, I'd looked at him and saw a protector, a parent and a friend.

I never doubted his loyalty to me, and even when he'd made decisions that hurt me, I knew he believed he was doing what was right.

It never occurred to me to question why he hurt others while placing me on a pedestal. Women were objects and money – all of them, except for me.

Buying time wouldn't just give me the opportunity to save the man who'd looked after me since I was a baby, it would give me the chance to ask the hard questions that, until now, I'd never had the strength to consider.

Staring down at me with curiosity and hesitation behind his cold, grey eyes, Elliot waited patiently for me to continue explaining the request I'd made. His hand still held the gun he'd used to threaten me. His body was still tight with lack of trust. But I had to forgive him for not readily believing a word I had to say. All I'd done is betray him in the worst possible ways.

"I want to know why he did the things he did," I admitted. "I want to know why I'm so special he would move the Earth and stars if that's what it took to protect me, yet he killed so many others without a single drop of remorse. I've never had the chance to ask him those questions. I don't know, Elliot. I just don't see him as the same monster that you see. If he has to die, I want to be the person that is there when he takes his final breath, if for nothing else but to say goodbye."

Shaking his head, Elliot finally broke the focused stare he'd held on me. Tilting his head up into the night sky, his throat moved to swallow down whatever lump of emotion choked him. His jaw twitched as he ground his teeth and his fingers tightened over the cold steel of the gun in his hand.

"You don't know what it is like to kill someone. It seems easy until it's time to pull the trigger. And it might seem easy to walk away and leave that decision behind you because you believed you had no choice, but the life you destroyed follows you. It tracks you day after day, constantly on the edge of your thoughts until it finds those moments of weakness to step in and haunt you."

Angling his head back down, he opened his eyes and blinded me with the despair that had settled behind them. A sob threatened to crawl up my throat, the pain in him so palpable I would have sworn it was my own.

"He's your father, Maggie. You love him and he loves you. I have no doubt about that."

"It's why I want to be the one to do it," I admitted, that damn desperation tackling me again and making itself known in my voice. "I know you don't think he deserves to leave this world with compassion. I get that. But I don't agree. At least not for the part of him that I know."

Indecision was obvious in the strict lines of his face. He wanted revenge, he wanted retribution and he wanted blood. Watching him closely, I realized there was a battle raging inside.

"We should get on the road and drive back to your house," he finally said, exhaustion evident in the way his shoulders withered. A cloud of dust kicked up when he settled his body onto the ground. Blowing out a breath filled with all the hate, anger and pain he'd been feeling, he shook his head again.

"For the last fourteen years, there has been nothing left of me," he confessed, his voice so calm and soft that it scared me more than the screaming had. "I didn't know who'd taken my family, not for the first several years at least. Each day of not knowing tore another piece of me away. I was afraid I would eventually die without the answers I needed to make sense of what had stolen away my life."

His eyes closed and opened again, waves of debilitating emotion crashing behind the glint of steel in his gaze. "You can't possibly understand what it feels like – how not knowing is the worst fate you can be given. But then one day there was a light that shone down and illuminated the void of not knowing. It wasn't an answer that screamed in my face. It wasn't the proof I needed to make everything right. It was more of a whisper, a trail of breadcrumbs left out that dared me to follow. But follow them, I did. Directly to your front door."

Settling myself on the ground facing Elliot, I toyed with an errant twig that sat on the ground at my knees. "You knew, didn't you? On the first day we met, you knew what my family had done."

Nodding his head, his eyes darted away from me. I took that as a sign of guilt, but I couldn't hold it against him. We'd both been playing each other since the very beginning.

"Yeah, I knew. I was hoping you'd tell me something that confirmed my suspicions." A bark of sad laughter burst from his lips. "I have to hand it to you, Maggie, you're damn good at keeping a secret."

I would have laughed with him if the subject weren't heartbreaking. "I learned from the best," I replied, my voice empty of any solace or humor. "I was drilled by my fathers and brothers since the moment I made them aware I knew what they were doing was wrong. For years, lies have been shoved down my throat until I could regurgitate them under torture, if need be. I guess the only reason I was good at telling the lies was because there was a grain of truth in all of them. And if a question was asked where the answer held no truth, I learned how to change the subject."

Placing the gun in his lap, he flexed the hand that had been holding it. Just seeing him relax helped me relax as well.

His mouth opened a few times, but he closed it again without saying a word. He was battling himself again, questions and comments floating around in that head of his that bothered him more than he wanted me to know. Finally shaking away the emotions that held him prisoner within himself, he glanced up at me and gave me a downhearted smile.

"Those things we did at the other farm, when I touched you and –"

"Elliot," I tried to stop him before he got the words out. I knew he'd used me, but I wanted to hold on to those memories as they were without knowing the truth of why he'd kissed me, held me or touched me in ways that made my body sing. If he never explained why, then I could go on convincing myself that he'd wanted to be with me in that way. I could keep lying even when I didn't believe my own lies.

"No, Maggie. Let me say this."

Turning my head, I attempted to avert my eyes, but he grabbed my chin and carefully directed my gaze back to his. The warmth of his skin on mine was staggering, the rough texture of his fingers reminding me of what they'd felt like on my body. A breath shuddered from my lungs, but I didn't attempt to turn away again.

"I didn't do those things only because I was using you for information. Technically, yes, it started out that way. But, over the days that we sat talking, I started to care about you. I didn't want to. Hell, I wanted to hate you as much as I hated your family. But I couldn't do it no matter how hard I tried. You're a victim of your family just as much as every person they stole from the world. They used you and abused you in ways that are unforgiveable and cruel. Yet, despite everything they put you through, despite every horrible bit of suffering you've had to witness in your life, you still have a light inside of you that is breathtaking when you allow it to be seen."

My eyes widened in response to his confession, my heart beating harder in my chest with hope rekindling itself in my veins.

"You remind me so much of Katelyn because of that light. And I pray to God, to the universe, to the heavens above that you never lose that light. I wasn't lying when I told you I wanted you to run away, to get married and to have babies and raise them to be as beautiful as you. The only thing I was lying about was the fact that I could be the man by your side."

He'd fed the fire inside me just seconds ago, but with the words he was voicing now, he'd doused the warmth of the flames.

"Is it because of what happened to your family? For the part I played?"

Another tragic smile pulled at his lips, his eyes shadowed by memory and hidden thoughts I feared he'd never reveal fully. "You were only four at the time. There was no way you could have known what your family was doing. I don't blame you for what happened to them." Swallowing hard, he reached up to rub his eyes. His head fell back and my gaze followed the long line of his throat, my hand itching to reach out to feel the rough surface of stubble against my palm.

"I can't be that man because I don't plan on living once I'm done. When they took my family, they took my life. All I've been doing for the past fourteen years is going through the motions of what living actually means. But I haven't been alive since the day my wife and son died."

A tear slipped from my eye and I could no longer tolerate the distance between us. Pushing forward from where I sat, I moved slowly over the ground, crawling on hands and knees, and ignoring the way Elliot protested with his eyes when I climbed into the warmth of his lap. The gun fell between his legs, and at first, he attempted to keep from touching me back, but within a few seconds I felt him lose his resolve. I released a breath I'd been holding when his arms wrapped around my body.

"I don't want you to die," I whispered. "I never want you out of my life."

His arms tightened around me, his chest moving rhythmically with his breath. Breathing in, I inhaled his masculine scent, memories of the times we'd shared beating down on me with the threat that they would never happen again.

The tears fell harder, but I fought against them. For once, I wanted to be brave. I wanted to save someone. And I wanted that someone to be the man who held me close despite everything we'd done to one another.

If ever two souls had been fused together through violence, despair and pain, it was Elliot and I. He might be able to let that bond go, but I wouldn't go down without a fight.

"Damn it, Maggie," he whispered. "I wasn't supposed to like you this much. It's wrong in so many ways."

Soft laughter shook my shoulders. "Well, you better get used to it. And you better stop talking like you're dying any time soon."

"There's not much you can do to stop me, beautiful."

I didn't want to pull away from him and lose the warmth that surrounded me, but I did just enough that I could look him in the eyes.

"There's a lot I can do, Elliot. And I'll start with refusing to help you find your way back to my house. We'll go right back to where we were an hour ago. Then what will you do?"

His lips twitched in response to the silly threat. "Well, as soon as you crawl off my lap again, I guess I'll grab my gun and we'll be right back where we started."

"You wouldn't do that," I argued, "Shooting me would just destroy my light."

Angling his head forward, he pressed his forehead to mine. "You're getting better at standing your ground, little girl. But this is just another conversation we'll have to save for another time. We need to get going. We've got a long drive to make, a woman we need to save, and three Crows that need to die."

I agreed with him about two of those Crows. It was the third one – my father – that still tore at my heart. I'd come up with a plan on the way back to the house. I'd figure out something to make things right.

Pushing away to stand up, I was surprised when Elliot pulled me back to him, and I was even more surprised when his lips fell on mine.

CHAPTER THIRTY

ELLIOT

Is it possible to cheat on a lover if they no longer occupy the same world as you? What if that lover was a soulmate? A person so indelibly attached that they'd become a part of who you are?

If any person had asked me those questions even twenty-four hours earlier, I would have answered yes.

The first time I kissed Maggie, I'd gone home and drowned myself in alcohol just to chase the guilt away. I'd apologized to the woman I'd lost, the woman who'd stolen my heart just when it learned how to love in the first place. Convincing myself that I wasn't falling for the girl who's family had destroyed the best parts of me – convincing myself that kissing her had simply been a means to an end – I'd indulged in the act of enjoying her without fear of the guilt creeping back in when I laid my head on my pillow each night.

There wasn't any excuse for the way I was kissing her now. I wasn't an operative in search for covert information. My actions were no longer a means to an end. She knew the truth of all the secrets and lies I'd kept between us, and there weren't any walls erected that kept my heart from beating again.

For as much as it hurt, I couldn't let her go. I didn't know if that made me crazy or just stupid, but regardless of the answer, I pulled her closer so that the warmth of her body could seep into my skin.

Lost in the way her lips moved against mine, I couldn't shake the feeling that I was cheating on my spouse, but at the same time, I couldn't continue lying to myself that Maggie didn't matter.

She'd crawled her way into my thoughts and heart. She'd melded herself to my soul while I hadn't been aware of what she was doing.

Her confession tonight had rocked me to the core of my being. She didn't want me to die. She didn't care that I would hurt her family. All she wanted was for me to remain by her side and lead her into a new and beautiful life.

The girl had more faith in me than I had in myself, but I was thankful for that faith despite not knowing whether I could deliver what she needed when all was said and done.

I caught myself questioning the possibility of a future with the woman in my arms, but I there was still one truth staring me in the face – a truth that had me breaking off the kiss and pushing her from my lap: Until I had my revenge and closed the final chapter on the woman I'd loved in the past, I was in no position to begin a life with the woman who could be my entire future.

Death might not have to be the final answer. Rebirth could be found in Maggie's arms.

Wiping at her lips with the back of her hand, she flashed me a hesitant look, a thousand unspoken questions flowing behind the lush green of her gentle gaze.

"Did I do something wrong?" she finally dared to ask.

Giving her an easy grin, I slid my thumb along the line of her jaw. "No, beautiful, you didn't. You did nothing but help me pry open my pain-swollen eyes."

🔻🔻🔻🔻

"Did you have to drive entirely across the damn state to drag me away? Damn, woman, my ass is numb from how long I've been sitting in this seat."

Taking my eyes off the road for a moment, I noticed Maggie sitting passively beside me. We'd been driving for two hours now, and it was only when we stopped to ask for directions that we were informed she'd taken me over state lines and practically crossed another before stopping for gas. If I hadn't woken up when I did, we'd be in another country by now.

Several times, I thought she was drifting off to sleep. The radio wasn't playing and the windows were rolled down – the soft hiss of wind enough to knock any person unconscious while being lulled to rest by the soft vibration of tires against the smooth asphalt of the highway.

Shaking herself of whatever thoughts had her caught in their silent grasp, she turned to look at me with eyes that were downcast with emotion.

"It's like a told you before," she finally answered, her voice rough with the sleep she refused to allow herself, "I tried to get as far away as possible, as fast as possible." Shrugging a tired shoulder, she yawned.

"I thought if I took roads that weren't familiar to me, I'd get myself so lost that you couldn't force me to take you back immediately."

Seconds of silence passed before a sullen laugh filled the space between us. "Guess I was wrong. I never figured you for the type that would threaten a woman with a gun to her head."

A grin tilted my lips. "Well, that makes two of us, then." My eyes darted to her for a second hoping to catch her eyes, but she'd already turned to stare out the passenger window.

The silence was putting me to sleep, and I didn't have time to pull over and rest when there was a woman's life on the line. I'd left her family bound to their chairs, and I hoped they hadn't broken free, that they hadn't had the opportunity to do anything but wait for my return. If I was lucky, the woman had woken up and left, most likely run to the police, and those bastard Crows were sitting behind bars.

No. That wouldn't be lucky for me entirely. I wanted them dead, not locked in a barred box being fed by taxpayer money.

Clearing my throat, I filled the silence, repeating her words back to her. "I never figured you for the type that could knock a man my size flat on his ass and kidnap him."

From my peripheral vision, I saw her turn to stare at me.

"I'll admit you've got some brass balls, Maggie. Once again, you took me by surprise. You have a funny way of doing that."

"Doing what?"

Her voice was hesitant and unsure when she asked the question. It occurred to me then that not many people in her life had explained to her the effect she had on them.

"You're a strong woman. My mother would have said you were the type of woman who was full of piss and vinegar. The type that breaks rules and toes lines. She has a fondness for those types because they're the ones who leave their mark on history."

Seconds passed with her silent contemplation before she shook her head and returned her gaze to the forest that moved past us in a blur. "I've never known a woman like that."

A bark of laughter rattled my chest. "Yeah, you have. Every time you look in the mirror, you met a woman like that. You just didn't know it."

It broke my heart to realize Maggie had no clue about the type of person she was. Naked bravery wrapped up in a pretty package, she was a bird that had its wings clipped since the moment its captors realized it could fly. It boggled me how a father could cripple his own child. I would have never done that to my son. It would have made me proud to see him become a stronger man than me, to see him make his mark on

228

the world with power, grace and the loyalty I would have taught him if I'd been given the chance. The thought made me hate Jonah more for what he'd done. I questioned the reasons why he could love someone as much as he loved his daughter, but prevent her from becoming the powerful person she should have been.

"What's it like?" Maggie asked, the question so random and out of the blue that I wrenched my neck to look over at her.

Her head turned for only a second and her eyes met mine, but they closed again on some unspoken thought before she turned back to staring at nothing.

Training my eyes back on the road, I waited a moment to think about her question. Not having the faintest clue what she was asking, I finally responded, "What's what like?"

"Losing somebody you love. What is it like having to continue living when you know you'll never see that person again?"

Damn. Of all the questions she could have asked, why did it have to be that one?

The answers eluded me because there were no words to describe the amount of loss a person suffers when someone they love is stripped away. A part of your soul is sliced clean in that moment and your life is branded with the pain that flows in to alter you in unspeakable ways.

Learning to love someone, and to lose them, is a study in change and metamorphosis.

One morning you wake up and look in the mirror to see the man you've always been. You go out that day, completely unaware that destiny is coming, and you stumble upon a woman who smiles in your direction and attaches herself to your every thought.

The next morning you wake again, but that man in the mirror isn't the same. He has a smile on his face and a song in his heart and he's looking forward to a future where he would see that woman again.

Every day he changes. Every day he grows into the man he needs to be for the woman he loves, and for some unknown reason, loves him in return.

Her love strengthens the man. It molds him and builds him into everything nature has endowed him to be. Days and months pass by. He grows. He changes. He loves more fiercely than he ever imagined possible. And then something comes from that love. His child. Her child. Another life that forces him to look in the mirror once more and discover he'd changed again.

The man no longer lives for himself, but for that woman and child. His future is written in stone, his mind set on all the possibilities of what that future can bring. He loves with all his heart. His mind is consumed with ideas on how to be a husband and father. He breaks his body doing hard labor just to provide for the family he'd created. But the muscle pain is bearable, only because he knows that he'll go home and have it smoothed away by the kiss of the woman he loves, and by the hug of the child that had become his entire world.

To have that family ripped away, to have it stolen when his back was turned as he gave up his freedom to provide for that family – there are no words to describe what it does to that man.

I look in the mirror now and see nothing but an empty shell. Large holes cut out my heart and soul in the shape of my wife and son. Jagged edges left in their place that if I try to touch them slice into me until I have no choice but to pull my hand away.

Losing someone you love alters reality itself, because the world is no longer the same without them in it. There's always something missing, something you know will never be replaced.

There are no words, but I tried to come up with some anyway.

"Losing someone you love is the most painful experience you'll ever live through, Maggie. It's like taking a bucket full of happiness and peace, and emptying it out until it's vacant and hollow, only to stuff it full again with every negative emotion you can think of to fill up the insides."

She didn't speak when my voice started breaking apart on those words. She simply sat in still silence, waiting for me to gather enough strength to start talking again.

"I'd been alone before I met Katelyn. But I was never lonely. I had my friends. My parents. My hobbies and interests. I'd been satisfied with the world and didn't think I wasn't entirely whole. When I met her, I realized in that precise moment our eyes first locked that half of me was missing. And after finding my other half, I realized I had been lonely all along, I just hadn't understood what that meant."

Hating the smile that graced my lips when I thought back to her, I wanted to close my eyes and see her face, but it wasn't the right time to lose myself to that small bit of paradise. With my eyes still on the road, I let those images swirl in the back of my mind before allowing the storm clouds to come rolling in to chase them away.

"We were way too young for the strength of the love we had for each other. In truth, we'd known of each other since we were small kids, but we'd never really *known* each other. Not until we were a little older and we finally recognized we were two halves of the same whole.

"Losing her, losing Michael, it was like losing the largest part of myself. The best part of myself. And all that was left behind were slivers of memory that burned my skin when I reached for them because they were wrapped in a blanket of bitter cold."

I couldn't bring myself to look at Maggie, but I knew she was staring at me.

"Is that how I'm going to feel when my father dies?"

My fingers gripped the wheel in response to her softly spoken question.

Fuck if I knew how losing her father would feel for her, but that wasn't the answer I would give. She was suffering just knowing what was about to happen. I had to wonder if knowing your world was about to change wasn't worse than having it happen when you didn't see it coming.

"I don't know," I admitted. "I've never lost a parent."

"You don't think it's the same?"

Now that question I could answer.

"No. I don't think it's the same. Not entirely at least."

"How so?"

I glanced over at her before reaching out to take her hand. She was hesitant at first, but then finally entwined her fingers with mine. Two people on the road to an unknown future.

"There's a natural order to life," I finally explained. "We're born into a family and through the years we come to recognize that our parents will grow old and eventually leave us behind. If life is fair and good to you, you'll grow up and start a family of your own. You'll have people there to support you when you lose those that supported you from the day you took your first breath. And all the while, your kids will look up at you and know that the cycle continues – over and over again – because that's the natural order of life."

A breath shuddered from my chest, memories creeping in that I'd rather remain buried.

"It's not natural for your child to leave this world before you do. It makes you feel like you failed to protect them, and that failure stalks you through the rest of yours days. It's relentless in the way it never lets you go. I don't think losing a parent leaves you with that same sense of failure. It was never your job to protect them in the first place."

More silence fell between us, but we were still connected together through the warmth of our hands.

"I hope I don't become someone different when my father dies," Maggie whispered.

"You will," I admitted. "Losing anybody makes you a different person."

"Will you still want me when I change?"

She'd spoken so softly, I wasn't sure I'd heard the question. We turned to look at each other in that moment, and the question remained there blazing behind her tear filled eyes.

There was no possible way I could know the answer to that question. But after giving it some thought, I wasn't sure she'd asked it the right way.

"I don't think it's whether I'll want you that should be the question."

Her eyes met mine again and it hurt more than I'd ever believed it would to tell her exactly what I wanted to say.

"In all honesty, Maggie, I have to wonder if you'll still want me after you change."

CHAPTER THIRTY-ONE

MAGGIE

"Fuck."

The truck lurched to a stop, dust kicking up into a cloud from beneath the tires, the world outside the windows becoming hazy and obscured.

"FUCK!"

Elliot's hand slammed against the steering wheel of the truck, both of our eyes locked to the scene staged before us. Whereas it had been a surprise to the man now screaming out obscene words, it hadn't been much of a surprise for me.

We'd driven for another two hours after discussing what happens when a person dies. And in those two hours we'd barely spoken to one another. The miles traveled over the road felt like we were crawling towards a moment of reckoning, and only I knew the truth of what we were likely to find.

I felt guilty as sin when I looked out at the empty plastic chairs and a bonfire that was now just smoke and ash. A foul scent lingered in the air, something unrecognizable that turned my stomach, but left me with no doubts that death had occurred here.

The guilt kept me from looking over where Elliot sat, to see the angry lines that I knew marred his beautiful face. He stared out the window deathly still and I knew he was making decisions with absolute precision, that he was plotting what actions he'd take next. I wasn't sure how long we sat there just staring out at the wisps of smoke that danced up from the ash and coals of a once burning inferno, but in that time I became filled with a powerful dread, with the weight of my responsibilities for the heartache we'd find.

"I need to go look around, Maggie. But I don't trust that your family is gone, so I want you to stay in the truck –"

"They're gone," I said, interrupting the instructions he was barking at me. Weakness kept a stranglehold on my voice, my tongue tied up with all the lies that bounced around in my head. However, what I'd just told him hadn't been a lie. I knew my family well enough to know they wouldn't linger at the scene of a crime.

"Yeah?" he asked, "And how do you know that?"

Releasing a breath that was filled with the putrid scent that surrounded us, I nodded my head towards the far right of the house. "The truck is gone. My family is smarter than to stay here after you saw what they were doing. My bet is that they cleaned up as well as they could before hitting the road."

His hands slammed down on the steering wheel again, his face a mask of indecision and rage. "The woman?"

My shoulders withered. "I'm sure she's dead, Elliot. They wouldn't leave any witnesses behind."

"How the fuck did they get free?"

His head turned in my direction, his eyes full of accusations.

Shame sat on top of me like a heavy blanket.

In all the time that Elliot and I had known each other, we'd built a relationship on lies. Lies protected us from knowing about one another. Lies held up the walls we'd relied on to pretend like being together was all right. And it had been lies that damn near destroyed us until the truth came in and taught us what it was to accept the circumstances that brought us into each other's lives in the first place.

I couldn't lie anymore, not if meant returning back to that place where the walls kept us apart.

"After I knocked you out with whatever that drug was my family always kept on hand, I knocked my father out with it as well. Once I knew he wouldn't be waking up for a few hours, I cut his binds."

Elliot's silence following my confession held me by the throat and kept me from breathing. I was trapped beneath it, desperate to fight my way free, but too scared to make a move or a sound until I knew how he would react to an act of utter betrayal.

If the woman was dead, I understood that her blood was on my hands. Glancing down, I saw the dark, crimson stain that marred my skin and made me no better than my family.

It's funny how even a small passage of time can clear your thoughts and help you see clearly. My father was a monster. He didn't deserve to live. But the Maggie that existed only eight hours before hadn't understood that simple fact. I wished I could go back in time and tell myself the truth – to warn myself that it wasn't just my father I needed to save.

If the woman was dead, I was to blame. And I knew that hard fact was screaming in Elliot's thoughts.

"Why?" he asked before shaking his head, the indecision splitting him in two. "You know what? I don't care why. I don't fucking care. I just need to know where they would have gone. I can't –"

He paused mid-sentence, aggravation a deep, splotchy red that colored his skin. After taking a few deep breaths, his fingers relaxed over the wheel, his hand reaching out to touch my face. "I'm not going to hold this against you. I'm not, Maggie. I refuse. But you have to help me make this right. You have to tell me where they would have gone."

There were only two places I knew of where my family would have run. One was an abandoned pig farm – a place I'd hoped to never see again. The other was a few days drive away, so far and so deep inside a forest that only a few people knew it existed. Tucked safely beneath trees on federal land, my father had maintained the place every time we were traveling, but we never stayed there often. Only during the times when we needed to hide.

"I need to get out of the truck," Elliot growled. "I need to make sure they're not here."

Taking his words as a challenge to my honesty, I clenched my eyes shut to keep from crying. "I'm not lying to you, Elliot. I'm not. They wouldn't have stayed behind. I know them well enough to know that."

His door opened and he was halfway out of the truck before he paused, his eyes cast down at his feet and his jaw ticking with whatever it was he was feeling. "I'm not doubting you. I just need to see for myself what happened. I need to know."

Nodding my head, I sniffled, the damn tears leaking out despite how tight I'd closed my eyes. "Then I'm getting out, too."

I didn't give him a second to argue before I threw my door open and jumped down to the ground. We both rounded the front to meet in the middle and, in silence, we walked toward the bonfire to find out if we could see the ghosts of the past.

"I hope she was dead," he muttered, his hand reaching up to rub at the back of his neck before he jerked it back down and turned to peer out across the fields. Muttering more curse words beneath his breath, his body was as stiff and immoveable as I'd ever seen it.

While he looked out across the expanse of tall grasses and weeds, I stared at the vacant eyes of the woman I'd helped my family kill. Not eyes, really. Just two large holes in a charred skull where those eyes should have been.

Beside her bones lay the pieces of a second charred skull, and I had no doubts whose head that once had been.

"They killed Jack, too. It doesn't look like he had a peaceful ending."

Spinning on his heel, Elliot turned back to me and opened his mouth to say something, but his words failed him when the whisper of sound came creeping its way from the house. Every hair on my body stood on end.

"I thought you said they weren't home…"

His words sliced deep as his body took large, powerful strides in the direction of the run down structure. He'd almost made it to the stairs before he spun back around and stormed in the direction of his truck.

Wanting to ask him where he was going, I snapped my mouth shut instead. He was a volcano on the verge of erupting, a firestorm that was being fueled by the purest oxygen known to man. I knew better than to get in the way of a man on a mission.

Shifting my weight between my feet, I battled my own indecision. My head turned between the house and Elliot's truck. Before I understood that I'd made up my mind, I found myself walking in the opposite direction of Elliot and climbing the stairs to the house

"Maggie!" he screamed out, his voice echoing across the expanse causing a flock of birds to abandon the trees where they'd sat perched in silent observation.

My eyes darted to where he stood staring, and I ducked my head as I ignored the irritation in his expression to walk my trembling body inside.

Something crashed inside the house as soon as I entered, but I didn't allow the sound to scare me away. I needed to know who lingered in this place – who had been too stupid to run when the chance had been theirs to take.

Rounding the corner of the living room, I heard the kitchen door slam open, the sound of heavy steps closing the distance behind me until a warm body stood at my back.

Panic froze me in place at that moment, a meeting that I would have sworn would have been as violent and lethal as my imagination had promised me it would be.

I was taken by surprise by the silence and by the way time stopped moving for a brief moment.

"Maggie Pie," my father croaked, his large body seated on the middle of our threadbare couch, a wrinkled blanket pulled over his lap and belly as if he'd been woken from an afternoon nap.

Elliot stilled where he stood behind me, rage like electric waves flowing off his body until it became uncomfortable to have him so near. Wanting to move forward, I found that my legs were too heavy to take that first step, so I simply stared straight ahead expecting to see anger and betrayal in my father's eyes.

He held my stare for several seconds, his expression tight, but not as furious as I'd expected. Finally breaking the wordless connection we had, my father looked up into the face of the man whose life he'd shattered.

Clearing his throat, my father spoke slowly, his voice weak and his skin a pale white. "I know what you came here to do, son. I may be old, but I'm not stupid."

Elliot's hand fell over my shoulder. "Maggie, I need you to leave –"

"That won't be necessary," my father interrupted. "I don't plan to fight you. Not that I have much fight left in me either way."

He didn't sound right. His voice was too calm. His body was too still. I wasn't sure what changed between the time I drugged him and drove Elliot away, but this wasn't the man who'd raised me.

"Maggie," Elliot warned.

"No," I managed to answer despite the festering lump of uncertainty that clogged my parched throat. Keeping my voice as calm as possible, I spoke gently because I stood at the meeting point of two impossibly violent storms.

"You made me a promise, Elliot," I reminded him, my eyes never leaving my father.

Daddy didn't shift position, didn't move a damn muscle. Not even his eyes twitched as he sat in repose watching us from across the room.

"Maggie." Elliot's voice had softened. There was understanding in the way he'd said my name. Lowering his voice even further until it was barely a whisper, he asked, "Are you sure you want to do this?"

I wasn't sure of anything at that exact moment, but I put on a brave face. "I'm sure," I answered.

The cold hard steel of a gun was pressed into my hand before Elliot took a step away.

"Son," my father called out, his eyes glued to Elliot where he stood behind me. I felt Elliot stop in his tracks, knew he was turning to look back at one of the men who'd stolen his family. It surprised me that he didn't move quickly to break the promise he'd made to me in that dark field, that he didn't shove me aside to charge towards my father.

Clearing his throat again, my father's shoulders shook with a weak cough. His eyelids drooped like he was tired and his ashen skin appeared sullen and lifeless.

"I just wanted to let you know I finished what you couldn't."

Elliot's body stilled and I felt like I was standing next to a coiled serpent.

"What did you finish?"

There was thin ice beneath all our feet. One wrong move and we'd all plunge into icy water only to get sucked in by the current of misunderstandings and become trapped beneath the frigid surface that reflected our crimes back at us.

"I killed the bastard that carved his name into my daughter. Broke his head into so many pieces that he'd never touch another woman again."

Closing my eyes, I attempted to wipe the imagery of Jack's death from my mind, but I'd seen that level of rage before from my father. I knew it hadn't been a clean kill.

"Why are you telling me this?"

His cough was a phlegmy, sickening sound – the sound of death creeping up like a whispered promise. "Just thought you should know. Just wanted you to understand that you're not the only father willing to protect what's his."

"I wasn't responsible for what happened to Maggie," Elliot argued, the disgust in his tone obvious.

Giving Elliot one nod of his head, my father's eyes darted to my face. "I know. But I'm responsible for what happened to your child."

To hear it spoken aloud made tears well in my eyes. I'd known the truth all along, but until then, I'd been able to hide behind illusions.

"I don't have much longer to live. But I'm asking you to give me the one thing I wasn't kind enough to give you. I need one more moment with my daughter."

Elliot didn't answer, didn't dare give the slightest hint that he was granting my father his request. He tapped the gun in my hand before whispering in my ear. "I'll give you this moment, Maggie. But I'm not giving that man a damn thing."

I listened to his boots storm a path outside of the house, knowing full well that if I didn't make this quick, he'd be back to check on me.

Although my legs were still heavy with the weight of the world, I managed to cross the living room to stand in front of my dad. Tears streamed down my cheeks in hot paths of regret, pain and acceptance. I knew he needed to die, and I knew I had to be the person to finally remove him from this world.

I just hoped I would have the strength to do it.

"Hi, Daddy."

His bloodshot eyes peered up at me and he patted the couch at his side. "Take a seat baby. It's time we said goodbye."

My entire body trembled, but I managed to sit beside him, my hand landing in something cold and wet on the seat. Picking it up, I stared at my palm to see blood smeared across it. My eyes shot open at the crimson stain, and I looked past my fingers to see resignation in my father's stare.

"Your brothers decided I wasn't worth taking along, I guess." Flipping the blanket aside, he showed me the stab wound in his belly. His shirt was soaked through with blood, the tops of his trousers stained black with the evidence of his impending death. When I didn't immediately speak, he let out a soft laugh. "Don't worry about it, Magpie. It doesn't hurt much anymore. I drank enough to be numb from the top of my head down to the tips of my toes. Didn't help stop the bleeding much, but there's nothing that can be done about that."

I shook my head, unable to understand the strange reality that now held me in its alien grasp. Elliot hadn't been lying about how it changed you when a person died. Although, my father was still breathing, just the thought of him leaving was changing me in impossible ways.

"I need to tell you something, Maggie, and I want you to just sit there and listen. You need to know this, baby girl. I need you to know this because it will probably save your life."

"Daddy –"

He raised a shaky hand to place a finger over my lips, his eyes meeting mine before hazing over. Exhaustion was evident in the slouch of his body and the heaviness of his eyelids. I wasn't sure how much time he had left, but I knew I shouldn't waste it by arguing. I needed to know what he wanted to say.

Satisfied that I would remain silent, he reached down to take my hand in his own. It broke me to pieces to realize he didn't have the strength to squeeze my fingers tight. It rattled me to the core to feel how cold his body had grown.

"I don't know how to tell you this, baby, but it's your right to know." His hand shook against mine, and his eyes

242

caught my gaze for only a brief second before going out of focus again. "You're not my daughter, Magpie. Not by blood, at least, but that doesn't mean you aren't my little girl."

Shock tore through my body as a violent wave of disbelief crashed within my head, memories ebbing and flowing within churning waters as I struggled to understand what he was telling me. I can't say I was entirely surprised. Brody and Finn had hinted that they weren't my true brothers. But to hear it from my father – to understand that my fate hadn't been destined to the parent who created me, but by the man who raised me as his own – it sent chills along my spine.

When he coughed, the couch shook beneath us, and he raised a soiled cloth to his mouth to wipe the spittle away.

"I've always raised you to believe that family comes first, Maggie Pie," he said on words broken apart by the weakness of his lungs and body. "I've always believed that since I was a little boy, since the day I saw my sister brought into the world and swore I'd always protect her."

A tear slipped from his eye. It was the first time I'd ever seen my father cry.

"I protected her about as well as I protected you. I was a damn failure at both. She died giving birth to you in that old church. That part hadn't been a lie. The man my father married her off to had beat her within an inch of her life when she was pregnant with you. She barely made it to me, and I took her to hide her. But on the road, she went into labor because her body was too weak to support you anymore. We ran across that church and I dragged her inside. I brought you into this world while she took her last breath. I'm not even sure she had the chance to look at you before she closed her eyes for the last time."

More tears leaked from his eyes to flow down his sunken cheeks. My tears dripped along in response to seeing the strongest man I'd known so weak. It didn't occur to me until that moment that I relied on the protection my father had always promised me. To lose it meant I was losing a part of myself; the part that felt safe and secure and kept me tethered to the belief that I would live a happy life.

His breathing became wet and shallow, but he pushed himself up straighter where he sat, his hand still nestled in mine.

"I raised you the best I could, and I thought I could teach your brothers to love you as much as I loved my sister. Until this morning, I thought I'd at least accomplished that. But I was wrong, Maggie. So, very wrong."

"Daddy, I know," I began to say, but with one look he silenced me. He didn't have much time left, and he still had more to say.

"After stabbing me, your brothers told me what they have planned for you when they find you. And please believe me, baby, they'll never stop looking until the day they die. I'm not going to burden you with the details of what they plan to do to you, but you have to know that the evil I've always been trying to hide you from was living beneath our roof this entire time."

Pausing to catch his breath, he attempted to squeeze my hand. The effort was too much for him.

His voice even more frail than when I first walked into this room, he begged me to understand what he was telling me.

"They have to die, Maggie. If you're going to live a good life, you have to make sure they're no longer part of it. They won't stop. There's a sickness in them and they plan to unleash it on you. I don't know why. I don't know what went wrong. They left me to die with the fear that they would find you and ruin you like they helped me ruin so many others."

A crack in his voice gave away the fear he felt inside. "That man that waits outside for you now? I think he's a good one. I think he's a strong one and I think he can help you survive. You need to stick with him, Maggie. You need to help him find your brothers and you need to let him help you move on from the bullshit life I gave you. He'll never forgive me for the pain I caused him, but I think he's forgiven you. It takes a strong man to do that. It takes an honorable man. You've never known one of those in your entire life, and that's my fault. So, I'm asking you to listen to me now and stay with that man for as long as he'll have you."

He fell silent for a few minutes, both our hearts beating with the turmoil and agony of saying goodbye. Although I sat beside him with strength in my spine, inside I was withered and torn apart, afraid to move forward into the unknown.

"You have a gun in your hand," he finally said. "Is there a reason why?"

It was my turn for the words I spoke to break apart. "I think you know why, Daddy."

Images flashed in my head. Early mornings where I woke up to the smell of bacon and pancakes. Hot summer days where I had ice cream smearing my cheeks and cold winters where my father stoked a fire to keep away the chill. I remembered his warm, strong lap where I always felt safe, and the way he kissed away the scrapes and cuts when I hurt myself trying to climb trees. There were the days he took me fishing, and the long afternoons where he taught me all there was to know about the land around us. In a day long ago, my father had been my hero. I wished I knew exactly when I would have the ability to let all of that go.

To the world, my father was a monster. I understood that fact and I didn't hold it against the people who saw him as something different than who he was to me. But he still held a piece of my heart within him. When he died, he'd take that part and leave an empty hole inside.

"I don't have much longer, baby. And if by killing me, you'll earn the trust of the man outside this house, then it's what you need to do."

Sobs shook my body, pain like I'd never known reaching up to slap at every part of me. My hand trembled where I held the gun and my mind was racing with how horrible and unfair my life had become.

"I don't think I can do it, Daddy. I don't have the strength. Can't I just sit here until you go? I'll tell Elliot that you died before I had the chance. He'll understand, Daddy!"

Shaking his head, my father placed his hand over the gun, but he didn't attempt to take it from me.

"You have the strength, baby girl. You're the strongest person I know. Don't start your time with him with bullshit and lies."

"I can't," I cried, the sorrow inside me making it impossible to breathe.

"You can, Maggie. Because we'll do it together."

"Daddy –"

"Please, baby girl. Help me leave this world. Save yourself and show me that everything is going to be just fine. I love you, Magpie. I've loved you since the day you were born. And I'll continue loving you from whatever Hell I'm sent to when I die."

Wrapping his hand over mine where I held the gun, he lifted it up until the muzzle of the gun was pressed to his head. Both our hands shook as we held the cold weight.

"Baby," he said, when he saw I was breaking apart beside him, "It's time."

His finger slid over mine and pressed it against the trigger. His eyes closed tight, but his mouth opened one last time.

"I love you, Maggie. And I'm sorry I wasn't a better man."

Pressing his finger down on mine, he pulled the trigger. The blast of the gun was so loud that I screamed a terrible sound. I was still screaming when his body slumped forward, still screaming when Elliot ran inside to pull me away from the bloody mess that was left of my father.

The world rotated around me, the room spinning with the confusion and desperation I felt.

And there was that word again – that all consuming feeling. That damn desperation that had charged at me once again to leave me a pathetic rubble of regret and naked pain.

Elliot spoke to me as he carried me to the bathroom. He stripped me of my clothes and begged me not to look in the mirror as he carried me by. Settling me in the shower, he turned on the water. I knew he continued talking, but the sound was jumbled with the ringing in my ears. He might as well have been speaking from inside a long, dark tunnel for as indecipherable as his words were to me.

Slipping from his grasp, I fell to me knees beneath the warm spray of water. My body felt torn apart. My mind was too big for my skull. Everything hurt and was numb at the same time.

I never understood that love could hurt a person so deeply – at least, not until the moment when I'd been forced to take my father's life.

CHAPTER THIRTY-TWO

ELLIOT

I let Maggie sleep for a few hours while I cleaned up the mess of her father. It didn't take much to get the bonfire going again and I figured burning one more body wasn't too much to ask of the flames that roared into the waning light of the late afternoon sky.

Sitting in the plastic chair that held Jonah while he'd still been alive, I breathed in the putrid scent, my eyes glaring down at his skin as it was burned completely away from his bones. I had to stoke that fire over and over again to get it hot enough to continue turning that man to ash, but eventually there wasn't enough left of him to worry about.

It wasn't the cleanest crime scene and I was sure the cops would have enough to identify the people who had died on this property, but that wasn't my concern. I didn't know how long it would take somebody to come out this way to find the scene – or if anybody would, at all.

Wasn't it just like life to keep moving forward despite the chaos and pain that occurred on a bright, sunlit day? The birds still flew in formation in the sky. The wind still blew through the branches of the trees. The leaves still rustled their natural song and I sat back simply listening to it while attempting to clear my head.

In the fourteen years I'd been chasing after the men who stole my family, I'd convinced myself that their death would eventually heal the pain. It appeared I'd been lying to myself that entire time. Despite the smell of Jonah's death that lingered in the smoke of the fire, I didn't feel any better. If I had to be honest with myself, his death had simply brought the pain right back to the forefront of my mind, making it feel like it hadn't been a day since I accepted the hard truth that they'd died.

Behind me, quiet footsteps crept, the swish of dirt beneath shoes adding to the soft symphony of early evening. The sun was sinking past the horizon, rays of brilliant light painted across the sky in dazzling oranges, yellows and reds. The crickets had already starting chirping and the birds had settled into their nests. I focused on the miracle of nature as those steps grew closer. Remaining perfectly still, I choose to let her approach on her own time.

"Thank you for –" Her words broke apart behind me, and I couldn't stay still any longer. Pushing up from my chair, I turned to find Maggie bent over herself, her arms clutching her abdomen and her face twisted with such naked and raw pain that it forced me to her side.

Taking her into my arms, I held her close, but I didn't speak or attempt anything else to soothe her. I knew the feeling of loss that consumed her in that moment. I dared not disturb it with platitudes or kind words that would do nothing to chase that pain away.

Her body trembled against mine, her tears leaving wet spots on my shirt where her face was pressed to my chest. When it felt like her legs weren't strong enough to keep her standing, I picked her up and carried her to the chairs. Settling her in my lap, I simply held her and gave her time to collect her thoughts.

Time moves slowly when agony has you in its wicked hold. It pisses you off to know that life continues moving around you, when in your mind nothing remains. I knew that agony, and I knew that anger. So, to join Maggie, I stopped time in my world, slowing it down so that our realities were the same.

Hours could have passed while I held her, but it was probably just a few minutes before she found the will to finish what she'd been trying to say.

"Thank you for taking care of my father," she whispered. "I didn't want to see that again."

"I know, and you're welcome." My hand smoothed over her hair and I brushed the errant strands away from her face. "I don't want to rush you along until you're ready, Maggie. But it's probably best we leave here as soon as possible."

Nodding her head, she swallowed down a choked sob. "I already packed my bags, Elliot. I just need to put them in the truck and then we can go wherever you want."

"I hate to bring this up," I said softly, "but we need to keep looking for your brothers. Do you have any idea where they might have gone?"

I wouldn't rest until I'd killed each and every one of the Crows, and I wondered if the fact that her brothers were still walking around and breathing wasn't the reason Jonah's death hadn't brought me the closure I sought.

"There are two places," she admitted. "One is about a day's drive away. The other is three or four days depending on how fast you drive or how many times you stop to sleep. Those are the only two places they would feel safe enough to run."

"Are you sure?" I asked.

Nodding her head, she reached up to wipe the tears from her red cheeks. "Yeah, I'm sure. If my father had been with them, they would have been harder to find. He had a network of friends that would have hidden them out for as long as they needed. But those friends never liked Finn and Brody that much, and they would question why my father wasn't there."

Letting out a long breath, I stroked my hand over her hair once more, knowing that the small contact wouldn't completely soothe her. Only time would ease the pain she carried in her heart.

"Let's get your bags in the truck. I have one place we need to go before hitting the road. It's probably best we sleep there for the night. I've been up for two days straight and I'm tired."

Slowly slipping from my lap, Maggie stood up and offered me a hand. I didn't need the assistance, but I accepted her hand anyway if for nothing else but to keep her close. Within minutes, we'd retrieved her bags from the house and packed them up with my belongings in the truck.

Another half hour had us pulling into the driveway of my modest home.

"What is this place?" Maggie asked, her eyes wide open and curious.

"It's where I live," I admitted.

A bark of laughter flew from her lips, the sound sad despite the humor she'd been attempting. "This doesn't look like much of a farm, Elliot. What is it you really do?"

She'd taken me by surprise by the comment and my shoulders shook with laughter. Reaching up, I scrubbed my palm against the back of my neck to ease the tension of my shoulders. "Um, well…I'm a mechanic."

Her green eyes met mine, her head snapping around so fast it shook the black curls that framed her face. "You are one hell of a liar, Elliot –"

Her mouth shut before she could finish the thought, embarrassment shadowing her eyes. "Hell, I don't even know your last name," she confessed.

"McLoughlin," I answered, my voice soft because I understood her puzzlement at that moment. She was with a man she barely knew. She'd just watched the death of her father. And for the first time, it was becoming glaringly apparent that I lied to her about everything since the moment we first met.

In truth, we'd both lied – the only difference was I knew her truth before I'd ever met her. For the first time, Maggie was learning mine.

Shaking her head, she gave me a hesitant smile. "You're a mechanic and you didn't know to check your battery cable?"

A tacit grin pulled at my lips. "Who do you think loosened it in the first place?"

Her eyes met mine again, but instead of anger, there was the stirring of interest behind the forest green.

We didn't say another word before crawling out of the truck and making our way inside. Maggie fell asleep on the couch while I showered and put on fresh clothes, her small body curled beneath a blanket when I stepped out to offer her something to eat.

It took me a minute to rouse her, but I eventually got some soup and bread into her stomach. My eyelids became heavy as the minutes ticked by and I asked her to sleep with me in the warmth of my large bed.

She hesitated before crawling onto the mattress, but was asleep as soon as her head hit the pillow. Leaving her to her dreams, I tiptoed back into the living room to pick up the three envelopes I'd left for my parents, Henry, and Maggie. I wasn't planning on dying any longer and I wanted to make sure there was nothing connecting me to the disappearance of the Crows.

Finally settling on the mattress next to Maggie, I slipped my arm around her body and pulled her close. And for the first time since I'd lost my wife, it didn't feel wrong to have somebody else beside me.

ᴧᴧᴧᴧᴧ

The next morning I woke to discover my body was entangled with Maggie's. Staring down at her with wonder in my eyes, I smiled to hear the way she snored softly. I imagined a future where I could poke fun at her for the sounds she made while she was sleeping. If that future could exist, I knew I'd spend many hours simply watching her rest by my side.

Wishing that the day could be normal, I stayed in bed for as long as the soft light allowed me. But by the time the sun starting climbing higher in the sky, Maggie eventually opened her eyes. Her body startled to wake up in unfamiliar surroundings, but the second she glanced up, she relaxed.

"Good morning," she said, her voice groggy with sleep. It was the sweetest sound I'd heard in a long time.

"Hey," I answered back, regretful that it was time to leave the warmth of the bed to hit the road.

When I didn't say more than that single word, she pushed herself up into a sitting position and stretched. Twisting her body around to lock her eyes with mine, she flashed me a crooked smile before asking, "Is it time for us to go?"

I would have given anything to tell her we still had time to relax and enjoy just being together, but for every minute that passed, her brothers were getting away.

"Afraid so, beautiful. I can make us a quick breakfast before heading out. Do you think you can get yourself ready in time?"

Soft laughter flowed over her lips. "Yeah. I'm not one of those women who need hours to make themselves presentable. Fifteen minutes should be fine."

Forcing myself out from beneath the covers, I pulled a shirt over my head and padded barefoot into the kitchen. Breakfast ended up being as simple as they came with some scrambled eggs and burnt toast. Maggie didn't seem to mind the fact that I wasn't the world's best cook, and after packing bags with my clothes and getting dressed, we were out on the road within a half hour.

Maggie hadn't been lying when she said it would take a day to travel to the first place her brothers would go. She sat silently for most of the trip, and I had to fight just to get small bits of information out of her. I didn't want to push her too much after everything she'd just been through, so I asked easy questions every so often, simply making conversation rather than making it sound like she was being interrogated.

What little bit I'd learned was that the place we were going was an abandoned farm. She mentioned that the farm had been used mostly for livestock. When I asked what kind, she shut down on me for a few seconds before finally admitting that the farmer had mainly raised hogs.

I couldn't understand why she appeared frightened when we pulled up to the property. It must have had something to do with the nervousness she felt for possibly seeing her brothers. But I didn't feel any qualms about driving up to the dilapidated house that sat a quarter mile in from the dirt road that led to the overgrown driveway.

Maggie had seen far too much death in her young life, and I hated that she would see a little more. But as far as she told me, she wasn't too concerned about the loss of her brothers' life.

Bringing the truck to a slow stop, I peered through the dusty windshield to see a vast expanse of abandoned land and run down buildings. The house was a one-story shack with blue paint peeling from the exterior walls and a metal roof covered in dirt and mold. One side of the house was buckled and open to the environment. On the left side of the building were a network of beat down sheds, and on the right was a large sty where I imagined the hogs had been held.

Glancing around, I didn't see fresh tire tracks or much else that would have indicated Maggie's brothers came here to hide.

"It looks like this place hasn't been touched in years," I casually mentioned. Turning to look at Maggie, I found that her eyes were rounded and glued to the building in front of us.

Shaking herself of whatever unspoken thoughts held her captive, she swallowed hard before blinking her eyes and turning her gaze on me.

"There's something I need to tell you, Elliot. I haven't told you all there is to know about where we are."

My body stilled at the tone of her voice, my fingers lightly resting on the steering wheel as I averted my eyes to keep from seeing the devastation written all over her face. Not sure whether I wanted to know what she had to say, I braced myself to listen to it anyway.

"When I was a kid," she practically whispered, "my father brought me to this farm when we were headed out of town. He thought I'd like the animals that were here, and I did for the most part, but that wasn't the only reason we came here." Swallowing again, her tongue peeked out to wet her lips, and she dared a glance at me before quickly turning her eyes away.

Dread crawled along my spine, but I remained motionless. I didn't think I liked where the conversation was going.

"I don't know any other way to say this, so I'm just going to spit it out. This farm was the last place I remember seeing your wife and son. After driving me home from the park on the night she was taken, your son and I had a tea party while my father and brothers –"

Her voice trailed off, her mind lost to the memories that had haunted her since she was a small child. I'd never had the luxury of knowing what happened to my family, and it wasn't making it any easier to hear the truth of it now.

Gaining control of herself, Maggie released a breath. "Anyways, after that night, it was time to leave and we came here first. When we drove away, I watched your son standing in front of the house holding his stuffed rabbit. I don't know what they did with your wife, but at the time we left, Michael hadn't been touched. Not by my family anyway."

Unsettling calm took me over at that moment and I thought it was funny how the body has a way of protecting itself against the mind. My thoughts were an explosion of rage, hatred and violence inside my head, but my body settled into a necessary stillness, a cool calm that was in complete opposition of everything I was feeling at that moment. It was as if the pain was so great that it short-circuited something inside of me, and I couldn't feel a damn thing at all.

Several minutes passed before I found the ability to speak again, but even then my voice was dangerously hushed.

"You were only four, Maggie."

"I know," she answered quickly. "But I shouldn't have kept that information from you. It was killing me inside, but I was too afraid to say anything while you were driving."

Nodding my head once, I forced my hand to the handle of the door and took a steadying breath before stepping outside. On furtive steps, I moved forward, breathing deeply before surveying the land that surrounded me. I was in wide open space of which I was unfamiliar, and from a tactical standpoint, it wasn't looking good.

Maggie's brothers could be hiding out just about anywhere. Behind one of the sheds. Beneath the raised foundation of the ramshackle house. Or perched in a tree with the scope of their gun pointed right at me. Not liking the odds, I had no other choice but to step softly and investigate every nook and cranny of the run-down property.

Moving back towards the truck, I knocked on the glass of the driver's side door. Maggie turned to look at me and I motioned for her to lock up. She followed the instruction immediately without daring to argue or complain. I was thankful for that small bit of cooperation on her part, although I wasn't sure if it was because she was scared of her brothers possibly hiding out, or if it was because she felt too guilty to be around me.

Either way, I felt safer knowing she was behind locked doors, and I'd intentionally left the keys in the ignition in case she had no other choice but to drive away.

Rounding the truck, I dropped the tailgate and pulled one of my rifles from the duffle bags. With a powerful scope and high caliber ammo, I felt safer with a weapon that would take out an enemy several hundred feet away. However, close contact fighting could also be on the menu today, so I tucked a handgun into the back of my jeans, and stowed a large knife in a sheath hidden on the inside of my boot. As ready as I could be, I slammed the tailgate shut and closed the distance between the truck and the house that was falling apart.

Reaching the door, all I had to do was touch the rotting wood for the decaying partition to fall away. A cloud of dust kicked up from the wood hitting the ground and I stepped back to allow the mess to settle. Keeping my body as protected as I could behind the exterior wall, I peeked around to get a look inside the structure.

Littered with inches of dust and thick cobwebs, it was obvious no person had stepped foot into the house in several years. The lack of footprints on the ground made me feel more secure about walking inside and taking a good look through every room. The floorboards groaned loudly beneath my feet, so I treaded carefully over the rotting wood. It only took me fifteen minutes to look over the small space. The home only had one bedroom, and the furniture was so sparse that it was obvious nothing could have been hidden here.

Stepping back out of the house, I exhaled heavily to evict the dust from my lungs. My eyes darted toward the truck and from a distance I could see that Maggie was still safely sitting inside. The network of shacks would take longer to inspect than the sty that sat to my right. I decided to take a peek over the gate to quickly rule out that someone was huddled behind the wooden barrier.

What I found was even more depressing than I could have imagined. Although the years had ensured that the remaining flesh of the hogs had withered away, it was painfully obvious that after the farmer died, nobody had come out to tend to the livestock. Hundreds of bones littered the dirt, the skulls of the dead pigs lying where the animals had died, the teeth decayed with age and the mud having long run dry. I imagined most of those pigs had been eaten by their own, the last few remaining most likely dying of slow starvation. Disgusted by the evidence of cruelty and neglect, I swallowed to clear my throat of the dust that remained trapped inside.

All that was left to check were the shacks. As far as I could see of the remaining land, it was covered with tall weeds and broke down fences. There was nowhere her brothers could hide in that mess without worry of rattlesnakes or other nasty critters that were as dangerous to their health as they were to mine.

With the truck in my peripheral vision, I moved towards the shacks. A network of three, they were connected by a shoddily built pathway walled in by rotting plywood. I didn't understand the reason for those pathways, but it wasn't of much interest to me either. Reaching the first shack, I used the tip of my rifle to push the door open. I could see directly through to the last shack, the doors having been removed between them. It occurred to me then that, rather than buying a larger building, the farmer had simply connected the three into one long storage unit.

Walking through the first shed, I encountered all the typical items you'd expect to find on a farm: long handled garden tools that were now rusted and sinking into the floor, bags of animal feed that were rotting and torn apart, most likely by foraging critters. Nothing was out of place, and like the house, the tool benches and floor was covered in a layer of dust, while above my head, large veils of spider webs concealed the metal ceiling. The wooden boards of the floor were rotting through in places, so I stepped carefully in order to not push through and break an ankle.

The second shack held more items like the first, also things of use to a farmer, but nothing particularly shocking or unusual. There were a few cans of gas, a box of matches, and some water barrels that I'm sure had long run dry, but that was to be expected with farm life.

Finally reaching the third shack, I regretted not having grabbed a flashlight from my truck. None of the structures had windows and having walked so deep inside, the light coming in from the door to the outside was splintered and muted by the distance. Above my head swung a single bulb light source, but I doubted the property had any power to make the bulb fire to life.

The toe of my boot kicked against something heavy and metallic. Glancing down, I stared at the odd barred box, realizing after several seconds it was an animal cage of some sort. At the far end of the shack was a basket of cloth, or some other burlap that I couldn't make out. Above it was a wall with what looked like pictures nailed to the surface.

Curious as to why pictures would be kept in such putrid conditions, I used the butt of my gun to knock away at the rotting wall to my side, finally satisfied when I opened a hole large enough to let in significant light.

Turning around, I froze where I stood, my jaw falling open as anger and pain - horror like I'd never known - assaulted me on the inside.

My eyes scanned the images as fast as they could while tears welled and burned paths down my cheeks.

Children, at least a dozen boys from what I could tell, were barely dressed. Their faces were marked with bruises and cuts, dirt smeared over their skin, and their eyes so full of fear and agony that I felt it down to my core.

Closing my eyes, my body shuddered where I stood, my mind unable to handle what stared me back in the face with such raw truth that I wished I never had to know.

Forcing them back open, I ripped the pictures from the wall, staring at each face and memorizing the details despite the way my stomach lurched with dread and disgust. My thoughts screamed at me to back away before the final truth was revealed.

It was a moment where I should have listened to the instincts that warned me. A moment where I should have settled for not knowing rather than demanding the answers I'd lived without for a long fourteen years of my life.

Eight pictures had passed through my hands before a familiar face stared back at me, accusation in his eyes that he'd been left alone to the machinations of a depraved monster, that he'd been turned over to the worst form of torment, because his father hadn't been there.

At the moment of recognition, my knees and entire body gave out. I fell to the floor, my ribs aching from the beating of my heart as it threatened to rip clean from my chest.

Bent over myself, I struggled to remain lucid, the tips of my fingers turning white as the blood was forced out. Holding onto that image with the strength I wished I'd used to hold onto my family, I stared for several minutes while my brain fought to register the horror I was seeing.

Michael.

His eyes were the same color as his mother's, but in this picture they were stained red with tears. He screamed at me from behind the lens of a madman's camera, his throat shredded by the volume of his cries, his body broken by pure evil.

His hair had been the same dark shade as mine, but in this image, it was shaved off completely.

Missing his shirt, I was able to see the scratch marks that covered his body and the dirt that was caked to practically every inch of skin. His ribs showed through what had once been a healthy, intact body. His small legs barely holding up his weight where he was positioned against a wall.

And when I looked a little closer, I saw the large shadow that loomed over him from the man who'd been taking the picture. The shadow of his captor. The shadow of a stranger who was the last person to touch him, the last person to hear his voice, the last person he saw when he closed his terrified eyes.

I thought I knew pain. I would have sworn that not knowing was the worst form of torture.

I was wrong.

The worst form of torture was knowing the last moments of my son's life, and accepting the cold, hard fact that I'd been helpless to save him. It was the all consuming realization that I was a coward because my first thought was to wish I'd never discovered the truth.

It had been easy for me to believe my son died quickly, to hide behind the comforting lie that Michael hadn't suffered. And while the truth stared me blatantly in the face, I wanted to scrub the images from my mind because I wasn't strong enough to exist in the same reality of my baby boy's fate.

Every belief I'd conjured that I'd been a decent father was shattered at my feet, my body falling down upon the shards of injustice, inadequacy and failure until my skin was torn and bleeding, until my heart and soul were shredded by a nightmare from which I couldn't wake.

Desperate to scrub the truth from my mind, I raised my hands to my head and clenched the sides, as if that one motion could erase it all.

The scream that tore from my throat was unrecognizable to me. My voice carried all the agony and pain, the hatred and fury that my body was powerless to contain. A dam broken, I released all the rage inside me in that unholy scream. I fell to the floor on my hands and knees praying for an outcome I knew could never be.

The past was long gone, and along with it, my son. I didn't need to know the specific details to understand what happened to him. I didn't have to glance back at the cage to know the last place he'd slept. My mind provided those details to me, as horrible and frightening as what my son had endured. I didn't need to hear him scream to understand that he'd been calling out to me. I didn't need to see his body abused and broken to hate myself for being unable to save him from a cruel and horrible world.

He was so young, so innocent and pure, that he couldn't have understood why evil had locked its red eyes on him. I heard his cries for his parents echo within these wooden walls.

I felt the pain and torment, the crippling cold and fear of the dark that I now knew had been the reality of his final days. When I'd left him, he'd been a happy, chubby boy full of dreams, love and everything good. But what I'd found in the image that was now grasped between shaking fingers, was that his smile was gone, his heart had been broken, and he had been left feeling scared and betrayed by a father who'd been powerless to save him.

All I had left was an image of a boy who had no hope of survival once he'd been kidnapped and sold off. A boy who'd thought his father was a hero because he was a soldier. A boy who believed himself safe because his father had always sworn to protect him from the monsters in the dark.

Releasing the picture from my fingers, my tears dripped onto the image where it landed on the floor. Ripped open and struggling to breathe, I fought against the desire to reach for my handgun and force it to my head.

Death would have been the only release from the torment that now owned me, but I wasn't brave enough – or strong enough – to take the easy way out. I was a coward, a failure, a man that had left his child in the path of the wolves. I didn't deserve an easy death, not when my child had been tortured. It made me pathetic that I couldn't handle knowing what had been done to my son, while he was the one who'd lived through it.

Desperate to find any piece of him that might have been left behind, I began ripping at the burlaps sacks to discover what was inside.

Dozens of stuffed animals fell to the ground, and at the bottom of one rotting bag I found the last thing I had left of my son.

He'd called it Floppy Bunny, and I remembered it well. I'd bought it for him on the day I'd enlisted in the Marines. They were inseparable since the minute that stuffed rabbit had reached his small hands. He took it everywhere, including the bath, much to the dismay of his mother.

On the day I was deployed to go fight in the Middle East, my boy had been holding this rabbit tightly in his arms while I held the boy tightly in mine. My body shook as the memories came rushing back and I screamed again when that memory of the last moment I'd held him rebounded in my head. I remembered thinking there was a chance I'd never see him again, but I'd been selfish at the time because I believed it would be me that ended up dead.

I was the person who'd been heading into a battlefield, and yet it was my young son who'd paid with his life.

Collapsing down, I hugged the stuffed rabbit to my body, cradling it as if it were Michael himself. Memories flooded me, painful because they were too happy, too optimistic to bear. Everything I'd spent years blocking from my mind was suddenly standing in front of me, mocking me with the horrible truth that I would never touch my son again. I would never hear his voice or smell his skin. I'd failed him because I left him alone.

I'd failed him.

And I'd failed my wife.

There was no telling how much time passed as I laid on the ground helpless to the agonizing assault of memories that plagued me. I was crazed and crippled as the agony ran its brutal course. It leaked out of me with each tear I shed, with every scream and whimper that burst from my throat. As the pain ebbed slowly, the fury returned to take its place, the heat scorching me from the inside, the rage pulling me apart and stitching me back together again until the pain threatened to annihilate me.

Unable to contain the surge of that which destroyed me - the nameless, faceless reality that tore me apart inside - I pushed up to my feet, stripping everything from the walls, kicking over everything that lay littered on the ground. I punched walls until my knuckles bled. I destroyed whatever object lay motionless in my path. I beat my hands against the cage that sat rusting, but nothing lessened the fury – nothing would bring my son back.

Wanting nothing more than to destroy the place where my son had taken his last breath, I pushed up from the floor with the dirty, rotting rabbit still tucked under my arm, and I grabbed for the gas cans and matches I'd seen on my way inside.

I should have taken the photographs from the wall and given them to the police. There were other parents out there like me who were still seeking the answers of what happened to their children. But I wasn't thinking logically at the moment. All I wanted was vengeance, all I knew was that I needed the godforsaken place destroyed.

Throwing gasoline over wooden floors and splashing it on the walls, I doused the place until the smell was unbearable. Barely able to breathe oxygen through the fumes, I reached for a match, and stepped towards the door as I struck it and tossed it inside.

Years of decay burst into flames, and I watched with morbid satisfaction as it all came tumbling down in a brilliant display of chaos and fire.

Not even watching it burn eased the feeling of utter failure that tore me apart. I breathed in the smoke of its destruction, I allowed the flames to lick at my body. I stood there reveling in the pain of standing so close to its inferno because I deserved that torment. I deserved to burn because, by failing my son, I'd just been another monster, one who'd told him pretty lies before leaving him behind.

He was helpless.

I was his hero – his strong, protective soldier.

And I'd allowed him to die.

CHAPTER THIRTY-THREE

MAGGIE

The human body is a wonderful and terrible thing. Wonderful because its design is a marvel of nature and science. Sheltering our vitality in an effort to keep us alive, the body acts without conscious thought. Cells regenerate, injuries are cushioned by the rush of water and fluids, the blood distributes oxygen, nutrients, and energy to the parts of us that work constantly to breathe, to cleanse poisons, to create children, to fuel us through our everyday lives.

The body allows us to feel emotions, chemicals designed that lead us to laugh, to cry, to love, and to hope. The brain stores our memories. It allows us to dream. And it allows us to think beyond the ordinary to invent and develop, to become part of something bigger than ourselves.

But there are the terrible parts as well, the seemingly innocuous consequences to our very souls that are part of what it means to be human. I don't care what religion you subscribe to, because there is one belief that is common amongst them all: we continue to exist once our bodies die, that there is a light inside of us without scientific explanation that carries us into the afterlife. It can't be touched or seen. It can't be weighed or measured. But it does exist and it is trapped by the physical body.

That's how I felt while sitting in the truck outside the pig farm as Elliot walked from building to building: trapped.

My soul had been injured by the injustices of my life. Shredded and torn apart, my soul was begging to fly free. The need to escape was the frantic pulse that beat within my veins. The desire to forget was the headache that pounded within my fragile skull. I was tired and weary, disillusioned and forced to stare at the ugly truth that my life until now had been one, big, horrific lie.

No matter how desperately I wanted to flee this world and all the horror it encompassed, I was trapped within a network of organs, my soul tied down my tendons and veins, my very essence left with gaping holes and sharp edges because my body was too stubborn to die.

It was a lesson in counterparts, the desire to leave this world in search of something better as opposed to the instinctual and biological drive to survive.

I was selfish for feeling this way, greedy and weak for wanting to simply fly away.

I'd been complicit in my family's crimes. I'd turned a blind eye beneath stars on those long, lonely nights. My mind had shielded me from believing I was responsible. Hidden beneath the comforting blanket of a lie that I was too young to understand, I broke under the weight of truth that now stared me in the face. I hadn't been too young my entire life. There were plenty of opportunities where I could have tried to do what was right.

My hatred of this farm sickened me because it was part of the sin I'd committed by complacency. A beacon of remembrance left decaying where it stood, the farm had always been a place in my nightmares – a place I'd chosen to forget while others had died. How many times had my hand been near a phone? Saving people would have taken one call, one written letter, one word spoken to a stranger who strolled by.

When I looked out over the expanse of rotting buildings and neglected land, I watched the ghosts of my family's victims staring back at me, their spirits glimmering in the bright sunlight, their expressions twisted with anger for the way I'd turned my head. I couldn't look at them where they stood restless, I couldn't apologize to them because it meant I'd have to accept my part in their deaths.

And while the weight of their lives crawled along my shoulders, I mourned the man who'd stolen them away.

How fucked up did that make me?

Several times, my hand moved to unlock the doors. My body prepared to jump down from the truck and run away while Elliot was hidden within the buildings. We were two people on opposite sides of a line that had no way of intermingling. Victim versus monster. Good versus evil. A man desperate to reveal truth versus a woman who knew that truth but had chosen to remain silent.

But yet, I sat there watching him walk the grounds while remembering every horrible thing I'd done to him. He cared for me despite the lies. He protected me despite the pain I'd caused him. He respected me because he was an honorable man who knew he'd been seduced by evil, but refused to believe there wasn't something good inside.

He saw parts of me I never believed existed. His faith in me was true. And for the life of me, I couldn't see the same person staring back in the mirror that he swore he saw when he looked into my eyes.

I wept for the man who murdered Elliot's family, and yet Elliot was strong enough to feel sympathy for my tears.

He wasn't just a decent man, he was the bravest man I knew.

Watching him walk into the network of sheds that sat off to the side of the house that was falling down on top of itself, I waited in anxious anticipation. Never having been inside those sheds when I was a child, I remembered the disgusted feeling I had when I walked past them. The banging sounds of animals caged, the smell of sweat, blood and decay. Having been young, I'd assumed those scents were just an unfortunate consequence of a farm, but I knew better now, knew that hidden behind those walls were atrocities like I'd never known.

Minutes ticked past with furtive beats, time grinding to a halt as the sun stopped its slow path across the never ending sky. Every breath was a struggle as my eyes remained locked to that single, decaying door that led into what I imagined was nothing less than Hell.

The silence surrounding me was deafening, every small sound that escaped its grasp shouting at me to look away.

Trapped in what felt like a pressure cooker, I fidgeted where I sat, my hand finally breaking free of the demands of my mind, my fingers gripping down on the handle as I set myself free.

I hadn't made it halfway across the yard before the screaming met my ears, and I tripped over my stumbling feet as smoke climbed its way up from the buildings. The breath of a dragon, it danced in dark plumes, reaching up with wicked hands to darken the bright sky.

Running over uneven land, I tripped and fell to my knees. My mouth opened to scream Elliot's name, but the sound wouldn't come, the one word had failed me, and I was helpless to watch and wonder if the bravest man I'd known would emerge from the rubble to live another day.

Sinking down into the sand, my palms pressed flat over sandspurs and weeds, I ignored the pain while my eyes sought any motion within the flames. Every heartbeat was agonizing, every tear I shed burning, every hope I'd had dying, as I watched the buildings crumble into embers and ash.

"Elliot," I finally whispered, my voice trapped in the belief that he was dead. But then to the side of the destruction and rubble, I saw a man creep along the ground, a stuffed rabbit held beneath his arm, his face twisted in agony for whatever he'd discovered on the inside.

In that moment, I realized that bravery didn't always mean to walk blindly into danger without fear or concern about your life. Bravery was the ability to forgive, the willingness to see the truth, the promise to survive despite the horror that stared you in the face.

It was my turn to be brave, to push past the weight that held me, to shove all my own pain aside so that I could pull Elliot from the chaos that threatened to swallow him whole.

Pushing up to my feet, I found the strength to move forward, to rush to his side and fall down on knees beside him. Never before had I seen a man gripped by the power of pure agony, crushed into dust by the beam of light that revealed what existed in all the dark shadows.

Tears streaked down his face to mix with the soot and dust of the fire. His body collapsed forward, his mouth opened on a silent scream.

When I'd been left crippled and broken beneath the death of my father, this was the man who'd picked me up and carried me away. It was finally my turn to return to him the favor.

"Come on, Elliot," I pled. "We have to leave. If we stay here, we'll die."

The fire was spreading with the wind that blew the flames. Dead grass and debris caught and sparked, the inferno crawling across the ground with a vengeance to consume whatever was trapped in its path. Smoke replaced oxygen, burning ash rained down on our heads. If we didn't move fast enough, we'd become one with the evil that still lingered on this swatch of land.

"Dammit, Elliot!" I screamed, "We need to move!"

I recognized the emptiness in his eyes, the inability to move forward because he was trapped in the past. But I wouldn't leave him here to become part of it. I flat out refused.

Gripping his arms with my hands, adrenaline and tenacious will flowed through my body. Pushing up to my feet, I found the strength to pull him with me, to force him towards the truck despite his feet fighting not to move.

If I had to drag him, I swore to myself I would find a way to move mountains if for nothing else but to keep him with me, to take him to safety, and to repair the parts of him that were dying before my eyes.

Don't ask me how I managed to get him in the truck. All action without thought, I didn't pay attention that the odds were stacked against me. But I managed to move him, to buckle him in and to run around to take control of the wheel. And as an explosion rocked the property behind us, I slammed my foot on the pedal and left the scorched horrors of the past behind.

🐇🐇🐇🐇

Elliot didn't say a word as we drove for several hours. Keeping his eyes trained to the terrain that flew past us, he clutched the stuffed rabbit to his body. Every so often his jaw would tick with some unspoken thought. Pained groans rattled from his throat and his body would tense only to relax slowly again.

I was a fish out of water struggling to breathe as I continued on the path towards the only other place where I knew we could find my brothers.

Exhaustion eventually overtook me, my eyelids drooping down, the truck swerving over the road as I struggled to remain conscious. And even when I finally pulled over, Elliot refused to glance in my direction.

He hadn't told me what he found in those abandoned sheds, but it didn't take a genius to figure it out. What did take a genius was discovering a way to free him of the past that imprisoned him to bring him back to the present day.

"I can't drive anymore, Elliot. Would you like to take over?"

Silence was his only response. Reaching out to prod him to look at me, I snatched my hand away when he flinched at the feel of my fingertips on his skin. I realized quickly that every part of him hurt, as if his body had been burned in that fire. From what little I could see of his skin, he didn't have a mark on him, except for the dried blood on his knuckles.

"Elliot, I need you to help me here. We can't sleep on the side of the road."

Still nothing. Not a blink of his eyes, not a twitch of his lips, not a scathing expression that screamed at me to stay away.

He was practically frozen, and I was determined to be the ice pick that cracked the surface and pulled him free.

Reaching forward again, I wrapped my fingers around his bicep, my fingernails digging into his skin as I shook him to gain his attention. "Damn it, Elliot. Talk to me. Scream at me, if you need to, but stop sitting there on your ass doing nothing! You got me into this mess, and –"

The words died in my mouth in an instant as my body was pressed up against the driver's side door. Elliot's hand wrapped over my neck threatening to squeeze the life out of me. With wide eyes I stared back at him, happy that he'd finally moved, but scared shitless that I wouldn't be moving much longer.

"Elliot," I rasped while staring into violent, grey eyes. "You're hurting me."

"Oh yeah," he growled out. "How does it feel, Maggie? Knowing that death is staring you in the face. Because it sure as hell stared in mine today. Because of your family. Because of that sick fuck who owned that farm. Because of –"

"Me?" I finished the sentence for him. "Is it because of me, Elliot?"

I wasn't sure how he'd managed to understand me with my words as broken up as they were, but his fingers relaxed over my throat, his eyes blinking twice until something human had returned to them, and he abruptly pulled away.

His head turned so he wasn't looking at me, but I didn't dare move a muscle until I knew that he was under control. We sat there for several minutes before his breath evened out again and the ticking of his jaw quit its furious, bloodthirsty beat.

Speaking softly because I was frightened, I chanced casting out a line that kept him connected to the present moment while it appeared he was slipping farther away.

"If you need to blame me, I'm right here and ready to take it. But sitting there saying nothing isn't helping you, Elliot. I'm sorry I don't have the strength to pick you up and toss you in a shower like you did me, but I'm trying to pull you back from whatever edge you're currently standing on."

Shaking his head, he breathed out heavily, his shoulders shaking with the vicious emotions trapped inside.

Pushing away from the door, I leaned against the steering wheel. "Please, Elliot. Talk to me."

"I don't blame you," he spat, heartache and turmoil dripping from those four words. A finely honed blade couldn't have sliced me deeper than the pain implicit in his voice.

"So, who do you blame?"

His head spun on his shoulders and his eyes locked to mine. "I blame myself, okay? I blame me."

His words hit me like a ton of bricks. "What happened to your family wasn't your fault, Elliot. There was nothing you could have done. If anybody is to blame, it's me."

"You?" he scoffed. "You were four fucking years old. You had no idea what your family was doing. I was nineteen. I could have done something. I could have stayed home instead of running off to fight in a stupid war."

"It wasn't your fault," I repeated, making sure to add enough strength to my voice to make what I was saying believable. "It wasn't."

"Yeah, so who's fault was it?"

"My family's. My father. My brothers. That damn farmer. They're the ones you should be blaming."

His nostrils flared at the mention of my family.

"I hate your family," he snarled.

Slowly, I nodded my head in understanding. "Yeah, I know. And whether we like it or not, I'm part of that family. So, if you need me to get out of this truck right now and walk away so that you can heal, I will."

"No," he answered. "I just need...fuck..."

He was breaking down before my eyes, crumbling to pieces right there in front of me. But I was determined to pick up every single scrap of him and stitch it back together.

"What do you need? Tell me and I'll give it to you."

Silence filled the space between us for several tense seconds.

Speaking slowly and fighting for control, Elliot clenched his hands into fists over the dirty stuffed rabbit in his lap. "I need my son back."

"I can't give you that," I admitted on a helpless whisper. "But I can give you what you sought me out for in the first place. I can help you end this, Elliot. But I can't do it without your help, as well. I'm not God. I can't erase the past. But what I can give you is vengeance. I can lead you where you need to go to make sure what happened to your son never happens again."

His head shook again, his teeth grinding beneath his cheeks. "We can't stop all the monsters, Maggie."

"No," I agreed, "we can't. But we can stop two of them. We can stop the ones responsible for your wife and son. That has to be enough."

"I want them dead, Maggie. I want them crushed until there's nothing left of them. I want them buried beneath the dirt and I want them erased and forgotten."

Bravery was a funny thing. Just hours before I swore I was the weakest person alive, but when the opportunity presented itself for me to be the strong one, I was brave enough to answer the call. I guessed it was just another part of a person that they never understood existed until it was staring them in the face and demanding that they do anything it took to survive.

"Then let's erase them. I'll show you where they are. And you'll make sure they never see the light of day again."

More silence filled the interior of the truck. My hands gripped the wheel and my lungs held onto a breath as I waited for him to respond.

After the tension had climbed so high that I thought I'd be crushed beneath it, Elliot's shoulders softened, his head fell back against the seat and his hands stop clutching the stuffed animal in his lap.

"You promise me you're taking me to them? That we're on our way to end this?"

I released the breath I'd been holding.

"Yeah, Elliot, that's what I'm promising you. But I can't get there without you being here with me in the present. I can't stop them if you remained trapped in the past."

He released his breath as well before turning his head to look in my direction. "Do you still need me to drive?"

I didn't mean to laugh at the question, but my nerves were frayed and it slipped out of me before I could stop it.

"Not anymore. After almost being strangled, I'm fully awake."

His mouth pulled into a thin line and shame rolled behind his eyes. "I'm sorry, Maggie. I didn't mean to take that out on you."

Giving him a gentle smile, I reached to turn the key and start the engine. "Don't worry about it, Elliot. If it had been me, I'd probably have done the same."

I'd barely had time to pull off the shoulder of the road before light laughter shook his shoulders.

Glancing over, I gave him a questioning look.

The corners of his lips turned up into a sad smile. "No, you wouldn't have, beautiful. But thanks anyway, even though you are a horrible liar."

He was still sad as we continued down the road, but it was a hell of a lot better than catatonic.

🕯🕯🕯🕯

Two days passed along with several thousand miles, Elliot and I both allowing the tranquil silence to help ease some of the strain of the past couple days. In the moments we weren't lost to our own thoughts and emotions, we talked to each other about random subjects. I learned about Elliot's family and the normal life in which he'd been raised. He learned about the constellations I'd taught myself on the nights I'd escaped my family's parties, and he'd laughed to learn that I was scared of small spiders. I liked the sound of his laughter, even if it was still somewhat sad.

We'd crossed several state lines on our way to the family's secret hideaway, but we both were running out of fuel and in need of some rest and relaxation. Although Elliot was determined to end this nightmare as soon as was humanly possible, I'd convinced him that one good night's sleep wouldn't hurt him, and that it would help for the fight to come.

Within six hours of our destination, we pulled into a hotel that sat lonely on the side of a long, remote road, and after checking in with fake names, we let ourselves into the room to collapse on the first bed we'd seen since leaving Elliot's bed back home.

"Fuck, it feels good to lay down," Elliot muttered, his eyes half closed and his body stretched across the mattress.

Eyeing the way his shirt rode up and the muscles of his abdomen peeked out to say hello, I bit down on my lip and kept myself from exploring the way they would feel beneath my fingertips.

"You know what else might feel good?" I asked, a shy smile tilting my lips at the way he stared up at me.

"What's that?"

A shiver coursed through my body at the rough tone of his voice.

"A shower."

His eyes clenched shut, but his lips pulled apart into a wide smile. "Damn woman, it has been so long since I've had one of those, I'd almost forgotten what they are."

Laughing at his attempt at humor, I couldn't help but feel happy that he was no longer crushed. He never told me what he found in those sheds, and I didn't press him on the subject. I needed him here with me in the present moment and not plagued by the memories of what had been done.

"Well, you'll just have to wait, mister, because I call first dibs."

Thankfully, my monthly visitor had ended the day before, but it left me feeling gross and neglected for not having had the chance to freshen up.

Shuffling my tired feet into the bathroom, I turned on the water to let it heat up and gladly stripped my body of the clothes I'd been wearing for way too many days. I had no way of washing them, and didn't much care to remember all the places I'd been and the nightmares I'd seen while wearing them. Tossing them in the trashcan that sat next to the sink, I felt like a million pounds had been lifted off me before climbing in beneath the spray of hot, steamy water.

In all my years, I'd never enjoyed anything more than this shower. The stream of water was like hot fingers massaging away all the conflict and turmoil coiled inside me. Turning my face up into the spray, I stood still as the water traced down the lines of my face, eventually settling over my tired shoulders and washing the grime of my past from my skin. I imagined that all the pain, horror and torment I'd suffered both emotionally and physically was sucked down by the drain at my feet and after cleaning my body, I hated to step away from the warm safety of the spray to emerge back into the harsh reality that my life had irrevocably changed.

Fresh white towels hung in wait on the bar and I wrapped myself in their soft touch before turning to look at the woman who stared back at me in the mirror. Was it possible to have aged years within only a handful of days? My face seemed thinner, the angles harder and more mature. My skin glowing from the heat of the water contrasted sharply against the white towel. The curves of a woman's body were evident beneath the terrycloth that covered it, and my eyes flashed with a fiery resilience that I'd never seen before.

Opening the door, I stepped into the main room to grab my bag of clothes, the steam chasing after me like phantom hands that wanted to hold me within their warmth.

Glancing towards the bed, I laughed softly to discover that Elliot lay still on his stomach, his arms reaching up to hug the pillow that was nestled beneath his weary head. Unsure whether I should wake him so he could jump in the shower, I stepped lightly over the faded green carpet in search of my bag. With my back to Elliot, I pulled out a pair of panties, some sleep shorts and a weathered t-shirt that was worn in all the right places so that it was neither restrictive nor harsh against my skin.

Dropping the towel, I bent over to pull on my panties and damn near fell to the floor when Elliot spoke.

"The bruises are already fading," he noted on a voice thick with exhaustion.

Reaching for the towel, I hugged it to my body and spun in place.

"The bruises?"

A grin stretched his lips as he pushed up to lay on his side. With his head resting on one hand, he stared at me with grey eyes that were a contrast of lust and utter despair. I wanted to wipe the pain from the lines of his face, but I didn't dare move. I'd only been naked in front of one other man, and I refused to allow those memories to climb back up to the forefront of my mind.

"Yeah, the bruises that ran up your legs. And the…well…" His voice trailed off, anger a light that glowed behind his gaze.

"I would have killed that man if you hadn't distracted me. Would have done the same thing as your father if we'd returned and he hadn't beaten me to it."

Not knowing what to say, I chewed on the back of my lip, my weight shifting between my feet. I felt so exposed, but it didn't feel wrong when Elliot was my audience. Not like it felt with Jack when the choice hadn't been mine.

"I'm glad you didn't," I admitted softly. "You didn't need his blood on your hands. You're not a killer, Elliot –"

"Yeah, Darlin', I am."

Startled by the sincerity of his words, I stepped back out of instinct. He didn't release me from the intensity of his stare, didn't paint pretty pictures to seduce me closer.

"You need to know that about me before things progress further between us. I'm not the same kind of monster you're used to, but I'm a monster all the same. And when it comes to protecting what's mine, there's nothing out there I wouldn't do, even if it means I have to take somebody's life."

Shaking my head, I averted my eyes. It was impossible to look at the beauty of his face and to hear him tell me such wicked truths about who he was inside.

"I'd never ask you to kill for me."

"You wouldn't have to. And if your life was on the line, you couldn't stop me either. I'm a possessive, protective, man, Maggie. What's mine is mine and I will fight to the death if need be to keep it that way."

His words should have been comforting, but after what I'd been through in life, they shook me to my core. "What if I no longer wanted to be yours? What if I wanted to walk away?"

"I'd let you," he admitted. "But if that wasn't something you wanted, then you can bet I'd never let you out of my sight." He paused for a second, his chest moving with the inhalation of breath. "I'm sorry, but I'm not sure I'll ever move past what happened to Katelyn and Michael when I wasn't there to protect them. If you really want to try this with me, you need to know that I'll always be watching over you."

A smile tilted his lips, soft and sad. "I may actually be annoying as hell by how closely I watch you. But can you blame me? Just look at yourself, Maggie. You're absolutely breathtaking."

And just like that all the anxiety I felt melted away. Taking cautious steps in his direction, I felt like a bunny creeping towards a snake. His eyes were all seeing, his body lying in repose when I knew he could strike between one second and the next. Nerves had my knees shaking beneath me, but I ignored the desire to move away. If ever I needed to face my fears and learn to trust, it was right now, right here, and with this man who had stolen away my ability to think clearly.

Standing by the edge of the bed, I locked my eyes with his and allowed the towel to slide down my body.

He didn't move a muscle, didn't pull his intense gaze from my eyes. "Are you sure, beautiful? Are you sure you can do this? That you want to do this?"

Nodding my head slowly, I watched him with timid fascination. "You seem to ask me that question a lot, Elliot. And there hasn't yet been something I couldn't do when you were standing there next to me."

Rolling onto his back, he kept his eyes trained on mine, and only moved to crook his finger in my direction calling me to his side. "I'll let you lead this dance – for the first time, at least. I won't push you, Maggie. Not until you say that's what you want."

My knees were practically knocking together. Ignoring the trembling of my body, and the erratic beat of my heart, I climbed onto the bed, crawling on hands and knees until I was straddling his lap.

"What do you want?" he asked, his voice rough with desire.

There was only one simple answer I could give. "I want you to touch me. I want you to show me what you promised to show me all those times we met at that abandoned farm."

His mouth pulled into a grin and his hands slid slowly up my naked thighs. I gasped when his thumbs brushed between my legs, but then turned quickly to trace up the curve of my hips, the sensitive sides of my ribcage and breasts, up to my shoulders and then pulled me down until my mouth joined with his.

We kissed until we were gasping, but when he pulled away, his lips were still pressed softly to mine. "What if I lose control? Will I scare you? I don't want to be like that other man -"

Slipping my tongue out to slide along his bottom lip, I silenced all of his concerns with a long drawn out kiss. I understood then that I trusted Elliot more than I trusted myself at times, and that if any person could show me what it meant to be loved, it was the man who'd already promised he would always protect me.

Speaking against his mouth, I was breathless when I said, "I'm yours to do with what you want, Elliot. Tonight. Tomorrow. And for as long as you'll have me."

From that moment forward, there was nothing left I needed to say.

CHAPTER THIRTY-FOUR

ELLIOT

She weighed practically nothing. It was the first thing I noticed about her when she crawled up to straddle my lap. Struggling to keep my hands traveling slowly and carefully over her trembling body, I pulled her into a kiss that sealed the promise that I would always be there to watch over her. I tried to convey with actions instead of words the truth of how I felt about a woman who, through tragedy, had crept inside my fractured and weary heart.

Maggie wasn't just a bandage for the pain that almost destroyed me, she was a balm that healed the soul. Her innocence consoled me, her beauty reminding me that despite the horrors of this world, there were still experiences to look forward to, still people I could love and trust.

Our relationship hadn't started on the firmest of foundations, but once the facades were tossed aside and the truth about our lives was revealed to one another, I discovered another part of myself within the body of a young woman who was far older than the number of years she'd actually lived.

We'd been introduced through warfare and heartache, and yet we'd walked out stronger because we were united together in the promise that we could live on.

With my mouth pressed against hers, I allowed my hands to travel the length of her body, touching and teasing, but never giving her what I knew she begged for with those cute little moans that had me groaning in return. It was impossible not to let myself go to the lust that consumed me as soon as my palms met the warmth of her smooth, supple skin, but I restrained myself to lead her through a dance that started off slow, only to stoke the flames of desire so hot that she was left panting with need.

Tracing my fingertips down her shoulders, I stroked softly over the outside of her breasts, smiling at how her body bucked over mine. I wanted to watch her reaction to each and every touch I gave her, but found it impossible to pull away from a kiss that was filled with sweet passion and raw, breathless trust.

She jumped when I brushed my hands down her ribs, and I discovered how ticklish she was. Laughing against her mouth, I opened my eyes to find hers staring right back at me, humor sparkling behind the depth of green.

"Sorry," I mumbled, but it wasn't a true apology. Looking forward to a day where I could hold her down and tickle her until she begged me to stop, I gripped my hands over her thighs, pushing them apart until she was nestled over the hardness of my cock.

"Oh," her mouth opened on that surprised sound, her eyes widening before closing as she fell forward.

"No, you don't," I teased, my hands moving quickly to push against her shoulders and set her up above me so I could worship the view of true perfection. Black hair fell in waves from her head over her shoulders, and I pushed the tresses back to run down behind her so that my view was unobstructed.

Her entire body blushed when I studied her, the rosy color magnificent against the pale beauty of her skin.

"Are you scared?"

Shaking her head, she flashed me a shy smile. "Not with you," she purred, her lush lips kiss swollen and soft red.

Unable to continue this tormenting, slow rhythm, I gave into desire and cupped the weight of her breasts. Her head fell

282

back, her hair long enough to brush over my thighs. Surprising me like she always had the ability to do, she began to move over top of me rubbing herself over the length of my cock that was still painfully trapped in my pants.

"I want you, Maggie Crow. More than I think you realize. It was torture for me to keep from taking you every way I wanted when we first started playing these games."

Her lips pulled into a wider grin, her head angling down so that her eyes could meet mine. "Then stop torturing yourself. I'm telling you I'm yours. You're the one stupid enough not to take what's being offered."

It was all she needed to say to push me into being a slave to my desire. Flipping her over until she was flat against the bed, I laughed at the cry of surprise that burst from her lips. A man crazed and desperate for release, I kissed her all over her body, my teeth finding the sensitive, hard peaks of her breasts and tasting the warm heat between her legs. The moans that escaped her throat were a vibration against my cock, lengthening and awakening me until I couldn't stand it any longer.

Pushing myself up to my knees, I stared down at the trembling woman where she lay sprawled on the bed. Her hair was a river of midnight black splayed over pillows of white. Pulling the shirt from my body, I groaned when she reached up to run her hands down my chest and over my stomach, and we both reached for the button of my pants which I couldn't open fast enough.

Finally freed of my clothing, I nestled myself between her legs. My hands slipped down between the mattress and the soft mounds of her perfect ass and I lifted her hips to position myself at the opening of her body.

Pushing in with one slow stroke, I studied the expression on her face, every muscle in me tightening to watch her eyes close and her lips fall open on an erotic moan.

"That's right, beautiful girl. Damn, you feel amazing."

I wanted this to be slow and meaningful, wanted it to be something that took hours to complete, but I couldn't control myself once I felt the wet heat inside her. I warned her to hold on. Without question, her hands grasped the sheets at her side, and I moved inside her with the ferociousness of a starving man.

It only took minutes for her body to break apart beneath me and for her to scream out her release, but I wasn't quite done with this beautiful girl, wasn't quite ready to let her sleep.

My hands gripped her hips as I held her in place and I made love to her with a steady rhythm that was gaining in speed. Her body molded perfectly to mine, her muscles gripping me so tightly that it was impossible not to come.

I hadn't had time to protect myself, so I groaned on the last thrust inside her before pulling out on my release.

"Fuck," I muttered, my body falling over hers, the sweat of our bodies mingling as we held each other tight.

Her hand stroked over my hair, her lips planting soft kisses along my jawline. And I closed my eyes as I breathed in her scent, and smiled to realize that she was finally mine.

$$\mathbf{\lambda\lambda\lambda\lambda}$$

It was impossible to sleep that night, not with Maggie's naked body curled up against mine, but after making love to her three times over, I finally fell into a restless sleep that was enough to recharge me for the day to come.

Knowing what we were facing, we both moved about our morning, showering and packing, while refusing to talk about the fat elephant in the room that was staring us both in the face.

After stopping at a small diner that stood on its own in the middle of nowhere, we were back on the road heading towards a federal reserve. Maggie told me her father had long ago built a small lean-to when he'd been a hunter and had added to the structure over the years they'd visited there to hide. Sneaking materials in while the authorities weren't looking, he built it deep enough into the woods that he didn't have to worry about it being discovered.

From how she described it, the structure was nothing more than four walls and a plastic roof. There was no running water or electricity, or anything else that would give it away.

I was surprised that, through all the years, no person had stumbled across it, but Maggie explained that once the land had been set aside as a nature preserve, there were no hunters walking around that could have discovered it. Even on the seldom occasions that Maggie's family had chosen to hide there, they had to sneak onto the property using an overgrown trail that was barely wide enough for the trucks and equipment they hauled while traveling the country.

She hadn't been lying. Once we approached the turn off that led into the woods, I had no desire to drive my truck through what looked like a path of saplings and low lying bushes and shrubs. They scraped against the bottom of my truck with jarring sounds that made me wonder how much work it would take to repair the damage being caused. However, within minutes of making the turn, I noticed that the trail had recently been flattened down by another heavy vehicle.

"Any chance it was your brothers' truck that cut through the vegetation?"

I was simply making conversation to fill in the silence that was thick between us, however Maggie didn't respond. Glancing over at her, I saw her mouth moving where she was gnawing on her lip, and I recognized the fear behind her eyes that held her motionless in her seat.

Reaching out a hand, I grabbed her thigh. "Hey, Maggie. Are you okay? You look like you're about to jump out of the truck and haul ass the other way."

Her head slowly turned to look at me, fear and apprehension behind her beautiful eyes.

"Where'd you go just now?"

"I'm right here with you." The words were spoken steadily enough, but as usual she failed to convince me of the lie.

"No, Maggie. You're somewhere else. You've gone to that place you go when you can't face whatever is happening around you. I can't handle not having you here with me now."

She knew she was caught. She attempted to avert her eyes, but I refused to let her. Gripping her chin with my thumb and forefinger, I gently turned her head back in my direction.

"Talk to me."

Breathing out a frustrated breath, she pulled her chin from my fingers. "You should keep your eyes on the trail, Elliot. It zigzags and you don't want to run us into a tree."

Soft laughter shook my shoulders. "Well, then stop forcing me to bring you back to the present. Tell me what's on your mind."

Tense seconds passed in silence, but she breathed out again and gave up the fight. "I'm scared. Hell, I'm more than scared. I'm terrified."

"Of what?"

"Of you getting yourself killed. You don't know my brothers. They're evil. When something gets in their way, they don't care what it takes to survive. I've seen what they can do to another person. I saw what they did to my father, and they were supposed to love him. I'm not in the present with you at the moment, you're right about that. But it's not because I'm thinking of something from my past. I'm fast forwarding to the future, and I don't want to watch you die."

The truck lurched suddenly as I slammed my foot on the brakes. Throwing the truck into park, I twisted my body in my seat to look Maggie square in the eyes.

"I'm not worried about dying. And I've been in worse situations than the one we're heading into now. But, to be honest, I'm scared shitless right along with you. Not about losing my life. I'm not worried about that. I'm worried about the sons of bitches getting their hands on you. I wish you'd have listened to me when I asked you to stay at the motel."

In truth, I'd all but begged her to stay in bed. To stay under the blankets where it was safe and to keep the mattress warm until I got back. She argued until she was blue in the face and refused to stay where I told her. Maggie was just as stubborn as me in that regard. I wasn't even sure why I'd bothered arguing with her in the first place because before I even opened my mouth, I knew what her answer would be.

"You wouldn't have been able to find the place if I stayed behind. You needed me to lead you here."

"Yeah? Well, I know where it is now, so why don't I turn this truck around and drop you off at the nearest motel? It would certainly make things a hell of a lot easier on me in the long run."

"No," was her final answer, the strength behind that one syllable word enough to tell me there was no changing her mind.

"Why?" I asked.

"Because we're stronger together. I know the property where we're headed. I know the way to sneak up to it and I know all the crevices where my brothers would hide. I'm not letting you walk onto a battlefield where they have the advantage."

The smile that pulled at my lips pissed me off. I wanted to be mad at her for being a stubborn, stupid woman, but I couldn't ignore the bravery she was showing me. When I'd met her, she was a timid young thing, unsure of herself as much as she was with the world around her. But not anymore. The woman that looked at me now had steel in her spine and an unspoken determination that rivaled even the toughest of soldiers.

But even then, there was still panic rattling around inside her. Not for herself. No. She was far too selfless for that. The poor thing was working herself up inside because she was too afraid of losing me. I made a promise to myself that I wouldn't let that happen. That we'd walk out of these woods together, or we wouldn't be walking out of them at all.

"Take a deep breath, Maggie, and then leave all those fears right here in this spot. They won't do either of us any good. You have the maps we need locked up in your beautiful head, and I have the skill to bring down your sorry excuses for brothers. We'll accomplish everything we came to accomplish, and then we'll walk away from everything in our past. You hear me?"

Nodding her head, she went back to worrying her lip between her teeth. Ignoring the fact that she was still nervous, I put the truck into drive and inched along the trail towards our destination.

"How long is this trail anyway?" I asked.

She shrugged her shoulder. "We have at least another twenty miles. These woods stretch out forever, it seems."

Thinking about the best approach we could take to ensure we both stayed safe, I said, "Tell me when we're three miles away. At that point, we'll leave the truck behind and move the rest of the distance on foot. That way we become a smaller target and we have a better chance of not tipping them off to our approach."

"I can do that," she promised. Her hand reached out tentatively, and when I released the wheel, she entwined her fingers with mine. She didn't let go of my hand for the remainder of the drive.

It took another two hours to crawl the distance to the house, the sun beginning to set in the distant sky. I didn't mind the darkness, in fact, I believed we could use it to our advantage. Assuming her brothers would light a fire, it would give me a beacon with which to find them. A target where I knew they'd be waiting without realizing what was stalking them from behind.

After pulling the truck off the trail just enough to ensure it wouldn't be seen, I leaned over to give Maggie a long and lingering kiss. She relaxed when my mouth met hers and I hoped the gesture was enough to ease the fear that assaulted her mind. Pulling away had been difficult, but I realized we only had so much time to get the job done that we'd come here to accomplish.

"You ready?" I asked, my finger beneath her chin as I tipped her face up to mine.

"As ready as I can be," she confessed.

Giving her a single nod of my head, I turned off the engine of the truck and climbed outside. Maggie met me by the tailgate and waited patiently while I readied myself for the fight I knew was coming. Slinging my rifle over my shoulder, I grabbed two handguns, handing one to Maggie as I asked, "Do you know how to handle that?"

She looked up at me like I was complete idiot.

I shrugged a shoulder and laughed.

After strapping two knives to my thighs and tucking a third in my boot, I grabbed additional ammo to shove into the pockets of my cargo pants. Surprising me yet again, Maggie reached into the bag and grabbed my spare rifle, pulled the bolt to ensure it was loaded before grabbing a few magazine clips to stuff into her own pockets. For once, she wasn't dressed in one of those loose dresses she seemed to love and I had the biggest urge to dip my finger in the mud at my feet to wipe little smudges of war paint beneath her determined eyes.

"You look fierce when you're pissed off, you know that?"

Her smile was like wicked sunshine.

"You don't look so bad yourself. Now let's go prove we have what it takes to end this."

While we walked, I considered the opponents we were up against. It would be too fortuitous to believe that the universe would hand me such an easy target as it had before. I doubted those two fucks were three sheets to the wind this time, or busying themselves with raping some woman that was a hell of a lot weaker than them. I'd caught them by surprise the last time I'd found them, and I was sure they'd be on the lookout for me after everything that had already gone down.

Interrogating Maggie about all the weapons they had at their disposal, my lips pulled into a thin line to realize they were as well armed as me.

"Daddy taught us all to shoot since we were old enough to hold a gun properly," she explained. "It wasn't only for our protection, but because we lived off the land during the times we were off the grid and hiding. Brody is a much better shot than Finn, but Finn is better at hand to hand. He's strong, Elliot, so don't think for a second that he'll be easy to take down, if it comes to it."

Shaking my head, I reminded her that I'd already wrestled that son of a bitch in a puddle of his own piss. Her face scrunched up in disgust, which made me chuckle.

"The house we're heading to was built on higher ground. Daddy did that on purpose so that we would know if trouble was coming. The main trail to the place has few trees we can use to hide where we are, but if we circle around south, I think we have better cover and can sneak up closer to the property."

"I have no problem following your lead, Maggie. You get me there and I'll take care of the rest."

"I can fight if it comes to it, Elliot. I have no love for my brothers."

Not doubting what she said, I grimaced to think of another person's blood staining this girl's hands.

"What I need is for you to be watching my back. How are you at climbing trees?"

"Pretty decent," she admitted. "But you're not leaving me behind."

I wanted to stop in my tracks to have this conversation, but the waning light was making it difficult to cross the rugged terrain. "My fear is that you'll become a liability to me. What if one of them gets ahold of you? It'll stop me from being able to act quickly."

"I'll worry about myself, Elliot. I won't get close enough for either one of them to grab me. What I need is for you to make sure you're taking care of yourself. I won't leave this forest without you."

"Maggie," I warned, knowing full well that she wouldn't listen to a damn word I said, "If something happens –"

"Nothing's going to happen," she insisted, cutting me off at the knees.

We didn't speak again as we closed the three mile distance. As the sun set on the horizon the small house came into view. Her brothers hadn't started a fire like I'd hoped, and the land was far too still to feel safe.

Lowering her voice so it wouldn't carry on the wind, Maggie said, "It's now or never, Elliot."

I took a few breaths while I scoped the property. The old red truck I'd seen her family driving was parked outside the house, but there was no other sign of her brothers.

"What are the chances they're sleeping?"

"Slim to none," she answered.

"That's what I was afraid you'd say."

Creeping up the hill, careful not to step on any errant twigs or trip over exposed roots, we crouched low to the ground, our eyes focused on the house and the clearing of land that surrounded it. We'd almost made it within a hundred feet when a branch broke above my head, and I looked up just in time to see Brody's body falling on top of me. Maggie screamed, but I couldn't see where she was standing. Throwing my hands up to push the bastard away, my head shot to the right with the full strength of his fist. We fought for several minutes, his body taking as bad a beating as mine, but our battle was quickly stopped by the only thing I feared.

"I've got a knife to your girlfriend's throat, you stupid fuck. If I were you, I'd stop struggling."

There was sick satisfaction in Finn's voice, and the pained cry of a woman who'd just had the blade of a knife dragged across her skin. Allowing Brody to pull me up from the ground, I didn't fight when he bound my hands behind my back and turned me to face his brother.

Blood from a shallow cut dripped down Maggie's throat, but her eyes didn't betray what she was feeling.

Finn's eyes were another matter altogether, and behind the blue, I saw the promise of violence and suffering.

"What did I tell you, Brody?" He jutted his chin in my direction as a sick smirk pulled at his lips. "I told you the little bitch would bring him here. Now aren't you glad I made you wait in that tree all damn day?"

Brody didn't answer his brother. He just tightened the binds on my wrists until I felt my skin split beneath the pressure.

Returning his insane gaze back to me, Finn smiled as he ran a hand up Maggie's body. Angling his face towards hers, he whispered words to torment her.

"Would have been smart of you to run away with your boyfriend, Maggie Pie. But you've never known when to leave well enough alone. Guess that's good for me. I still haven't finished doing to you all the wonderful things I have planned."

His tongue flicked out to lick a trail up the side of her face, her eyes rounding with disgust. Tears slipped down her cheeks and Finn licked them up, one by one.

"Leave her alone, Finn. This is between you and me."

I knew what I said wasn't enough to get him to stop torturing his sister, but I hoped it would drag his attention back to me.

Laughter shook his shoulders, the sick sound echoing beneath the trees. "Is that so?" he finally asked. "And why is that exactly? Because you think we did something to your family?" More laughter, his brother, Brody, joining in.

Lowering his voice so that it was a deep rumble on the wind, Finn traced a finger along Maggie's shoulder, smiling when he saw how badly she trembled.

"You know," he said, as if lost in some important thought, "I've been thinking about what you said to us that night at my house. About the woman you swore we'd killed. She was your wife, right? Her and a little boy? I think I remember them."

My body stilled when he mentioned my family, my jaw ticking with the rage I couldn't contain.

"I don't remember much about the little boy. He wasn't exactly my *flavor*. But your wife, I seem to remember her. Took me a while to think back that far, but I have to admit, now that I took the time to think of her, she left one hell of impression."

Brody laughed from where he stood behind me, but I trained my expression to one of boredom and lack of concern. My refusal to react pissed Finn off, that cold fact evident in the expression that wrinkled his face.

"She begged for her little boy's freedom. Stupid kid with a stuffed bunny, right? Can you believe the little shit actually fought with us trying to protect his mama?"

My jaw ticked with how hard I ground my teeth, but I met his stare with venom in my eyes, my body rigid where it was held in place. My mind imagined every way I planned to kill this bastard.

"That wasn't until we dropped him off to the sick fuck who ran the pig farm. I think that's when he realized his mommy wasn't having fun at the party. But your wife..."

Shaking his head a low whistle emitted from his lips.

"...damn that bitch could give head. After we were done with her, I gave her an hour or two to cool down. You see, it had been hours that her body was used. Sneaking back into

293

the room with a glass of ice water, I mentioned I could save her son if she was nice and did me a special favor. She believed me and she sucked my cock like it was the best tasting dick in the world."

A grin pulled at his thin lips. "Did you teach her how to do that?" Lowering his voice, he ran his hand ran up Maggie's body. "Have you taught Maggie the same tricks?"

When I didn't answer, he shrugged a shoulder. "Guess I'll be finding that out in a little while."

Jutting his chin in the direction of the small cabin, Finn barked orders at his brother. "Take the piece of shit into the cabin. Strip him of his weapons and find him a comfortable seat to watch the show. Might as well let the fuck see what we did to his wife before he takes his last breath."

Maggie cried out when Finn's hand moved between her legs, the threat made obvious by the sickening lust in his eyes.

Grinding my teeth, I focused on the problems that surrounded me, and I hoped like hell I would find a way out of this mess before they killed me and had their way with Maggie.

CHAPTER THIRTY-FIVE

MAGGIE

I always knew it would end this way.

It was in the back of mind the entire time we'd driven, the crushing feeling that nothing would go according to plan.

After Brody stripped Elliot of his knives and guns, he tucked the weapons into his own pockets and slung the rifle over his shoulder. With a shove that almost sent Elliot to the ground, he forced him to take the first few steps in the direction of the cabin. Elliot didn't meet my eyes before allowing himself to be led away, didn't give any indication of what he was thinking or feeling.

Behind them, Finn led me along the same path, laughter rumbling from his lips every time I stumbled over a root, or my own feet. I hated to admit that I was scared shitless at that moment, but there was nothing I could do now that Finn had taken all my weapons.

It was an impossible situation, and one that I knew would end horribly. Elliot would most likely die a painful death tonight, but I wasn't sure my brothers would make it that easy for me. Brody might have after he'd gotten what he wanted from me. But Finn? He was too sick in the head to make things quick. It pleased him to drag out the inevitable, and I wouldn't have been surprised if he planned to fuck me for days until my body gave out and I died right there beneath him.

Remembering back to what my father had told me, I wanted to cry. From the minute I was born that man tried to protect me from the evil he swore was following me, but he was too blind to see the sickness in his sons' eyes. How long had they been planning to do unspeakable things to me? How many nights had they stayed up late, most likely drinking, and planned the worst kind of torture they could commit against my body?

I supposed the answers to those questions didn't matter much. It's not like they would save me. But the mind has a funny was of shielding itself from the horror that stood before it. It had a way of distracting you with nonsense, if for nothing else but to keep you from going insane. It was a one of the wonderful things about the human body, but terrible as well because it kept you from focusing solely on the problem at hand.

Before long, Elliot and I were led into the dark interior of the cabin, the scent of decay assaulting me as soon as I stepped foot inside. It was readily apparent that nobody had been here since the last time my father had taken us *camping*, and nature had begun the process of reclaiming the space that had once been hers alone.

"Be sure to tie him up nice and tight. We wouldn't want the fucker getting brave and interrupting all the fun we'll be having."

Finn continued to bark orders in Brody's direction, and it wasn't until that moment that I realized just how scared of Finn Brody was. How had I never noticed the way he followed every instruction his older brother gave without complaint or argument of any kind?

"It's pitch fucking black in this dump," Finn muttered while shoving me towards the ground. Once he had me settled in place, he didn't bother binding my hands or feet, just simply assumed that fear would keep me trapped in place, a helpless victim to whatever cruel deeds he had in mind. Rather than fighting against him, I played the scared little sister, the girl I'd once been while Daddy was still alive.

Anger blossomed inside me to remember the stab wound to my father's stomach. They'd betrayed their own family, a man who'd done nothing but love them, and I didn't know the reason why.

"Brody. Why don't you go outside and fetch some lanterns from the truck? I'd like our boy here to have a nice view of what a woman can do for a man if she's given the proper encouragement."

Knowing exactly what type of *encouragement* he had in mind, I kept my mouth shut and mimicked the blank expression I'd seen on Elliot's face. There was no better way to endure a battle than to learn from the soldier who'd seen plenty in his time.

Brody followed his instructions like a little punk. He didn't even scoff at the way his brother was ordering him around. Now that I was really watching how the two of them were with each other, I couldn't help but wonder what Finn had done to Brody to scare him into submission. I would probably never know the details, but it dragged Finn into an entirely new level of evil. It wasn't just women that he tortured and raped, it was most likely his brother, too.

While Brody was gone fetching the lights, Finn took the opportunity to toy with Elliot.

"Here we are, just the three of us camping in a dark cabin in the middle of nowhere. Who would have thought that so much would change between us in only four short days?"

That slimy laughter of his filled the room, sliding off the walls and dripping from the ceiling like some kind of malicious ooze.

The air moved when he knelt down beside me, a small gust that felt like Finn's fingers brushing across my skin, disgusting me. It wasn't long before I felt disgusted again. Except this time, I was being touched by the real thing.

His palms were sticky and warm, his fingertips tangling in my hair as he cupped my face. "You know, even in the dark, I can see the fear behind your eyes. I already told you what I planned to do you." He laughed. "You know what's coming."

297

My thoughts raced back to the night they'd whipped me. It struck me then that large parts of that night were hazy, mostly the pain of the beating. It was as if my wonderful mind and body had instinctively sheltered me from the worst parts. I couldn't help but wish my mind had been kind enough to also hide the details of the vile threats he'd made.

"I can't find the batteries." Brody burst back into the small cabin. Soft light shone in from the outside, illuminating Elliot where he sat. I studied his sitting position, the expression on his face, the distance he was from me, and every other detail that could be important. But when he looked up at me, his eyes locked onto mine.

"They're in the truck where the lanterns were stowed, you stupid shit."

"They're not there. I checked everywhere."

Pushing up from the floor with a huff of frustration, Finn crossed the room to the door. He pointed his finger in Brody's face. "I should kill you next for being so stupid. Watch these two while I go find them."

In the soft light, Brody's expression hardened. "I dare you to try."

My eyebrows shot up my head. For once Brody was standing up to Finn.

"You want to challenge me on that, little brother? I'm all yours." Raising his arms to his side, Finn took a step into Brody's space.

They glared at each other for a few seconds, and then both of them walked out the door. I stared open-mouthed as the door swung closed, returning us to darkness.

"Maggie, there's a knife in my boot that your brother didn't find. I need you to cut me loose."

Whisper-shouting the words, Elliot didn't waste any time.

Scrambling over the floor, I didn't think, I just moved. My hand wrapped over the handle of the knife and I yanked it free. Moving around Elliot, I sawed at the rope that bound his wrists, my hands working furiously to cut through it. I'd made it down to the last quarter inch of rope, but heard Brody and Finn just outside the front door. Shoving the handle of the knife into Elliot's hands, I crawled back to my place on the floor. The door burst open and the two men entered with lit lanterns in their hands.

"It's starting to feel like a party now," Finn shouted, his voice exuberant and loud.

Brody, on the other hand, was far more subdued, even with the line of anger that creased between his eyes.

"It's too bad we didn't think to pick up some beer while driving here. Would have made for a better night all around."

Canting his head to the side, he grinned at me. "And would you look there? Maggie is in the exact same place I left her," his eyes darted to Brody, "just like I said she'd be. It appears you were wrong about that, too."

Not surprised by his belief that I wouldn't move, I thought back to the woman I'd been before now. Timid and obedient, I never openly defied my family's demands. However, I wasn't that person any more. The timid mouse in me had been chased away by every act of violence I'd endured. The naïve girl opened her eyes to the evil that constantly surrounded her. And the hopeless romantic, who thought all romance was happy and carefree, had learned that a stronger form of love could be forged through tragedy.

Elliot's love strengthened me by making me feel secure; not because I thought he would always save me, but because I knew he was the type of man who would stop at nothing when he tried. Nothing but death would ever stop him.

Swallowing down a festering lump in my throat, I breathed deeply and slowly, attempting to settle my heart and mind. Darting my eyes between Finn and Brody, I chanced a glance at Elliot. One small muscle frantically twitched in his arm, his grey eyes locked to mine. Before I had a chance to process what he was doing, he winked at me before dropping to his back on the floor and taking out Brody's legs with his feet.

Brody dropped to the floor with an audible thump. The room was suddenly filled with the sound of Finn's voice screaming at his brother to get up.

CHAPTER THIRTY-SIX

ELLIOT

Brody was fast, but I was faster, and thankfully he was easy to take by surprise.

Falling down like a sack of bricks, he grunted when his body impacted the floor. Recovering quickly, it only took a second for him to turn over and push himself from the floor.

I lunged forward before he had the chance to balance on his feet and pulled him back to the ground. With one hand, I held him in place, smiling down at the shock in his expression. It was unfortunate there wasn't any time to tell him everything I thought of him, and I hated that this lucky fuck was going to get a quick death.

Finn started towards me as my free hand swung around. He didn't grab me in time. The knife I held angled down to Brody's face, and I shoved the steel blade into his eye. His body twitched a time or two, but the steel lodged deep in his brain killed him within seconds.

"You son of a –"

Throwing his weight on me, Finn tackled me to the ground. I was at a disadvantage with my feet still tied together, but I took Finn's weight and rolled him to the ground using his own motion against him. Pinning him with my hands on his shoulders, I brought my forehead down a few times against the bridge of his nose, blood bursting when it broke beneath his skin.

He roared out his anger and managed to slip out beneath me, immediately moving towards Maggie. For a split second, panic raced through my veins, but my beautiful girl hadn't missed the opportunity to prepare herself. A hunting knife in hand, her feet were planted in a battle ready pose, her lips pulled up into a snarl as she faced down her brother.

Kicking out with my bound legs, I barely missed his feet. The bastard turned like the coward he was and bounded for the door, Maggie's knife slamming into the wood just as Finn made his escape.

"Throw me the knife, Maggie!"

Without hesitation she dislodged the steel from the door, tossing it my direction, handle first. I caught the knife in mid-air and moved quickly to saw away at the binds across my ankles. Pushing up from the floor, I shoved Brody's body aside and removed my rifle from where it was still slung over his lifeless shoulder.

"Elliot," Maggie cried out, stopping me before I ran outside in pursuit of Finn.

Glancing over at her, I nodded my head once before saying, "I'm taking him down, Maggie. I want you to arm yourself with the guns they left laying around and if anybody comes through this door, I don't want you to hesitate to shoot them."

"What if it's you?" Her eyes were rounded with panic and trepidation.

"I'll yell out to you before I come in. If you don't hear my voice, don't trust what's walking inside."

I was proud of her for moving quickly to follow my instructions and I knew I didn't need to worry about her refusing to pull the trigger if it came to it.

Making my way outside, I scanned the distance looking for Finn. The forest surrounding us was far too still for this hour and I wondered why even the nocturnal creatures hadn't yet scampered out from their beds. The wind blew softly through the boughs of the trees, the leaves rustling gently. From the corner of my eye, I saw movement behind a thick stand of trees and I crouched down to eye my target. From one second to the next the forest was still and then one large son of a bitch was making his run for it.

Finn was fast, I'd give him that, but I had patience and training on my side. Realizing that I was simply in another type of battlefield, I scanned the perimeter as I stalked my prey, identifying and categorizing every shuffled sound and frenzied movement. I wasn't moving slow until I lost sight of Finn, and I crouched down again waiting for him to make his next move.

Knowing he was unarmed while I held a rifle put a smile on my bruised face.

Maggie hadn't been wrong about his strength in hand to hand combat, but I had surprise on my side and, together, we'd managed to run him off without too much of a fight. Keeping my distance, I decided to use his lack of a weapon to my advantage.

Settling myself behind a low lying shrub, I was a hawk watching for a foraging mouse. With one eye closed, I scanned the forest around me through my scope waiting for the smallest movement or sound.

"You know," a deep voice called out, the echo through the trees making it next to impossible to pinpoint where the sound was coming from, "I didn't get to finish telling you what I remembered about your family."

Finn's voice was breathless, most likely from running. I was sure he was resting to regain his strength. Why the fucker would call out was beyond me, but I decided it proved that the son of a bitch was crazy.

"Your boy, he told me his daddy would come save him. He actually tried to hit me when he heard his mother cry. I broke his hand for it."

My teeth ground together so hard that pain shot along my jaw, but I refused to let Finn rattle me. Still unable to pinpoint him on sound, I kept my eyes trained on any movement in the distant shrubs and trees.

"That boy squealed like a pig when his fingers popped. Bet he squealed again when the farmer had his way with him. Did Maggie take you to the farm?" His sick laughter drifted maliciously through the forest. "Bet there's a lot in those shacks you'd want to see. I used to love dropping off a new one, just so I could go inside and shove him in the cage the farmer kept them in. Your boy cried so hard when that happened. And you should have seen his face when we dragged his mother away for the last time."

More laughter crawled through the darkness, clinging to my skin like fungus.

"But Daddy didn't come and save him, did he? You left him there to be the farmer's new pet. You should have seen the things he did to those kids. Even my father was disgusted by it. But not me. I thought it was fascinating. Even tried some of those tricks on my kid brother."

This fucker wasn't just crazy. He was certifiable.

The one thing he wasn't was stupid, and I wouldn't let him rattle me enough so that I spoke or moved and gave away my location.

Every so often, I'd see a shadow bound from behind one tree to another, and I set my sights on those trees waiting for when he made a run for it. While moving quickly to stay hidden, he wouldn't let me have a clear shot of him. But as soon as he took off running, he was mine.

A few seconds passed with weighted silence, but Finn wasn't able to keep his trap shut for long.

"And your wife. Man, I wasn't lying about how sweet she was. After she dropped Maggie off to our house, we invited her inside. She didn't want to come in, but we forced her regardless. Your stupid kid walked off with Maggie like nothing was wrong, and that's when the party started."

It took all the self-control I had not to charge through the trees straight towards him. Forcing myself lower to the ground, I peered through the scope and waited.

"Jonah had her first, as usual. Fucker always was selfish. But Brody and I didn't mind the sloppy seconds. Her body was prime, too. And that blond hair? I enjoyed wrapping my fingers around it. Kept her exactly where I wanted her."

My finger slid behind the trigger guard and landed squarely on the trigger. With my other hand, I searched the ground at my feet for anything heavy and a grin tugged at my lips to feel the smooth, cold surface of a large rock.

"That woman could scream. I remember that. She cried out your name a time or two. At least, I think it was yours. But who the fuck knows, right? You never can trust bitches. They always run around playing when their man isn't there to see what they're doing. Fuck man! My dick's hard now just thinking about her. Best pair of tits I've ever held in my hands."

Lifting the rock from the ground, I threw it in Finn's direction. It hit a tree hard enough to knock away some bark, and the Crow I was after flew out from its dark nest.

As soon as I had him in my crosshairs, I pulled the trigger. The Crow went down with a cry of pain, his body impacting heavily with the ground.

My grin widened and I pushed up from my crouched position to stalk towards him like death itself was walking.

Finn wasn't talking anymore and the silence was music to my ears.

Approaching him on slow steps, I gazed down at the man cradling his blown out knee.

"Bet that hurts," the stock of my gun slammed down on the injured knee, a horrifying roar emitting from Finn's mouth.

"Bet this will hurt too, you sick fuck," Another blow to the thigh bone rendered a loud crunch. His thigh bone snapped easier than I'd expected, so I had some fun and took out the other one as well.

Slowly working my way up, I was breaking every bone in his body. He continued screaming out in pain and I sucked in a breath, filled with joy for the sound of it. Turned on by the slow death I was handing him, I broke his hips apart – left and then right – and continued working my way up until every rib was fractured.

I'd intentionally shot him in the leg just to bring him down, but not kill him. And the pain I delivered with each crushing blow was worth not taking a head shot.

Barely able to breathe and writhing around in agony, Finn gasped as blood leaked out of his mouth. Knowing that his organs would shut down soon enough, I took out his arms from the shoulders down to the delicate wrists. With each bone I crushed, I told him why he was getting this beating.

"That's for treating your sister like garbage."

My gun hit his right hand crushing every small bone down to his fingers.

"And this is for pissing me off."

His left hand went next, his throat so torn apart, he was no longer able to scream.

There was only one part left on him intact, and once that was crushed, Finn would no longer be moving.

"And this, you sick son of a bitch, is for ever touching my wife and son."

The butt of my gun came down on his skull, the bones cracking apart with a putrid crunch. But one hit wasn't enough, not when it felt like I was possessed by a reaper.

I'll admit I lost control as I smashed his head in. My muscles flexed, sweat dripped down my brow, and my teeth were gnashed together. Hit after hit rained down on his head until there was nothing left that was identifiable as human. Blood, bone and brain tissue burst up in spurts as my gun rained down blows. Not caring that parts of him were dripping from my arms and legs, I continued beating him into the ground, pulverizing his body into mush.

"Elliot!"

Maggie's voice rang out through the forest, but it didn't stop me from beating him some more.

"Damn it, Elliot, stop. He's dead. You killed him, Elliot. Stop!"

Jerking my gun up to hit him again, I paused with it raised in the air. But my fingers loosened, my tight jaw released, and I looked down at the mess that had once been a man.

A hand touched my bicep, soft and hesitant, and I turned to Maggie to see concern written across her features.

"He's dead," she whispered, her eyes meeting mine. "You can stop now, Elliot. It's over."

EPILOGUE

Dear Katie:

It's been two years since I've written you. But it's time for me to finally leave the past in the past. I don't really know what there is to say anymore. I still dream about you sometimes. I see the brilliance of your beaming smile. I see the love in your eyes that was always there when you looked at our son and me. I see you dancing in rainbows and throwing your arms up in the air as you twirl through streams of sunlight. You always were so carefree, so glorious because you recognized the beauty that existed in life.

For so many years, you were the light that balanced out the dark parts of me, and when I lost you, the shadows crept in to turn me into something even I didn't recognize. Nothing mattered when you were gone. Nothing could hold me to this world that hadn't been the same once you were no longer a part of it.

I don't want to bother you with the details of what I've done. And I don't want to hurt you with the truth of what happened to Michael. There are no words for the horrors that happened to you both, and I'm still so sorry that I wasn't there to protect you. I don't blame myself anymore. I know it wasn't entirely my fault. I never found your remains or Michael's, so I buried what I could in your place.

Do you remember the clearing where we used to escape to on the days we skipped school? The one that sat in sunlight beside a pond so shallow we could lay in the water without fear of drowning? I buried you there with Michael. Floppy Bunny now lies beneath four feet of soil in the place where we fell in love – in the place where Michael was most likely conceived. Sunlight shines down on the small patch of ground and I knew on the day I buried it that what I was really burying was my heart.

But I had to let the two of you go. It was the only way I could move forward.

You told me once that even within the worst of circumstances, there is some good that can be found hiding among the evil. I thought you were crazy then, and I remember telling you so, but you laughed because you knew I was too blind to see it. I know now that you were right, Katelyn. And in the deepest, darkest crevices of the evil that stole my family, I found something so pure and true, that the word 'good' doesn't even cover it.

Maggie saved me when nothing else could. She surprises me on a daily basis, even though I've now known her for years. We've settled in another state, in another small town just like that one we grew up in. I think you would have liked it here, and I know you would have liked Maggie. People look at us funny for our difference in age, but I swear to you that girl is far older than her years. She knows tragedy. Hell, she was forged in it. And the love we have for each other was forged in it, too.

Like two cards balanced on our sides to create an upside down V, the only reason that either of us remain standing is because we lean on each other for support.

She cries at night sometimes. But those moments are becoming less and less frequent as times moves forward. As we move forward with each other.

You were my world for so many years, but I knew you would have never wanted me to be alone. It took me several months to come to that realization, to not feel wrong for loving another. But once I did – once I remembered who you were and how much you loved me – I was able to truly love again.

I want you to hug our son for me, Katie. I want you to tell him his father is proud of him and will love him forever. And I want you to know that I'm not alone anymore. A strong woman found me and pieced all the broken parts of my heart back together.

It's amazing to me how the spirit is so resilient, how despite the bleak tragedies that suffocate our lives in undeniable pain, we find the means to move forward and to seek out happiness again. So, perhaps you were right to tease me when I was pissed off and moody. Perhaps you were the smarter one all along to believe that even in the darkest corners, there is light.

I should have listened to you all those years ago, but I guess I had to go out and figure it out for myself. I always was a stubborn ass. You'll be happy to know that hasn't changed much, and that Maggie's the type of woman to remind me.

Until the next time I see you in dreams.

Elliot

🗡🗡🗡🗡

Tearing the page out of the notebook on which I'd scrawled my last letter, I tossed it into the flames that flickered softly in the fireplace. It was my final goodbye to a past riddled with heartache, a dividing line and defining moment where I could say I finally let go.

Two years had passed quickly since the night Maggie and I walked out of that forest together. Returning to town, we packed up everything we considered important, said our goodbyes to the town – to Henry – and we moved north.

We've been living together ever since, learning about each other, learning about ourselves, and coming to the understanding that we were stronger for being together and that we'd never let go of one another again.

I still suffer some hard times, especially when the nightmares creep in and disturb my sleep, but the pain of those memories are becoming less and less frequent, the passage of time a soothing balm on a heart that was no longer weak.

After watching that letter burn to nothing but ash, I stepped away from the small office I'd set up in the back of our house. Banging from outside drew my attention, and I pulled aside the curtain to discover the source of the racket.

Maggie's feet were sticking out from beneath a '69 Mustang, a rundown car we'd purchased as a project to restore. Although I believed she was running just fine with all the work we'd put into her, Maggie wasn't convinced. She reminded me of Henry in that way, always in search of perfection. It's the reason I'd made her my business partner when I opened my auto shop on the outskirts of town.

Huffing out a breath of frustration, I swore under my breath and stormed through the house. The door slammed open from how hard I tugged it and dirt kicked up around my feet as I took long legged strides in the direction of my wife.

"What in the hell do you think you're doing under that car? Have you lost your damn mind?"

This woman was going to give me a heart attack one of these days, and I loved her more because of it.

Pushing out from under the car, she smiled up at me from the mechanic's creeper on which she laid. Her hair was a mess of black curls around her head and there was a small smudge of dirt and oil running across her cheek. She looked just as fierce beneath a car as she did on the hunt against evil. I couldn't stay mad at her for long.

"I took the car out to grab us lunch, but I heard something rattling around. I'm just checking that everything you installed is bolted in right."

My lips pulled into a wide smile. "Uh, huh. And you're so sure it was me who messed something up? There isn't a possibility it was you?"

Her grin matched mine, her green eyes sparkling with humor. "Hell no. I'm the one who saved your ass when your truck broke down years ago. Or don't you remember?"

Laughter shook my shoulders. Even knowing that I'd intentionally loosened that battery cable just so I'd have a reason to talk to her, she still wouldn't let me live down the fact that she'd *rescued* me.

Reaching down with my hand, I said, "Here, babe, let me help you up."

She placed the wrench down on the ground beside her, wiped her hands on an old dirty rag and entwined her fingers with mine. A small surprised cry flew from her lips from how fast I pulled her to her feet.

Kissing her forehead softly, I kept my lips pressed to her skin. "You know you won't be able to fit under that car much longer. I don't think you should be stressing yourself out or working so hard in your condition."

Pulling away from me, she cocked a single eyebrow up. "The doctor said I can work as long as my body lets me. I'm not big enough yet to throw in the towel. I can still turn wrenches and you're not stopping me."

Spinning her around, I pulled her back to my chest, my hands reaching down to cradle the swell of her stomach. She was only twelve weeks along, and just barely showing, but I knew the time was coming where her body would round out with our growing child.

"Has anybody ever told you that you have a special gift for pissing a man off?"

Laughter vibrated through her body. "I think you've mentioned it a time or two."

"More like a hundred times, but who's counting?" I grumbled.

Grabbing her hands in mine, I led her into the house determined to convince her to lie down and take a nap. After feeding her lunch, and massaging her shoulders, I finally tucked her into our bed. She was snoring softly by the time her head hit the pillow and I chuckled knowing how angry she'd get when I teased her for it.

312

A long, deep breath blew out of my lungs as I looked down at the woman who'd become my future. We were two people who'd endured evil, one for a lifetime and the other for a handful of years. Somehow, within the shadows we'd found each other and we'd clung on like the other was the only lifeboat in a sea of unspeakable pain. Through her eyes I saw myself more clearly. And through her heart I'd learned to live again.

Every day I thanked God for the woman beside me because she was the perfect example of everything that is good and true.

Despite the injustices we suffered, despite the nightmares that threatened to tear us apart, it was only because we'd found each other that we were able to love and move forward into the light.

THE END

If you are interested in reading additional books by Lily White or would like to know when new books are being released, Lily White can be found on:

Facebook and

Twitter

Join the Mailing List!!!

If you are interested in receiving email updates regarding additional books by Lily White or would like to know when new books are announced or being released, join the mailing list via this link.

http://eepurl.com/Onoeb

Join the Facebook Fan Group!!!

If you are interested in receiving exclusive previews for upcoming novels, or to participate in giveaways, join the fan group for Lily White Books.

FAN GROUP LINK

www.ingramcontent.com/pod-product-compliance
Lightning Source LLC
Chambersburg PA
CBHW051237260626
47162CB00002B/475